SOMETHING SENSATIONAL

SOMETHING SENSATIONAL

Anne Marie Forrest

POOLBEG

Published 2002
Poolbeg Press Ltd.
123 Grange Hill, Baldoyle,
Dublin 13, Ireland
Email: poolbeg@poolbeg.com

13579108642

A catalogue record for this book is available from the British Library.

ISBN 1-84223-072-7

Cover designed by Slatter-Anderson
Typeset by Patricia Hope in Goudy 11/15
Printed by Cox & Wyman

www.poolbeg.com

About the Author

Originally from Cork, Anne Marie Forrest now lives in Dublin having spent the last few years in Australia and in Asia on a trip not dissimilar to Genevieve's *et al*, though she never actually bumped into them.

She is the author of two previous novels, *Who Will Love Polly Odlum?* and *Dancing Days*.

*To my daughter Lucy, without whom this book
would have been completed a lot sooner.*

Portrea woman held in Bangkok on drug charges

by Laura Tobin, Bangkok

ALTHOUGH LESS THAN twenty-four hours since her arrest at Bangkok airport on suspicion of drug-smuggling, Genevieve Price, the twenty-four-year-old woman from Portrea, Co Cork, is already showing the ill-effects of her detention. When I visited her in prison this morning, her baby-blue tracksuit was filthy, her carrot-red hair greasy and her plain, broad, freckled face was streaked with grimy tears.

Yet underneath the tears and the grime there lay a frightened, innocent-looking face, a face hard to conceive as belonging to a criminal. But then there are, it seems, many faces, many sides to Genevieve Price.

That of lover:

"I'm in love with Andrew Clancy. There. I've finally said it. And it's the truth though I've been denying it all along even to myself. But I am in love. I am. I, Genevieve Price, am in love with Andrew Clancy. I love him. I do, I really do."

That of deceiver:

"Genevieve changed once she started travelling and met up with Andrew Clancy. Before that she wanted the same things as I did – a big wedding, a nice little bungalow, children. But once Andrew Clancy came on the scene it was like her head was completely turned."

– Theo Whitlam, Price's jilted boyfriend, in conversation with this reporter.

That of the other woman:

"It was obvious right from the start that Genevieve was interested in Andrew but I didn't take it seriously. I mean Andrew and I have been together for such a long time and I never imagined he would be interested in Genevieve as she's an awfully silly girl."

– Mei Fan, Andrew Clancy's ageing oriental mistress.

And that of drug user:

"I like it. It makes me feel sort of free and relaxed and I stop worrying about everything and suddenly it's like I haven't a care in the world. Nothing seems scary any more. All I want to do is to laugh out loud though there's precious little to laugh about."

So many sides to Genevieve Price, sides which this reporter finds almost impossible to reconcile with the Genevieve Price she's known since childhood.

For I grew up with Genevieve but that Genevieve was just your average, small-town girl and if she was remarkable for anything it was perhaps for being especially unremarkable. But maybe that was just one more face she wore, one more mask, and who knows what was really going on behind that dull façade she portrayed.

But, in light of recent events, it seems likely to have been a lot more than any of her old classmates, myself included, could ever have imagined.

How could we have foreseen that one day Genevieve Mary Price would be languishing in a Thai prison, her fate resting in the hands of the Bangkok courts? How could anyone ever have imagined such a future was in store for her when she set off just three months ago to Asia on what was to be a trip of a lifetime? A trip she's now looking unlikely ever to return from, for if the Thai authorities decide against her, as seems likely, then Genevieve will face a charge of execution though as a foreigner it's possible that her sentence will be commuted to life imprisonment.

Execution or life imprison-ment, such is Price's bleak future now.

1

I never travel without my diary.
One should always have something sensational to read in the train.

From THE IMPORTANCE OF BEING EARNEST – Oscar Wilde

From: "Tobin, Laura"<lauratobin@hotmail.com>

To: "TonyHoward"<editor@idolmagazine.co.uk>

Subject: My column

Date: 15th Oct, 16:29:10

[Reply][Reply All][Forward][Delete]

Dear Tony,

Now that we've agreed payment, I've started working on my first column. I'm glad you like my idea of doing a few entries leading up to our departure, not least because it will allow me an opportunity to provide some background information on the girls.

Your suggested title, *An Asian Diary*, sounds fine. One other thing, Tony, I'm sure you'll agree that it would be better if I'm not identified as the writer. I just don't think this sort of thing fits in with my existing profile and I feel it would be better to keep them separate in the public's eye.

Regards,

Laura.

16th October

Genevieve

These are the very first words of my travel diary. Who knows what the last will be . . .

To mark our great adventure I bought these diaries for the three girls and myself which were originally priced at 12 euro but I got them for the bargain knockdown price of 4 euro as they're shop-soiled though there isn't much the matter with them really except that some of the pages stick a bit and there are grubby paw marks all over the back cover of one which I'm going to give to Maeve as she's the least likely to notice. I'm keeping the best one for myself which is only fair really seeing as how I bought them but I can't wait to give the girls theirs and it's really not all that long now till we'll be meeting up and heading off.

Well, at long last I've nearly everything packed. To make things easier to find when we're on the road I've divided all my stuff into these extra large ziplock freezer-bags I found down in the kitchen. I've put all my underwear in one, my tops in another, jeans in a third and so on and so forth. All I've left to do now is to stick some labels on the bags and to sew some little pockets in the insides of my socks so that no matter what outfit I'm wearing I'll always have somewhere safe to keep my money for you can't be too careful especially when you consider where we're going.

My cousin Caitríona came into work today and I had to show her the ropes for she's going to be helping Dad out while I'm away but to be honest she didn't seem all that interested and I just hope she doesn't turn out to be a <u>complete</u> <u>disaster.</u> When I was explaining to her how the whole filing system worked she just didn't seem to get it <u>at</u> <u>all</u> and despite what she says I think it makes prefect sense to file people under whatever pest we first treated their premises for like Mr Duane under C for cockroach and Mr Harrison under R for rat and so on and so on. And as I said to Theo, it's very easy for Caitríona to just come waltzing in and to start picking holes in everything for of course she has no idea of the amount of effort I put into setting up the whole system in the first place. Theo says he'll pop in from time to time to keep an eye on her while I'm away. Not too close an eye I hope! Somehow I don't think I have any need to worry on that score! But really, how am I going to stick being away from Theo for three whole months? I am going to miss him something awful no exaggeration.

It's only three more days to go now . . .

An Asian Diary

Sometimes, dear reader, I wake in the middle of the night in a cold sweat at the thought of just what I've let myself in for. Every now and then I feel a panic attack coming on and I ask myself what the hell I was thinking when I agreed to go on an extended trip to Asia with Genevieve, Debbie and Maeve, three old school friends.

I say three old school friends but I guess "three girls I used to be in school with" would be a more accurate description.

First there's Genevieve. Now, reader, what can I say about Genevieve? Well, for a start you're sure to know the kind, there's one in every class. She's the one who's always left over when the teams have been picked. The one nobody wants to sit beside. The one who sucks up to the teachers but even they can't stand the sight of her. I haven't seen Genevieve since the night of our debs when she turned up with our classmate Theo, a male version of herself who, I gather, she's still going out with. Of course I am a little curious to see what Genevieve's like nowadays. Curious but anxious also. And even more anxious at the prospect of spending almost three months in her company.

So what's Genevieve been doing in the interim since school? Well, poor Genevieve wasn't exactly the smartest when it came to the books, or when it came to anything else for that matter, and 'plain thick' I think would have been the staffroom consensus. Not for our Genevieve the heady lights of London or Dublin but, staying put in our home town of P–, she went to work in her dad's pest-control business and is still working there, so Maeve tells me.

Maeve also tells me that Genevieve's duties are strictly administrative and she's not actively engaged in the control side of things although, if her father had any sense, he'd capitalise on her amazing ability to bore. He could sit her in the middle of an infested building, give her a topic and let her drone on and on, and pretty soon the rats, woodlice, & cockroaches would be tripping over one another, desperate to escape.

17th October

Genevieve

I've been thinking about it and I suppose I can see Caitríona's point for if Mr Duane for example comes in while I'm away with say a rat problem well Caitríona's not going to know to look up his file under 'C' for cockroach not having the background knowledge I have. I mean it's easy for me for I've been working with Dad for over seven years now so I know everything there is to know about the customers and have all that knowledge stored away in my fingertips and I suppose it's not really fair of me to expect Caitríona to be able to grasp everything in a matter of days.

But what am I like writing about cockroaches of all things in my travel diary when I should be writing about travelling! So let me see. Well, Maeve rang this morning wanting to know if I was all set and I told her that of course I was though needless to say she was far from all set herself and I swear I've never met anyone so disorganised. And I wish now I hadn't said a word about sewing the little pockets in my socks or about how she should do the same for of course she only started mocking me and going on about how she'd never heard of anything so stupid in her

9

whole life. Just wait until she gets mugged and then we'll see what side of her face she's laughing on!

She was telling me she was on the phone to Laura Tobin earlier to arrange about meeting up in Heathrow. I wonder what Laura's like nowadays. I don't think she's been back to Portrea since she left school which must be terribly hard on her parents but then I'd say she never really got on with them for though they're nice people and all, they're quite ordinary really whereas Laura always had <u>big</u> <u>notions</u> for herself. Maeve says she's <u>very</u> <u>sophisticated</u> nowadays. Of course Maeve's in touch with her all the time but though it's hard to believe I haven't actually met her since the night of our debs which is over seven years now. Time really does fly. Of course I've seen her articles in *The Argus* from time to time not that I've ever actually read any of them for they usually seem to be about politics and whatnot. Now that I think about it, I can't remember seeing her name or the little photo that goes with it on any of the articles in *The Argus* for quite some time.

I must remind Mam to get some spare knickers when she goes to town tomorrow for they'd be the one thing it'd be a fright to run out of.

Only two more days to go . . .

An Asian Diary

The second member of our little party is Maeve. This whole trip was her idea. She's the one who's meant to be organising it all. But, trouble is, dear reader, Maeve couldn't organise the proverbial piss-up in a brewery though she'd be the first in line to go to one. Way back in the not-so-halcyon days of school, some misguided teacher once gave her the task of running the Christmas raffle and, being Miss Popularity herself, Maeve did manage to sell a record number of tickets but her downfall was the prize. She just didn't get around to organising it in time and, on the day of the big draw, the winner went home with a turkey far more alive than she could ever have bargained for.

And what's Maeve been doing since school? Well, as soon as we'd finished, she hightailed it out of P– almost as quickly as I did but, whereas I went to London, she headed to Dublin where she took up a long succession of dead-end jobs, the last of which was that of hostess in an infamous Dublin nightclub. A fitting job I think for a girl who almost got expelled in fourth year for smoking cigarettes behind the school bike-shed; in fifth for getting up to what she shouldn't have been getting up with Pat O' Toole behind same bike-shed; and, in sixth, for drinking behind, you guessed it, the very same bike-shed.

To come on this trip, Maeve chucked in her nightclub job for she's not the sort to let work interfere with leisure and has been known to hand in her notice for much less – to go to a concert, to go shopping and, most frequently, to nurse a hangover.

18th October

Genevieve

The latest on the trip front is that Debbie was on the phone earlier and started rabbiting on about how we should try and fit Cambodia into our itinerary. I mean for crying out loud! Cambodia! What is she like? Who's ever heard of anyone ever going on their holidays to Cambodia? As far as I know they're in the middle of a famine or a war or something for if it's not one thing with those kinds of countries it's another and anyway why on earth does she want to go chopping and changing things now at this late stage? God help us if she's going to be carrying on like that when we're away. And then she started reminding me to be sure to pack a sleeping bag and some insect repellent. Like I needed to be told when I'm probably the most organised of the lot of them.

I am mad about Debbie but sometimes she really does go on like I'm stupid or something. And of course she can be bossy out too if she's let get away with it which is something I'm going to have to watch out for while we're travelling.

But Cambodia! Like really! And the last time she rang she was going on about this other country called Laos or something like that but I'd say she was all mixed up for I've never heard of such a place and when I asked Theo he hadn't either but told me to be sure to ask her was it County Laois she was talking about! And anyway even if this place Laos exists which, as I say, I <u>seriously</u> doubt, there's no way I'd go for there's no telling what it'd be like. I mean China and Vietnam and Thailand are enough for anyone. Especially China and to be honest wild <u>horses</u> wouldn't get me going there if it wasn't for the fact that Maeve's dad who's been living in Beijing for the past five years will be meeting us off our flight and we'll be staying with him to start with. I don't know whether I should do my legs now or hold off. I suppose I should do them and of course there's nothing to say I can't do a quick job on them again before we go. I wonder are the baths in China the same as they are here. I guess I'll find out soon enough.

Only one more day to go . . .

An Asian Diary

And lastly there's Debbie. Despite being complete opposites, Maeve and Debbie have been best friends ever since they first espied one another as babies peeping from prams when their mothers stopped to chat. Scarcely a cross word has passed between them since or at least it hadn't, not until they became aware of the opposite sex and discovered that they had this unhappy knack of always falling for the same man. Right now Maeve is going out with Dylan. The very same Dylan who Debbie used to date. In fact, Dylan was the love of poor Debbie's life. Tragic then that he dumped her for Maeve though not immediately and, for a spell, it looked like this trip was in serious jeopardy when Debbie found out she was sharing him but somehow Maeve talked Debbie around and, as only Maeve could, she managed to keep Dylan as her boyfriend, Debbie as her best friend and this trip on the rails.

But for how long, dear reader, that's the question.

Best friends they may be but Maeve and Debbie are like chalk and cheese and while Maeve was busy doing everything she could to get herself expelled, Debbie was at home studying. Which she needed to be. I'm not saying she was in the same league as Genevieve, but she was what teachers euphemistically refer to as a hard worker and, sadly, her ability fell somewhat short of her ambition.

But she put the hours in and post-Leaving Cert had the offer of a place in the army which was probably her true calling as there's always been a lot of the Sergeant Major about Debbie. However, in order to be close to best buddy Maeve in Dublin, she opted instead to work in an insurance agency in the city centre where she remains to this day.

To come on this trip, she's added up her holiday leave for the last four years but then she's had little need of it given that her only extra-curricular activity is hill-walking. Boyfriends certainly don't take up much of her spare time. Apart from her doomed relationship with Dylan, she's been boyfriend-free most of her life and not through choice either.

I say they're best friends but it would be more accurate to say Debbie is the best friend Maeve's ever had and, in fair weather, Maeve's as good a friend to Debbie as she's likely to be to anyone.

Let's just hope the weather stays fair.

19th October

Genevieve's room. Late evening.

Genevieve

I'm still not convinced Caitríona is going to be able to manage when I'm gone. At least Dad will be there to help and Theo for it's no exaggeration to say he nearly knows as much about the world of pest control as I do myself for he's listened to me yapping on about it on the spin home in the evenings often enough. When he was here this evening I told him to be sure to give her all the help she needed.

But I really just don't know how I'm going to survive for so long without Theo for in all the time we've been going out, hardly a day has gone by without us seeing one another. He said that I'm not to phone him from abroad as it would make him feel too lonesome and anyway it'd just cost too much but what I am going to do instead is send him a postcard every week to keep him up-to-date.

I know Theo and Trevor are close and you'd only expect that what with them being twins and all but I really don't know what Theo was thinking when he brought Trevor along with him tonight seeing as how it was our last evening together. And of course Trevor the eejit has absolutely <u>no cop on</u> and he just sat there on the couch beside us all night long gaping at the television so that Theo and myself never really got a chance to say a <u>proper</u> <u>goodbye</u> <u>if</u> <u>you</u> <u>know</u> <u>what</u> <u>I</u> <u>mean.</u> And though I was blue in the face from telling Trevor to go and join Mam and Dad in the front room he just didn't get the hint and wouldn't budge because he said the picture on the telly in there was all fuzzy.

I was hoping Theo would come to the airport tomorrow to see me off but he says he can't afford to take the day off as they're too busy which of course is disappointing but if it can't be helped then it just can't be helped and I know he'd come if he could. So it'll just be Mam and Dad seeing me off which I'm sure will suit them fine. I'd say the only reason they're happy that I'm going on this trip at all is because it means I'll be separated from Theo for they've never approved of him. He's not exactly the dynamic young businessman they'd have picked themselves for a son-in-law but although Theo might not set the world on fire he suits me just fine. We've been together almost seven years now and in all that time we haven't fought so much as once so Mam and Dad are fooling themselves if they think three months apart will change a thing between us.

I've decided that as soon as I get back I'm going to start organising the wedding and my parents can just go and lump it if they don't like it. I know Theo and I aren't actually engaged or at least not officially but we're as good as and from what I hear you really need to book things like the church and that way ahead of time to be sure of getting what you want.

No more days to go! Tomorrow we're finally off!

An Asian Diary

So there you have, it dear reader. Our little travelling party and quite a mixed bunch it is too with only Maeve and a shared school history in common. Every time Maeve rings and I start panicking and asking her what the hell she's talked me into, she reassures me and tells me that at the very least it'll be interesting.

She's right and she doesn't know the half of it.

She doesn't know, for example, that her darling boyfriend Dylan doesn't seem entirely satisfied with dating first one friend, then a second, but seems quite keen to move onto a third judging by the advances he was making on me on that one occasion we met when I stayed with Maeve whilst over in Dublin carrying out research for a story.

Neither does she know that, at fourteen, I was her father's very own Lolita and had more than a little to do with her parents' break-up. What can I say? Even at that age men found me irresistible. I wonder if he still has the hots for me? No doubt there'll be plenty of opportunity to find out when we stay with him in Beijing . . .

And Maeve isn't the only one who's not in command of all the facts.

Debbie, for instance, doesn't know that Maeve and Dylan are already plotting for Dylan to come and join up with us along the way. How cruel to spring such a surprise on Debbie especially as she's just beginning to come to terms with being dumped by Dylan. I am tempted to tell Debbie but Maeve has sworn me to secrecy and I can hardly betray her trust, now can I? Besides, it'll be more fun to watch Debbie's reaction when Dylan appears out of the blue. And Maeve's reaction, when she begins to realise that Dylan just can't keep his hands off me.

Not surprisingly, Genevieve, being Genevieve, doesn't know a lot of things.

She doesn't know that Maeve has been in and out of detox more times in the last few years than Elizabeth Taylor, Matthew Perry and Robert Downey Jnr. combined and that one of dutiful Debbie's reasons for coming on this trip, despite the awkward timing and bad feeling, is to keep an eye on Maeve as Debbie is the desperately loyal kind even if Maeve doesn't always deserve it.

Neither does Genevieve know that when Maeve was vacillating between saying yes or no when Genevieve asked could she come on the trip, it was I who persuaded Maeve to say yes. I can't say my reasons were exactly altruistic. Something about seeing how someone as gormless as Genevieve would cope with roughing it in Asia appealed to my perverse sense of humour.

But, most importantly, what none of them know is that, for the next three months, their day-to-day concerns are going to provide regular entertainment for you, dear reader.

20th October

Debbie

9.00 *a.m.* Our big trip is under way. Genevieve, Maeve and I have flown in from Dublin and are waiting to meet up with Laura and then fly out to Beijing.

Genevieve has given us each a diary to mark the occasion, which was quite a nice thought and it's what I'm now writing in.

Genevieve

Well so far so good and here we are in Heathrow which is absolutely <u>jam-packed</u> but at least we've managed to find a nice quiet corner for ourselves though this woman did ask just now if we'd mind taking our bags down from the seats to make a bit of room but I was quick enough to let on we were keeping them for some friends who were in the Ladies as otherwise we'd have been crowded out and anyway we'll be needing one of them for Laura when she arrives so it wasn't a complete lie. Of course if it was just the woman on her own I wouldn't have minded but she had this mob of howling, snotty-nosed children hanging off her, plus an old lady who must have been a hundred if she was a day and who I'd say was probably the grandmother as well as I don't know how many bags and suitcases and prams and whatnot. I don't know how she thinks she's going to be able to manage everything.

I gave Maeve and Debbie their diaries and I must say they were very pleased with them. Debbie's even started writing in hers already. I must go and find a toilet for I am <u>bursting.</u>

Debbie

9.35 a.m. "Would you look at what I've found!" Genevieve emerges from the crowd propelling a startled-looking Laura and her even more startled-looking boyfriend Felix along in front of her.

Losing no time, she zooms in on Felix. The inquisition begins.

"A radio presenter! Well! And tell me, how much would a person earn at that game?"

The questions come hard and fast until Maeve interrupts to ask, "What's, like, with the Queen Mother accent?"

No doubt it's Genevieve's attempt to impress Felix who is very posh.

Genevieve

It's great to meet up with Laura again after all these years though it only feels like the other day. It's funny how it's so easy to lose contact but then I guess Laura and I were never very close not like the way Debbie and Maeve are for instance despite all that brouhaha there was between them over that fellow Dylan. To be honest I was always a bit in awe of Laura and a bit wary of her but she seems far nicer now than she used to be. I guess we've all just grown up. And she's looking a <u>million</u> <u>dollars</u>. She's blonde out now.

Debbie

9.45 a.m. "Aren't you gone fierce blonde altogether, Laura? Weren't you nearly as mousy as Debbie there?" Genevieve says, grabbing a fistful of Laura's hair and holding it up to the light.

Genevieve

And I'd say money is <u>no object</u> with her.

Debbie

9.48 a.m. "I wouldn't say they came cheap!" she cries, bending down to get a good look at Laura's Gore-tex boots.

Genevieve

And she has the most amazing figure though that doesn't mean to say she used to be fat or anything like that in school because she wasn't. Just a bit hefty maybe especially her backside but then weren't we all carrying a bit of puppy fat back in those days. In fact if you ask me she's probably even a little <u>too thin</u> now not that I said that to her, of course.

Debbie

9.55 a.m. "And look at that, not an inch of fat!" she screeches, grabbing Laura's underarm.

Genevieve

On the other hand she says I haven't changed a bit, that I'm the same old Genevieve.

Debbie

10.00 a.m. What was it Maeve said again when I voiced

my worries about such a motley crew travelling together? Something along the lines of, "Get along! Of course we'll get along! Why wouldn't we? Haven't we all been friends for years?"

Which isn't strictly true. Just because Maeve is friends with each of us doesn't necessarily make us friends with one another.

Genevieve

I'd say it's getting near our boarding time so I'd better start reminding Maeve to have her passport ready this time for she absolutely mortified us back in Dublin by holding up the queue for ages while she searched through all those small little bags she's bringing with her as well as her rucksack which of course is way too big but when I tried telling her that she nearly bit the head off me no exaggeration and wanted to know what good was there in pointing that out to her at such a late stage. She didn't need to be quite so cross as I was only trying to help but Maeve can be very hotheaded sometimes. I suppose all the travelling has her feeling a bit stressed and I read somewhere lately that it's meant to be one of the most stressful activities and that more people fall stone dead from heart attacks in airports than in any other public place. Which is another good reason why that woman with all the children and whatnot should have thought about leaving the granny at home. To my mind she's far too old to be travelling and it would've been a kindness to have left her behind but then maybe they'd no one to look after her. But I mean to say how does she expect to manage that walking frame of hers for instance? I've never seen such an awkward-looking contraption. If she's not careful she'll do somebody an injury.

Debbie

10.30 a.m. Genevieve is out of her seat and is on at us to start queuing. Maeve is trying to tell her that it's much too soon, that there's at least an hour before boarding. Reluctantly, Genevieve resumes her seat.

10.50 a.m. Genevieve is on her feet again and is once again insisting that we queue though no one else seemed gripped by such urgency apart from a single over-anxious traveller who alone constitutes the "queue" she keeps pointing over to. Now she's bundling Maeve's things back into her bags.

I'd better get my own bits and pieces together before she turns her attention to me.

Some hours later.

Genevieve

Apparently there's some problem with fog so we're bloody well still stuck here in Heathrow and we don't know how long it'll be before our flight which to my mind is an absolute <u>disgrace</u> and of course there isn't a <u>sinner</u> around to complain to. No doubt they're all hiding out in some coffee-room somewhere for fear they'd have to give us the public some answers. God Almighty!

24

An Asian Diary

*I*n order, dear reader, to be a good diarist one needs to have a little, snouty, sneaky mind, as someone famous once said and I tend to agree. I've always been a little suspicious of people who keep diaries. I've just never really seen the point of them for, by their very nature, life's important moments tend to commit themselves to memory and I can't help but wonder if any of the usual daily minutiae – "Got up early. Very warm, at least 22°C. Brian called to collect his suit."– is really worth the bother of writing down.

Unless you're getting paid to do it of course, like I am, and have at your disposal, like I do, top of the range technology in the form of a palmtop computer. Paper and pen is just so yesterday.

I also tend to think that there's an inverse relationship between how boring a person's life is and their penchant for recording it all so it was no great surprise then to learn that Genevieve is a diary-keeper extraordinaire and it was somehow so very apt that she should present us each with a diary of our own so that, how did she put it again, "in time to come, we'll each have a memento of this very special time".

Very special time? I don't think so. Not when we're grounded here in Heathrow due to fog. One might think that there hasn't been an awful lot to write about thus far but that hasn't stopped Genevieve scribbling for a moment.

No doubt she feels compelled to write down every thought that enters her vacuous little mind. Which is bound to take some time. Not because such thoughts amount to very much but because she writes so slowly and laboriously. I fancy I've even noticed her mouth move as she deliberates over each spelling.

As well as Genevieve, dull-as-ditchwater Debbie has been busily writing in her diary and again, that figures and ties in with my theory about dullness and diary keeping being related.

A short time ago, noticing that I was using my palmtop and not the crappy, cheap diary she'd given me, Genevieve peevishly observed that I probably didn't have much mass on it so I told her that I loved it and that I was only using the palmtop to jot down some rough notes before carefully transcribing them.

But apart from Genevieve, I'm beginning to think there can be few things in life more frustrating than being delayed in an airport. Well, one other perhaps. Being delayed in an airport with Maeve, Genevieve and Debbie. On average, Maeve is mentioning Dylan every five minutes; Debbie is pretending not to notice; and, both of them are gritting their teeth as Genevieve gives out about the lack of soft toilet paper in the loo, the disgusting lump of gum stuck under her seat and the myriads of other things that are annoying her.

Now she's on at Maeve, demanding to know why she hasn't written in her diary yet. She's wasting her time. Maeve never so much as managed to finish an essay in school so I can't imagine why Genevieve would think she'd suddenly take up diary-writing. Maeve isn't exactly the world's most reflective person.

21st October

Maeve

G gave me this diary.

1st pressie I ever got from her 'cept for a bk of poetry on my 18th which she'd been given on hers.

Only know this cos she forgot to tear out the, "To dearest Genevieve with xxxxx's on your B'day from U. Pat & A. Maura".

The diaries cost her 12 euro each as she's just happened to mention oh, at least 1/2 doz. times which is (come to think of it) a bit of a swizz – they're Pretty Grotty.

Never had a diary before.

Only good girls keep diaries, bad girls don't have the time – as someone once said (I think).

Never quite got what it is you're meant to write in them *exactly*.

Like, should you write as if someone is standing there, looking critically over your shoulder? Or, should you pour your Heart & Soul & *all* your secrets out onto the page?

Don't know.

Which is why I asked G for some tips but she thought I was teasing her & maybe I was.

Just a little.

It's hard not to sometimes.

Only writing now cos we've been stuck in the airport since yesterday (cos of this, like *pea-souper* of a fog) & G's been going on & on & on & *on* at me the whole time, wanting to know if I, like, was *ever* going to use it.

Debbie

10.00 a.m. Twenty-four hours later and the fog still hasn't lifted.

Maeve sighs and tells us all how much she's missing Dylan.

Genevieve groans and complains that the woman next to her is playing her Walkman too loudly and that it's driving her insane.

Laura spins some yarn about how she felt it was time to move on from *The Argus* even though everyone knows, bar Genevieve it seems, that she was more or less fired because of the whole Devereux Affair and what happened to that poor woman Lily Buchan.

Maeve

Since it *is* a travel diary guess I should start with me leaving.
Just awful!
Having to leave Dylan was heartbreaking.
The worst!
As for Mum – Complete Hysterics!
She even came up from Portrea esp. to be with me for my last few days.

Drove me *nuts*.

Like, at 4.00 a.m. (while I was *still* trying to pack) she was following around after me with ciggie (55th of the day) in one hand & vodka (20th) in the other, telling me these incoherent stories from my childhood & trying to catch a hold of me to give me (yet) another hug.

This guy just passed by & I swear for a sec. I thought it was Dylan – he was like, the Dead Spit of him.

From the back anyway.

I am *sooooo* missing him already.

But back to Mum.

In the taxi on the way to the airport she started, like, crying her eyes out all cos I hadn't told her I loved her enough times. To cheer her up, agreed that her flying out to Thailand for a wk. in Jan. to meet up with us when we get there was, like, a fab idea.

Debs will go *mental* when she finds out.

Annoyed enough as it is about me letting G & L come along on "our" trip which we've been talking about going on since we were, like, fourteen or fifteen.

And she doesn't know about Dylan coming out yet!

This diary-writing lark isn't so hard after all when you get into it.

But enough for now.

Think I'll go & ring Dylan.

Debbie

> *11.30 p.m.* Maeve is sighing and telling us how lonesome Dylan sounded on the phone and how she doesn't know how she's going to survive the next few months without him.

Genevieve is complaining about the way the man sitting opposite her is eating his sandwich with his mouth wide open. She wants us all to watch and see how he's "dropping lettuce and whatnot all over the place". I hope he doesn't understand English for she's talking very loudly.

Laura is bragging about some book she says she's been commissioned to write on Asian culture.

And I'm cracking up.

Genevieve

We're still stuck in Heathrow and have been here for over twenty-four hours now which I think is an absolute disgrace and an outrage fog or no fog and as soon as I get a chance I'm going to write a letter of complaint. You never know I might even get a free flight out of it. And given how much they're paid you'd think pilots would be trained to cope with a bit of fog especially with all the technology that's out there nowadays.

I notice that the woman and her mob from yesterday are still up and down and in and out for they're scattered all over the place. They're really getting on my nerves and if they weren't so cross then people might just make more room for them so they could be all together but at least now the old lady's got a seat to herself. Two of the children are sitting on the floor behind me and I have to say they're making it very hard for me to concentrate with all their whingeing and whining and I'm beginning to get a fierce headache from them and it's not like they're the only ones in this awful boat. I wonder where the father is. I wonder why the woman couldn't have left the granny behind with him. But maybe he's already gone ahead and they're flying out to meet him. Or maybe he's long gone out of the picture altogether. He could even be remarried by now and have a completely new family. I wouldn't blame him for his old ones are <u>such</u> <u>whingers.</u>

The diaries are definitely proving to be a <u>big</u> <u>hit</u> and worth the money for I noticed that Maeve has started writing in hers too now. Laura hasn't gone near hers yet and is more interested in that little computer she has with her although it can hardly be up to much for I've seen bigger calculators! Of course it's not just a holiday for Laura and she was telling me earlier about this book she's been commissioned to write as she put it, on something to do with Asia though I didn't really get what it was about exactly but it sounded interesting and she's getting a huge advance for it.

Debbie

1.05 p.m. Maeve is sighing.

Genevieve is groaning.

Laura is bragging.

How did I ever let Maeve persuade me to go through with this trip?

Why didn't I pull out after all the hassle over Dylan?

2.10 p.m. Maeve is sighing.

Genevieve is groaning.

Laura is bragging.

Or pull out after Maeve told me that Genevieve was coming as well?

3.15 p.m. Maeve is sighing.

Genevieve is groaning.

Laura is bragging.

Or even more so pull out after Laura announced she was coming?

Genevieve I can take. When all her complaints, frets and neuroses get too much I can just tell her shut up as she never takes offence. But Laura? Now she's a different matter entirely.

An Asian Diary

"Together again, eh lads?" Genevieve keeps repeating, as if we'd spend the years apart doing little else but long for this moment. Thankfully she stops short of slapping us all on the backs – just about. I don't know how many times Maeve and Debbie have told her to shut up but they're not words Genevieve seems to understand. Funny that, when she probably hears them more than most people.

But here we are, dear reader, still living out every traveller's worst nightmare; still stuck in this hellishly crowded airport; still with no idea as to how long more our flight is going to be delayed.

That we checked through our luggage and so are left without toiletries or a change of clothes exacerbates the situation. But for once Genevieve has shown herself to be resourceful and, ordering Debbie who wasn't exactly pleased to be ordered thus to guard our seats for fear they'd be nabbed in her absence by the hordes unlucky not to have one of their own, she dragged me off to the nearest shop. Once there, she scuttled in, checked left and right, picked up a can of deodorant, stuck it under her jumper, sprayed one armpit, then the other, put the can back on the shelf and scuttled back out again. What was the sense, she demanded to know when she saw me looking at her askance, in buying deodorant when she already had a can in her luggage? And then, on our way out of the shop she hovered for a scarily long time amongst the toothbrushes, eyeing them up, no doubt considering whether or not she'd get away with some quick freebie dental hygiene. Thankfully she thought better of it.

Not that she was quite finished her grooming yet and en route back to Maeve and Debbie, she detoured by the Ladies where I was unlucky enough to witness her solution to the problem of sweaty feet. Off came the shoes and socks and into the wash hand basin went said feet.

But there can be nothing more boring than waiting in airports. It's like they're deliberately tormenting us and it seems like every hour they announce they expect the fog to lift soon and flights to resume.

But, in the meantime, Debbie is poring over maps and plotting routes and terrifying Genevieve with talk of places we should include. Maeve has disappeared into the smoking room with a crowd of hippie-travellers and hasn't been seen for a couple of hours now. As long as she stays in the smoking-room and doesn't decide to pay a visit to the bar for a quick gin. Or two. Or three. And, for the last couple of hours, Genevieve has been reading an old magazine someone left behind. And eating. Somehow she managed to talk one of the ground staff into giving her twice as many food vouchers as she's entitled to and she's determined to use them all up. Mumbling through a full mouth, she keeps going on about how it's the last bit of decent food she's likely to see for a long time.

They've just announced our boarding call. Finally. Thankfully.

22nd October

Debbie

5.05 *p.m.* We're in the air – finally. The stewardess has just ordered Genevieve, who's restless already, to please return to her seat and to stay there until the seatbelt sign has been switched off.

Genevieve

Do they think it's only midgets who need to fly? I'd have expected a plane going all the way to Beijing would be a bit roomier but instead we're all squashed in like flaming sardine sandwiches and I'd like to know where the hell they think our legs are supposed to go and it's not like I'm fat or anything but I'm bloody well <u>wedged</u> <u>into</u> <u>my</u> <u>seat</u> and I've nowhere to put anything and I'm already beginning to get cramps in my legs and my neck is stiff out.

Debbie

5.15 *p.m.* The seatbelt sign's been switched off and Genevieve's out of her seat like a bullet and straight over to us. She wants to know why she's stuck beside a total stranger whereas we three got to sit together.

5.25 p.m. She's back again. This time to complain about how she's feeling very boxed in and how flying is far worse for her on account of her being so tall.

5.30 p.m. And again. Now she wants us to know that she suffers from claustrophobia, or at least she thinks she does.

5.45 p.m. And again. What's more, she tells us, the stranger beside her is really beginning to get on her nerves, though hardly as much as she's getting on his for every time he picks up his book and looks set to continue where he left off reading, she's at him to either leave her back in or back out again.

The stewardess has just come to tell her that she's going to have to sit down and stay sitting as she's causing an obstruction in the gangway.

6.00 p.m. The flight attendant's words have fallen on deaf ears and Genevieve is back again and is listening open-mouthed as Maeve deliberately adds to her woes by giving her an in-depth account of an article she read lately about the numbers of people who die each year from blood clots they develop whilst flying economy class on long-haul flights.

The attendant has now come storming down and has told Genevieve that if she doesn't sit down immediately she's going to get the pilot to come out to see to Genevieve personally. Muttering to herself, Genevieve has reluctantly resumed her seat.

At least worrying about clots will give her something to occupy her mind.

Maeve

Beginning to wonder if I'm *completely* Off My Head.

Like, what am I doing going away like this when Dylan & I have been together for such a short time??????

But how could I *not* go when Debs & I had been planning our Big Trip for yrs & yrs & yrs?

If I'd pulled out or if I'd let her pull out then it would have been Curtains For Our Friendship – no doubt. And despite our ups & downs that means everything to me.

I mean things are *still* a bit fraught b'tween us as it is but at least this trip will give us a chance to get back to the way we used to be – I hope.

Altho' it might not help (Understatement Of The Year) if Dylan comes out & joins up with us.

Not that I'll be holding my breath.

Lately he can hardly get it together to buy himself a new jacket – so wouldn't bank on him arranging tickets, visas etc, etc, etc *&* getting himself on a plane at the appointed time. Funny, don't remember him being so outta control when he was going out with Debs.

But at least he's happy for me to be going away.

But will he feel diff. after a few wks all alone? Now *that's* the big qst.

For one, he's not exactly the type to be content to sit in on his own, watching T.V. on a Sat. night. His past record hardly instils confidence & Rick & the boys aren't exactly going to be interested in keeping him on the Straight & Narrow.

Funny that the reasons I'm attracted to him (v. good-looking, a bit mental etc, etc, etc) are the very reasons I've such qualms about leaving him now on his ownie-o.

Debbie

8.00 p.m. It's impossible to get any sleep with Laura going on and on about how she's flying out to Asia to research this book she's been commissioned to write. She's talking at the top of her voice of course so that everyone around is sure to hear her.

All the flight attendant asked was if she was off on holiday.

Maeve

But I just need to rem. that Dylan is nuts about me.

No doubt.

Everyone says so – least everyone bar Debs. She doesn't say anything.

So I mustn't be silly – of course I can trust him.

Course I can.

Course I can.

L is now leaning over, pretending to be reading what I'm writing.

– Dylan this, Dylan that, Dylan, Dylan, Dylan blah-de-blah blah blah. Big fat yawn.

Such is her summary.

Debbie

8.30 p.m. And Maeve is still going on about Dylan. You'd think she could be a little more sensitive and not mention him quite as much.

I know I was the one who broke it off with him but not because I'd fallen out of love with him, as Maeve knows, but for other very valid reasons. Like his out-of-control drinking, his drug habit, his lack of any proper job, his run- ins with the law. I think that about covers it.

Genevieve

I'm not really complaining but how come the others got to sit together and I got stuck next to this fellow who is just <u>unbelievably</u> <u>annoying</u> and it's almost impossible to write when he's practically up on top of me like this and I really feel like turning to him and asking him did he ever hear of personal space. He's Australian I think and I have to say that it's just so typical of Australians to take up as much room as they like for I suppose they'd be used to the space what with having the outback right on their doorstep and that. And why can't he just keep his knees together? What is it with men? Why do they always sit like that with their legs sprawled all over the place without the slightest bit of regard for the people around them?

The back of my left calf is beginning to feel sort of funny and sort of dead with this kind of odd numbing ache. I hope it's not a clot.

Debbie

10.00 p.m. Genevieve is making all sorts of wriggling movements and strange faces at her neighbour. He's staring back at her with a completely bemused expression on his face. She's gesticulating furiously at his elbow. I think she wants him to move it.

Genevieve

I wonder how long a clot would take to travel to a person's heart. God Almighty! How much longer do we have to stick this? I've hardly room enough to write but at least I think I've finally got it through the Australian's skull that the arm-rest isn't just his and that he's <u>meant</u> <u>to</u> <u>be</u> <u>sharing</u> <u>it</u>.

Anyway what I was going to write about before I got sidetracked was how strange it is to think that here we are, us four old classmates, heading off together like this after all these years. It's funny but to look at Laura now you'd never guess in a million years that she came from somewhere as countryish as Portrea. She hardly has a trace of an Irish accent now not to mind a Portrea one. She really leaves Debbie and Maeve in the halfpenny place and I used to think <u>they</u> were the height of sophistication!

Of course my parents never really approved of Laura when we were young and I'd say they used to think she was full of herself but in the end didn't she show them all by making a bit of a name for herself in the world of journalism. Her boyfriend Felix is also in the media and presents a radio show in London so he was telling me when we met him in Heathrow so I guess you could say he's a bit famous even if I've never heard of him myself. I must say I thought he was <u>very good-looking</u> and <u>very well-spoken</u> though I couldn't say I really warmed to him as such. I just didn't like the way he kept forgetting my name even though I must have reminded him I don't know how many times. You'd think having such a bad head for names would be a terrible handicap for someone in his line of work. And you wouldn't call him outgoing either though you'd expect he should be and honestly I had to drag the information out of him. I hate to say it but I actually found him <u>quite cold.</u> And I got the distinct impression that Laura was trying to hurry him away, like she wasn't too keen for him to meet us. I'd have said she was embarrassed by her old school friends if I didn't know any better!

Debbie

11.00 p.m. Laura certainly hasn't grown out of her desperate need to impress. She's now going on about her book to a girl sitting in the seat in front.

But what I don't get is why she's coming away with us. She's not exactly the backpacking sort so how come she's happy to rough it with us? Especially given the huge advance I just heard her saying she's getting.

Maeve

Ho hum. Dying for a ciggie.

And another drink.

Already had a couple – if I have any more Debs will start on at me.

Sometimes she seems to think she's my mother. Or like a mother should be.

You'd swear I was, like, a *total* alkie the way she goes on.

Wish I could get some sleep.

Maybe I should follow G's example & do some exercises.

She's been marching up one aisle & down the other for over 1/2 an hr now, puffing & panting as she goes, pausing every now & then to do a few squats all the better to ward off the dreaded clots.

Think more people are watching her than the official in-flight entertainment.

Debbie

Sure Genevieve is daft and sure she's making a show of herself right now doing laps around and around the plane but if Laura thinks I'm going to be giggling with her behind Genevieve's back she's got another think coming.

41

I know I was concerned about Laura coming on this trip but I think I'm going to find it even harder than I imagined.

Genevieve

I'm <u>knackered</u>. The sweat is just <u>pouring</u> off me no exaggeration for I've been doing some exercises but hopefully they'll put a stop to those clots lodging. I'll do some more again in an hour or so.

I must admit that at first I was worried about travelling with Laura for as I say I just hadn't seen her in so long and we were never really close but now I think it's probably for the best as Maeve is a bit too laid-back and I'm afraid Debbie is the other extreme altogether and will have us going from morning to night if we're not careful. God Almighty! I see she has her nose stuck in her guidebook yet again though she must have the whole thing learned off by heart by now. She hardly put it down the entire time we were in Heathrow and kept reading out bits she thought were interesting though what other people think and what Debbie thinks is interesting are two <u>very</u> <u>different</u> <u>things.</u>

Maeve

Arragh!!

How many more hrs??

Could really do with another drink.

Or something stronger.

Am Going Completely Out Of My Mind!!!!!!!

Genevieve

I'd like to know just who the hell that air hostess or

stewardess or flight attendant or whatever it is you're meant to call them nowadays thinks she is. Telling me that I was getting in her way and ordering me back to my seat like that at the top of her voice! She'd do well to bear in mind that it's <u>us passengers</u> who pay her wages and if I die from a clot <u>I</u> <u>will</u> <u>sue her</u> <u>personally.</u> And she can threaten me all she likes but it'll take more than a few words from her precious pilot to scare me.

And if it's not bad enough having her harping on at me and being cooped up here like this and being forced to breathe in the same air as everyone else over and over, now the Australian's feet have begun to <u>stink</u> no exaggeration and I thought Australians would be particular when it came to hygiene what with their love of the beach and that. But now that I look at him he doesn't seem at all well. He's awfully pale for an Australian. I just hope he doesn't go getting clots. Him collapsing on top of me is all I need right now. He has the look of a heavy smoker and I already know for <u>a</u> <u>fact</u> he's a heavy drinker for Ms Hoity-toity Air Hostess can't pass up or down the aisle without him calling her over and demanding yet another gin and tonic. But at least it's giving her something to do besides fixing her hair and filing her nails. Some people are just <u>so</u> <u>vain</u>. I mean she's not even all that good-looking and I'd say she must be forty if she's a day though from the carry-on of her you'd think she was about half that age and her manner leaves a lot to be desired so don't ask me how she ever got to be an air hostess.

Debbie

3.30 *a.m.* Genevieve's just woken us to tell us her latest concern. She's afraid that her neighbour is going to fly off into one of those "so-called air rages" at any moment

43

for it seems he's a drinker who's drinking a lot and a smoker who isn't allowed smoke – a lethal combination according to Genevieve.

Genevieve

For crying out loud, why should I have to put up with this? I can't breathe with the smell from the Australian's stinking feet. God Almighty, he's now asking for yet <u>another</u> gin! And there's something very odd about his face. I think it's the shape of his eyebrows though I can't be sure for every time I try to get a good look, he stares back at me really rudely.

There! I just knew he was an alcoholic. Three swallows and he's finished his gin! And where on earth is he off to now?

Debbie

4.00 a.m. We're all wide-awake now. This flight seems to be going on forever. Laura's just overheard Genevieve's neighbour complaining to one of the attendants about Genevieve. It seems he's not very happy for a number of reasons: she keeps staring at him, shoving his elbow off the shared arm-rest, tut-tutting loudly every time he takes a sip from his drink and fanning his feet with the in-flight magazine. It seems he wants to change seats and is prepared to take anything at all.

Maeve

Debs told me to stop fidgeting & just go & write in my diary or something.
Am going insane!!
Truly.

44

In-flight entertainment rubbish.

Thought Morecambe & Wise were dead.

Miss Dylan so much already.

He is *such* a cutie tho' a wee bit dumb sometimes.

Take our last day in town for e.g. when I pointed out these Ray-Bans to him in a shop window & he took the hint (or so I thought) & went hurrying inside but – 5 min. later – came back out with a (wait for it . . .) torch!

Said he thought it'd be of more use on our trip!

That I'd *hardly* be pointing out designer sunglasses to him if it was, like, a torch I secretly hankered after hadn't occurred to him.

Oh but I miss him *soooo* much.

Genevieve

I think I misjudged that air hostess for she obviously has some cop-on as she's just moved old fatso Mr Australian to another seat. I suppose she must have seen how awful it was for me to be stuck next to the likes of him. As soon as I get an opportunity I must be sure to thank her.

Anyway, what I was going to write about before I got started on him was boyfriends and how one of the worst things about going away is having to leave them behind. I'm leaving poor Theo and Maeve is leaving Dylan and Laura is leaving Felix. Debbie's the only one of us who isn't going out with anyone at the moment but then it's always been the same old story with her for although she's quite nice-looking in her own way she never seems to be able to hold onto one. She even went out with Dylan for a while before he and Maeve got together which I gather was the cause of the big falling-out between herself and Maeve. Not that either of them told me much about it but for a while there it seemed like the whole trip was going to be off until I managed to talk them both around.

But I'd really love to see Debbie settled with someone nice. I've always thought Theo's brother Trevor would be ideal and we'd get on really well as a foursome and I know he's interested in her but despite my best efforts whenever she's home from Dublin for the weekend I've never been able to get them together. At least not yet but fingers crossed! As Trevor says, she's just acting mean to keep him keen. And he is. <u>Very keen</u>. Of course if we are to have a double wedding they'd want to hurry up about getting together. Ha ha!

Maeve

Just found a strip of passport photos of Dylan in one of my pockets.

Guess he must have slipped it in before I left.

What a softy!

Can just see him. Racing off to the photo-booth (all excited with his great idea) then sitting there with his hair tidied & his face all smiley.

Snap. Snap. Snap. Snap.

Definitely a cutie.

Now I'm embarrassed! G just passed on her way to the toilets & saw me kissing the photos. Of all the people! Can't imagine her *ever* acting so foolishly!

Should try & sleep but it's imposs. & we have hrs to go . . .

Genevieve

At least Laura and Debbie managed to get some shut-eye though Laura is wide awake now and is tapping away on that little computer of hers again but poor Maeve's been awake the whole time like myself. When I passed by on my way down to the toilets a little while ago she was sighing over some photos of Dylan and kissing them which is something I can't ever imagine myself doing with photos of Theo though that doesn't mean to say that I'm not every bit as fond of him as she is of Dylan. Theo and I have been together for seven years after all and though I hate to say it, I doubt if Maeve and Dylan will last even a <u>fraction</u> <u>of</u> <u>that</u> <u>time</u>. To be honest I don't know what she sees in him but maybe I'm missing something for Debbie used to be cracked about him too. I mean I can see he's very good-looking and all that but he's just too off-the-wall for me.

The air hostess is going around with some wet cloths and waking everyone up and it looks like they'll be coming around with the trolley again soon. I'm not really all that hungry but I guess I should eat whatever's going as God only knows what kind of food we'll get in Beijing. There can't be more than a hour left to go now.

Debbie

6.30 *a.m.* Ever since the attendant announced we're coming in to land, Genevieve's been poking around, packing up everything she can find to take away with her. And I mean everything. Earphones, in-flight magazine, socks, even the little pillow and blanket they supply for the duration of the flight.

Not that she can have all that much room left in her bag. Laura says that after dinner she watched her stash away the plastic cutlery set, two little bottles of wine, a mini can of Coke, a portion of cheese as well as a bunch of face wipes.

47

An Asian Diary

*I*t's funny how little some people change. Genevieve for one hasn't, not a scrap. Ever the wide-eyed country girl. I can only imagine what the other passengers must make of her. Not to mention the flight attendant. I know Genevieve hasn't flown before, not least because she insists on telling anyone foolish enough to make eye contact, but you'd still presume that even she should be able to figure out that pressing the overhead button is sufficient to gain attention and that, sitting there, frantically waving her arms in the air and yelling yoo-hoo, isn't actually necessary.

It's odd but I'd forgotten how she used to think I was the bee's knees, as she might say herself, back in school but it's all coming back to me. If I came to class wearing purple leg warmers on Monday, Genevieve would be wearing them by Tuesday and, if I troubled myself to notice and told her they'd look better stuck in her ears, she'd thank me for the advice and promptly pop one in each.

Honestly, reader, the way she's been fawning all over me since we met up again is positively embarrassing. Telling me how fantastic I look – like I need to be told. And how handsome she thought my boyfriend was. What does she expect? After all like does attract like. And rabbiting on about how come she couldn't find a pair of boots like the ones I'm wearing when she went looking. That she shops in P – and I shop in Kensington might have something to do with that. That and the small matter of our respective budgets.

Debbie hasn't changed much either. Still her same old steady, sensible self. I don't think she's quite lost the chip she used to have when it came to me. Jealousy? Perhaps. In fact, probably, though it's impossible to know what Debbie's ever thinking. Except every time Maeve mentions Dylan that is, which is approximately every five minutes or even more when I prompt her – just for the fun of it. And then I swear Debbie's left eye twitches ever so slightly and her mouth becomes clenched, super-glue tight. Of course, Maeve, being Maeve, is completely oblivious.

But I have to ask, what kind of person would be stupid enough to go on holiday with the very person responsible for breaking up the only serious relationship she's ever been in, even if they have been best friends forever?

But it's good to see that Maeve doesn't seem to be drinking so much at the moment. It's good to see that she's back to being the bouncy, bubbly girl she was in school after going through a few rough years in the interim. She's in far better form, for instance, than she was eighteen months ago when she turned up out of the blue on my doorstep in London in the middle of the night, looking for somewhere to kip. But it is good to see she's settled down a little and, surprisingly, going out with someone with the alcohol and drug dependency problems Dylan has, doesn't seem to have disrupted her fragile equilibrium. At least not yet.

23rd October

Debbie

10.00 a.m. Maeve's dad hasn't shown.

10.30 a.m. He still hasn't shown.

11.00 a.m. Maeve is demanding to know how Genevieve could possibly know that her father is going to turn up at any second, as she keeps insisting.

11.30 p.m. Still no sign.

12.00 p.m. Maeve is beginning to get upset.
"Stop hugging me, Genevieve. It's not helping, you know? Just get the hell away from me! All right!"

12.30 p.m. Maeve is very upset.
Assuming she's just being brave, Genevieve continues to offer comfort in the face of some pretty strong resistance. "Will you ever just get out of my face, Genevieve!"

2.00 p.m. Still no sign.
Things have come to a head between Genevieve and Maeve. Maeve is now poking Genevieve in the chest and warning her that she'd better not say another word if she knows what's good for her.

Sadly Genevieve never knows what's good for her.

Genevieve

God Almighty! I hope Maeve's mood is going to improve for she's being a <u>right</u> <u>bear</u>. If she's going to be carrying on like this the whole time we're away then this holiday is going to end up being a compete disaster! And anyway I don't know why she should take her bad mood out on me. Going on about how I'm crowding her out like that. I was only trying to comfort her. It'd be worse if I didn't care. And anyway if she's going to lose her temper with anyone though I'm not saying she should then it should be with Debbie for she's the one who said that Maeve's dad not showing was hardly a surprise seeing as how Maeve is always complaining about how unreliable he is. All I did was agree with her and that was just out of politeness more than anything for I can hardly even remember the man.

Maeve should be thankful that we're still even talking to her given that it's her fault we're here in China, stranded, all on our own, no one to meet us, with no idea of what we're going to do or where we're going to sleep and not a single word of Chinese between the lot of us apart from Chicken Chow Mein. It's just as well Theo doesn't know the predicament we're in or he'd be worried out of his mind.

Maeve

Don't think I've ever felt *so, so, sooooo* let down in my whole life.

Expecting Dad to collect his daughter & her friends when they'd travelled $1/2$ way round the world was hardly, like, expecting *that* much.

Genevieve

And not a bite to eat. It's a bit much really. And I don't even know what time of the day or night I have between all the coming and going.

Maeve

I mean I thought he was looking forward to seeing me as much as I was him.
Like, it *is* over 18 mths since he was back in Ireland last.
Mum's right.
I shouldn't expect anything from him.
At least that way I wouldn't be lining myself up for a disappointment.

Genevieve

I just remembered the cheese and the other bits and pieces I took from the aeroplane but if I offer them around they'll go nowhere.

Debbie

3.00 *p.m.* Maeve still can't reach her Dad. She's now got into one of her huffs and has decided that we're going to take a taxi and look for somewhere else to stay. When we can find Genevieve that is. She seems to have disappeared.

Room 303, Golden Dragon Hotel, Beijing.
Several hours later.

Genevieve

This place is the <u>pits.</u> I wish I'd thought to pack some pellets and the like from Dad's warehouse but not for a moment did I think we'd end up staying in somewhere like this. It is just <u>filthy</u>. Even worse than that B&B outside Dingle run by the queer baldy woman with the extra thumb where we stayed the time of Auntie Maura and Uncle Pat's silver wedding anniversary. The fact that it was the sixth place we tried but the first to have rooms at a reasonable rate should have sounded warning bells in our heads. The sheets on my bed are covered in these greyish stains and I can't even bear to think what they might be and the floor is all sticky and there aren't any windows in the room though for some unknown reason there is a dirty old rag of a curtain hanging on the wall over my bed. We're all stuck in the one room but at least it's dead cheap, about seven euro per head but still, if we'd stayed put in the airport until we'd managed to get in contact with Mr Clancy like I said we should then we wouldn't have had to shell out a penny or put up with such filth but of course no one had any interest in listening to me.

I am absolutely exhausted but it's pointless even trying to go to sleep for I know I won't get so much as a wink in this dreadful place but maybe I should try for I really am hanging.

Debbie

6.00 p.m. Genevieve announces she's going to go for a snooze.

6.01 p.m. Preparations for the snooze commence.
Stage one: She stands by the bedside and stares hard at it in order to detect any movement of "ticks, lice, maggots and whatever else might be crawling about in there".

Stage two: She removes the blankets and lays a clean towel over the bottom sheet then covers the pillow with a second towel so as to prevent her catching anything off the "manky bedclothes".

Stage three: Fully clothed, so as not to go "contaminating" her nightie for she's only brought the one and "can't be washing it every day" she finally lies down.

6.05 *p.m.* Genevieve is sound to the world.

Maeve

Met these Scottish guys earlier when we were booking in so we're going to head out with them to check out Beijing's nightlife.

When L is finished on her palmtop.

I'm, like, *gasping* for a drink

G's not coming.

Despite all her complaining 'bout the state of the bed, she was asleep the sec. her head hit the pillow.

Some hours later.

Genevieve

Oh for God's sake! How is anyone expected to sleep in this place! Is there any privacy at all? Just now this pimply spindly English youth wandered into our room wearing nothing but a scrap of a towel around his waist and he'd that whipped off and was clambering into Laura's bed before I was finally able to make the dope understand that he was in the wrong room. Bad and all as this place is you'd think they'd at least be able to come up with a couple of locks for the doors.

I think the others must have gone out with those Scottish fellows we met earlier when we were checking in and who asked us to go for a drink with them. I have to say that I'd no interest in going though the others were fierce anxious to go of course and no surprise there. I know she's single and all but I hope that doesn't mean Debbie's going to be going around picking up fellows every night of the week. We don't know these fellows from Adam and no doubt the girls will end up paying for everything as the Scottish are notorious for being mean.

But I just don't know how I'm ever going to get any more sleep tonight between doors banging and toilets flushing and people clattering up and down the hall non-stop and screeching laughing and calling out to one another like it's the middle of the day. And if I actually do manage to go back to sleep, how can I be sure that someone won't sneak in during the night and go pilfering through our things? That English fellow knows the lie of the land now and could easily find his way around the room in the dark.

[Save Address(es)][Block]   [Previous][Next][Close]
From: "Tobin, Laura"<lauratobin@hotmail.com>
To: "Howard, Tony"<editor@idolmagazine.co.uk>
Subject: Column for "The Idol"
Date: 23 Oct, 23:52:16
[Reply][Reply All][Forward][Delete]

Hi Tony,

I've taken on board your point about not using the girls' real names. It's something I should have thought of myself and, as you'll see, I've amended what I already sent you and have given each of them a pseudonym. Maeve is now Mags, Debbie is Deanne and Genevieve, Geraldine. I've also given some of the other characters nicknames. I trust these minor changes aren't going to delay including my column/ diary in your magazine any further.

Regards,

Laura.

24th October

Genevieve

Maeve managed to contact her father first thing this morning so now he's on his way to get us out of this <u>hellhole</u> and not a minute too soon. My ankles are covered in these bites which I'd say are from <u>fleas</u> of all things and it's a pity Dad isn't here for he could tell straightaway just by looking at them. But at least nothing was stolen during the night or at least as far as I can tell but earlier when I was showering in the bathroom down the hall someone stole the fresh knickers I'd laid out for myself. I ask you! What kind of <u>weirdo</u> would steal someone else's underwear of all things? And they were one of my most comfortable pairs too, one of the few that didn't catch.

I had a dream about Theo last night all about him coming to collect me in the van except the van was red instead of blue. I wonder what that means. I really do miss him even if I don't go on about him all the time like Maeve does about Dylan. I'd love to give him a ring but I suppose he's right and it'd cost a fortune and anyway I don't know how the phones work in China and if I ask any of the others they'd just think I was stupid and start laughing at me though I'm sure I'll be able to work them out in my own good time.

A little later.

Maeve

Please Dad, just please, please, *please* hurry up.

Don't think I can *bear* listening to G any longer. I do love her but sometimes she, like, does my head in.

Like, does she think I'm only joking when I keep telling her to shut up about her fleas & about the place being full of robbers (tho' what it is they're s'posed to have robbed she refuses to say) & esp. about how she was right all along about there being a perfectly reasonable explanation for Dad's non-appearance yesterday?

As it happens – there was.

Turns out he had to go on a mercy dash to the hospital with his housekeeper's 10 yr old son who'd accidentally taken some pills & by the time he'd it all sorted out & had finally managed to get to the airport, we'd already left.

Don't mean to sound hard-hearted but couldn't he have, like, called an ambulance for the boy? It hardly sounds like a life-&-death situation.

This Asian girl has come to our door & is trying to hand G a pair of knickers. She's saying they got mixed in with her things in the bathroom & seems to think they belong to G. G is refusing to take them.

Says she's never set eyes on them before.

Can't say I blame her (they're a right pair of bloomers) but I bet they're hers – they've Genevieve written all over them.

Debbie

11.30 a.m. Genevieve is whining on about the "bites" on her ankles.

11.45 a.m. She's still whining.

12.00 p.m. Still whining.

12.15 p.m. Still whining.

1.15 p.m. Maeve tells her she's the "moanest" person in the whole world. Laura points out that there is no such a word as moanest. Genevieve begins to whimper. She says that nobody cares about her pain.

1.30 p.m. Mr Clancy comes to collect us. Alleluia!

Living-room in Andrew Clancy's penthouse apartment. Late afternoon.

Debbie
5.00 p.m. We've arrived at Mr Clancy's apartment which is very impressive.
Laura of course is trying hard to give the impression that this sort of luxury is exactly what she's used to. Genevieve too is so impressed that I think she's finally forgot her bites.

Genevieve
I don't really remember Mr Clancy from long ago for we were only about fourteen or so when he ran off but I must say he's much younger than I thought he would be and much nicer than you'd expect for a man who deserted his young wife and child even if it was years ago. I must say his apartment is absolutely out of this world and the longer we can stay here the better for it's costing us nothing and if the truth be told I'm in no hurry to repeat our experience of last night. I get the shivers even thinking about all those dirty, filthy creatures just gorging

59

themselves on my body as I lay there asleep. A few tins of pellets and what-have-you and Dad and the lads would have that place sorted out in no time. But I have to say that the room Laura and I are sharing is fantastic. It has its own enormous balcony and a huge en suite bathroom which is completely white. White tiles, white fittings, white towels, white bathmats, white everything. It is simply <u>divine</u>! The bathtub which is also a jacuzzi is absolutely colossal. Laura's been in there for the last half an hour and when she comes out I'm going to have a go if we still have time before dinner. The one drawback is that Laura and I are going to be sharing a double bed which is something I'm not very comfortable with as having grown up an only child I'm used to my own space but I guess it's all part of travelling together, all part of bunking in you could say. But then maybe it won't be so bad for Laura and myself are getting on way better than I thought we would and way better than we used to when we were in school and I find I could listen to her for hours for she has some amazing stories for she's led such an interesting life especially when you compare it to mine for example which I'm sure some people could consider a bit boring though I'm not complaining of course for it suits me fine. Maeve and Debbie's room is even bigger than ours and I must try and have a peep into Mr Clancy's for I can only imagine what that must be like!

I wish Laura would hurry up. If she doesn't come out of the jacuzzi soon I'm not going to get a go for we're meant to be having dinner at half past six.

On the terrace. A couple of hours later.

Debbie

8.00 p.m. After a delicious dinner we're all sitting out

on one of the terraces, enjoying the view, too full to move, just relaxing. It's quite cool out here but that's only to be expected as it's coming into winter.

Maeve's just arrived out wearing an Aran sweater belonging to Genevieve something Genevieve doesn't look too happy about. She's not saying anything but is just sitting there, glowering over at Maeve. It seems like Maeve has packed all the wrong clothes and didn't listen when I tried telling her before we ever set off that it was going to be cold until we got down south.

Genevieve

Theo warned me before I went away that if I'm going to enjoy this holiday then I can't let small things annoy me. Like Maeve taking my jumper out of my rucksack for instance without asking. We're going to be away together for almost three months and annoying things like that are going to happen all the time and I'm going to ruin the trip for myself if I let them get to me. But would it have been too much trouble for her to have just asked? I'd better start thinking about something else otherwise I'll start getting really annoyed. Like this place for instance. Honestly I've never seen anything like it, except on the telly. Mr Clancy doesn't actually own it and in fact it's owned by the American company he works for who've sent him over here but he must be <u>very</u> <u>important</u> if they've given him somewhere like this to live and a driver and a housekeeper to boot. Maeve's going to ruin the sleeves of my jumper if she keeps pulling them down like that but like I said I'm not going to get annoyed. The housekeeper's name is Mei and she seems nice enough though she's very quiet but then I suppose she must be worried about her son being in hospital and that's understandable too but at least the doctors say he's out of danger. The meal she served up tonight wasn't too bad and not too Chinese-y.

Debbie

8.45 p.m. Mr Clancy asks Maeve if her room's ok.

Genevieve tells him that hers is "just gorgeous" and that she loves it.

It's touching to see how anxious Maeve's dad is to impress her, not that she even notices.

Maeve

Phoned Mum earlier.

Killed me cos I hadn't phoned for all of, like, one day.

Had to play down Dad's plush pad tho' I let it slip that he had a driver & a hsekeeper.

Big big *big* mistake.

How could I have been *so* stupid?

Started her off on this huge moan about how well it was for some people to have their every need taken care of, blah-blah, blah-blah, blah-blah.

Even *more* stupidly, I then said something like how it was time she stopped being so resentful of Dad given how long they've been apart.

I'm going to be apologising for that one *forever*.

Debbie

9.00 p.m. Mr Clancy asks Maeve what she thinks of the apartment.

Genevieve tells him that "Honest to God, it's like

something off the telly," and that she just can't get over the staircase, that it's "just huge."

I don't think I've ever seen Genevieve flirt before, not even with Theo, but she is definitely flirting with Mr Clancy but then being so handsome, I'd say he has that effect on most women.

Maeve

And then – just as I was about to hang up – Mum started on about Dad's hsekeeper *again* asking me did I think there was anything between her & Dad.

As if!

To ease her mind, I explained that Mei was about ½ Dad's height, almost as old as him, not exactly fair of face, barely able to speak a word of English &, that she has a 10 yr old son.

Hardly the catch of the century & *definitely* not his type.

Debbie

9.15 p.m. Mr Clancy asks Maeve what she thinks of the view from the terrace.

Genevieve says she's never seen the like of it.

I don't think Genevieve is setting out to flirt and I'd say she just can't help herself as Mr Clancy is very charming. But she is excruciating to watch she's so bad at it.

I wonder what Mei, Mr Clancy's girlfriend, makes of it.

9.30 p.m. Equally oblivious to Mei, who really is as quiet as a mouse, Laura has begun to vie with Genevieve for Mr Clancy's attention. It's only now coming back to me how Laura had this major crush on him when we were kids.

Right now, she's doing her best to impress him with insider titbits on British politics. She really can go on and whether any of it is true or not it's definitely more interesting than what Genevieve has to say. She keeps butting in with talk of bugs and bites and the cockroach infestation her father successfully dealt with only last week though it's hard to imagine why exactly she should think Mr Clancy might be especially interested though he is sitting there politely, trying to listen to both her and Laura at the same time.

10.00 p.m. I'm beginning to think Mei's silence isn't related to her command of English for she seems to be smirking an awful lot at the carry-on of Genevieve and Laura.

10.15 p.m. Genevieve's moved onto a new topic. Her stomach and how it "isn't the best".

Genevieve and Laura's room. Many hours later.

Genevieve

I feel sick out. I know Mr Clancy's housekeeper, Mei, went to a lot of trouble with our meal tonight but it's really upset my stomach and it's just as well we've an en suite for I've been out to the toilet <u>six</u> <u>times</u> <u>so</u> <u>far</u> tonight no exaggeration and I'm not really well in either end and Laura keeps rolling into the middle of the bed which is <u>driving</u> <u>me</u> <u>mental</u>. I just can't get her to stay on her own side.

An Asian Diary

*I*t turns out that Mags' father, Mr C, has done frightfully, frightfully well for himself. In a country where the average home is the size of a shoebox, even I'm impressed by his triple terrace, five-bedroom penthouse in the heart of the city.

I think Geraldine is overwhelmed by it all. Ever since we got here, she's done nothing but wander around, salivating, just touching everything, sighing and babbling on about how this table or that sideboard is exactly the kind she's going to have one day when she and the Country Bumpkin are married and have a house of their own.

I don't think so. Somehow I don't think Mr C's period pieces are available as flat packs from the furniture warehouse in P–! And her getting married might not be quite as soon as she thinks. My memory of the Country Bumpkin was that even at seventeen he was a very happy bachelor boy.

But back to the delectable Mr C. Besides his obvious wealth, the other important point of note is that he's still absolutely gorgeous. And I don't mean in a gorgeous-for-someone's-father or gorgeous-for-a-man-in-his-late-forties sort of way. I mean he's just absolutely drop-dead gorgeous. Like George Clooney gorgeous. It pleases me to see that even at fourteen I had excellent taste in men.

In a way he should be thankful to me for I was the reason he left P – in the first place. If it wasn't for me, dear reader, his excuse of a marriage might never have broken down and he'd still be living his semi-life in his semi-d, sleeping night after night in one twin bed, his ageing and increasingly alcoholic wife across the room from him in the other. But instead, thanks to me, here he is living the life of a high-flying ex-pat in his swish apartment with a coterie of servants at his beck and call.

But things could have been very different if he'd had his way. If he'd had his way, we'd have ended up living together over the local newsagent's in a poky flat but, young as I was, and handsome as Mr C was, even then I'd the sense to realise that that wasn't the life I'd in mind for myself and broke his heart by finishing things. Have you ever seen a grown man cry? Have you ever seen a grown man on his knees, clinging to the hem of a schoolgirl's skirt as she tries to walk away? Not a pretty sight.

But that was years ago. And here is Mr C now – incredibly handsome as I say and evidently very wealthy. And from the looks he's been giving me all night, it wouldn't take much to have him clinging to my hem once again. But should I go down that particular path? After all, I have a boyfriend waiting at home for me. An even handsomer, younger and much, much richer man than Mr C. But a handsomer, younger, much, much richer man who isn't exactly accessible right now.

Whereas Mr C is right here, right now and very accessible. Hmmm . . .

25th October

Living-room of Andrew's apartment. Early morning.

Debbie

8.00 a.m. As soon as Maeve is finished getting ready we're going to head out sightseeing for the day.

I'm glad we're going to get such an early start as we've an awful lot to get through. There's just so much to see in Beijing.

Genevieve

As soon as Maeve's ready we're going to go and do a little bit of sightseeing though don't ask me why we're going so early and I don't know what Debbie expects to be open at this hour of the morning but that's Debbie all over.

Mr Clancy's just left for work. I think Maeve was a bit mad with him last night when he told her he couldn't come with us today as he's some important meeting to go to this morning and then afterwards he has to go to see the housekeeper's son in hospital but he promised he's going to take tomorrow off and spend it with us. I was just thinking how strange it is to think that Mr Clancy was married to Maeve's mum once for they don't seem at all suited as he's just so free and easy whereas she's as uptight as I don't know what. Except when she's out socialising that is and I swear she could drink for Ireland. I remember seeing her last Christmas Eve in Hurley's at closing time and she was on her ear no word of a lie but to be fair, that time of the year must be an especially lonely time for people like her. Of course it must have been even worse for her in the early days when Mr Clancy and that American girlfriend of his who was young enough to be his daughter were shacked up over the newsagent's on the main street in Portrea. I'd say Mrs Clancy was well pleased when she hightailed it back to America. I think himself went to Dublin after that for a couple of years and then came out here I guess.

Debbie

8.20 a.m. Maeve finally came downstairs wearing a sleeveless top and skimpy little skirt so I took her over to the window and pointed out that the reason all the people below were decked out in their woolly winter clothes was because it was winter.

She's gone back upstairs to change.

Genevieve

But what's gas to watch is the way Debbie and Laura carry on with Andrew as he's told us to call him. They're forever asking him what he thinks of this, that and the other. I suppose you could excuse Debbie in a way for at least she's not in a relationship and she's probably getting a little anxious what with the three of us having steady boyfriends and of course it's not like she's getting any younger. I wish she'd just relax and stop ranting on about what's keeping Maeve now. Haven't we got the whole day ahead of us? Laura on the other hand has been going out with Felix for over a year now and I overheard her talking to Maeve about how well things are working out since they moved in together a couple of months ago so it's hardly a fitting way for her to be going on though I'm sure it's harmless enough and that she doesn't mean anything by it but an older man like Andrew might not realise that.

Debbie's in a right tizzy now and has gone stomping upstairs to get Maeve.

Debbie

8.45 a.m. When I went up to find out what was keeping Maeve this time, I found her in Genevieve and Laura's room with Genevieve's clothes strewn all over the bed. She was looking for something warm but couldn't find anything she was willing to be seen wearing in public, like anyone here knows her.

So I asked her to show me what was in her own bags and there was nothing apart from bottles of suntan lotion, bikinis, beach-wraps & skimpy little outfits. In the end I had to loan her some of my clothes.

All I have to do now is make sure Genevieve doesn't go up and see the mess Maeve has made of her things otherwise we'll never get going.

Genevieve

But one thing I will say about Debs is that I really admire the way she pulled herself together after Dylan dumped her. I hadn't realised how badly she'd taken their break-up but Laura was telling me she went <u>completely</u> <u>off</u> <u>the</u> <u>rails</u> and that she used to ring Dylan up dozens of times a day for ages after and pester him at every opportunity and it sounds like she made a right nuisance of herself. In the end Dylan had no choice but to get his number changed.

Debbie

8.55 a.m. There was one other thing in Maeve's bags. An album full of photos of her and Dylan which she started trying to show me.

How could she possibly think I'd want to see happy snaps of her and Dylan when I haven't yet got to a point where I can bring myself to throw out ones of him and me?

Genevieve

It's funny what with Debbie normally being so sensible she's the last person you'd expect to behave like that but when it comes to love you just never know how people will react. I'd better finish up for they're all heading out the door. It was fine for us all to spend the morning waiting for Maeve but none of them are prepared to wait even five minutes for me

Back once again in Andrew's living room.
That evening.

Maeve

Think Debs is afraid we'll stay with Dad for too long & fall behind schedule.

I swear she, like, seems to have our every move planned out for the next few months.

But it is nice staying here.

G definitely thinks so – if she'd her way we'd end up spending all our time in Beijing

Just now she started on about how *huge* his en suite was &

when L asked how she knew she had to pretend Dad had brought her in to see it (since she could hardly confess to snooping) & nearly died when L said she was going to ask him to show it to her too.

I wouldn't put it past L. She's great fun but she can be a real bitch sometimes.

Like on the way back to Dad's this evening G started telling us one of her yawn-inducing Theo stories but L butted in & began doing this take-off of Theo & what he was like back in school.

And she was brilliant too – spot on.

The way he used to hop from side to side, mumbling like a moron, trying desperately (& usually unsucc.) to come up with an answer to the teacher's qst.

Course it was mean to laugh but she *was* priceless.

But then when Debs told her to shut up & reminded her that Theo *was* G's b'friend, L acted like she'd forgotten (which is rubbish – L *never* forgets *anything*).

And how could she when G is forever going on about her Theo & what things are going to be like when they become happy-ever-after Mr & Mrs?

I don't think G even realised L was being mean.

She can be *sooooo* thick at times.

I swear she thinks the sun shines out of L.

Meanwhile, out on the terrace.

Debbie

8.00 p.m. After a hectic day's sightseeing followed by a delicious dinner, I've come out onto the terrace to get a break from the others for a while and especially from Maeve as she's started on about Dylan. Again.

8.30 p.m. I've been spotted. Concerned that I might be "a bit lonesome out here on my own" Genevieve has come trundling out after me and has pulled up a seat.

I'll keep writing and she might take the hint and go away.

"I always thought it was a pity, Debbie, that Dylan dumped you for Maeve . . . of course they're far better suited than you and he ever were . . . and everyone knows musicians never make a penny . . . no spring chicken yourself, Debs, if you don't mind me saying . . . age differences don't seem to matter so much nowadays . . . at least thirty years between Michael Douglas and Catherine Zeta Jones . . . Andrew got divorced five years ago . . . he must be absolutely loaded and he's just lovely too, isn't he?"

I have tried interrupting her, to tell her I wasn't the one who got dumped but it's impossible to get a word in edgeways when Genevieve is in full flight and besides she has this extraordinary capability to only hear what she wants.

And is she seriously suggesting that I should consider Maeve's father a potential boyfriend?

9.00 p.m. Genevieve leaves.

9.01 p.m. Genevieve returns.

Expressly, it seems, to point out that I could be Maeve's stepmother which she thinks would be "gas!".

At least Andrew Clancy makes a nice change from her own boyfriend's twin Trevor who she's forever trying to foist on me.

9.20 p.m. Maeve wants to know if I'm coming out with them to some Irish pub. I may as well.

Genevieve and Laura's room. Later.

Genevieve

The others have gone out to some Irish pub but I didn't bother for I'm just wrecked. We've been going non-stop all day. We went to see the corpse of this fellow Chairman Mouse or something like that who's this dead Chinese leader which I have to say I thought was a <u>sick</u> thing to do but Debbie says he's a huge tourist attraction. It was her idea to go of course and if you ask me you'd have to wonder who in their right mind would want to go gape at someone who's been dead for centuries and who should have been buried long ago but apparently the Chinese are mad for that sort of thing. I must admit I got an awful fright when I saw him lying there all pale and waxy because nobody had told <u>me</u> what we were queuing up for and of course what with the shock and everything I let out a scream which caused everyone in the place to turn around and stare so that I was absolutely mortified and it didn't help that Maeve and Debbie got into a fit of giggles which caused all the Chinese in the place to keep on staring and staring at us like <u>we</u> were the floorshow or something.

And the way Maeve can't let things go sometimes drives me crazy and I know Debbie's right and I shouldn't take any notice but it was really annoying the way she kept on asking me what I thought it was we were waiting in line for but to be honest I didn't actually know but I didn't want to ask and show myself up and earlier we'd been talking about getting a bite to eat so I figured that maybe that's why we were queuing. I mean everything is just so different here and it's hard to know what's what and it's not like a dead body would be the first thing to spring to mind exactly.

Maeve messed up all my things this morning and didn't even apologise for doing so. It took me ages to put everything back in the right place and when I gave out to her about it she just started mocking me and mocking all the little labels I have on the ziplock bags. I know I said I wouldn't let myself get annoyed at small things for I don't want to go spoiling this trip for myself but I think that was <u>out</u> of <u>order</u>. Laura says that if I let Maeve get away with that then she'll start thinking she can walk all over me but what can I do? I wonder what time the others will be back. It must be nearly midnight.

[Save Address(es)][Block]   [Previous][Next][Close]
From: "Tobin, Laura"<lauratobin@hotmail.com>
To: "Howard, Tony"<editor@idolmagazine.co.uk>
Subject: Column for "The Idol"
Date: 25 Oct, 23:00:18
[Reply][Reply All][Forward][Delete]

Hi Tony,
I think you're worrying unnecessarily about the girls' sensibilities. First, it's unlikely they'll come across an issue of *The Idol* in Asia. Second, even if they do and they recognise themselves, it's not like they can sue for defamation. We're not even using their real names.
Regards,
Laura.

[Save Address(es)][Block]   [Previous][Next][Close]
From: "Tobin, Laura"<lauratobin@hotmail.com>
To: "Wilson, Felix"<felix@fmsounds.com>
Subject: I'm missing you already
Date: 25 Oct, 23:15:17
[Reply][Reply All][Forward][Delete]

Hello my darling Felix,
Here I am in Beijing – finally. Getting here was something of a nightmare. Just after you left me they announced the flight was delayed so I was stuck in Heathrow until the following day which was a drag although I did have those girls we bumped into for company, the ones I went to school with back in Ireland. I'm not entirely sure if that was a blessing or a curse. Have you ever met anyone like that girl

Genevieve? Isn't she completely nuts? Imagine having to put up with her for fourteen years in school! No wonder I left for London as soon as I could.

I survived the flight, just about. It helped that NCRR Publishing sent me business class. I don't know how all the sad souls, including Genevieve et al, coped with being stuck in cattle class.

Unfortunately Andrew Clancy, my contact here in Beijing, was called away unexpectedly so he didn't make it to the airport but he did arrange for me to be collected and brought to his place which, I have to say, is super, just out of this world. All in all, I'm enjoying myself though I haven't managed to get down to work on the book yet but then that's hardly surprising as it's early days and I'm still finding my feet.

It's a pity I've only managed to get your answering machine so far but I'll try ringing you again in the next day or two.

Love you,

Laura.

[Save Address(es)][Block]   [Previous][Next][Close]
From: "Tobin, Laura"<lauratobin@hotmail.com>
To: "Kane, Christopher"<kaneliteraryagents@aol.com>
Subject: Book Proposal
Date: 25 Oct, 23:52:30
[Reply][Reply All][Forward][Delete]

Hi Chris,

Thanks again for agreeing to consider my book proposal at such short notice.

It was disappointing we didn't get to meet up and discuss it when I dropped it into your offices before I left for Asia but if you've had a chance to look at it and want to go over any aspect of it, e-mailing is probably the easiest option as I'm moving around quite a lot.

Regards,

Laura.

26th October

Andrew's living room. Late morning.

Maeve
Wonder what L is going to do for cash now that *The Argus* has fired her.

Hers & Felix's lifestyle can't come cheap. She's forever going on about all the swanky parties & fancy-pants restaurants they go to.

Yesterday – when G & her were enjoying one of their cosy tête-à-têtes – I heard G suggesting to L that she should do some articles on our trip but L just broke her face laughing. Pointed out that she was, like, a serious journalist & that she did, like, have a book to write.

Then she tells G that she's actually on leave from *The Argus* – like, *Hello!*

Does she think we don't read newspapers in Ireland? *Everyone* knows she was fired – maybe not, like, technically but as good as.

But I guess writing about her & her friends backpacking 'round Asia would be a letdown after all the high profile political stuff she's done.

Debs says she's going to find it v. hard to find work again

with any of the papers cos of the whole Devereux Affair.

And I don't think any of us know what L's book is actually s'posed to be about. Not *even* L.

One minute it sounds like it's meant to be a travel book, the next it's all about Chinese literature.

All v. vague.

Debs thinks it's all nonsense & that L's just bullshitting – which is why she keeps trying to pin L down on what the book is about *exactly*.

Must rem. to get some aspirin.

Have this *splitting* headache – think I overdid it last night.

Don't think Dad was too pleased with me.

Debs certainly wasn't.

Debbie

11.45 a.m. Laura was hard to take in school but she's far worse now. It's hard to believe but I think she brags even more than she used to back then. I'm not sure why she feels such a need to impress us with all her talk about this book she's meant to be writing.

But I am surprised at how well she's getting on with Genevieve given how bitchy she was to her in school. She is still a bitch however. Just after breakfast, I overheard her telling Mei she'd dropped a plate. She wasn't saying she'd dropped a plate meaning she was sorry but that she'd dropped a plate meaning Mei should clean it up. But, quiet as Mei may be, she was well able for Laura and just handed her a pan and brush and walked away. With her son in hospital, Mei has enough to deal with without having to put up with rude guests as well but at least Shao is coming home tomorrow.

I wonder what's keeping Laura? We'll get nothing done if we don't get a move on soon.

Tearoom in the grounds of the Summer Palace. Early afternoon.

Genevieve

Another thing I remember about Mrs Clancy was that she always very highly strung and that she'd eat you if you came into the house and forgot to hang up your coat or wipe your shoes or whatever. Maybe that's why Maeve went the other way and is so disorganised and messy now. This morning she came and messed all my stuff up again and took a loan of my red jumper with the green pattern which I was going to wear with my cords today. When I asked her to take it off she just laughed and told me to stop fretting and said I'd so many jumpers I could kit out the entire population of the Shetland Islands and have enough leftover for all the sheep which of course makes no sense whatsoever. Sometimes I don't get her at all. I'd say she'd a few too many last night for she looked <u>very</u> <u>ragged</u> this morning.

But I guess you can't really blame Mrs Clancy of course as running a house and bringing up a child especially on your own can't be the easiest thing in the world and I wouldn't envy anyone in that position. But she definitely was very highly strung from what I remember and you can see why Andrew might have been inclined to leave her though I'm not saying that what he did was right. And I don't know what it was about Mrs Clancy but she never took to me when I was young and I used to be calling around to the house for Maeve.

Debbie's at me to get a move on. What is she like? I was hoping she'd let me stay here and just collect me on the way back out but she says they won't be coming back this way. I don't know why she can't take things a bit easier. It's fine for her, she doesn't suffer from fallen arches.

An Asian Diary

Although it's impossible to imagine what he sees in her, it turns out the delectable Mr C has this live-in, quiet-as-a-mouse girlfriend who barely speaks a word of English, or of anything else, and comes encumbered with a ten-year-old son. Quite a catch indeed!

What have I done to the poor man? Did I break his spirit so completely to cause him to give up on love and settle instead for this Ms Mouse?

We're taking the Chinese equivalent of serious hillbilly here and I think little Ms Mouse would be far more at home in the fields of provincial China, sowing and reaping, or whatever it is peasant farmers do. And I swear she's so quiet that at first I didn't even notice her pottering around in the background, not until she dropped a plate and then I just assumed she was the housekeeper, and an incompetent one at that.

It was only when I saw Mr C give her a peck on her red cheek that I realised she was more than the hired help. Poor man! I don't think he could have looked any more embarrassed when he noticed me watching.

But it seems Ms Mouse and I aren't the only ones aware of Mr C's charms. Neither the presence of Ms Mouse or the existence of Geraldine's boyfriend has stopped Geraldine going all out to try and impress Mr C. Geraldine is definitely more than a little smitten with him but when I dared say as much she took umbrage and told me not to be so stupid and weren't she and the Country Bumpkin practically engaged. News to him, I'm sure.

It is, of course, possible that she doesn't realise Ms Mouse is Mr C's girlfriend. After all, I didn't at first and I think it's reasonable to credit myself with somewhat superior powers of observation than Geraldine.

In fact, I don't think Mags yet appreciates the intimate nature of their relationship. I did consider telling her but Mags is a shoot-the-messenger kind of girl and I don't need her giving me a hard time.

And besides, I think it would be better to let things take their natural course. More fun. More fun to watch Mags gradually realise she's been supplanted in her father's affections of which she's always been ridiculously jealous.

27th October

Maeve
Debbie's been missing for, like, bloody ages.
Wish she'd come back.
Can hardly be *that* much to see.
L's all huffy with me.
Overheard me starting to tell G about how she lost her job
at *The Argus* and interrupted to tell me I was mistaken &
that she'd resigned in order to write the book & do some
freelancing.
Sure!
She can't, like, exactly be up to her eyes in freelancing
assignments if she can come travelling with us for so long –
book or no book.
That housekeeper of Dad's is doing my head in – she's just
being *unbearably* nice to me all the time – good to get away
from her for a while.
And her son came home this morning – fully recovered
from his overdose.
He's a right nuisance – one of those hyperactive kids.
How does Dad *stand* having him about the place?

Genevieve

You can really tell that Laura doesn't scrimp when it comes to clothes and grooming and that but then I'd say she's doing very well for herself and that money is no object with her. She even resigned from *The Argus* which I think is very brave though it's not something I'd do myself if I were in her shoes seeing as how she was permanent there but she says she wanted to do more freelancing and to write that book about whatever it's about for I never seem to be able to remember but it sounds far too clever for me. But fair play to her for I don't remember her being all that smart in school but I guess she must have been.

I was telling her earlier about the work I do in my dad's office and she said she couldn't imagine how they were coping with me being away and that it seemed to her like I practically ran the place single-handedly and I was obviously very efficient and she just hoped Dad appreciated me.

It's nice to have someone to be able to talk to about things like that. Maeve and Debbie never want to hear that kind of stuff and I know they think the work I do for Dad is boring yet Laura is very interested though she leads a far more exciting life than either of the pair of them what with working in the media and earning a fortune and living the highlife in London and going out with someone who is practically famous and of course being practically famous herself.

Debbie's just arrived back and is hurrying us all up and going on about how we're not going to have enough time to fit everything in. How can she say that when we have practically three whole months to go?

Back at Andrew's, Genevieve & Laura's room.
That evening.

Genevieve

The girls have gone out with Andrew to some night market but I've given it a miss for if the truth be told I've had more than my fill of sightseeing for one day. I am knackered! Apart from the break we had in the park Debbie had us marching about all day like we were a troop of girl guides or something. I swear my whole head is throbbing like mad which is why I've taken myself off to bed early but I've been calling and calling out to Mei all evening for some aspirin but she hasn't come near me though I know she can hear me for I've had to put up with listening to her yakking away on the phone all night. Between her and her son Shao I can't get a wink of sleep. He came home from the hospital today and it's like he's wound up. He's in and out of here like a yo-yo, wanting to show me all these pictures he's drawn though what they're meant to be I have absolutely no idea and if you ask me he should be gone to bed hours ago but she's too busy nattering away to care though she'd want to watch it or next thing she'll find him head first in the cleaning cupboard helping himself to whatever takes his fancy and she can <u>forget</u> <u>it</u> if she thinks I'll be taking them to the hospital for the last thing I need right now is a crash course in driving on the wrong of the road.

And though I haven't said anything to Andrew, I know for <u>a</u> <u>fact</u> that either Mei or her son have been at my things. There's nothing gone missing I don't think but my diary was put back in the wrong ziplock bag. And it wasn't Maeve either looking for a jumper or whatever for if it'd been her she'd have just left everything in a right heap. But at least neither Mei or the boy would have been able to understand

86

what's written in my diary. But still I can't think of anything more despicable than reading someone else's diary. I think I'd better call it a night. I just hope Laura won't go turning on the light and waking me up again. I think I'll put a sign on the door to tell her as much.

Maeve and Debbie's room. Some hours later.

Maeve

Rang Mum when we got in this evening.

She always sounds so *desperately* lonesome whenever I ring.

Started on about the housekeeper – again.

Wanted to know if there was anything b'tween Dad & her – again.

Told her there wasn't – again.

What I *didn't* mention is that I'm beginning to think poor Mei has the hots for Dad.

I swear she's forever hovering about him like she owns him & is always trying to start up these conversations with me – the old getting-in-with-the-daughter trick – though it's *agony* having to sit there waiting as she gropes 'round, trying to find the right words in English.

Feel like telling her she's wasting her time, that 18 yr old airheads are Dad's type ever since he left Mum – *not* plain, desperate, middle-aged women.

Rang Dylan next.

Must have been onto him for at least ¹/₂ an hr! How I miss him!

Can't wait until he comes out.

Shouldn't hold my breath tho' – he hasn't even got his ticket yet.

An Asian Diary

As might be expected I guess, there's a certain tension between Mags and Deanne for Mags' only topic of conversation appears to be her boyfriend. I swear the girl is obsessed. I've stopped counting the number of times she sighs per day, tells us all how desperately she's missing him and wonders what he's doing right at this very moment. Most likely he's asleep regardless of the time for Mags' boyfriend doesn't make the same distinction between day and night as the rest of us and has been known to sleep right around the clock. And it's not laziness of course. It's the – ahem – artistic temperament, so Mags says.

You see, dear reader, Mags' boyfriend is a musician. Well actually he's a cycle courier who plays the guitar and manages to get the very occasional gig but in his and Mags' imagination he's a musician – up there with the Greats. Move over Bono!

And what's Deanne doing when Mags keeps going on about her wannabe-a-rock-star? Well, Deanne is the still-waters-run-deep sort and while the casual observer might think she either doesn't hear or doesn't care, the keener observer will notice that the smile is more of a grimace, that the fists are clenched tight and that the knuckles are blanched as she stares fixedly into the distance, a tightly controlled smile on her face. Mags of course sees none of this and thinks everything is just fine.

And if Deanne is finding it tough going now, she's going to find it a hundred times tougher when the wannabe arrives out to join up with us. I wonder how long she'll manage to carry on suffering in silence then.

28th October

Andrew's living-room. Early evening.

Genevieve

I am just <u>wrecked.</u> It was all go-go again today but at least I got a break from Debbie for Laura and myself spent the morning in the city centre looking around the shops while Debbie dragged Maeve off to see some historic thingy and then we all met up again for lunch in this really posh restaurant. Andrew was meant to come too but didn't as something came up at work. But I must say that lovely and all as the restaurant was, lunch was an out-and-out <u>disaster</u> but I'm not going to go into that.

It's funny how I used to think Maeve's job as a hostess at Vichy's Nightclub was fierce glamorous but it's nothing compared to Laura's as a journalist. When we were going around the shops together today, every now and then and not that she was boasting or anything, Laura would just happen to mention in passing something like say, the time Bill and Hilary Clinton were at the same party she was or how she happened to be sitting beside our very own Taoiseach at some function which of course is just mill-of-the-run stuff to her but to someone like me it's <u>absolutely fascinating</u>. And from the sounds of it she's on very good terms with Chelsea Clinton no less and when the hassles of being the famous daughter of an ex-president of the United States get too much for Chelsea she just picks up the phone and who's at the other end for her to talk to only Laura.

We're heading out to dinner as soon as Maeve's ready. In one way I'm in no mood to go for as I say I'm wrecked but at least I had a go in the jacuzzi as for once Laura didn't hog it. I am absolutely starving though and the place Andrew is taking us to is meant to be the most expensive restaurant in the city so it'd be stupid to miss out especially after that fiasco of a lunch.

Debbie and Maeve's room. Later that evening.

Maeve

At dinner this evening had to listen to G moaning on & on & on & *on*.

How there isn't a part of the animal they don't throw away.

How Chinese food is full of MSG – tho' I'd say she, like, doesn't even know what that means – it's prob. something she heard L. say.

How Mei's Shao was staring at her all the time – she's convinced he's suffering some after-effect from those pills he took tho' he seems perfectly normal to me – just v. taken with her for some peculiar reason for G's not exactly a natural with kids.

But the worst part of the whole evening was having to watch Dad flirting with all & sundry *&* all & sundry flirting with him.

He's pathetic!

And the girls are even worse – the way they were cajoling him, getting him to tell them all about his time in China & laughing themselves silly at all his (pretty dire) jokes.

Not that he needed much encouragement. He was even flirting with Mei.

How did Mum *ever* stick him?

Think I'll go & ring Dylan.

Debbie

10.30 p.m. Because we were all so young when Mr Clancy left I hardly remember him at all. He was just this genial, shadowy father figure who dropped us and collected us whenever and wherever Maeve wanted him to.

It's funny but from the way Maeve, and even more so her mum, have gone on about him since he left, I expected him to have turned into this loud-mouthed, flamboyant playboy type but he isn't at all. He's just very nice.

I wonder what the full story is with him and Maeve's mum. All Maeve will ever says is that he ran off with Miss American Teen Queen "end-of-story", but I just can't see him making the decision to leave lightly.

But it is nice to see that at least one of them is happy with a new partner.

Maeve

Thought the phone call to Dylan might cheer me.

Didn't.

Just thinks the way I'm going on about Dad is funny & that I'm exaggerating.

That's easy for him to say – he's never met Dad.

Had told Mum I'd ring her too – didn't.

It's crazy to be ringing her so often & I just didn't feel up to her usual inquisition.

Meanwhile in Laura and Genevieve's room.

Genevieve

At least the meal we had this evening made up for lunch and I swear I could have eaten a horse I was so hungry. Andrew paid for everything and absolutely nothing was too expensive. I'd say it was the dearest meal I've ever eaten in the whole of my life though of course it's the sort of place Laura eats in all the time so it was no big deal to her.

I happened to mention to Laura on the way to the restaurant how I thought someone was reading my diary. I wasn't going to say who I thought it was but she kept on and on at me until I finally told her I suspected Mei. I half expected her to tell me I was imagining things but to my surprise she said I could be right and said it had struck her that there was something very odd about the woman and that though she couldn't put her finger on why exactly she definitely wouldn't trust her. And I swear her son is driving me bananas for he'll hardly leave me out of his sight and he keeps giving me these little paper animals he's made for me which is kind I suppose but I don't know what I'm meant to do with them all?

An Asian Diary

Regardless of her matrimonial hopes vis à vis the Country Bumpkin, I've never seen Geraldine quite so dolled up as she was today for our luncheon date with Mr C.

All decked out was she in her 1980's style suit with its pleated A-line skirt and its jacket with enormous shoulder pads and labels. Sad she should own such an outfit. Even sadder she should consider it her best. And even sadder still that she should have taken the trouble to pack it so carefully in a ziplock bag and label it – *CLOTHES FOR GOING OUT i.e. baby blue suit with matching blouse*. So tightly had she packed the suit that it took her over an hour of very vigorous ironing this morning to take out all the wrinkles.

So, when something came up at his workplace and Mr C rang the restaurant with his apologies, Geraldine was disappointed on two accounts. First, because she'd lost the chance to dazzle him with her looks and with even more stories from the world of pest control. Second, because she'd lost out on a free lunch.

But, what Geraldine somehow missed was that when Mr C rang the restaurant to say he wasn't coming, he also gave the manager his credit card details and so, while the rest of us ate as much of whatever we fancied in this top class restaurant, Geraldine stuck to a glass of water and a minuscule starter and spent the entire lunchtime with her brow all furrowed, casting surreptitious glances at the menu prices which were exorbitant even by my standards and, fretting over how much it was going to cost her.

I don't think I've ever seen anyone look quite so distraught as she did when she finally realised Andrew was picking up the tab.

29th October

Living-room in Andrew's. Early evening.

Genevieve

I came back early from dinner with Mei and her son but the girls and Andrew carried on and went for a drink somewhere though I honestly don't know how they managed to keep going for I was just <u>hanging</u> with the tiredness as we'd spent the whole day traipsing along the Great Wall which to my mind wasn't really all <u>that</u> great though of course we didn't get to see the whole thing and I'd say if Debbie had her way we'd be walking yet. I know she's really nice and all but sometimes she'd do your head in with all her bossing.

Because there were so many of us on the trip out to the Great Wall we had to travel out in two cars and don't ask me how but I got stuck going with Andrew's driver and Mei and her son whilst the others all got to go together in the car Andrew was driving. Well, all I can say on that score is that I most certainly <u>did</u> <u>not</u> enjoy it. The whole way there and back the driver and Mei were gabbing away and it was like I was completely invisible and of course I couldn't understand a single word they were saying and they were laughing like mad and for all I know it could very well have been me they were laughing at and talking about and I half suspected it was most of the time. As for that child! Give me patience! I was stuck in the back seat with him and he just spent the whole time sitting

96

there, gawking away at me like I was from outer space, the mouth of him hanging wide open and the eyes popping out of his head. You'd think I was the most fascinating thing he'd ever seen in his whole life. And he was just as bad at dinner tonight. I got put sitting beside him again worst luck and honestly he hardly had time to swallow he was <u>that</u> busy staring at me.

I think I hear the others coming in though it's not even ten yet. Maybe the bar closed early for there's no way Maeve would be coming home before she had to.

Out on the terrace. Later.

Debbie

10.00 p.m. I'm on the terrace again on my own. We've just arrived back after having a couple of drinks. We'd probably still be sitting in the pub except that Maeve insisted we leave which definitely must be a first.

She is such a drama queen sometimes. There we were, having a grand old time, until she suddenly got into one of those moods of hers where she's just itching for a fight and out of the blue she told me to stop flirting with her Dad and wouldn't listen when I pointed out to her that flirting with my best friend's father was hardly my style. Not that she let the best friend thing stand in her way when it came to Dylan, as I might have reminded her. I'm not saying I'm blind to Andrew Clancy's charms, I doubt if any woman could be but it's Laura she should be annoyed with as she was the one doing most of the flirting. I don't think Laura's quite got over her schoolgirl crush.

Maeve's now taken herself off to bed in a huff which is why I'm out here waiting until she goes to sleep as I know she'll start on me if I go in.

[Save Address(es)][Block]   [Previous][Next][Close]
From: "Tobin, Laura"<lauratobin@hotmail.com>
To: "Wilson, Felix"<felix@fmsounds.com>
Subject: Your e-mail?
Date: 29 Oct, 22:34:56
[Reply][Reply All][Forward][Delete]

Hi Felix,

I'm having such an amazing time. This country is incredible though it is very poor and the facilities are shocking but if you have money you can avoid the worst and NCRR Publishing are being very generous in terms of expenses.

I haven't met too many westerners so far, just the odd backpacker. I keep meaning to get in contact with those girls we met in the airport, the ones from Portrea, and arrange to meet up with them again as I think it would be interesting to see how they're getting on but I just haven't had the time between all the interviews and the research I'm doing for the book.

I really wish you were here with me, Felix, as I know you'd enjoy it all. Like the marvellous restaurant Andrew Clancy took me to this evening to meet a couple of young Chinese writers he'd set up interviews with. And the luxury of his penthouse where I have my very own en suite bedroom complete with jacuzzi, moonlit balcony and king-sized bed – such a waste when you're not here to share it.

Oh well, I'll just have to make do with dreaming about you though I'll have you know that I'm sleeping alone by choice for the very handsome Mr Clancy seemed very reluctant to say goodnight! But don't worry, our relationship is strictly business.

Don't pine too much.
Love you,
Laura.
P.S. I didn't get a reply to my last e-mail so write soon. I can't believe I've only managed to reach your answering machine. Are you ever home?

30th October

Overnight train, Beijing – Xian. Late afternoon.

Debbie

4.59 p.m. We rushed onto the Beijing – Xian train with exactly one minute to spare. Our hasty departure was at Maeve's insistence though she remained tight-lipped as to her reasons. Could it have anything to do with her discovering the true nature of the relationship between her father and Mei? Attempts to engage her in a rational discussion have proven useless as Maeve doesn't, "want to talk about it, all right? So just drop it okay! Just drop it! You're beginning to bug me, Debbie, you really are".

5.00 p.m. We walked up and down and up and down the train searching for our compartment but our search was hampered by our inability to read the signs, all in Chinese characters.

5.05 p.m. Genevieve accosted one of the passengers and demanded to know if he, "Speak-e English? You speak-e English?" in what I guess she thought was a Chinese accent and though he was staring at her blankly she went on to ask, in English again, but again with that odd accent, where seats 33a, 33b, 33c and 33d were.

Given that he didn't understand her first question, it was unlikely he'd understand this more complicated one, something which didn't seem to have occurred to Genevieve but it soon became obvious to all but her that he'd absolutely no idea what she was talking about yet she persisted and repeated her question again and again in increasingly louder tones as if she believed that this would somehow make things clearer.

5.06 p.m. A crowd began to gather, all fascinated by the six-foot, red-haired foreigner that is Genevieve and who was by then practically yelling in her increasingly desperate attempts to be understood.

5.07 p.m. A middle-aged man in the crowd stepped forward and seemed to understand what she was saying. He signalled us to follow.

5.10 p.m. At first it seemed that this man had brought us to the wrong section of the train but gradually it began to dawn on us that we did not have a sleeping compartment to ourselves as we believed we would but were in fact sharing a carriage with hundreds of other people.

Sleeping accommodation is in the form of what can best be described as rows upon rows of triple-decker bunk beds, the bottom ones of which are currently being used as seating for the passengers. Overall the carriage has the air of a rank, over-crowded prison and as the only foreigners in the entire carriage, we're proving to be of huge interest to the other passengers.

Genevieve

Staring. Staring. Staring. Staring. Everywhere we go we're bloody well stared at. It is driving me insane! What is it they all find so fascinating? I really just don't know how I'm <u>ever</u> going to stand being cooped up in this dreadful place with all these people for the next <u>sixteen</u> hours. I mean if one of the four of us so much as scratches, everyone else just stops whatever it is they're doing to have a right good gawk for themselves. Miss Know-it-all-Debbie says the people are like that because until recently foreigners weren't even allowed into the country so we're probably the first lots of them have ever seen. Well I don't care what the reason is. I still think it's downright rude. I swear things are so bad I can hardly bear to even write about them.

The reason we're stuck on this train in the first place is because Maeve suddenly got it into her head that we were leaving Beijing. Just like that. With <u>no</u> explanation, <u>no</u> discussion, <u>no</u> nothing. And we've no bloody room whatsoever as Maeve, Laura and myself are all squashed into the one seat and Debbie and these two men are sitting opposite and are so close they're practically up on top of us and I can't so much as move my knees without knocking against theirs and there is absolutely no doubt about it but I am <u>definitely</u> claustrophobic.

It's bad enough now but it's set to get even worse later on when the seat we're sitting on becomes Laura's bunk and I'll have to climb up onto the bunk just above our heads though I have no idea how I'm supposed to manage to do that and Maeve will have to climb up onto another bunk even higher still. And as the two fellas will be sleeping in the bunks opposite we're not going to have any privacy whatsoever though I'm going to ask Debbie to try and make sure she takes the middle one for that way she'll be directly opposite me so at least I won't have either of them lying across at eye level, gaping over at me all night. Even so, it's far from a satisfactory arrangement.

Maeve

Right now we're on the 1st train we could get seats on going to Xian & all cos of my father.
I hate him.
Hate him.
I am *so* mad.
Don't even know where to start.
Just calm down, Maeve, just calm down.
Breathe in. Breathe out.
Breathe in. Breathe out.
Slow-ly.
OK I'm calm.
I'm calm now.

Debbie

7.00 *p.m.* One of the Chinese men sharing my seat leaves the carriage but soon returns carrying a pot of water which he puts on a little stove to heat and to which he gradually adds some meat and some rice. All the while he is being watched by Genevieve whose horrified expression might lead one to believe she imagines him to be carrying out some dark, satanic ritual and not just making himself a bit of dinner.

Maeve

OK, so, here's the story.

Last night Debs, L, Dad & myself go to this bar where Dad spends all his time talking to Debs & L. So much so that – at one point – when L is in the loo & Dad is up at the bar, I let fly at Debs & ask her how would she feel if I carried on with her father the way she & L were flirting and carrying on with mine.

Course she thinks this is terribly funny & says I'd be very welcome and that she's sure he'd be only delighted.

Ha-bloody-ha-ha.

Then she tells me that I'm being stupid & that she's just behaving like any normal woman would towards a generous, entertaining, attractive (like, pleeaase – pass the sick bag) man but that doesn't mean she's trying to hop into bed with him & anyway – as far as she can see – he already has a girlfriend.

So I ask her what does she mean by *that* exactly which starts her off on this spiel about how I need to wake up & not be walking around with my head in the clouds & thinking of nothing but Dylan all the time (who has *nothing* to do with any of this but I guess she just couldn't miss the opp. to drag all that up *again*).

Anyway, an hr or so later when we leave the pub, Debs & L walk on ahead & Dad & myself stroll along behind, chatting away & I'm feeling v. pleased to have him all to myself for once.

So I start nattering on about Mum & how well she's looking blah-de-blah & so he, like, starts asking me is she seeing anyone & so I laugh & say that no, she isn't, & tell him she's young(ish), free & single & ask him why the interest, is he hoping for a chance to get back with her?

So he says that that's hardly likely given the circumstances.

So I say, what circumstances, & that's when he drops the bombshell & tells me he means his relationship with Mei *of course* (like this was something I should know!).

At 1st I think he's joking.

I mean she's hardly a looker or in the first flush of youth which is more or less what I say to him which gets him into a right snot but then *he's* the gall to tell me that looks or youth aren't everything (*this* from the man who left Mum for that silly American barely outta high school).

So then I tell him how I thought this woman Mei was meant to be his hsekeeper & so he says that's how they'd met originally but that she'd be his wife now if only she'd agree to marry him for he'd asked her often enough (like I need to hear this!).

And so I say I should prob. be thankful that at least he isn't going to tell me Shao is his son & he says that no, he isn't, at least not biologically, but that he means as much to him as a real son ever could (quick, quick – the sick bag).

So then I ask him how come he hasn't, like, told me any of this before and he says he, like, wanted to, but thought it better to wait until I'd got to know Shao & Mei but was surprised I hadn't already figured it out for myself.

I guess it must have been about then that I called him a sad, lonely old ex-pat, hitching up with the 1st woman who'd have him as soon as he set foot in China & who must be delighted with her fine catch.

And I guess it was about then he called me a selfish, stupid, prejudiced little girl.

So there!

Anyway, the upshot of it all is I've had enough.

Suddenly I'm presented with a de facto stepmother &

stepbrother & Dad expects me to turn around & embrace this newly discovered family.

Yeah – right!

Dream on, Daddy-o!

That's why we're now on this train.

Haven't told the others yet tho' they prob. have some inkling of what happened.

At least Debs & prob. L as well.

But they're sure as hell not going to get any confirmation from me.

Debbie

7.30 p.m. At the top of her voice, Genevieve announces that, "it's beginning to stink to high heaven in here," and hopes, "we don't have to put up with these fellows cooking all night".

She wants to know, "what in heaven's name do they have boiling in there anyway?" and suspects it could be, "bears' paws or fish lips for it certainly smells bad enough".

7.32 p.m. One of the men smiles over at Genevieve and in perfect English assures her it's neither and is in fact a simple chicken dish with rice.

7.33 p.m. Blushing a bright red and stuttering, Genevieve tells him he misheard her and assures him that of course she knew it wasn't bears' paws or fish lips as, "nobody in their right mind would eat such things". At this the man laughs and tells her that both are in fact considered delicacies here in China but unfortunately he hasn't yet had the pleasure of sampling either though it is an ambition of his to do so.

7.34 p.m. At first Genevieve thinks he's joking and begins to laugh but the expression on his face remains serious and under his unwavering stare she blushes even brighter red and buries her head in her diary.

Genevieve

All I can say is that I do not like these two Chinese fellas at all. They're a right smart smarmy pair. They're now offering around some of the food they've cooked but needless to say I passed for whatever about food from a restaurant there's absolutely no way of knowing where theirs comes from. But of course the other three are gobbling away like mad especially Debbie. I swear that girl would eat anything and though these fellows might say it's chicken we only have their word for that. I must say it's seems like complete madness to me to allow those little stoves on the trains for they can't be safe and they certainly wouldn't let the likes of them on the trains back home.

But at least I thought to bring along half a dozen apples and a couple of packets of rice crackers so I won't starve for I don't think I fancy eating in the dining-room car either and when we passed through it earlier it didn't look at all clean but quite the opposite. In fact, I would go so far as to call it dirty and the <u>last</u> thing I want to go getting right now is the runs what with being stuck on a train and all.

Debbie

8.00 p.m. At last it really feels like we're travelling.

Maeve may have been a bit rash in deciding to leave her dad's place so suddenly just because she got into a huff over his relationship with Mei but I'm glad.

And, given the way Laura was coming onto him last evening, it was probably just as well. She's got such a nerve.

When I came down from the terrace after writing in my diary last night, just she and Mr Clancy were in the sitting-room and Laura, in her skimpy little pyjamas shorts and vest, was sitting so close to him she was practically on his lap and was all hands and fluttering eyelids and girly giggles. Neither of them saw me but it looked like she'd stepped things up considerably from harmless flirting. I hurried away just as she put her hand on his knee and began caressing it so I don't know how far she got but Mr Clancy looked absolutely stunned.

It's as well it was me and not Maeve who came across them for Maeve would tear Laura's hair out if she'd witnessed her carry-on last night.

Genevieve

Correction. I thought to bring along half a dozen apples and a couple of packets of rice crackers which Maeve has just seen fit to take out of my bag without my say so and is now offering around to our two new "friends". I could kill her. What does she think I'm going to eat for the rest of the journey? And of course our two boyos aren't exactly slow in helping themselves either. No, sir!

And I've never heard anyone ask so many questions as this pair. I'm beginning to think there's something <u>very fishy</u> about them since they claim to have never been out of the country yet they can speak English fluently but say they picked it up from listening to the radio. Dad always had Raidio Na Gaeltachta on in the background at home but you don't see me sprouting off *as gaeilge*. One of them has just asked Debbie what my name is and of course she's gone and told him so now he's calling over, trying to get my attention, making sheep's eyes at me but he's got another thing coming if he thinks I'm going to spend the evening chit-chatting with him and his buddy for I've <u>no</u> intention of doing anything of the sort. I know Debbie's single and all but her drawing these fellow on us like this is just about the last thing we need right now. I just hope she doesn't fancy either of them.

Oh yes they're delighted with the crackers all right. I've never seen anyone get through a packet so quickly. And the apples are long gone.

God Almighty! I can hardly hear myself think with all the noise the girls and our two fishy friends are making. They've been at it for over an hour now and it looks set to continue for the two boyos have opened a bottle of some kind of spirits which the girls are more than happily taking their turn at and are knocking back like there's no tomorrow. I tried warning Maeve that it mightn't be the wisest thing in the world to be taking drink from strangers as for all she knows it could be very potent and anyway sharing a bottle like that is hardly the most hygienic thing in the world but of course she had absolutely <u>no</u> <u>interest</u> in listening to me and is happily guzzling it back like there's no tomorrow and as I say it looks like they're all set to continue for quite some time and it definitely won't be an early night for any of them.

So it's just as well I have so much to write about for you see I heard the strangest thing this afternoon from Laura when we were having coffee while the other two were queuing to get our train tickets.

It started when she began asking questions about Theo and me. I guess because she's a journalist she's very interested in other people and is forever asking all sorts of things. Now I have to admit that at first I was wary when it came to answering her for she used to be a right mocker in school but I've come to see that she is in fact genuinely interested. She really is much nicer than she used to be back in school. Anyway, at one point she asked me if I was still crazy about Theo after all this time and so I said I was although crazy wouldn't be the word I'd use myself but I knew what she meant. Then she asked me what kind of man I'd like if I wasn't going out with Theo so I said I didn't know because it wasn't something I'd given much thought to for why would I? But she told me to think about it now. And so I did. And after a while Andrew Clancy came to mind because I do really think he's an attractive man though that's not to say I'd like him over my Theo because that's not the case <u>at</u> <u>all</u>. Anyway Laura laughed when I mentioned Andrew and at first I thought she was laughing at me for being so cheeky as to name him but I was wrong and in fact she had a different reason entirely for laughing which was as follows.

You see at one point last night when Andrew and the girls were on their way home from the pub, Laura found herself on her own with Andrew and as they chatted away my name happened to come up in the conversation which caused Andrew to say something about it being a pity I hadn't come out with them for the night as I was such a lovely girl and very good company or something like that. Anyway hearing him say this and being the kind she is Laura started teasing him and saying how it sounded to her like he'd a crush on me, a remark which she said made him go all red much to her surprise. But of course that only made her tease him all the more and he started getting all embarrassed and began stammering and stuttering and going on about how he didn't have a crush on me for wasn't I one of his daughter's friends and that all he was saying was that I was really nice. But Laura said she got the distinct impression that wasn't quite the truth and she felt he was <u>definitely</u> <u>attracted</u> <u>to</u> <u>me</u> as she put it.

They're still at it! Knocking back the drink and yakking away at the top of their voices. They've been carrying on now for over two hours. It's nearly ten o' clock and I really want to go to bed for I'm absolutely hanging with the tiredness. And Maeve will be on the floor any minute now for I swear she's taking a couple of swallows for one of everyone else's.

For crying out loud! Now Debbie is trying to learn Chinese from our two friends. I wish she'd just shut up. She's been repeating the word "ma" over and over. Who'd have thought it could be that hard to get one single word right but I swear she's driving me bananas.

I'm not sure why I wrote down all that stuff about Andrew Clancy only that I guess it's flattering to be considered attractive by a man like him.

I'm in my bunk finally though the others haven't budged yet and are still talking rubbish with their new "friends". It was a real struggle to get into my nightie because my plan was to get changed in the toilet at the end of our carriage but that didn't turn out to be a very good idea I realised as soon as I saw the state of it. <u>Disgusting!</u> I couldn't even face using it for what it was originally intended for so let's hope I can hold out for the night. In the end I had to get undressed underneath my bedsheet which wasn't at all easy but it was the only way I could get any privacy what with those two fellas looking on and hardly daring to blink for fear they'd miss something.

It's gone past eleven now and they're all still up talking and there's just no way I'm going to be able to get any sleep until they go to bed. The way Debbie is going on, laughing and joking to beat the band, makes me think she definitely has her eye on one of them. And Maeve of course always has to be the life and soul of every party though she'll be in foul form tomorrow no doubt about it.

Twelve o'clock and they're still up talking nonsense. I am <u>wide</u> <u>awake.</u>

Twelve thirty and at last they've gone to bed though they're all giggling like mad now. <u>For</u> <u>crying</u> <u>out</u> <u>loud</u>!! Would they ever all just bloody well <u>shut</u> <u>up!</u>

Maeve is singing now at the top of her voice. I don't think she cares who's looking at her.

Twelve fifty and at last they've settled down though I'm still wide awake for it's impossible to sleep what with so many people close by and having to put up with them all coughing and snuffling and shuffling up and down to the toilet not to mind the noise of the train itself. I can just imagine what kind of disgusting state the toilet will be in by morning and even if I'm <u>absolutely</u> <u>fit</u> <u>to</u> <u>burst,</u> I'm definitely going to have to hold it in until we get off this stupid train.

Debbie

12.55 a.m. I just love this. Being carried safely through the night, lulled to sleep by the motion and sound of the train. That sound has to be one of my favourites in the world.

And so to sleep, perchance to dream.

Genevieve

God Almighty! Debbie is snoring like a <u>pig!</u> It's nearly two now and I can't get to sleep <u>at</u> <u>all.</u>

Honestly it seems like we're stopping at every goddam station there is between Beijing and Xian. I don't know how anyone is meant to get any sleep what with people hopping on and off all night and dragging suitcases and bags and crying children along behind them and clomping up and down the corridors looking for their bunks. What are they doing bringing children onto trains at this time of the night anyway, that's what I'd like to know. Debbie is <u>still</u> snoring. I've never heard the like of it.

Nearly four now and we've bloody well stopped <u>yet</u> <u>again!!</u>

I know it's silly to be going on about it but it really is flattering to hear someone like Andrew Clancy say he thinks I'm attractive. I wonder what Theo would make of it if I told him. I wonder if he'd be jealous. Probably not.

Nearly six in the morning and I still haven't slept a wink although Debbie is having a fine night's sleep from the sounds of it. She should really think about getting an operation done on her adenoids or tonsils or whatever it is that causes people to snore like that.

Just when I'd <u>finally</u> fallen asleep, this big bossy train official came around at a <u>quarter</u> <u>to</u> <u>seven</u> and made us all get out of our bunks so that she could collect up the sheets. And now though it's only half past seven I have to sit propped up on this hard old seat so it's impossible to sleep though I'm absolutely knackered and we've hours and hours yet to go as far as I know. The others have gone with their two shifty friends to get some breakfast.

An Asian Diary

We left Beijing sooner than expected at Mags' insistence. She wouldn't say what precipitated such a hasty departure but only a fool couldn't guess it was because she'd finally cottoned onto the relationship between Ms Mouse and her dad. Speaking of fools, Geraldine of course has no idea.

I actually feel a little sorry for Mr C's girlfriend. I imagine she must be feeling very satisfied with herself for having managed to snare such a rich, handsome, intelligent man who is willing to take on her and her horrid little son. But I don't think she'd be feeling quite so satisfied if she'd witnessed last night's scene.

Just as I was about to go to bed, I realised I'd left the book I was reading in the sitting-room so I went back down to get it and who was sitting there in the dark? You guessed it – Mr C. "I hoped you'd come," he said in that sexy deep voice of his. So, quickly, I began explaining what I'd come for, picked up my book and turned to go but found that he was blocking my way. What came next, dear reader, was positively embarrassing for he launched into this spiel about how his life had been a misery since we split up; how he couldn't help but compare every woman he'd met ever since to me; how the reason he'd come to China was to try and made a fresh start for once and for all; and, how the only reason he'd got involved with Ms Mouse in the first place was because he was lonesome.

What an interesting prospect I thought, a little illicit love affair. Nothing serious, at least not on my part. But, no need to rush things I decided and far better fun to let him sweat a little first. To play it cool. To tease him. After all, as far as I was concerned, I'd all the time in the world to play around with his feelings. How could I have known that Mags was going to get it into her silly head to suddenly up and leave?

Not that it matters. It would only have been a bit of sport, something to pass the time. For why would I be interested in him now? Why, when I have an eminently more eligible boyfriend of my own age. Far more sophisticated. Far better looking. Far more successful. And far richer. Richer by a couple of million in fact, not that I care to discuss such base matters.

As I say, it would only have been a little fun but a pity all the same for I hate to miss an opportunity.

31st October

Room 4, Friendship Hostel, Xian. Late evening.

Debbie

9.00 p.m. Genevieve is lying on her bed as stiff as a poker with all her clothes still on, staring morosely up at the ceiling. It's hard not to feel a little sorry for her. She does look so very sad and this hostel really is pretty horrible.

9.20 p.m. In the most sorrowful little voice imaginable, Genevieve's just announced that this is a far cry from the kind of place she expected to be staying in, even if this is China.

9.25 p.m. Maeve catches my eye and we get into one of those laughing fits where it's impossible to stop. Genevieve is demanding to know what we're laughing at.

9.35 p.m. Genevieve is still demanding to know what we're laughing. Neither of us have the heart to tell her it's her.

Maeve

I'd *swear* it was poitín those two guys were drinking on the train last night. I have this raging hangover – still.

It hurts to even laugh.

And G's not helping. I wish she could be quiet for once but no chance! She is very, very *very* upset about this place we're staying in tho' Debs says it was the only place she could find. Debs suggested that writing in her diary might cheer G up but G says she's too down even for that!

Debbie

10.00 *p.m.* A sob issues forth from poor Genevieve who's now a bundle in the bed, face to the wall.

Maeve

Christ! I wish G would give over moaning.

Course she blames me for making them all leave Beijing so suddenly – don't see that I had much choice given the circumstances.

She'll get over it.

She should expect to rough it a bit. We are, like, meant to be backpacking after all.

Checked my e-mails earlier. One from Dylan. Says he went in to collect his ticket today but found it was 200 euro more than he'd been quoted – wants me to get my bank to transfer the same amt. into his account.

Was annoyed at 1st but guess he *is*, like, spending a fortune to come out here to see me so maybe I should be prepared to help him out a bit.

Debbie

10.35 *p.m.* The silence of the night is broken. Why are we being so mean and why won't we tell G what we were laughing at?

[Save Address(es)][Block]   [Previous][Next][Close]
From: "Tobin, Laura"<lauratobin@hotmail.com>
To: "Wilson, Felix"<felix@fmsounds.com>
Subject: Travel update
Date: 31 Oct, 23:29:02
[Reply][Reply All][Forward][Delete]

Hi Felix,

I've left Beijing and have now arrived in Xian. I thought it was time to bid Andrew a hasty adieu as he was beginning to get the distinction between business and pleasure a little blurred. Typical male!

I made the trip down last night on the overnight train. First class was very comfortable and spotlessly clean – which couldn't be said for the rest of the train.

There weren't any single cabins so I ended up sharing a double with this young woman from Hong Kong. We must have been up half the night talking and in the end she asked me to stay with her family in Xian but I passed and booked myself into this hotel instead which is very swish although nowhere near as nice as Andrew's place. I did however take her up on her offer of dinner tomorrow.

My work on the book is going very well. I've collected some good material from the interviews I've already carried out and I've several more interviews lined up for the coming week.

E-mail me soon. Nothing has come through from you yet!

Love you,

Laura.

[Save Address(es)][Block]   [Previous][Next][Close]

From: "Tobin, Laura"<lauratobin@hotmail.com>

To: "Kane,Christopher"<kaneliteraryagents@aol.com>

Subject: Book Proposal

Date: 31 Oct, 23:47:30

[Reply][Reply All][Forward][Delete]

Hello Chris,

I'm not sure I quite understand what you mean exactly but of course I can clarify whichever aspects of my book proposal you find confusing. As for the scope of it being all-encompassing well, it's that way by design.

I don't think my ability to write is at issue considering my credentials though I'd have preferred to have had more time to tighten up the submission however I'm sure you'll appreciate that the lead-up to my departure was pretty hectic and I was anxious to get it to you before I left.

Apropos an academic background being necessary for what I propose, I'd have to disagree with you on that score. In fact I feel it might even be a hindrance for I see the book as having a broad appeal.

Regards,

Laura.

1st November

Room 4, Friendship Hostel. Early morning.

Maeve

G has gone in search of somewhere else for us to stay.

Finding somewhere with all the comforts of Dad's apartment but at YMCA rates won't be easy.

She is so *not* the backpacking/hostel/travelling type as L's just pointed out tho' that's a bit like the pot calling the kettle black & I'm not sure who's more outta place – G or L.

You'd think we were checking into the Sheraton the way L was carrying on down at the front desk yesterday – even asked for her bags to be brought up & (just for a sec.) the young guy behind the counter (flustered by her regal manner no doubt) looked as if he was about to oblige but (in the nick of time) recalled the class of plc. he was working in.

In the end, G (the eejit!) bought up practically all L's stuff as well as her own.

G would want to watch out or L will turn her into her own personal little handmaiden. She's never happier than when she has an adoring sidekick.

Just checked my e-mails.

Nothing from Dylan.

I hope the money I transferred gets through okay.

Room no. 208, Aviation Hostel.
Later that morning.

Genevieve

All four of us are now sharing the one room in this backpackers' which is far from perfect but at least it isn't working out too expensive although I don't think I'll ever get used to all this bunking in together. At least it's a lot cleaner than the place we stayed in last night plus there's a sink in the room which is very handy as it gives me a chance to wash out some of my things even though you're not really meant to for there's a sign up saying so which also says the management will do it for you for the equivalent of fifty cents. Per item. They have got to be kidding! I mean that's just throwing money down the drain. I thought we'd be getting value for our money in China but we seem to be going through it like water

The others have just left to have a look around the city and to visit a pagoda whatever that might be when it's at home but I stayed behind and to be honest I'm far happier here doing my bits and pieces than I would be racing about the place after Debbie, trying to keep up with her. No wonder Laura calls her the Sergeant Major behind her back which is a bit mean though I don't think she really means to be and she's just being funny.

I'm glad Laura's on this trip for we really are getting on like a house on fire. I could listen to her talking for hours. Her life is so different from my own which I suppose is why she finds mine as interesting as I find hers. It is nice to have someone to talk to like this. Sometimes I feel quite lonesome and I've never really had a best friend. Of course I've been friends with Debbie and Maeve for years now but it's always been them and then me. And Theo's my boyfriend so I can't very well call him my best friend though if he wasn't my boyfriend he probably would be. Not that I'm claiming Laura is my best friend or anything for someone like her must have hundreds of friends.

I noticed they sell these little pots of noodles in the shop downstairs so I'm going to buy a couple and have a nice bit of lunch for myself up here in the room. It'll be a change to know what I'm eating for once or to be actually able to eat it for I always seem to order the wrong thing when we're in restaurants. At least with pot noodles you know where you stand.

Some hours later . . .

Maeve

Debs does my head in sometimes.

If her guideb'k mentioned an interesting toilet block, she'd have to drag us off to see it.

In the end I called it a day & bailed out early for who knows how long more she'll be pestering that young guide who took us to the pagoda for answers to all her qsts.

But if G doesn't stop moaning 'bout me smoking in the bedroom I might just go back out again.

Would she *ever*, like, give it a rest?

I'm not, like, complaining about how *she's* stunk the place out with her pot noodles *or* how she's turned the room into a launderette while we were out.

Guess she thinks she's exempt from the massive sign hanging over the sink – *Honoured Guests! Please! No Washing Of Personal Apparel!*

And, like, how many pairs of knickers has she brought with her anyway? There must be at least 2 doz pairs dangling over our heads.

123

Now L's just come back in & has managed to get herself entangled in a fine big navy pair. Lovely!

She says Debs was driving her crazy as well & that she left her off on her own.

G is pestering L now, wanting to know if she can see what she's writing in her palmtop.

L does seem to be forever tapping away on it – writing her book I guess – but she'll never let G see what she's writing tho' G's forever asking.

I know L keeps talking about this book of hers but I don't get it. I mean what does she know about Chinese literature or whatever the book is meant to be about? It's not like she even speaks the language.

And it's not like she's doing any research either – she's with us all the time.

Sometimes I think it's all bullshit..

Whenever I ask Debs what she thinks about L's book, she just throws her eyes to heaven & mutters something about L's mind being a complete mystery to her.

No e-mail from Dylan to say the money got through. Did ring him but he was out with Karl & Seanie.

[Address(es)][Block]   **[Previous][Next][Close]**

From: "Tobin, Laura"<lauratobin@hotmail.com>

To: "Wilson, Felix"<felix@fmsounds.com>

Subject: Your e-mails

Date: 1 Nov, 17:22:18

[Reply][Reply All][Forward][Delete]

Hi Felix,

It's a pity I haven't managed to reach you by telephone yet. You're obviously as busy as ever but I'll try again later on this evening.

What news? Well, the book is going brilliantly. There's just so much research to do but I'm getting there although finding the time is a problem as there's just such a lot going on.

Last night I went for dinner at the house of that girl I met on the train. It turns out she's great friends with this woman who's one of China's best-known actresses. I can't remember her name but you know her, she was in *Farewell My Concubine* and a few other big Chinese films as well.

Anyway, this other one, this actress, turned out to be an absolute doll. Very charming and very, very witty. But the funny thing is just before her acting career took off she stayed in the UK for six months and immediately recognised my name when I introduced myself to her. She used to read the papers to help improve her English and said she particularly enjoyed my articles and that they gave her a great understanding of a lot of the issues of the day. She could even quote bits of them back to me! So, my fame spans the continents!

Anyway, when she was leaving she gave me her assistant's

phone number and made me promise to ring her and to let her know when I'll be in Chengdu as she has a house there and wants me to stay with her. She knows a lot of the up-and-coming writers and artists and the like from around there who she says she'll introduce me to so I'm definitely going to have to make a point of visiting her.

I'll try ringing you again tomorrow, hopefully with more luck. I still haven't got any of your e-mails.

Love you,

Laura.

2nd November

Room no. 208, Aviation Hostel. Early evening.

Genevieve

One thing that's beginning to annoy me is how the girls are forever splitting the bill four ways so I nearly always end up paying way more than my fair share. Theo and I always pay separately and we're practically engaged so I don't see why it should be any different with the girls.

Like just now when we went for something to eat in the restaurant next door, I decided that for once and for all I was going to put my foot down and only pay for my share which as usual I'd barely touched but at least I was able to buy a couple of tubs of pot noodles in the shop downstairs when we got back here so I'm not absolutely starving. Anyway after we'd finished eating or not eating as the case may be in the restaurant, I made the mistake of paying a quick visit to the toilets and when I came back out the bill had arrived down and of course the others had gone ahead and split it so I tried telling them once again that I just wanted to pay for my own share but they all pooh-poohed that suggestion as if it was the most outlandish thing they'd ever heard in the whole of their lives and then Debbie started on about how it all evens out in the end which is not at all the case and is in fact precisely the problem as I tried explaining to her but she and the others weren't paying the slightest bit of attention and started getting up to go so I had no choice but to put my money down on the table and follow out after them. And I even got caught for a quarter of the cost of the beer too even though I didn't drink so much as a single drop and I'd say Maeve probably guzzled at least three quarters of it. Of course it's all right for them for they seem to have way more money than me.

I think I'll sort out my rucksack before I turn in for the night. It's well overdue for my things are getting all muddled up and it doesn't help that Maeve goes and messes everything up whenever she goes and borrows anything that takes her fancy. Like this morning she took one of my jumpers which I hadn't even worn myself yet without so much as asking me and needless to say mixed everything up when she was looking for it and then didn't even apologise when I said as much to her. And of course it'll stink of cigarette smoke when she gives it back to me for do you think she'll wash it? Not likely!

Maeve

Just rang Dylan on the way back from the restaurant.
Told me he got the cash transfer & paid what was outstanding on the ticket.
Can't believe he'll be here soon.
Says he'll e-mail me with the finer details in the next day or two.

Debbie

7.00 *p.m.* For reasons best known to herself, Genevieve has decided to explain to us how she's organised her backpack and, seemingly under the impression that her system is quite complex, she's going into considerable detail.

7.10 p.m. We're all steadfastly avoiding eye contact so as not to encourage her for this is the kind of thing Genevieve could talk about all night.

7.15 p.m. She drones on. Now she's reading out the various labels she's stuck on the ziplock bags and is trying to get us to look at them.

HANDY BITS AND PIECES *i.e. pens, torch, sink stopper, washing line, alarm clock etc.*

WOOLLIES i.e. *heavy socks, scarf and hat, gloves, terminal (sic) leggings etc.*

7.20 p.m. Maeve, who for some reason seems in extraordinary good form, tells her to put a sock in it and collapses into hysterical laughter at her own joke. Genevieve ignores her and drones on.

7.25 p.m. Laura says she wishes she'd thought to organise her things in such a fashion. Missing the sarcasm, Genevieve smiles smugly across at Maeve and drones on.

7.30 p.m. Maeve leaves the room. Not discouraged, Genevieve drones on.

7.35 p.m. Laura leaves the room. Genevieve continues to drone on and on.

7.40 p.m. I think it's time for me to leave.

[Save Address(es)][Block]   [Previous][Next][Close]
From: "Tobin, Laura"<lauratobin@hotmail.com>
To: "Kane, Christopher"<kaneliteraryagents@aol.com>
Subject: Book Proposal
Date: 2 Nov, 18:15:38
[Reply][Reply All][Forward][Delete]

Dear Chris,
No, it's not meant to be some kind of a highbrow guidebook
either. It's intended to be an interesting, informed slant on
Asian issues and I think the fact that I am in Asia whilst
writing it will give it a certain feeling of immediacy and
relevancy that other books of a similar nature might lack.
Regards,
Laura.

3rd November

Room no. 208, Aviation Hostel. Early morning.

Genevieve

It's the bloody crack of dawn and Debbie has woken us all up already. No doubt she has about a hundred and fifty things lined up for us again today. Why can't she just give us a break? This is meant to be a holiday for crying out loud but there never seems to be any let-up whatsoever. As it was she kept me awake half the night for I could hear her out on the balcony at all hours of the night with some Chinese girls practising how to order in a restaurant and they were going over and over the same sentences until my head was done in. I don't know why she just can't be happy with pointing at the menu like the rest of us.

She's just been in again telling me to get out of bed and I would too only that I left my slippers behind in the last place or should I say Maeve left my slippers behind and the floor here is freezing cold & all sticky & there's no telling what you'd catch and I hate walking on it barefoot so I'm waiting until Laura is finished with her slippers so that I can take a loan of them for the last thing I want to go getting right now is a verruca off of the filthy floor.

She's yelling again. Bloody Sergeant-Major! All she's missing is one of those bugles.

Back once more in the hostel. Evening.

Maeve

Bought Dylan this lighter today which is très, très cool – it plays this marching song & has a picture of Chairman Mao on either side.

G was, like, completely baffled as to why I was buying presents so early on & even more so by the fact that it was a lighter as Dylan doesn't smoke. (At least not ciggies but I wasn't going to get into *that* with *her* – there are certain things G doesn't need to know.)

So I tried explaining that the reason I'd bought it for him was cos I knew he'd be amused at seeing a communist icon like Chairman Mao being exploited by upstart capitalists & stuck on cheap souvenirs destined for the West.

From the blank expression it was obvious she'd no idea what I was talking about so I tried explaining the irony of how the lighter stands for everything Chairman Mao was against yet his face is smiling out from it.

Nah, still nobody home. I'd lost her – way back.

So then I told her that Dylan has a gas cooker in his flat & he'll be able to use the lighter for that.

Finally she was happy.

Can't believe I'll actually be able to give it to him in person in a matter of days.

Guess I'll soon have to tell Debs he's coming which will *not* be fun.

I wish G would stop asking me if I'd rung Dad since we left Beijing – she keeps going on about his hospitality and how nice he was to us.

I did get an e-mail from him asking me to ring but I don't think I will – not just yet – he deserves to be left hanging for a while.

Christ Almighty! G's just asked me to check the soles of her feet for verrucas. Doesn't she, like, understand there are certain boundaries in every relationship?

Genevieve

I am exhausted. We spent half the bloody day trailing around some stupid bird market though why Debbie made us go there I have <u>no</u> idea for it's not like we could actually buy anything since we're hardly going to take birds home to Ireland with us although that didn't stop the stall owners from <u>hounding</u> us. And the crowds were just something else and people kept bashing into us all the time and I don't think a single one of them had ever so much as heard the word sorry. And if the stupid bird market wasn't enough she then dragged us off to see these houses which she said were of historic interest. Historic interest my eye! Boring old falling-down shacks more like.

I'm killed from telling Debbie that she's going to have to slow down a little and that there's no need to be rushing around like a mad thing. If she carries on at this pace we'll be suffering from burn-out in no time. As it is the weight is just falling off me for I'm hardly eating a thing. Laura says I'd want to be careful or I'll fall away to nothing.

And then just when I thought we were <u>finally</u> coming back here, Debbie bumped into these foreigners, Danes or Dutch or something like that, who she'd already met yesterday for they're staying on the floor above us and who were on their way to see some monument and of course Debbie told them that we'd all just love to go along with them and since I didn't know the way back to here, I'd no choice but to go even though listening to Debbie and some bald Danish lad yapping their heads off about the cultural significance of this stupid monument was about as much as I could take. I think Debbie must have fancied him and definitely someone like him would be much more her sort and I don't know how she ever got together with Dylan.

My stomach is rumbling like crazy. After all our tearing about I specifically mentioned to the girls that I wanted to go to this Kentucky Fried Chicken I noticed yesterday where I'd at least be able to get something decent to eat for a change but before I knew it Debbie had hauled us all off to some food market instead which turned out to be <u>the</u> <u>most</u> <u>revolting</u> place I have ever been to in the whole of my life. Disgusting! Seeing all these people walking around, chewing away on frogs and scorpions and whole squids on sticks, the half of which were probably still alive. It was all I could do to stop myself vomiting. The other three had no such problem of course especially Debbie and within minutes of arriving she was chomping away on every sort of disgusting thing there was on offer as if she'd been raised on nothing else.

I'm never going to be able to get to sleep if my stomach keeps rumbling like this. It's going bananas. It's a pity they were all out of those noodles in the shop.

Maeve
Just checked my e-mails.
None from Dylan.
Shouldn't get too excited about him coming – be just like him to change his mind & sell off the ticket or mess it up somehow.
L says I shouldn't say anything to Debs until the day he's due in.

Maybe she's right – no point in creating hassle for myself until it's absolutely necessary.

If G mentions once more how she's not eating a thing, I'll swing for her.

It's not even true.

She's downing tubs of instant noodles by the new time. She's even cleared out the shop downstairs.

And it's beginning to show – for all her talk about falling away to nothing, I'd say she's putting it on.

Maybe not quite the kilos L's says, but she definitely is heavier than when we started out.

It suits her tho' – she looks better than ever.

And she's getting *heaps* of attention – much to L's annoyance!

An Asian Diary

The downside of heading away like this for several months is that I've had to leave behind my beloved who I've been going out with for over a year now and who, after an awful lot of persuasion, had finally talked me into moving in with him just a few months ago. As you can imagine, he's gutted by my absence.

Now some people might say I'm crazy for leaving him on his own. After all, he is movie-star good-looking and as a student in college (college being Cambridge) he even earned a little pocket-money modelling. Not that he needed it. Hardly, when his family own one of the biggest supermarket chains in Britain. Others think I'm crazy because, as I say, he's pretty wealthy. In fact he's a bona fide millionaire in his own right though he's not the first millionaire I've ever gone out with. Others think that someone as well known as he is (for yes, he is quite famous and you would almost certainly recognise his name if I were foolish enough to give it) will have women throwing themselves at him when attending the multitude of parties and functions he goes to as a matter of course each week.

You'd imagine someone like that, with such a lot going for him, wouldn't worry about me getting up to anything while I'm away. But my beloved does. Every time I phone, all he does is moan. He moans about how he's missing me so much he can hardly sleep. About how it's been ages since I phoned him. About how I never reply to his e-mails. He just moans on and on and then, when he's finally through moaning, the questions start. Have I met many men? What was Mr C like? Is Mags leading me astray? And I've lost count of the number of e-mails he sends per day. Sad really, even if a little flattering.

Just as well I didn't tell him about Mr C coming on to me or about all the attention I'm attracting along the way for a tall thin blonde doesn't exactly go unnoticed in China much to the chagrin of the other three girls and I think they're more than a little peeved I'm getting all the attention.

But I'm not going to be the only one with man problems for much longer. Pretty soon Deanne will too though problems of a very different nature for, soon, we're going to be joined by Deanne's old boyfriend. Not that Deanne knows that yet for typically Mags is putting off telling her until the very last moment.

4th November

Coffee Conscious Restaurant. Afternoon.

Maeve

Hooray!!!!

Within the next couple of hrs, Dylan will be winging his way to China – looks like I did him an injustice after all & underestimated his organisational capabilities.

I just checked my e-mails & there was one from him, telling me how he'd got a last min. cheapie flight.

Which is odd – he'd definitely said he'd paid for his flight as soon as I got my bank to transfer money to his a/c.

Better not think about things like that right now. The main thing is he's coming.

He'll be arriving in Beijing tomorrow where he's going to try & arrange to get a flight to Chengdu ASAP & meet up with us there.

He'll keep me posted by e-mail.

Now all I have to do is work up the courage to tell Debs – groan.

She's going to go nuts!

Got *another* e-mail from Dad as well, asking me to ring him. He'll be waiting.

What the hell is keeping Debbie anyway?

Like, how long can one possibly spend going around a bell tower?

Genevieve

Those Danish people Debbie got so pally with flew back to Denmark today. In a way I wish I was them. I don't mean I wish I was Danish or that I was going back to Denmark but what I mean is that in a way I wish I was going home. They left a packet of rice crackers behind in the hostel kitchen so I took them as there's no point in letting them go to waste. They're barbecue flavour which isn't my favourite but beggars can't be choosers and we're just racing through our money. I'm going to have to be very careful with it if I'm going to be able to make it last.

[Save Address(es)][Block]   [Previous][Next][Close]
From: "Tobin, Laura"<lauratobin@hotmail.com>
To: "Wilson, Felix"<felix@fmsounds.com>
Subject: Your e-mails
Date: 4 Nov, 16:23:54
[Reply][Reply All][Forward][Delete]

Hi Felix,
Are you receiving my e-mails?
Laura, XX

[Save Address(es)][Block]   [Previous][Next][Close]
From: "Tobin, Laura"<lauratobin@hotmail.com>
To: "Lewis,Timothy"<lewissolicitors@lineone.net.ie>
Subject: Your e-mail of the 3rd
Date: 4 Nov, 16:30:21
[Reply][Reply All][Forward][Delete]

Dear Timothy,
Signing that agreement presents no problem. Believe me,
I've no ambition to ever seek work again with any of the
Argus Group in Britain or elsewhere.
Thanks again for all your help over the past few months.
You've been a brick, both on a personal and on a professional
level. I don't know how I'd have got through it all without
you and please, don't take this the wrong way, but I do hope
I won't need your services again! Let's hope no more relatives
of Lily Buchan turn up out of the woodwork!
Kindest regards,
Laura.

5th November

Genevieve

I went and bought myself a little notebook today which I think was quite cheap though I'm not sure for I still find it very hard to figure out how much these blasted yuans are worth exactly and Debbie keeps yakking on at me about how I'm probably getting conned all the time and that I'm a sitting duck the way I carry on in the shops and markets.

As the others don't seem to be on any kind of a budget it makes it very hard for me to keep an eye on what I'm spending but hopefully this notebook will help and I'm going to use it to keep a record of all my outgoings. Of course none of the others have the expense of a wedding in the not-too-distant future and with such good jobs they all earn a lot more than I do. Well at least Laura and Debbie do what with Laura being a journalist and now writing a book and all and Debbie being whatever she is in insurance though what exactly that is I can't say even though she's explained it to me often enough. And I've no idea what a hostess in a club earns but I wouldn't have thought it could be very much yet Maeve never seems short of cash.

There was a load of our meal left over tonight so I asked the girl serving us could I take a doggy-bag away with me for

141

I thought I might eat it for my lunch tomorrow as it'd save me a couple of bob but she'd obviously never heard the phrase before and kept repeating it over and over and howling laughing. Then she started saying it to her colleagues and so of course they all started laughing their silly heads off and I'd be waiting still if I hadn't gone and emptied the food into a napkin myself.

I never thought about it before but I can see how my life might seem boring to someone like Laura for as she says it hasn't exactly been action-packed and she wasn't being mean when she said it or at least not deliberately and she was just making an observation. And she's right. In fact nothing has really changed since I left school. During all that time I've been going out with Theo and living at home and working for my Dad. Not that I'm saying I'd want things to change for I'm more than happy with the way they are. But I can see what she means.

Debbie

9.45 p.m. One of Genevieve's obsessions is how little she's eating. She keeps telling us that she's falling away to nothing but I think she's never looked better. Her hearty, robust good looks are really coming into their own compared to Laura for example who's beginning to look pretty rough now that she's without the regular services of her beautician and hairdresser.

In fact, Genevieve attracts far more attention than the rest of us, which isn't surprising really, given her red hair and the fact that she is almost six foot tall but, instead of taking all the attention as a compliment, she gets really annoyed.

Take this morning for instance. When we were in the market she completely cracked up and started shouting at this bunch of people, demanding to know what they were all gawking at but, the more she shouted, the more there was to see, so the bigger the crowd grew and the more they stared and stared at the antics of the crazy foreigner and the crazier the foreigner became. Poor Genevieve!

In the lobby of the Overseas Chinese Hotel.
Later that night.

Maeve

The phone in our hotel isn't working so I'm waiting here in the lobby of the hotel next door as L asked me to come with her while she tries to phone Felix.

Again!!

He must have *the* most hectic social life for he *never* seems to be there.

Why doesn't he, like, get himself an answering machine?

Imagine – Dylan should be landing in Beijing 'round about now!

An Asian Diary

Not a day has passed without Geraldine sidling up to me to ask if I'm getting much use of the diary she gave me.

Am I? Well – yes. I've filled pages with shopping lists, to-do lists, reminders to self and outlines of possible articles. I've inserted tickets stubs and the like in between pages for safe-keeping. I've torn out scraps and used them to wrap old gum, to leave notes for the others and, on one occasion, I've even given some to Deanne to use as – there is no way to put this delicately – toilet paper – when she was caught short. So yes, I have found it useful.

As I say, part of the problem is I've never really quite understood what it is you're meant to write in them exactly. I mean, should you write as if someone is standing there looking critically over your shoulder? Or should you pour your heart & soul & all your secrets out onto the page? I just don't know.

But I do have a confession. On occasion, when I've happened upon Geraldine's diary lying there unattended, my hand has hovered over it, my eyes have darted towards the door, and I've been sorely tempted to take a peek. But I've resisted though admittedly my resolution hasn't come entirely from nobleness of character. It's just that I think Geraldine's diary would be too boring for words.

If her usual topics of conversation are anything to go by, I suspect it contains little more than a record of her bowel movements, what she's eaten that day, her ailments and, the condition of every single toilet we've come across. The girl can't come out of a toilet without going into the greatest detail as to just how disgusting it was. No doubt she feels the same compulsion to write it all down for posterity. As for her ailments, she always seems to have several on the go. Today, for example, her head is throbbing; she's just killed from her "arches"; and, she suspects she might be suffering from, amongst other things; verrucas, claustrophobia and asthma.

As I say, why would I bother?

6th November

Victory Restaurant, near the Temple of Grace. Morning.

Debbie

10.00 a.m.   Genevieve is driving me bats. Whenever I so much as say hello to a male she thinks I'm trying to chat him up and whenever Maeve mentions Dylan, which she does, all the time, she gives me these sympathetic little squeezes if I'm not quick enough to move my hand out of the way.

And she keeps sidling up to me to tell me she's there for me if I ever need to talk though Genevieve wouldn't exactly be my first choice of confidante. And I just wish she'd get it into her head that I dumped Dylan and not the other way around!

I'd better get going. I've a lot I want to get through this morning before I meet up with the others again. I don't know why any of them weren't interested in seeing the temple.

Room no. 208, Aviation Hostel. That evening.

Maeve

Still haven't told Debs about Dylan.

I am *such* a coward!

Another e-mail from Dad.

"Please-oh-please ring me, we need to talk."

Ah – I definitely don't think so.

The last thing I want is to ring up & have *her* answering the phone.

Debs also giving out cos I haven't phoned him – like it's any of *her* business. She keeps on about how I should go back up to see him at the end of our trip before we fly home.

Hmm – don't know.

Maybe.

Maybe not.

Maybe I'll feel diff. about things when I've had a bit of time to get used to them but right now I have absolutely *no* interest in seeing him again.

Or his *girlfriend*

Cost of the flight back wouldn't be a prob. esp. when G's forever getting us to eat in the cheapest places possible.

Feel a bit mean.

Cos G was *so* annoying tonight, going on & on & *on* about how I should give Dad a ring, I started teasing her in front of everyone about how she'd probably been cheated when she bought that notebook.

Which is true.

But I needn't have been so mean but she is just *sooo* gullible & always ends up paying 'bout 4 times over the odds.

Still, she'll get over it soon enough.

Genevieve

Debbie and Maeve's habit of forever drawing complete strangers on top of us is fierce annoying. Like those Birminghammers we met this afternoon. Nothing would do Maeve and Debbie but to invite them to come along with us when we were going for something to eat though I noticed neither of them asked Laura or myself if we minded though I certainly did for they were just the pits. The girl kept going hee-haw hee-haw like a donkey at everything everyone said even when it wasn't meant to be funny and I don't think the fellow said so much as a single word throughout the entire meal. I think Debbie must have had her eye on him but he was obviously going out with the hee-haw girl which I'd say Debbie mustn't have realised until I pointed it out to her which of course annoyed her but I felt I had to. I just didn't want to see her making a fool of herself.

And if it wasn't bad enough having to listen to that girl all evening, I think Maeve had a bit too much to drink and started telling everyone how I'd finally splashed out and bought a notebook like it was a big deal or something. And then she started talking like I wasn't even there and started telling everyone how she could just see me, standing in the shop, ignoring the queue building up behind me while I muttered away to myself as I tried to convert yuans to euro but getting it all wrong so that I ended up paying way over the odds but came away thinking I'd got a bargain.

I am really fond of Maeve of course I am but she can be very mean sometimes. Like the way she mocks me like that and whenever I try telling her I hate it and ask her to stop she just laughs it off like I'm not serious or something. What she doesn't seem to realise is that I have feelings too. It's easy for her to go on about how stingy I am but I just don't have the kind of money she and the others have. Laura says I shouldn't take any notice

It's funny but before we started off I'd never have

thought for a moment it'd be Laura who I'd get along best with on this trip. I mean she's used to mixing with much more interesting people than myself such as Richard Branson and Chelsea Clinton and that woman on the news with the funny-shaped head whose name I can't think of but who just happens to live on the floor above Laura and Felix. The nearest I've ever got to anyone famous, besides Laura herself and Felix for you could say both of them are a little bit famous, was Ned Toner who used to be a minister in the last government though for what I can't remember. Theo and I were sitting behind him at a concert up in the Town Hall once. Or at least I think it was him though Theo kept saying it wasn't and that it only looked like him.

I never realised it before but I think Laura's right and Debbie is a bit jealous of her for when Debbie overheard Laura telling me all about a party she went to in one of Richard Branson's magnificent mansions she told her to just give it a rest. Laura says that Debbie was always like that towards her even when we were at school. I'd never have thought Debbie was the jealous type before but I can see what Laura means and I suppose Debbie has good reason to be jealous for Laura really has everything going for her.

I keep getting this funny smell. I bet it's coming from Maeve's bags for you wouldn't know what she'd have in there and I don't think she's washed a stitch of clothes since we left home but then why would she bother when she can wear everyone else's?

[Save Address(es)][Block]   [Previous][Next][Close]
From: "Tobin, Laura"<lauratobin@hotmail.com>
To: "Wilson, Felix"<felix@fmsounds.com>
Subject: Phone call
Date: 6 Nov, 22:34:56
[Reply][Reply All][Forward][Delete]

Hi Hon,
I don't know if you're getting any of my e-mails for nothing
is coming through from you.
If you are receiving mine then I'm writing to tell you that
I'm going to ring you again tomorrow at 10.00p.m. (your
time) Be there – please!
I can't believe I haven't got to speak to you yet.
I love you.
Laura.

[Save Address(es)][Block]   [Previous][Next][Close]
From: "Tobin, Laura"<lauratobin@hotmail.com>
To: "Kane, Christopher" <kaneliteraryagents@aol.com>
Subject: Book Proposal
Date: 6 Nov, 22:45:11
[Reply][Reply All][Forward][Delete]

Dear Chris,
I'm not sure I'd agree that everyone seems to be travelling
right now and to be writing about it and saturating the
market but as you're the expert I guess I'll have to defer to
your greater knowledge.

In any case, thanks for taking the time to consider my proposal and in the meantime I'll mull over the unique angle you think is necessary for a book to succeed.

Kindest regards,

Laura.

7th November

Genevieve

Actually I did see that fellow with the white hair who does those house renovations programmes on telly doing an interview out near Portrea Strand once. I suppose he'd be more famous than Ned Toner even if I can't remember his name. The fresh air out here on the terrace is lovely and I just had to get out of the bedroom for the smell is getting worse. I wish Maeve would empty out her bloody bags but she says it's got nothing to do with her.

I really don't feel like doing anything today for I'm just not in the best of form. I know Debbie and Maeve laugh at me and think I'm a fusspot and a moaner and maybe I am but things just seem so much easier for them. The pair of them would eat absolutely anything that's put in front of them and they aren't a bit fussy when it comes to where they sleep. And it doesn't bother them in the slightest when people stare at us and they do <u>all</u> <u>the</u> <u>time</u> which is something I find really hard to put up with.

And they have absolutely no fear whereas I'm scared of everything. I'm scared of what lies in store for us when we arrive into each new place. I'm scared of the strangers we meet for fear they'll attack us or rob us or whatever. I'm scared of getting into every wonky old bus and taxi in case the brakes fail or the driver is a lunatic. But to the others it's all mill to the grist.

And having travelled so much more than I have and being more experienced in life, the others no doubt had a much better idea of what to expect on this trip. And of course they're all used to bunking in with other people which is something I'm not and never will be no matter how long I live. Being an only child I've never even had to share a room and this whole communal living is just not my cup of tea.

I guess the truth is I'm a routine sort of person. I just like waking up in my own bed each morning and knowing exactly what the day ahead has in store for me. What I can't stand is not knowing what horrible dive we'll end up sleeping in from one night to the next. What I can't stand is having to lug around that stupid monstrosity of a rucksack full of crumpled clothes. What I can't stand is this whole trip.

As well as getting me away from Theo for they've never really approved of him, I know another reason Mam and Dad were anxious for me to ask Maeve could I come on the trip was because they thought it'd be an education for me and maybe if I was genuinely interested in the sights then all this racing about here, there and everywhere would make sense to me but I'm just not interested in learning about these places. It's as plain and simple as that for I mean to say a temple is a temple is a temple and a mountain is a mountain is a mountain and a statue is a statue is a statue and when you've seen one bloody mountain or bloody temple or bloody statue you've as good as bloody well seen them all. Full stop end of story.

Now Debbie's on at me to come with them to some old market. Is there any let-up? I've had markets up to my eyeballs. Well for once I'm not going to budge and I told her I'll meet up with them at lunchtime instead.

**Pavement outside a food stall near the Big Goose Pagoda.
Lunchtime.**

Debbie

1.00 p.m. The woman behind the stall actually understood me when I ordered in Chinese so all my practising is paying off!

These dumplings are delicious though poor Genevieve doesn't seem to have much of an appetite. She's looking very down. I don't think she's enjoying herself anywhere near as much as the rest of us on this trip. She wouldn't even come with us to the market this morning. She said she wasn't interested. But how could she not be interested? I mean there was just so much to see. But even now sitting here, when there's so much going on around us, she hasn't so much as looked up even once.

It's a pity really for she misses out so much. Whenever we're travelling along and there's something worth seeing from the window of the bus or train, Genevieve's attention is sure to be elsewhere. She'll be busy either poking about in her bag looking for something or staring crossly at one of the other passengers trying to catch them staring at her.

Take the other evening for example. We were coming back to Xian on the bus from the Banpo Museum and as the sun began to set the sky went through the most amazingly beautiful array of yellows, reds and oranges, holding everyone spellbound. Or rather, was holding bar Genevieve spellbound. She alone was looking out the wrong side, the only one oblivious to the beauty.

Genevieve

I only wish people would stop knocking into me and would stop staring at me. I don't know why we couldn't have gone somewhere to eat where there was room to sit inside.

Back at the Aviation Hotel. Evening.

Maeve

No e-mail from Dylan so don't know if he's managed to get a flight down to Chengdu.

Definitely, definitely, will tell Debs about him coming before we arrive there ourselves.

Debs just made G empty her bag – there was a wicked smell coming from it.

The cause?

Some food G took out of a restaurant over 3 days ago in a napkin!

[Save Address(es)][Block]   [Previous][Next][Close]
From: "Tobin, Laura"<lauratobin@hotmail.com>
To: "Wilson, Felix"<felix@fmsounds.com>
Subject: Your e-mails
Date: 7 Nov, 22:18:59
[Reply][Reply All][Forward][Delete]

Felix,
Between my inability to contact you by phone and the lack
of e-mails coming from you, I could imagine you're trying to
tell me something – if I were the paranoid type.
I'm going to try ringing you again at 7.00 p.m., Irish time, so
please be there.
Love you,
Laura.

8th November

Genevieve

Well that's the last we'll be seeing of that place which is just as well for I had just about enough of it but then I've had just about enough of this whole travel business for it is nothing like I imagined it would be and I am completely fed up. And it's all just costing so much as well and far more than I thought it would.

We went on a trip out to see the Terry Cotter Warriors this morning but to be honest I couldn't see what the big deal was about. One thing I really wish is that Debbie would stop trying to make me take an interest in stuff but as she was telling me when she was in her tour-guide mode as Laura calls it, is that there's about eight thousand of these lads in all but it turns out you can't see half of them for nobody has even bothered to dig them up and of the ones you can see a load of them have heads and arms and whatnot missing and are just lying about higgledy-piggledy all over the place. And to top it all we weren't allowed to use our own cameras so if you wanted a photograph you had to pay an official photographer something outrageous like ten American dollars which has to be the biggest swizz ever and you'd want to be completely out of your mind to fall for it!

157

I did manage to sneak a shot with my own camera though I'm not sure if it'll come out as there were guards all over the place watching us like hawks so I had to hold it down by my side and take it really quickly and I couldn't use the flash as that would've attracted too much attention. Still it was worth a try.

Maeve

Poor L.

Seems like it's curtains for herself & Felix.

Not that she's said anything to me.

Doesn't even know I know.

But, here's the story.

This p.m. came back from Terracotta Warriors, collected bags from the hostel, went straight to station to catch this overnight train to Chengdu, train was late, went to stretch my legs, wandered about, heard person shouting, looked over & there was L *roaring* into a phone & from what she was saying it was pretty obvious she'd been dumped & wasn't exactly finding it easy to deal with. (Judging from the horrified faces of those around, many English swear words do *not* require translation to be understood in China.)

So not wanting to embarrass her, I beat a hasty retreat.

In all the time I've known L I've never, *ever* seen her lose control.

Can't believe Felix has given her the heave-ho.

They were the perfect couple personified with their matching blond hair & year-round tans, their his & hers perfect clothes, their so, so sexy jobs, their swanky apt.

Your ideal couple.

So: –

Shd I tell her I know Felix ditched her?

Shd I wait until she decides she's ready to talk about it?

Shd I tell the others?

Ahhh – no, yes & no in that order.

No (cos I'm a coward).

Yes (cos I am a coward).

No (cos 5 secs after G swears herself to secrecy she'd be off in search of L to comfort her & tell her it's prob. for the best).

But how is L (who's always had, like, *everything* she's ever wanted fall into her lap) going to deal with this blow? Getting fired from the job of her dreams was bad enough & now this as well! Things like this just don't happen to L. Or at least they didn't use to.

But in a way I was kinda surprised Felix stuck around this long given the whiff of scandal surrounding Laura.

She's not exactly flavour of the month in the newspaper business – hardly the ideal girlfriend for an up 'n' coming hot young radio star.

Maybe he wanted to wait until he was outta harm's way before breaking it off.

Can't say I blame him given her reaction.

Can't believe I'm going to be seeing Dylan in 12 hours time!

Several hours later.

Debbie

7.30 p.m. Genevieve's just sitting there, staring out the window with this dreadfully wounded expression on her face. Laura's just let fly at her. It was only a matter of time really. What was odd was how well they were getting along. Genevieve used to drive Laura around the twist in school so

I don't know why anyone should have expected it to be different now. People don't change that much.

Genevieve

I don't know what's got into Laura. Earlier Debbie asked me was I coming with them to the dining car for something to eat but I told her I didn't think I'd bother for there's never anything for me to eat in China and I'm not joking when I say I'm falling away to nothing. When Maeve heard me saying this she started on about how I should really eat something seeing as how we're going to be stuck on this train for at least the next twelve hours and so <u>once</u> <u>again</u> I tried explaining that there probably wouldn't be anything I could face eating and it was then Laura suddenly lost it. Out of the blue she lit into me and started shouting about how she was fed up with having to put up with my complaining day in day out and she wanted to know why I'd bothered coming away in the first place seeing as how I seemed to hate everything.

Debbie

9.00 p.m. I don't think I can stomach looking at such miserable faces for much longer. I'm taking myself off to bed.

Genevieve

And I thought we were getting on so well together and all.

An Asian Diary

I know people are travelling more and more these days but you really have to wonder why someone as half-witted and crabby as Geraldine even bothers. Ever since we set off, it seems like she's done nothing but moan, moan and moan. She's been miserable the whole time, apart from when she's complaining that is, for that does seem to give her a certain grim satisfaction.

Absolutely nothing about travelling seems to interest or amuse her and she sees every question put to her as an opportunity to complain. "So how was your walk?" – "Way too long." "Isn't the weather getting warmer?" – "It's bringing out the flies." And she's obsessed with the lack of hygiene on public transport and always inspects the seat before seating down as if she suspects that the last passenger almost certainly peed on it.

But as the days have passed and she's become more and more miserable, I felt compelled to ask her why she'd bothered coming away in the first place. And her reasons? Well, she had two. 1) Because we (her three old school friends) were going and she didn't want to be left out; and, 2) Because it would be her last chance to spread her wings before she marries and settles down for good. Sadly pigs will fly before that happens.

Broadening the mind certainly wasn't one of Geraldine's reasons, and, as she says, "a temple is a temple is a temple and a mountain is a mountain is a mountain and a statue is a statue is a statue and once you've seen one bloody mountain or bloody temple or bloody statue well, you've as good as bloody well seen them all. Full stop end of story."

And it's true. Nothing, absolutely nothing, impresses her. I think she's found every one of China's great historic sites sadly lacking. She took one look around Tiananmen Square and immediately suggested we go for a bite to eat. She didn't think the Great Wall was "all that great" and the Terracotta Army or the Terry Cotter Army as she calls it (as if that collection of thousands of life-sized clay soldiers was single-handedly created by a migrant sculptor from Cork who somehow just happened to find himself in Han Dynasty China) was, in her opinion, the pits.

And it's incredible how much she misses out. Whenever we're travelling along and there's something worth seeing from the window of the bus or train, Geraldine's attention is sure to be elsewhere. She'll be busy either poking about in her bag looking for something or staring crossly at one of the other passengers trying to catch them staring at her.

The other evening for instance, as the sun was setting, the sky went through the most amazingly beautiful array of yellows, reds and oranges, holding everyone on the bus spellbound. Or rather, was holding everyone bar Geraldine spellbound. She alone was looking out the wrong side, the only one oblivious to the beauty.

9th November

Debbie

9.00 *a.m.* We've been up since six on account of a pressing urgency on the part of the railway staff to get the bunks undressed. We expected to arrive in Chengdu at eight this morning but it seems we might be still some hours away though just how many I can't be sure for I've got as many different answers as the number of people I've asked. I suspect that the few who did actually understand the question hazarded a guess out of a simple desire to please.

10.00 *a.m.* There's still no sign of Chengdu. It wouldn't surprise me if we'd passed through it in the night without knowing.

10.30 *a.m.* Will this journey ever end? Laura is still in crabby form. Genevieve is still acting all hurt. Maeve is the only one who's in good mood, in very good mood in fact. She's really giving Genevieve a hard time and keeps teasing her about this old fellow with great wolf's teeth and bottle-bottom glasses who's taken a shine to her and who's been pestering her all morning.

11.00 *a.m.* It doesn't matter where poor Genevieve goes to try and get away from the old man for he just follows

163

after her, sits down opposite, and stares and grins at her in this all-the-better-to-eat-you sort of a way whilst offering her sips of vodka from a little bottle he has and scraps of some unidentifiable food from a crumpled brown-paper bag. Staying in our compartment doesn't render her safe either for he just comes shuffling in after her.

11.15 a.m. Genevieve says she's getting off at the next station even if it isn't Chengdu as she's fed up with Maeve teasing her and the old man pestering her.

Maeve

Meant to be in Chengdu hrs & hrs ago.

Still no sign.

Sigh!

Cannot wait.

Cannot wait.

Cannot wait!

Imagine I'll be seeing Dylan this *very* day.

(Maybe) this *very* hour??????

Did begin trying to tell Debs about his impending appearance but everyone's in such foul form that I changed my mind – it's not like I know for *definite* he'll turn up.

Knowing Dylan he could easily have met up with some people in Beijing & decided to stay on there for a while.

Or headed off somewhere completely different.

So, what's the point in bringing Deb's wrath down upon me until I absolutely have to?

Debbie

12.10 p.m. It's now four hours later than the time we

expected to be arriving into Chengdu and still no sign of the place. Genevieve's still being pestered. It's funny how out of the four of us, she's proving to be the biggest hit with the Chinese men which has definitely put Laura's nose out of joint.

In fact, now that I look at her, Laura's looking particularly rough this morning. I've never seen her looking so bad.

Maeve

Still no sign of Chengdu or (more to the point) Dylan – I'm going outta my mind!

Notice that L *still* hasn't said a word about her phone call with Felix yesterday but (no doubt) that accounts for the rotten mood she's in.

Like, she's the only one who knows Dylan is going to be waiting for me in the station but she hasn't even bothered asking me if I'm excited or anything.

I know she's upset but I can't believe she could be, like, *sooooo* selfish.

Debbie

1.00 p.m. Genevieve's new-found friend has a wife who he's now brought up from wherever she was sitting to meet Genevieve. Mrs Wolf, for she's not unlike her husband in the dental department, has taken up position beside her husband on the seat opposite Genevieve and seems every bit as fascinated by Genevieve as he is. Both of them are now nodding and grinning madly at Genevieve.

1.15 p.m. Mrs Wolf is practically shoving some of Mr Wolf's food into Genevieve's mouth but Genevieve is not at all impressed by these strangers' generosity and "Look!" she doesn't want any of that, "disgusting stuff, all right! Now, stop it! Just stop it! Get away! Get away from me!"

1.45 p.m. We pulled into a station and back out again while Genevieve was in the toilet so she missed her chance to get off. When she did finally return, Maeve reminded her that the toilets aren't supposed to be used while the train is stationary.

"Shut up, just shut up," was her hysterical response.

Maeve

Are we ever, ever, *ever* going to get to Chengdu?
What if Dylan isn't there?
I don't think I could *bear* that.

Genevieve

Laura has just apologised for eating me last evening. She explained that the reason she was in such a bad mood was because she'd rung Felix just before we got on the train so she was feeling very lonesome as she really misses him an awful lot. I told her there was no need to apologise whatsoever and that it was like water off a duck's back and under the bridge and that I understood exactly how she felt as I was in an identical situation with regards Theo.

Unfortunately I had no choice but to use the toilet. Absolutely <u>disgusting.</u> No toilet paper and no running water. Surprise. Surprise.

Debbie

4.00 p.m. At long last I think we're pulling into Chengdu.

An Asian Diary

Within the next few hours either Mags or Deanne is going to be very upset and it's even money as to which one it'll be.

You see, as I write, our train is heading towards Chengdu station where Mags is expecting her boyfriend, the wannabe-a-rock-star, to be standing on the platform waiting for us to arrive.

If he is there, then, it's Deanne who's going to get the nasty shock for she has absolutely no idea of his plan to come travelling with us for the next few weeks. Mags was going to tell her but in her usual gutless way she kept putting it off and off until she finally decided that there was no point in upsetting Deanne by saying anything in case he didn't show. But what if he does, I asked Mags, what then? Her answer? Classic Mags – to deal with it when the time comes.

If he does turn up, then, to say Deanne is going to be upset is something of an understatement. Remember, this was the one true love of Deanne's pathetic love life. Given that her face starts twitching like crazy whenever Mags so much as mentions the wannabe's name, it'll be interesting to see what contortions it'll go through as she tries to control her emotions as the two lovers reunite.

Of course there is every possibility that Wannabe won't make an appearance. There's every possibility he mistakenly booked a flight to Chile, not China for they probably sound similar enough to someone as fuzzy and spaced out as he is. There's every possibility he blew the money Mags gave him on a mad weekend with his so-called band. Every possibility that, having made it as far as Beijing, he met up with some guys in a bar and all plans to make it to Chengdu just went right out of his head. What then? Maybe Mags will go off the rails which she does from time to time.

Come to think of it, she's never much fun to be around when that happens so, on balance, I guess I hope he shows. But as I say, it's fifty, fifty.

10th November

Debbie
   1.40 p.m. Maeve is such a snake! Dylan was waiting at
the station when we arrived into Chengdu yesterday.

Genevieve
   The big news is that when we finally arrived into
Chengdu yesterday, Maeve's boyfriend Dylan was waiting at
the station. Needless to say the rest of us were pretty
annoyed about him showing up like that. After all this was
meant to be an <u>all girls' trip</u> and if we'd known Dylan was
going to arrive out on top of us then we could all have
invited our boyfriends along. Or at least Laura and I could
have. Not that Theo would have come but that's not the
point.
   None of us have seen hide nor hair of the pair of them
since and the weather is just rotten today and it's absolutely
bucketing out of the heavens so we're stuck here in the
guest house and I have to say Debbie and Laura are a right
pair of old misery guts. I've never seen such long faces.
They're driving me crazy. I'm mad about Laura of course I
am but she definitely can be a bit moody sometimes and of
course I can understand Debbie being so sour for she must

be just <u>gutted</u> about Dylan arriving out like that. Being Debbie she's trying to act as if she doesn't care but as I said to her she doesn't have to put on a brave face in front of me and when she wants to talk about it I'm right here for her.

Debbie

2.00 p.m. And I don't know how many times Maeve must have asked me when we were looking for this place last night if I minded Dylan turning up like that. As if she cares!

Genevieve

To be honest I can't see for the life of me what either of them see in Dylan. Personality-wise he's a complete loop-de-loop but I guess you'd have to say he is very good-looking though not quite the oil painting I'd say he thinks he is and I swear he's nothing but skin and bone and there isn't a pick on him and I have to say I can't stand fellas like that and I prefer them to have a bit of meat on them like Theo for instance though I suppose some might regard Theo as being too fat but then there's no accounting for taste.

I know Debbie hasn't had too much luck when it comes to romance but still, you'd imagine she'd be getting over Dylan by now but honestly she looked just miserable when Maeve and himself were mauling each other on the platform yesterday.

Debbie

2.30 p.m. Do I mind? What does she think? Like she even has to ask!

And I've never met anyone so thick-skinned as Genevieve. I don't know how many times she asked me this morning if I was "absolutely gutted?"

She's driving me crazy. If only it'd stop raining and I could get out of here.

Genevieve

And the way he dresses doesn't do him any favours either. All those old baggy jumpers and little knitted hats. Dreadful things altogether. As for that fuzzy head of hair of his well, that would drive me around the bend and if I were Maeve I'd make him chop the whole lot off but then maybe she likes him going around looking like Shirley Temple for as I say there's no accounting for taste.

Debbie

2.55 p.m. I mean it's barely six months since I broke it off with Dylan, and Maeve knows better than anyone how badly that affected me.

And she was the one who kept saying we shouldn't cancel this trip, that we needed to stick with our plans for the sake of our friendship. She might have thought of our precious friendship before she invited Dylan to join us.

Genevieve

And I'd say he's just using Maeve. As Laura says, it must be very handy to have Maeve around to pay for everything. How else could he have afforded to come out to China on the little he makes? You'd think that coming up to Christmas would be the busiest time of the year for a cycle courier and the one time he'd actually stand to make some money yet it's the very time he decides to take off! I'd say he doesn't make much from his music either for he doesn't seem a bit serious about making a career out of it despite all his talk. I asked him earlier how much he charges for weddings for if he was any good I was thinking I might book him myself as it'd be nice to put a bit of work his way but he just laughed like he thought that what I was saying was the most ridiculous thing he'd ever heard. I mean to say you'd think he'd be grateful to me!

Honestly I just don't get him at all. When I asked him how long he was going to be here he just laughed again and said he didn't know, that it depended on which way the wind blows! Like what's that supposed to mean!

Debbie

3.25 p.m. But Dylan must have been planning to come out even before we left Ireland, not that Maeve's ever going to admit that to me.

Typical Maeve, she thinks she can charm and bluster her way out of every situation. Not this time.

4.00 p.m. And I'm not going to start worrying about Dylan or looking out for him either in case he gets into trouble. I did enough of that when I was going out with him.

Genevieve

And as I say Laura is almost as big a misery guts as Debbie though heaven only knows what's up with her. I know she apologised to me for her outburst on the train yesterday but I don't know why she even bothered as she's snappy out again today with me. I thought she looked almost as sad as Debbie when Maeve and Dylan were making such a show of themselves yesterday in the train station but when I asked her was she okay and asked if she was missing Felix she nearly bit the head off me. <u>Yet</u> <u>again</u>. It's not like she's the only person in the world missing her boyfriend. And we were getting along so well and all. I've never really had a best friend as such before though I've had lots of friends of course and I really thought that Laura and myself were getting to be very close though we're very different but, as she says, the best friendships are often between people who are complete opposites though I can't help thinking we're a bit too opposite, much and all as I like her.

Debbie

4.30 p.m. I'd like to know just how much our friendship means to Maeve? A lot less it seems than her short relationship with Dylan.

4.45 p.m. I wouldn't expect much more from Dylan. I'm sure he doesn't see a problem with any of this, having no doubt filed me neatly away under either the Former Girlfriend or Best Friend Of Current Girlfriend categories. Maeve's the one I'm furious with.

Room 11. That evening.

Genevieve

I heard Laura say there's a phone downstairs so I've decided I'm going to go and give Theo a ring. I know we agreed I wouldn't phone while I'm away as it's just so expensive but seeing Maeve and Dylan together is making me feel fierce lonesome.

Debbie

8.00 p.m. Maeve just came in for a chat. She wanted to explain things. She says she knew Dylan was thinking of coming out but that she never encouraged him or thought he actually would which is why she didn't say anything to me.

This is the nearest I'm going to get to an admission from her. The other reason she didn't say anything to me was because she was afraid I'd be angry with her. Did she think I'd be any less angry if he showed up without any warning? She can be so thick at times.

Genevieve

Honest to God I'd have been better off with a couple of yoghurt cartons and a piece of string the line was that bad and it took me forever to get through and when I did eventually it was Trevor who answered and he kept me talking for ages, asking me question after question about Debbie and how she was doing. When I did finally manage to get him to put Theo on eventually Theo hardly asked me a single question about the trip but kept on fretting about how much the call was costing me though that didn't stop him telling me about every little thing that happened him since I've been gone like how he got two fillings at the dentist and how he bought a pair of navy cords in Ward's sale at a third of their original price and how Toby slipped his leash and was missing for a couple of nights. He really is a terrible one for rambling on and on even though as he kept saying himself I was ringing from China which must it must be costing me a fortune and how right he was. I noticed he made sure to tell me how Caitríona was getting on at Dad's and how the place was running so smoothly you'd hardly notice I was gone. I know I told him to keep an eye on Caitríona but I hope he hasn't been keeping too close an eye.

Across the hall in Room 12.

Maeve

Dylan is here!

Dylan is here!

Dylan is here!

Dylan is here!

When we arrived into Chengdu yesterday afternoon he was standing on the platform waiting. With all the people around I didn't even see him, not until he came right up & tapped on the window.

To see his lovely face looking in at me.

He's lovelier than I remembered.

How could I ever, ever, *ever* have left him?

I love him.

I love him.

I love him.

I love him to pieces.

I have never been *so* happy in my *entire* life.

An Asian Diary

Mags wins. Wannabe showed up. Apart from a very public and uninhibited reunion on the station platform, little of them has been seen since for they've holed themselves up in their room. Judging from their performance at the train station yesterday, they've a lot of catching up to do although they made a very good start there and then on platform no. 5. Unless I'm very much mistaken, however, that didn't stop him throwing the odd admiring look my way.

As yet, there hasn't been sufficient opportunity to fully gauge Deanne's reaction though if Geraldine had any sense, she'd ease off on the expressions of sympathy. Can she not read the signs? Can she not work out that the clenched jaw and the bulging veins at the side of Deanne's temples are not good?

But to me, the great mystery of it all is that even one person could love Wannabe. But that two do beggars belief. There he was as our train came in, standing on the platform, looking the epitome of cool or so he thought and if this were the sixties then perhaps – guitar, long scraggly hair, raggy jeans, sandals. Yes, sandals. Like, "Hey Man!"

For someone who's forever complaining that people here stare at us all the time, Geraldine wasn't exactly shy in showing her own interest in Wannabe. A visitor from outer space couldn't have come under closer scrutiny, I almost expected her to start prodding and poking at him. And it's not like she hasn't met him before but I guess he does look particularly outlandish out of his natural habitat.

When she'd finally examined him to her satisfaction, she moved on to making conversation. She began by asking him about music. Poor Geraldine. She was trying hard but I thought I'd choke when I heard her ask him if he agreed with her that Kate Winslet should have been allowed to sing the theme song from *Titanic* instead of Celine Dion. Now it was Wannabe's turn to stare. Somehow I don't think that's his kind of music. But the best was yet to come and his face was a picture of unmitigated disgust when she proceeded to ask him if he charged a flat rate or by the hour for wedding gigs with, no doubt, her own wedding in mind and, did he, she wanted to know, give reductions to people he knew. Somehow I don't think wedding gigs are where Wannabe's professional aspirations lie.

Geraldine and Wannabe? Chalk and cheese. At least one friend of Mags is safe from his amorous attentions.

11th November

The Pink Curtain Café, Chengdu. Morning.

Debbie

9.00 *a.m.* Maeve and Dylan are gazing into one another's eyes and smiling, touching, hugging, kissing and looking as if they just can't believe they're actually back together again.

9.10 *a.m.* Maeve and Dylan are gazing into one another's eyes and smiling, touching, hugging, kissing and looking as if they just can't believe they're actually back together again.

9.20 *a.m.* Maeve and Dylan are gazing into one another's eyes and smiling, touching, hugging, kissing and looking as if they just can't believe they're actually back together again.

How am I going to stick it? It's enough to put me off my breakfast.

Genevieve

When we were having breakfast Laura disappeared but now she's turned up with a beautiful silk painting and some

Chinese sweets she's bought for me by way of an apology for her recent outbursts. She said she hoped she hadn't ruined things between us seeing as how we've been getting along so well together. The sweets are very sickly-sweet though of course I didn't say that to Laura and I'm not all that gone on the painting but I'll keep it and give it to my mother as a present when I get home. It'll save me having to buy her something which is just as well as my money really isn't going anywhere near as far as I thought it would. Anyway since Laura had the decency to apologise over being so cross I told her that all was forgiven and forgotten.

Debbie

10.00 a.m. I am sick to death of the pair of them already.

[Save Address(es)][Block]   [Previous][Next][Close]

From: "Tobin, Laura"<lauratobin@hotmail.com>

To: "Wilson, Felix"<felix@fmsounds.com>

Subject: Two of a kind!

Date: 11 Nov, 16:23:11

[Reply][Reply All][Forward][Delete]

Hi Honey,

I guess we're two of a kind. Both too hotheaded for our own good. But I know you and I know all that nonsense you had on the phone about us finishing is just you speaking rashly.

It's hard being separated like this and we're bound to say things we don't mean. It's understandable that you might be feeling a little jealous being stuck in London while I'm gadding around Asia courtesy of NCRR Publishing and no doubt it seems to you like I've been away forever but in the greater scheme of things it isn't really all that long, not when you consider we've a whole lifetime together ahead of us.

So let's just forget that silly phone call, okay?

I love you so much.

Laura, XXXXX

[Save Address(es)][Block]   [Previous][Next][Close]

From: "Tobin, Laura"<lauratobin@hotmail.com>

To: "Kane, Christopher"<kaneliteraryagents@aol.com>

Subject: Book Proposal

Date: 11 Nov, 16:57:21

[Reply][Reply All][Forward][Delete]

Dear Chris,

I didn't expect to be back onto you quite so soon but I've

been mulling over your contention that the book needs a truly unique slant to capture the public's imagination and though it's an even greater departure from the sort of work I'm known for I have another idea I'd like to pitch at you.

What about a light-hearted fictionalised account of an extended trip through Asia written from the perspective of a ditzy female character in her mid-twenties who is completely unsuited and unused to travelling but who finds herself in Asia with three friends?

I can picture her exactly, a great big tall country redhead who stands out like a sore thumb in Asia. While her companions are enjoying the experience of travelling, she's sitting there, hunched up, head bent, scribbling all her woes and worries into her diary. And I know exactly how she'd sound, or write rather, too: in a rambling, almost pointless fashion, jumping from one subject to another, scrawling down whatever pops into her mind at that moment without reflection.

Obviously it's a huge departure from the factual reportage with which I've made my name but who says I can't diversify? If you like I can scratch down a few pages, give you a better idea of what I'm talking about.

Regards,

Laura.

12th November

Genevieve

The carry-on in public between Dylan and Maeve is absolutely <u>mortifying</u> and Laura says the same. She says she's never seen such pathetic, juvenile behaviour and she's right for they can't kept their hands off one another, not for a second. This afternoon when we went to the zoo to see the pandas they spent the whole time there just groping one another and the Chinese are bad enough for staring at us tourists when there's nothing to see but when there actually is then they are the <u>pits</u>! Everyone and I mean everyone was staring at the pair of them no exaggeration.

And of course the way Dylan dresses doesn't help for his clothes are <u>screaming</u> <u>out</u> <u>for</u> <u>attention.</u> Instead of wearing a warm jumper or a jacket like any normal person would as it was quite chilly today, he was wearing about five layers of raggedy old long-sleeved t-shirts plus a pair of baggy old, half-hanging-down so-called combat pants and a pair of bright red socks and he had one of those little beanies on his head. It was Debbie's idea to hire out bikes to go to the zoo and an idea I was not at all in favour of and I have to say it was very embarrassing to be cycling along and to see all these people turning around and staring at us though I must

182

say I was glad not to be the focus of attention for once. Some people were even laughing at Dylan and <u>actually pointing</u> <u>him</u> <u>out</u> <u>to</u> <u>their</u> <u>children.</u>

And he keeps on and on asking me if I'm happy with the cost of this or that though what's perfectly obvious to me is that one of the girls and most likely Maeve said something to him about how I'm a little bit cautious when it comes to spending money. And so what if I am? What business is it of his?

Poor Debbie is still looking a bit down but of course it's very hard for her having Dylan and Maeve around her all the time smooching.

Maeve

I love G.

She's just *so* nosy – like today asking me qsts no one else would dare but thinking she's being v. discreet.

When we were cycling back from the zoo she wanted to know (tho' she hastily assured me I needn't answer unless I wanted to) if myself & Dylan had any plans to get married & if (she continued not giving herself time to draw breath or me time to ans. her 1st qst.) we had then wouldn't we find it hard to manage what with Dylan not having a proper job & what *did* he want to do with himself anyway?

Surely – she pointed out – he didn't think he could actually make some cash out of playing the guitar & it's not like he was going to be able to keep going as a cycle courier forever. I assured her she'd be the 1st to hear of our plans.

Debbie

8.00 p.m. I don't think Genevieve is all that enamoured with Dylan. "Debbie, I know you used to go out with him before but tell me, what do you really think of Dylan?" she asked me earlier today which of course meant that what she was actually asking was, "Debbie, can I tell you what I think of Dylan?"

As it turns out, she thinks he's, "All right I suppose but no offence, I wouldn't fancy him myself. He's a bit too smart-alecky for my liking and you're definitely better off without him. You know Debs, it's probably time for you to move on and of course there's plenty more fish in the sea."

Pop psychology from Genevieve is just about the last thing I need right now.

Maeve

Marriage?

Dylan?

Yeah right!

I can just see him waiting at the top of the aisle!

We've never even talked about it & it's not like we're in much of a position to marry at the moment. A fly couldn't live on what Dylan makes (as G pointed out with char. bluntness) & I've just given up my job tho' I'm sure they'll take me on again when I get back.

But I just can't imagine a future without Dylan.

I know we've only been together for a short time but in a way it's like we've been together 4ever.

Sigh!!!!

But then I can't imagine the pair of us playing happy hubby & wifey either.

Funny how L *still* hasn't said anything about her break-up with Felix.

With all the excitement of Dylan arriving out, it kinda slipped my mind.

Guess I should try talking to her about it tho' I can't say I fancy the prospect.

Maybe I'll wait until my headache is gone – I've a *killer* of one after last night & I think all the fresh air we got today made it even worse.

Dylan & myself ended up in this bar with some Americans until 4 in the a.m.

And there I was, managing to be reasonably sensible when it was just us girls.

Oh well!

Only young once.

Eat the peach.

Seize the day.

Blah-de-blah.

Dylan should have been back by now. Said he was only popping out for half an hour.

[Save Address(es)][Block]   [Previous][Next][Close]
From: "Tobin, Laura"<lauratobin@hotmail.com>
To: "Wilson, Felix"<felix@fmsounds.com>
Subject: [none]
Date: 12 Nov, 22:12:58
[Reply][Reply All][Forward][Delete]

At last an e-mail from you! Though not exactly the one I was hoping for. I can't believe you're still going on about us splitting up? Can't you see how stupid it is especially when I'm thousands of miles away? What we need to do is to wait until I come home and then we can sit down and talk things through, calmly, sensibly.

If you genuinely felt like this for ages, Felix, then I think you would have said something to me before I left. You're just upset because I'm so far away.

13th November

The Pink Curtain Café. Mid-afternoon.

Maeve

I know Debs isn't too happy with Dylan being here but what can I do?

I'm sure she'll come 'round with enough sweet-talking – she always does.

L is like a pig as well.

Of course splitting up with Felix is a bit of a bitch but she could at least *try* & be happy for me.

Like, it's not every day someone's boyfriend flies all the way to Asia to be with his girlfriend.

Like, this a.m. she told me she didn't want to hear another word about how wonderful it was to have Dylan here – you'd swear it was, like, all I *ever* talked about.

And why hasn't she told any of us about Felix dumping her?

I just don't get it.

But if she doesn't want to confide in us then I'm not going to waste my time worrying about her.

Esp. with Dylan around – don't want to waste that precious time.

Wonder where Dylan is now. He's been missing for ages.

Genevieve

Dylan's gone off somewhere and I wish Maeve would stop fretting about where he is and personally I hope he stays away for the rest of the day for I've had enough of his sarcasm for one day thank you very much.

What I will say for him though is he's not tight with his money. Practically the only thing I can eat in this whole country are those pot noodles so I always like to have a couple of tubs spare for at least then I won't starve but yesterday when I stopped to buy some I'd spotted in this little stall I found I'd left my money belt back at the hostel which is very unlike me for I'm usually so careful but straight away Dylan stepped in and paid for the noodles and then when I tried to give him the money back this morning before he disappeared off he told me not to bother. Laura says it's easy for him to be generous since it's probably all Maeve's money in any case. Still, I thought it was nice of him all the same.

Back at the Chengdu Guest House, assorted bedrooms Evening time.

Maeve

Dylan's just arrived back but went straight to bed – told me to stop annoying him when I tried asking him where he'd been.

Don't know why he was being such a pain.

Told Debs 'bout Felix dumping L this afternoon when we were coming back from the museum. Not sure why – it just sort of, like, came out.

Wish I hadn't.

Debs started on about how I should talk to L cos I'm closest to her.

I don't know why Debs should care for it's not like she even likes Laura, not that she'd ever say.

And when I said as much to her she denied it – of course – but it's always easy to tell when Debs doesn't like someone for she just avoids them as much as poss. or is overly polite to them when she's no choice but to be in their company.

But the way I figure it is that if L wanted us to know about her & Felix then she'd have told us but she didn't. So why should I go sticking my nose in where it's not wanted?

Debbie

9.00 p.m. What a horrible day. Everyone is driving me crazy.

Maeve and Dylan for the obvious reasons.

Genevieve because she kept sympathising with me so much that in the end I had to take her aside and carefully explain yet again that it was I who broke it off with Dylan. From the pitying smile she gave me, I don't think she believed me.

And Laura because she's in even worse form than I am. Maeve says it's because she and Felix have broken up but I'm not meant to know and in typical Maeve fashion she's made me swear not to say a word to Laura.

9.30 p.m. Laura's just asked me to walk into town with her. She says that Felix is expecting her to ring which is very odd given what Maeve told me earlier.

Since Laura's about as fond of me as I am of her, the only reason she's asked me to come with her is because Maeve and Dylan are otherwise occupied and Genevieve is "only crippled from her feet".

I don't want to go. Her company is about the last thing I want right now for all she ever seems to do is bitch about whichever one of us isn't around. She's poison when it comes to Genevieve so I can only imagine what she's like behind my back.

[Save Address(es)][Block]   [Previous][Next][Close]
From: "Tobin, Laura"<lauratobin@hotmail.com>
To: "Kane,Christopher"<kaneliteraryagents@aol.com>
Subject: Book Proposal
Date: 13 Nov, 22:24:10
[Reply][Reply All][Forward][Delete]

Your comments regarding my latest book idea not exactly being my first foray into fiction are highly objectionable. It's a cheap jibe, Chris, and completely unfounded.

The Argus stand over everything I wrote on the Ronald Devereux Affair. The only reason they settled out of court with Lily Buchan's brother was simply to assuage public feeling, something I have always maintained they were unwise to do for I think it has wider ramifications vis à vis the freedom of the press.

I have forwarded your e-mail to my solicitor, Timothy Lewis, for his consideration. Expect to hear from him in due course.

[Address(es)][Block]   [Previous][Next][Close]
From: "Tobin, Laura"<lauratobin@hotmail.com>
To: "Lewis,Timothy"<lewissolicitors@lineone.net.ie>
Subject: Following on from our phone conversation . . .
Date: 13 Nov, 22:45:59
[Reply][Reply All][Forward][Delete]

Dear Tim,
Further to our telephone conversation, I'm attaching Christopher Kane's e-mail for your consideration.

Can you advise me as to what legal redress I have as regards the comments contained therein?

Regards, Laura.

14th November

Genevieve

I'm knackered. I don't know why I ever let Debbie persuade me to walk out to that monumental garden with her and for the life of me I couldn't see what the big deal was about but at least my arches held up okay though I think I definitely have a verruca or something on my left foot. There's a little hard white lump there that's quite painful to walk on.

I really just don't get Dylan at all. Yesterday he very kindly paid for my pot noodles but then earlier today on our way here I actually saw him <u>steal</u> a kebab from one of the stalls in the town just for sport and after taking one bite of it he threw it away. When I told him he shouldn't be robbing like that he laughed and said I was mistaken. But I know I saw what I saw which is what I was telling him when Maeve came over and stuck her beak in and began wanting to know what was going on and so I told her and all she had to say was that Dylan should have got one for her too and then she started laughing like mad like it was a big joke or something. And they mock me for being mean! At least I don't go around stealing from people who probably can ill-afford to be stolen from.

Debbie

2.00 p.m. I can see why Genevieve isn't all that impressed by Dylan. There really isn't an awful lot to him underneath all the posturing. He is shallow. He is silly. He is full of himself and he isn't exactly the sharpest tool in the box. I know all that. At least I do until I see him smile.

I just have to keep reminding myself that I was the one who dumped him.

2.10 p.m. But when I see the way his hair curls at the back of his neck . . .

Remember I dumped him.

2.15 p.m. Or when I hear him humming in that absent-minded way he has . . .

Remember I dumped him.

2.20 p.m. Remember I dumped him.

Remember I dumped him.

Remember I dumped him.

Lounge, Chengdu Guest House. Evening time.

Maeve

For someone so hapless as Dylan appears to be, he's proven to be very resourceful.

The reason he's been going missing so much is because he was on a "mission" as he puts it.

He's only been in China for a matter of days yet he's already found a supply of dope!

Amazing really.

Esp. when he'd be hard pressed to figure out how to go about buying train tickets or finding us a hotel or doing anything else of a practical nature.

Genevieve

I went back to the kebab stand after we left that café and bought a kebab and told the woman to keep the change which will cover the cost of the one Dylan stole. I didn't eat it of course for you can never be too careful with meat and especially off the street like that. And then when I arrived back here Dylan had the <u>cheek</u> to turn around and ask me for a loan but I told him where to go.

Laura wants me to walk into town with her for she needs to phone Felix but the phone downstairs isn't working. God knows what time of the day or night it is at home. That Felix seems to have the most hectic social life of anyone for I don't know how many times she's tried ringing him especially over the last few days but he always seems to be out. The last thing I want to do right now is walk into town on account of my verruca and how my arches are acting up again but sometimes it's very hard to say no to Laura.

[Save Address(es)][Block]   [Previous][Next][Close]
From: "Tobin, Laura"<lauratobin@hotmail.com>
To: "Wilson, Felix"felix@fmsounds.com>
Subject: You're pathetic!
Date: 14 Nov, 11:59:00
[Reply][Reply All][Forward][Delete]

I suppose I should thank you for taking my call. But you know something, Felix, I have never heard such bullshit in all my life.
What do you mean by saying you had to wait until I went away before you felt you could break it off? Are you that much of a coward? Am I that scary?

15th November

Lounge of Chengdu Guest House. Morning time.

Debbie

11.00 a.m. "I'd be really happy if you and Dylan could get along for my sake. Could you not just try, Debbie?" So Maeve said to me this morning.

11.25 a.m. "We are still friends, aren't we Debbie?" Dylan's just asked me.

Can't he understand how that's not an option? He and Maeve really are one of a kind. I don't know which one is blinder.

An hour later.

Genevieve

Is there <u>ever</u> any let up? I swear I can get no peace whatsoever from Debbie. She was in here just now going hup, hup, hup like I was a cow or something and demanding to know what I was doing lying about in bed so late in the day when it was so fine outside especially as we'd such an awful lot to get through today. I told her I'd a pain in my stomach which is kind of true too but I don't think she believed me but I am just knackered and I really am not up to doing any sightseeing today. In fact I am <u>sick</u> to my eye-teeth of sightseeing. And why did she have to go opening the curtains? Why couldn't she have just left them be? She just doesn't get the notion that holidays are <u>meant</u> to be for <u>relaxing</u>. Well I'm going to stay put and she can come in here yelling all she wants and yanking at the bed clothes but for once I am <u>not</u> going to budge.

An hour later.

Genevieve

I think they've all gone out now and good riddance for it's good to get a break from them. Especially Dylan for he's bloody well doing my head in. One thing I hate about him is the way he treats me like I'm as thick as a plank and he's forever mocking me though I'd say he thinks I'm too stupid to realise. And it's not like he's some kind of Einstein either though he seems to think he is. I'd say he never even finished secondary school.

And he's always trying to get a rise out of me. And sticking whatever disgusting thing he's in the middle of eating under my nose and asking me if I want some of it knowing full well I wouldn't touch whatever it is with a ten-foot bargepole.

Maeve of course seems to think that every word he utters is just about the funniest thing she's ever heard in the whole of her life. I have to say I like Maeve much better when he's not around. Seeing Maeve stuck with someone like him makes me realise just how lucky I am in having Theo. I guess I should think about getting up.

Room 11 once again. That evening.

Genevieve

Well the latest on the Dylan front is that <u>he</u> <u>does</u> <u>drugs</u>.

I know this for a fact. How I found out is as follows. Just now on my way back to my room I got lost and ended up in this little courtyard at the back of the hotel and who was sitting there in the dark only Dylan so I tried to sneak away before he saw me for I was just not in the mood to listen to any more of his sarcastic comments. But before I managed to escape he spotted me and called me over so I didn't really have much choice but to go. He was in great form altogether and even livelier that usual and was all chat chat chat like we were best friends though I could hardly hear a word he was saying for all the time he was strumming away on that stupid guitar of his like he was Kurt Cobain or one of those other fellas he's forever rabbiting on about. But then I noticed something odd which was the fact that he'd a cigarette in one hand and so I said something to him about how I never knew he smoked which sent him off into howls of laughter. Well I'd had enough of him by that stage so I left as quickly as I could but it was only when I reached my room that it dawned on me that his cigarette didn't smell like an ordinary cigarette at all and that it must have been dope he was smoking!

In a way Dylan doing drugs doesn't come as much of a surprise. He has all the signs. The long hair. The ratty clothes. The guitar. He's just the kind really.

But I think he'd want to be a bit more careful when he's out foreign whatever about at home. I mean to say he hardly brought that stuff with him on the plane so where did he get it? And who did he get it from? It could have been anyone even an undercover policeman and what would happen if he was caught by the authorities? And what would happen to the rest of us?

And then just as I reached my room, I bumped into Maeve coming out of hers and the first thing she asked me was had I seen Dylan and I was about to say I had and to tell her under what exact circumstances too but then he appeared and put his hands around her waist and started kissing her on the neck despite the fact that I was standing there trying to hold a conversation with her not that he even seemed to notice me for no doubt he was as high as a kite and of course people on drugs have <u>absolutely no inhibitions.</u> And of course as soon as he appeared Maeve lost all interest in anything I had to say but maybe it's just as well I didn't say anything for she would have been <u>gutted.</u>

I think the thing for me to do is to talk to Laura and find out what she thinks I should do about this whole tricky situation.

An Asian Diary

Wannabe certainly has diverse taste in women. Deanne. Mags And now me. Although he's only been with us a matter of days, he's already skulking behind Mags' back telling me how, from the moment he met me that weekend in Dublin he's had, as he put it, the "serious hots" for me, ever since.

You'd imagine people would know when someone is out of their league but not this sad fool and he actually seems to think he might be in with a chance. I can just see myself dumping the Millionaire and turning up at one of my circle's dinner parties back in London on Wannabe's arm! And I can just see him at the dinner table, boring everyone with his talk of the tragedy of Kurt Cobain dying so young and how he shares his pain and the angst of being an artist.

Pity he doesn't share his talent. Don't laugh but he's composed a song about me. Apparently he's been working on it ever since our first meeting but it's not quite finished yet for he's having trouble with some of the lyrics. That didn't stop him getting out his guitar however and singing it for me when we found ourselves on our own today. As soon as he'd finished, he asked me what I thought of it and, being the kind soul I am, I held back and settled for telling him that I thought it was a little clichéd. For a second he looked confused but then nodded his head in satisfaction, deciding, I guess, that clichéd was a good thing. But I was being kind. I think Billy Joel has already made the phrase 'uptown girl" his own.

So what am I to do with this attention? Although Wannabe might not sing like an angel, he does have the face of one. Big blue eyes, full pouting lips, dimples, and, when washed, a fine head of curly hair, which all combine very pleasingly. And the body's not bad either, even if a little on the skinny side. The clothes are a bit off-putting but that could be taken care of easily.

You see, it does get a little lonely sometimes being so far away from my own beloved. And it's not like anybody, apart from you, dear reader, need ever know.

16th November

Debbie

9.00 a.m. I thought that being on this tour with thirty strangers might give me some breathing space from each other but we're still stuck with just ourselves to talk to since everyone else is Chinese and only Ralph the guide has any English.

Genevieve

Maybe Laura wasn't the best person to ask for advice as regards Dylan and the drugs. I stayed awake especially last night until she came back from ringing Felix but before I got to it I just asked out of politeness if she'd managed to get through to him and if she did how was he keeping and I swear she nearly bit the head off of me no exaggeration and called me a <u>nosy</u> <u>little</u> <u>bitch</u> which of course was completely uncalled for and then she snapped at me again and told me to spit out whatever it was I was waiting to say to her and so I started telling her about Dylan and the drugs and she just went, oh for crying out loud, and then stormed off to the bathroom so really I still have no idea as to what I should do.

But I've been keeping a close eye on Dylan all morning

and though it's hard to tell if he's high or not for he's always a bit hyper at the best of times I think he's fairly okay today from what I can tell. Of course himself and Maeve are <u>all</u> <u>over</u> <u>one</u> <u>another</u> and have absolutely no regard for the old people on the bus who wouldn't be used to such behaviour but then there's nothing new in that. But poor Maeve would be <u>absolutely</u> <u>gutted</u> if she knew what kind Dylan really was for she's <u>cracked</u> about him no exaggeration. I know she was always a bit wild herself but drugs are a <u>whole</u> <u>different</u> <u>ball</u> <u>game</u> altogether. I still don't know whether I should tell her or not. Maybe I should just have a talk with Dylan and see if I can make him see sense and convince him to give them up.

I wish the old people would shut up. They're doing my head. They've been singing non-stop for bloody ages and my head is absolutely <u>pounding</u> from them.

Maeve

Debs organised for us all to go on this bus tour.
Wished she'd, like, looked into it a little better – seems we're the only people under 70.
A bit dull & boring to say the least.
All the oldies are singing already.
I swear it sounds like "The Fields of Athenry" in Chinese.
Dylan bought some dope with him – which *mightn't* necessarily be a bad thing.
Know I swore I'd ease off but at least it'd relieve the boredom.

Genevieve

My head is <u>splitting</u> and it really is like being on an outing from some Chinese old folk's home with all the old folk singing like mad and jabbering away at the top of their voices and even leaving aside the whole worrying business of Dylan and the drugs I just know I'm not going to enjoy this tour at all though we're paying a bloody fortune to come on it. As for Ralph the tour guide, well it seems to me like he thinks he's <u>God's gift to women</u> though he's a right little pip-squeak with heels on him that are at least <u>three inches high</u> no exaggeration.

I notice Laura's very quiet in herself but I certainly am not going to be stupid enough to ask her if anything is up for though she's fierce nice and all most of the time she can be very snappy when you happen to say the wrong thing to her. If you ask me she hasn't really been herself since Chengdu. Up to that we were really hitting it off but she seems to have gone into herself since and is still <u>very touchy</u>. Maybe she has her period or something.

Debbie

12.10 p.m. I think I should suggest to Maeve that she and Dylan lay off the lovey-dovey stuff for I've noticed quite a few startled glances being thrown in their direction.

12.15 p.m. I shouldn't have opened my mouth. Maeve just laughed and demanded to know who could possibly object to a couple simply expressing their affection for one another. From the look she gave me, I'd say she thought I was just jealous.

Genevieve

God Almighty! Our tour guide Ralph is <u>crackers!</u> We

just stopped at this hotel for a break so I went to the toilet and when I was coming back out I ran straight into him and it's a wonder I didn't do him an injury for he went flying to the ground. When I asked him what the hell he was doing hanging around like that outside the Ladies like some kind of a pervert he said he'd noticed I was gone for quite a while and was worried in case there was something the matter with me! Like it's any business of his! I told him he'd little enough to be worrying about! Then when we got back on the bus Maeve started teasing me about how he fancies me and then Dylan joined in! But I can tell you that him fancying me is just about the last thing I need right now!

But I am beginning to get a bit worried for I haven't actually <u>gone</u> now for two whole days and I just hope there isn't anything the matter with me down below. At least I managed to have a quiet word with Dylan when we got off the bus and I warned him about the dangers of taking drugs and how he should really consider giving up as otherwise he's letting himself in for major problems in the future through ongoing drug-dependency and the like. He said that I'd given him a lot to think about and that he'd certainly take what I'd said on board though I don't know whether he was being sarcastic or not for you can never tell with Dylan.

[Save Address(es)][Block]　　　[Previous][Next][Close]
From:　　　"Tobin, Laura"<lauratobin@hotmail.com>
To:　　　　"Lewis, Timothy"<lewissolicitors@lineone.net.ie>
Subject:　　Your e-mail of the 15th
Date:　　　16 Nov, 20:43:23
[Reply][Reply All][Forward][Delete]

Dear Timothy,
Thanks for your advice. I guess you're right but I can't help being annoyed by the fact that Christopher Kane thinks he can get away with saying whatever he likes.
As regards payment for your work on my behalf in respect of *The Argus*, I've directed my bank to transfer the money required to your account.
Regards,
Laura.

[Save Address(es)][Block]　　　[Previous][Next][Close]
From:　　　"Tobin, Laura"<LauraTobin@hotmail.com>
To:　　　　"Simmons, Alma" <alma@syncyrecords.com>
Subject:　　Hi!
Date:　　　16 Nov, 20:59:12
[Reply][Reply All][Forward][Delete]

Hi Alma,
Great to get your e-mail!
Yeah, I'm having a fantastic time and the book is going very well.
I'm missing Felix of course and thanks for telling me what's being said but rest assured there's no truth in it. I'm not sure how such rumours start but that's all they are – rumours, and

I'm afraid I've no hot update for you. Felix and I are still very much together.

I have to go now but I'll send you a longer e-mail with all my news when I have more time.

Love and kisses,

Laura.

17th November

Day two of the coach tour. Morning time.

Debbie

10.00 a.m. Dylan actually had the nerve to ask me for a loan just before we got on the bus this morning and when I refused he seemed genuinely surprised and had the cheek to point out I'd never refused him before.

I had to explain that things were a bit different now than when we were going out together.

Genevieve

It's obvious Dylan didn't mean a word of what he said to me yesterday about quitting drugs and from the carry-on of him today I'd say he's as high as a kite. He's now teaching some of the old people a song all about how they were going to go to school but then they didn't because they got high and how they were going to clean their room but then they didn't because they got high and so on and so forth and they're all singing it to beat the band though of course they've <u>no</u> idea of what any of it means.

Debbie

11.30 a.m. Now Dylan has everyone on the bus singing like crazy. If I didn't know any better I'd swear he was stoned out of his head. But how would he even know where to get his hands on anything here in China? And anyway, even he'd hardly be stupid enough to risk it.

But it's probably not a bad thing one of us is proving so popular for Laura seems determined to alienate everyone on the tour. She's so snappy. I noticed one of the old ladies offering her some sweets earlier and she just completely ignored her.

I don't think she's taking being dumped by Felix very well. I'd like to say something to her but I know I'm the last person she'd want offering her sympathy. I keep telling Maeve she should talk to her and she keeps promising me she will but then does nothing.

Maeve

I'm so, so, *sooooo* mad with Dylan.

Course he doesn't care. He's just ignoring me.

Earlier he just, like, happened to mention in passing how he *somehow* managed to sweet-talk Yvonne in Tyson's Travel into debiting my Visa card to pay for his plane ticket to Beijing.

Which means I've paid for his ticket *twice* now since I already transferred money from my account to pay for it.

Says he spent that money on a new backpack & all the other bits & pieces he needed for the journey.

But what Yvonne did must be illegal.

Like, how can she take money from my account like that?

And how did he manage to persuade her?

I mightn't mind *so* much if he'd told me about it before but it just came out now as a by-the-way.

And he's smoking his head off too tho' I don't think

anybody has noticed. The girls prob. think he's being his usual off-the-wall self.

Well, maybe not Debs but she hasn't said anything to me.

Debbie

12.05 p.m. Aside from the understandable feelings of jealousy, I really hate seeing Maeve and Dylan together. They're just not good for one another. They seem to spend all their time either groping one another or going out at night getting wasted or fighting just so they can make up again. It's all highs and lows with them. I think they enjoy the drama.

Genevieve

I was going to go to school but then I got hi-high. It really is a catchy tune. I just can't get it out of my mind.

Well so far nothing's happened in the you-know-what department yet and I'm really beginning to worry for it's been days now and I'm going to have to talk to one of the others if things don't start moving soon and if that and the whole worrying situation with Dylan and the drugs isn't enough to have to deal with right now, there's the food they're giving us which is just pathetic. You wouldn't dish the breakfast we got this morning up in a zoo.

And lunch wasn't much better. When we pulled into this little village Ralph herded all of us down off the bus and along this alleyway and around the back of a building and into this room which he called a restaurant though aside from a couple of tables scattered around it looked exactly like a squash court to me and smelled like one. So anyway he sat us down around these huge roundy tables and I'd say we must have been there for at least an hour before these grumpy, greasy-looking waitresses came and slapped plate after plate of food down in the centre of the table. Well all I have to say is that I've <u>never</u> seen anything like the way the others on the tour set upon the food and what with Chinese people being quite small and all you wouldn't expect them to have such big appetites but honestly they could well have just finished that Long March Debbie was telling us about earlier. Laura's right. She can be really boring sometimes. I mean to say I spent enough time in school having Irish history drummed into me without having to put up with Chinese history lessons of all things on my holidays. Anyway because this Ralph fella was sitting so close to me I could hardly move my elbow so it was hard to pick things up with my chopsticks and the whole lot had practically disappeared before I got a chance to get at any of it. Not that I would have eaten much in any case but that's not the point and I just think the others could have been a little bit more considerate and of course I'm starving now and I could eat a horse although I should be careful about saying something like that for you never know and I might have already without realising.

But I just don't get Laura at all. One minute she's all over me and is acting like we're best friends and then the next minute she's biting the head off me. Why can't she just make up her mind once and for all and decide to be either one thing or the other? Nice or not nice? And stick to that? It'd be easier for everyone if we all knew where we stood.

Like, after nearly <u>eating</u> me when I asked her what I should do about Dylan and the drugs, now she's suddenly all interested again and just now she made her way up the bus to me and wanted to know had I said anything to him and so I told her I had and that he'd promised he'd lay off them but when she heard this she laughed and said I shouldn't believe a word that comes out of a drug addict's mouth for they'd sell their own mother for a fix. I guess she's right though I don't think Dylan has quite got to that stage yet.

Laura seems to think I should try talking to him again though what good it would do, I don't know.

Common room, Emei Shan Hotel. Evening time.

Maeve

Poor Dylan.

He's a bit strung out.

Don't think he feels too much like singing now!

And I don't think he's going to find what he's looking for in this one-horse town.

I think G's losing it.

Says that our tour guide Ralph is stalking her but (funny thing is) Dylan says it's she who's stalking him.

He says that every time he looks around she's just standing there, staring at him, like she's insane or something.

Genevieve

That Ralph is doing my head in. All day long he was hovering about and whenever I turned around he was standing there right behind me grinning at me like he was completely <u>insane</u> or something. And all evening he's been sitting beside me and asking me questions about my country and what we eat there and what kind of clothes we wear and what do the young people like to do. I've never met anyone with such an interest in Ireland.

Dylan's eyes are definitely a bit bloodshot-looking. The drugs? I saw Maeve examining them just now. I just hope she doesn't suspect anything.

Debbie

8.45 p.m. Our guide Ralph definitely fancies Genevieve but when I pointed out as much to her earlier today, she got really annoyed.

But she must be blind if she can't see it. He's been sitting beside her all evening, smiling at her, delighted when she throws a look his way, no matter how cross.

Genevieve

God Almighty! Ralph is now trying to teach me Chinese. I tried offloading him onto Debbie for she's interested in that sort of thing but he was having none of it and though I keep telling him I've no interest whatsoever he doesn't seem to hear me for he just carries on pointing at things and repeating their names over and over and prodding me in the shoulder and trying to get me to repeat them after him. And he has this <u>disgusting</u> habit of clearing his throat and spitting and when I say spitting I mean spitting even when he's in the middle of talking to me without so much as bothering to turn away. And in between the spitting he's smoking and seems to think he's the flaming Marlboro man or something and that I'm bound to be fierce impressed at the sight of him puffing away like a chimney. I think I'm going to have to go to my room to get away from him and anyway we have a very early start in the morning and if I want to wake up bright-eyed and bushy-tailed as Debbie keeps saying I really should go to bed now.

An Asian Diary

Sometimes, dear reader, I ask myself what century Geraldine is from. The other day she came across Wannabe smoking a joint but from her reaction you'd swear she'd found him injecting heroin whilst simultaneously snorting lines of coke and popping E's.

We've been on this bus tour these last few days and because she's sitting at the front of the bus and he's down the back, she has her neck permanently craned around, keeping him under constant surveillance. I don't know what she expects to happen. His head to suddenly explode? And every time the bus stops and we all get out to stretch our legs, it's like she's stalking him. I've even noticed her following ten paces behind when he went looking for the loo at our last stop this afternoon. All she's missing is the long trench coat and the shades. I can only guess what the other people on the tour make of her.

So worried was she about the "situation" that she came to me asking for advice as to what she should do. She'd already had a word with him, she told me, but she didn't think he'd taken her all that seriously. So what else could she do? Should she tell Mags? Or would I perhaps take Wannabe aside and try talking some sense into him?

Now Wannabe's just a pothead, nothing more. A sad, sorry pothead who didn't have that many brain cells to begin with so the loss of a few more isn't going to make much difference to him; mean of me then to tell Geraldine that, given the gravity of the situation as Wannabe's habit is very likely spiralling out of control, she'd no choice but to do her utmost to try and convince him to give them up immediately. She'd a moral duty, I told her and she nodded gravely, taking to heart all I'd said.

So now, no doubt, she'll be driving Wannabe crazy, chasing after him, pestering him with her pearls of wisdom which should provide some light entertainment on what is otherwise proving to be a very boring couple of days. I know what Geraldine means when she says, "We've flaming historic monuments coming out our flaming ears".

18th November

Day three of the coach tour. Dawn.

Debbie

4.00 a.m. It's the middle of the night but we're on the bus already, on our way to Mount Emei Shan which we're going to climb to watch the sunrise from the top. My guidebook says it's a must-see.

We're already running late. Genevieve held up our departure by refusing to budge from her bed. Not until Dylan threatened to get in alongside her did she budge and then she was out of there like a shot.

Back at the Emei Shan Hotel. That evening.

Genevieve

The others have all gone out to have a look around the town but I'm going to have an early night as I'm absolutely knackered for Ralph had us all up at the crack of dawn climbing some stupid mountain and I just don't know how he managed it seeing as how he smokes at least forty a day.

I can't say I'm enjoying this tour at all. In fact if I'm to be honest the only part of this entire trip I've enjoyed so far has been the time we spent with Andrew at the very start. I was asking Maeve again today if she's been in

216

contact with him since we left Beijing but she hasn't which I think is a bit mean. He was just so good to us when we were there. I have thought a couple of times about giving him a call myself just to let him know how we're getting on but I haven't as the last thing in the world I'd want is to have him thinking I was being <u>overly</u> familiar

Someone's just started knocking on the door and no prizes for guessing who either. That Ralph is absolutely <u>hounding</u> me. Maybe if I keep quiet and don't answer he'll go away. Honest to God I've had just about enough of him for one day. At every meal he plonks himself down beside me and keeps on and on at me, trying to get me to eat and I end up having to pick at this and that to keep him off my back and I have to say I find it impossible to eat any of the stuff especially as he uses his own chopsticks <u>the</u> <u>very</u> <u>same</u> <u>ones</u> <u>that</u> <u>have</u> <u>just</u> <u>been</u> <u>in</u> <u>his</u> <u>mouth</u> to shovel all sorts of mush onto my plate. And even if I didn't have to put up with that then the way he eats would definitely put me off my food. I know I'm a fussy eater but I can't help that and having him slurping away beside me just puts paid to any appetite I might have. This evening at tea for example when most of the flesh had been picked off this enormous fish they'd put in the centre of the table for all of us to share, Ralph grinned over at me and then leant forward and yanked off the head of the fish with his chopsticks and popped it into his mouth whole and when I say whole I mean whole. Eyes. Mouth. The Lot. I nearly vomited. And then he chewed and chewed for five minutes or so before spitting all the little bones back out onto the plastic table cover right beside me. How could <u>anybody</u> eat with the likes of that going on?

I've been keeping a close eye on Dylan all day and as far as I can tell he hasn't been taking any more drugs. The knocking has stopped so I think Ralph has finally got the message that there's nobody at home.

An Asian Diary

We spent the day climbing Mount Emei Shan, one of China's sacred mountains. Deanne of course had all the right gear – the climbing boots, the lightweight pants, the waterproofs – and set about climbing that mountain as if her very life depended on it. She'd people scattering left and right desperate to get out of her way.

Geraldine took a somewhat easier option. Just where the mountain started to get very steep, there was a group of local men hanging about and, for a fee, they were offering to carry people the rest of the way in these basket seats which pairs of the men hoisted up on their shoulders and then carried between them. Those availing of this service were the frail and the elderly with one exception – strapping Geraldine who probably equalled the combined weight of her two carriers. Not that that bothered her and like a satisfied reclining little Buddha, all tucked up in her thick padded jacket, she relaxed back as they panted and puffed under her weight, their stick-like legs buckling at the knees, all the while being passed by their colleagues who were lucky enough to be carrying Chinese-light-as-a-feather septuagenarians.

Mags and Wannabe made it to the top in their own leisurely way, their progress hindered somewhat by Mags stopping to kiss her "honey" every couple of minutes much to the annoyance and embarrassment of the other climbers who were forced to make their way around them.

And then when we eventually got to the top of the mountain, Wannabe, in an attempt to cool down a little, began undressing his top half. First his beanie, then his green army jacket, then his denim jacket, then several t-shirts, until, eventually, he was standing there, bare-chested. From the stares and sniggers of those around, his blond curly chest hair proved to be something of a novelty. Not that he cared in the least. Not even when one old lady came up to touch it, as warily as one might come to touch the antennae of a creature from outer space.

19th November

Day four of the coach tour. Early morning.

Debbie

10.00 p.m. "We had some good times together hadn't we, Debbie?"

What does Dylan expect exactly? That we sit around and reminisce about the good old days?

Genevieve

No obvious signs of drug use either today. But then if he's a committed long-term user the effects mightn't be all that easy for the layman to spot.

And as if I hadn't enough worries on my plate what with Dylan and the drugs and the horrible food and the lack of activity in the you-know-what department, Ralph has now declared his love for me first thing this morning. I swear I got such a shock that the only thing I could think to do was pretend I didn't understand what it was he was trying to say to me.

I swear it's no exaggeration to say I am <u>just</u> fed up! And not just with this bus tour we're on right now either though I'm fed up with that too but at least it's nearly over although it doesn't look like we'll <u>ever</u> get back to Chengdu for there's some hold-up on the road. It's boiling in the bus and the sweat is just pouring off me and to make things worse Ralph has plonked himself down beside me and is rabbiting on again about how he loves me. I'm killed from telling him about Theo and how we're as good as engaged but he just doesn't seem to care and keeps going on and on about how my hair is so beautiful and my eyes are like miniature lakes whatever that's supposed to mean. I thought he might take the hint when he saw me writing in my diary but not a hope and he just keeps trying to peer into it.

Victory House, lounge. Evening.

Genevieve

Well we've finished with the bus tour and I've seen the last of Ralph and no harm either. But honest to God I am just so fed up with this whole trip for it's been nothing but a nightmare from start to finish. When I said as much to Laura earlier she wanted to know why I'd decided to come in the first place but sure how was I to know it was going to be like this? I'd just imagined the good times the four of us would have, travelling around together, and had absolutely no idea what the reality would be. But I hate it all. I hate the disgusting food. I hate the horrible places we end up staying in. I hate having to pack and unpack that stupid rucksack every day. I hate never being able to find anything no matter how well-organised I try to keep my things especially now some of my ziplock bags have burst and it's impossible to fit everything into the ones that are still intact so everything's just getting all muddled up and none of my labels really apply any more.

I just don't know how I'm going to stick much more of this.

And things are set to get even worse! They're now all talking about going horse-trekking of all things up in some mountains. For <u>three</u> <u>whole</u> <u>days</u>! I can't think of anything in the whole wild world more awful.

Debbie

7.00 p.m. "Dylan thinks you're still odd with him. I really wish you'd be a bit nicer to him, Debs. For my sake." What planet is Maeve on?

Later.

Genevieve

These two Americans came looking for Dylan just after he and Maeve left to go for a drink. They said he owed them money so I told him I didn't know where he was which was true as I didn't know where he was <u>right</u> <u>at</u> <u>that</u> <u>moment</u>. I mean I knew which pub he was in but I didn't know if he was in the toilets or if he was sitting at the counter or whatever so I wasn't lying as such. When he and Maeve got back at a reasonable hour for once I told him about them but he just shrugged his shoulders like he didn't care and said good on me for covering for him. But if he owes them money then he really should just pay up and I don't want him thinking that he can involve me in any of his shady activities. Next thing he'll be sending me out to score for him or whatever it is they call it.

I was thinking again about Andrew and about how Maeve hasn't bothered to contact him after all his generosity to us and in the end what I've decided to do is to send him a postcard. It seems more fitting than a phone call and not as forward.

[Save Address(es)][Block]　　　　[Previous][Next][Close]

From:　　　　"Tobin, Laura"<lauratobin@hotmail.com>

To:　　　　　"Jefferies, Jeanie" <jeanieje@bbc.uk>

Subject:　　Hello there!

Date:　　　　19 Nov, 23:51:10

[Reply][Reply All][Forward][Delete]

Hi Jeanie,

I was delighted to get your e-mail and thrilled to hear you got that job with the BBC. Things are going very well here too and the book is coming along wonderfully even if my research is becoming far more involved than I imagined it would.

Of course Felix and I haven't split up. He'd some reservations when I was leaving and, understandably, felt that too long a time apart might not be a good thing for our relationship but we're finding it's working out fine. Of course we are missing one another desperately.

Keep in touch,

Laura.

20th November

Genevieve

I think those Americans must have caught up with Dylan for he arrived down this morning with a black eye! He says he tripped but that's a likely story if you ask me. I wonder if he owed them money for drugs. I'd say it's something like that. He'd want to be careful for there are forever articles in the newspapers about people disappearing and then turning up later in the boot of a car or what-have-you.

I know drug suppliers are the scum of the earth and I wouldn't mind him cheating on the likes of them like I would a regular person but he should have paid up if he owed them money if only for his own safety. I asked Maeve what happened to him but she just said the same thing about him tripping. Poor Maeve. She might think she's very sophisticated but she really hasn't a clue.

And if all that wasn't bad enough, I really am sick to the stomach with worry for Debbie has gone and booked us all on that horse trek in the mountains. Ever since a horse threw me off when I was seven and we were on a family holiday in Kerry I've been terrified of the creatures which I <u>tried</u> explaining to Debbie and the others but none of them

225

took the slightest bit of notice and Maeve just told me to stop whining for once. The only good thing about this whole trekking business is that at least it will keep Dylan out of trouble.

Maeve

Had to give Dylan money today.

He got some hash from some travellers he got friendly with & then skipped off on that tour to Emei without paying them – think he thought they wouldn't be here when we got back.

But they were.

And they beat him up.

Not badly but he does have a fine shiner.

Serves him right.

So I'm now paying for his dope as well as for his plane ticket (twice) & for practically all his day-to-day costs for it turns out he hasn't a penny.

No big surprise there – I guess.

Says he's expecting a cheque to come thru from a couple of gigs he played just before he came out.

Yeah – right!

We've catching a bus tomorrow to Songpan where we're going to go horse trekking – least that should keep him out of harm's way.

[Save Address(es)][Block]   [Previous][Next][Close]
From: "Tobin, Laura"<lauratobin@hotmail.com>
To: "Crean, Sara-Mari"<sara-mari@magenta.uk>
Subject: Hi!
Date: 20 Nov, 20:12:34
[Reply][Reply All][Forward][Delete]

Hi Sara-Mari,
Lovely to hear from you. Seems like I'm just about the most popular person around at the moment.
No, Felix and I haven't split up. We're just having a lovers' tiff. He's mad at me for going away. That's all.
Love and kisses,
Laura.

[Save Address(es)][Block]   [Previous][Next][Close]
From: "Tobin, Laura"<lauratobin@hotmail.com>
To: "Mee, Marsha" <dailyimpact!@compuserve.com>
Subject: Possible series of articles
Date: 20 Nov, 20:29:45
[Reply][Reply All][Forward][Delete]

Dear Marsha,
Greetings from far-flung Asia where I'm travelling for a few months whilst researching a book I've been commissioned to write.
But you know how some of us are, Marsha, never happier than when we've several projects on the go which leads me onto my reason for e-mailing you. You see, I'm moving around a lot over here – China, Vietnam, Thailand, Cambodia, Laos and wherever else my research takes me

and I was thinking of doing a series of articles, each about 2,000 words, on such subjects as the architecture, history, culture, etc, of the various countries I'm visiting. Given your paper's extensive travel section, I thought I'd approach you first to see if you might be interested.

Do you think you could use something along those lines? Looking forward to hearing from you.

Regards,

Laura Tobin.

I do have an assistant based in Beijing but because I'm moving about so much the easiest way of contacting me is probably via e-mail. I'm using a palmtop with a modem connection so communication couldn't be simpler or more immediate.

21st November

Genevieve

This bleeding bus is packed and being squashed in alongside Maeve and Dylan in a seat meant for two people is <u>no</u> <u>picnic</u> I can tell you and I swear they've been at it like jackrabbits ever since we left Chengdu at whatever ungodly hour it was this morning. The pair of them take the biscuit. I just can't understand them at all. One minute they're at each other's throats and the next minute they're all over one another. I wish they'd just give over! And I've nowhere to put my feet for Dylan's stuck his guitar case on the floor in front of me and I don't know how I'm expected to write what with Maeve knocking against me all the time and of course she doesn't even hear me when I try telling her to cop onto herself and certainly doesn't take any notice though the whole bus is gawking at them. When they're not getting sick that is for I swear at least half the passengers have puked their guts up no exaggeration and the smell of vomit is so bad now it's a wonder I'm not throwing up myself especially seeing as how the road is fierce bumpy and every spring in our seat is busted and we haven't seen so much as a single house or a single human being in I don't know how long and heaven only knows where we'll end up.

I think I'll go and talk to the others. At least that'll take my mind off things.

Debbie

11.00 a.m. Genevieve has come and squashed herself in alongside Laura and myself and for reasons known only to herself, she's begun explaining to us some of the finer details of the pest-control business.

11.10 a.m. Like how by going through an English distributor for rat poison, her father saves 15 per cent which he then passes onto the customer. And he saves 3 per cent by importing cockroach pellets from Germany and 8 per cent by importing Finnish flea powders.

And of course Laura's leading her on and encouraging her by acting as if everything Genevieve says is fascinating whilst at the same time winking over at me. She is such a bitch.

11.30 a.m. Genevieve just doesn't see it at all. She really thinks herself and Laura are the best of buddies.

On the bus once more. After lunch.

Genevieve

I am just <u>bursting</u> to go to the loo. I did try using the toilet around the back of the restaurant for want of something better to call it where we stopped for lunch but when I closed the door I was left in the pitch-black and there were all these flies buzzing about absolutely dozens of them all great big black lads and the smell was fierce altogether and I could hardly breathe and I couldn't even bear to stay in there long enough to do what I'd gone in there to do. And now we've hours to go yet and I don't know how I'm _ever_ going to survive and it'll probably be ages before the driver will be stopping again other than at the side of the road which he's done a couple of times to let some of the passengers out to do their business in the fields but I'd sooner _die_ than do that and have everyone on the bus sitting there gaping out at me. Not that lack of privacy appears to be of much concern to any of the other passengers including Maeve. That girl has no shame. We're really in the back end of nowhere now. Where are we going to end up at all?

And as if I didn't have enough on my plate, when I was coming back to get on the bus after my unfortunate visit to the so-called toilet, I noticed Dylan lurking around the side of the restaurant looking _very_ _shifty_ and I'd swear on my mother's eyes he'd just been smoking some dope though when I confronted him about it he laughed and said that of course he hadn't and that he'd taken my warnings on board and would never touch the stuff again but I'm not sure I believe him. And then right after I'd spotted Dylan I bumped into Maeve who was looking for him but I managed to ward her off.

Poor Maeve. After all the trouble with her mother and her drinking, it's tough that she now has a boyfriend who as Laura says is at risk of developing a serious drug addiction problem.

And doesn't Dylan realise how dangerous his carry-on is here in China? Didn't he hear Debbie telling us yesterday how there were over _fourteen_ _million_ prisoners being used as slave labour in Chinese prison camps which sound like terrible places and I can't see Dylan lasting for very long in one of them.

Maeve
Why can't G *ever* mind her own business?
Wanted to get a few drags from Dylan's joint at lunchtime as otherwise I don't know how I'm going to be able to stick the afternoon on the bus but she intercepted me on my way over to him & (taking me firmly by the arm – despite my protests) she more or less frogmarched me back onto the bus.
And boy does she have some grip!
There was *no* escaping her.
So now – while Dylan is sleeping soundly – I'm forced to sit here wide-awake.

Genevieve
I wonder what being stoned is like. It seems to do wonders for Dylan for he's sleeping like a baby now even though the road is getting rougher and rougher all the time and we're being thrown about all over the place so much so that I don't think I'm going to be able to go on writing any longer. I really wish that lady in the seat opposite would stop throwing up for it's just dreadful having to put up with it and the noises she's making are something else.

Assorted bedrooms, International Hotel, Songpan.
Many hours later.

Genevieve
On the bus here I'd made up my mind I was going to stay put while the others went off on the horse trek tomorrow

but now having seen what this hotel is actually like, I don't think I've any choice but to go with them for this is definitely not the safest place in the world for a girl on her own and it seems that whoever takes a fancy can just wander in off the streets and I've seen some right oddballs going up and down the corridors and they're not guests either for I think we're the only people staying in this godforsaken hellhole and it really has got to be <u>the most miserable place I have ever stayed in my life</u> and that's saying something. International Hotel, my eye! International hovel more like.

The window in our room is so dirty you can't even see through it and there's a gap in the corner of it which has been stuffed up with an old woolly, dirty-grey sock belonging to God-only-knows-who and I found an ashtray down by the side of my bed which was overflowing with butts and mouldy apple cores and gobs of pink bubble gum. Plus I found a long curly blond hair on the sheet and despite what Maeve might say I did <u>not</u> go looking for it. And the single toilet in the place is up on the roof and miles away from the bedrooms and you can only get to it via an outdoor stairs and it's not exactly somewhere you'd chose to linger <u>to say the least</u> and in actual fact it's <u>putrid</u> and worst of all Debbie saw a <u>rat</u> scuttling along the stairway though she didn't let on to me and even denied seeing it when I quizzed her about it but I overheard her telling Maeve and Dylan.

And all I really want to do right now is to go home but instead I'm forced to either stay in this revolting hotel or go horse trekking <u>in the snow</u> of all things for yes there is in fact actual snow on the mountain tops. Is there any end to this hell?

Maeve

This town is mental.

There are throngs of mountainy people in fur hats & thick, embroidered clothes on the streets & horses, yaks, chickens & dogs wandering all over the place.

Think it must be market day or something.

It's Dylan's kinda place & he disappeared off the min. we got sorted out with a (pretty grotty) hotel. I think we must be its sole occupants – haven't seen any other tourists about.

But it's, like, bloody *freezing*.

Like, there's actual *snow* on the mountain tops surrounding the town – *the* very mountains we'll be heading into tomorrow!

G is beside herself with worry – fret, fret, fret, fret.

Later.

Genevieve

Talk about being stuck between a rock and a hard place. If the hotel is bad then the town itself is even worse. I have <u>never</u> been in such a rough place in all my born days and it's exactly the kind of place where young tourists like ourselves could get mugged at the drop of a hat and where nobody would so much as bat an eyelid if we did or lift a finger to help and we could easily disappear off the face of the earth without a trace, never to be heard of again.

And right beside our so-called hotel there's an abattoir and earlier they were killing a cow on the path outside it and to keep going the way we wanted to we'd to step over a stream of blood which was flowing right across the footpath and of course when Dylan saw it he started smacking his lips and going on about how he'd like nothing better for his dinner than a fine big juicy rare steak just dripping with blood and that he wouldn't have to worry about it being fresh or not. I just pretended not to hear him of course for he was only trying to get a rise out to me.

But honestly my stomach is just churning at the thought of what's in store for us tomorrow. I haven't felt this nervous since the morning I started my Leaving Cert though at least I don't have the runs this time. I <u>really</u> <u>am</u> <u>just</u> <u>about</u> <u>at</u> <u>the</u> <u>end</u> <u>of</u> <u>my</u> <u>tether.</u>

[Save Address(es)][Block]   [Previous][Next][Close]
From: "Tobin, Laura"<lauratobin@hotmail.com>
To: "Wilson, Felix"<felix@fmsounds.com>
Subject: A little bit of space
Date: 21 Nov, 20:18:18
[Reply][Reply All][Forward][Delete]

Dear Felix,
Some friends have persuaded me to go horse trekking with
them for a couple of days. The area we're going to is very
remote and I intend using the peace and quiet to try to
come to terms with what's happening between us.
L.
XXX

[Save Address(es)][Block]   [Previous][Next][Close]
From: "Tobin, Laura"<lauratobin@hotmail.com>
To: "Chunn, Bryan"<bchunn@ westernalliancebanks.co.uk
Subject: Standing Orders
Date: 21 Nov, 20:29:35
[Reply][Reply All][Forward][Delete]

Dear Bryan,
I'm in two minds as to whether the Internet is a blessing or
a curse. A blessing I guess though I have to say the last
person I imagined I'd be corresponding with while away is
my bank manager.
But you're right, it is as well to get everything sorted as soon
as possible and I trust funds have now been transferred to
my current account to cover all standing orders.

I also have a request, Bryan. Could you arrange to have the limit on my Visa card extended? You see most places here don't accept travellers' cheques so I'm finding I have to fall back on my Visa more than I expected.

Regards,

Laura Tobin.

237

22nd November

Somewhere in the mountains near Songpan. Evening time.

Maeve

This trekking is mad!

Had this idea when we set out this a.m. that *we* were in charge of our horses.

Hah!

Soon learnt we're no more to them than the tent, food, cooking utensils or any of the other luggage they're carrying. *Our cries of "Whoa" & "Gee up" are completely useless & our 2 guides are their only bosses. But I just love this.* Me, my boyfriend, my 3 oldest friends gathered around this huge campfire in the middle of nowhere. Sitting here – watching Dylan's breath fog in the cold air. Watching the smoke & the sparks fly up from the fire & disappear into the dark.

It's just so, so, *soooo* prefect.

Debbie

8.25 p.m. Since we headed out from Songpan at seven this morning, we've rambled along on horseback, gradually climbing higher and higher into these deserted mountains in the middle of which we've now set up camp for the night.

And now, here we are, smack-bang in the middle of nowhere, sitting in the dark on some logs around a blazing fire, waiting until dinner is ready.

Despite the aches and pains this has got to have been the best day of the entire trip so far.

Genevieve

If I <u>ever</u> manage to get back to the town of Songpan alive which I seriously doubt at this moment then I'll be getting on the very first bus out of there and back to civilisation. A.S.A.P. I am <u>fed up</u> to my back teeth.

This whole horse trekking business is <u>complete madness!</u> I don't know how many times I could have actually <u>died</u> today as Laura's stupid horse kept nipping my stupid horse in the bum which of course sent him galloping off every time and no matter how much I screamed and screamed and pulled at the ropes he wouldn't stop so all I could do was close my eyes and hold on for dear life until our two guides finally decided things were becoming serious enough for them to throw down their cigarettes and come galloping after me.

And now I'm aching <u>all over</u> and just <u>hanging</u> with the tiredness and all I want to do is go to bed but where our beds are to be heaven-only-knows for the two boyos are far too busy puffing away and gabbing with one another and warming themselves by the fire to be bothered doing what they should be doing which is <u>putting up our tents so that we can go to bed and finally put an end to this awful day</u>. I've tried telling them that I'll put up my own tent if they'd only show me where to find it but their English is hopeless and somehow, and don't ask me how, they got the notion that I

239

was demanding more dinner as if <u>anyone</u> would be <u>insane</u> enough to want extra of that mush and one of them even started ladling it onto my plate until I pulled it away so it went all over me and now I'm all sticky and I just <u>stink</u> <u>to</u> <u>high</u> <u>heaven</u> <u>of</u> <u>cabbage.</u>

I swear if I'd any idea that there was going to be camping involved I'd <u>never</u> <u>ever</u> in a month of Sundays have come. It's all very well for the others to be laughing at me now and for Maeve to be asking me if I thought there'd be a string of five-star hotels dotted across the mountains but I just hadn't really thought about it. And camping is bad enough at the best of times but who's ever heard of anyone doing it when there's actual <u>snow</u> <u>on</u> <u>the</u> <u>ground</u>.

And if all that wasn't bad enough, when I went looking in my bag for the spare fleece jacket I've been lugging around ever since we left home I found it wasn't there and at first I thought I must have left it behind somewhere along the way but then whatever look I gave, what did I see only Maeve plonked in front of the fire, all wrapped up in it and cosy out she is too and Dylan is sitting beside her with my fleece hat on his head looking completely ridiculous for it's way too small for him. And what do they think I'm going to wear?

Maeve

Dylan thinks it's hilarious how all 4 of us are *so* different.
He gets on well with Debs – or used to, & I guess time will heal & all that.
He thinks G is a total basket case but likes her – maybe 'cos she *is* a total basket case.
He thinks L is a snobby cow – which she is. Course it

doesn't help that she's been in such bad form since he arrived out, due – I guess – to the Big Bust-up (which weirdly she *still* hasn't mentioned).

In any case she doesn't do friendly without good reason & a lowly, p-time courier, p-time musician has nothing much to offer her. Dylan just can't get what she's doing backpacking around Asia with the likes of us.

Speaking of weird. I overheard her & G talking earlier today & from the way L was going on, she was making it sound like she & Felix were still together.

Très, très, très weird!

I don't know.

Maybe she's hoping they'll get back together once this trip is over & that's why she's not saying anything.

If it were anyone else I might bring the subject up but L's so *terribly* private & anyway I'm not in the mood to get involved with other people's complicated affairs of the heart.

With Dylan being here, I just don't want to waste this precious time.

Both Dylan (who thinks the amt. of diary writing that goes on is *insane*) & L are now laughing at the fact that G, Debs & myself are all busily scribbling away.

Genevieve

I am just <u>so</u> <u>miserable.</u> And I'm <u>cold</u> and I'm <u>tired</u> and I'm <u>damp</u> and I'm <u>starving</u> as I've had nothing to eat since this morning for I could hardly stomach any of the stuff the two lads have been giving us. And who knows what wild animals are lurking about out there in the dark but there's definitely something for I can hear whatever it is rustling about and I most certainly won't be going to the toilet unless I'm fit to burst for there's no way I'm going wandering around in the pitch black looking for a suitable spot for <u>that's</u> what we're reduced to.

Debbie

9.45 p.m. There's complete darkness now except for the light of our enormous campfire. There isn't another soul for miles and miles around.

Things would be perfect but for Dylan's presence. Sometimes I can almost convince myself I'm over him but when he's sitting opposite me, looking so lovely in the firelight, it's a different story. It's the way his hair curls and falls so softly against his neck that always gets to me.

But remember I dumped him and with good reason.

In the tent. Much later that night.

Genevieve

I am absolutely suffocating. The five of us including Dylan are crammed into the one tent and when I say tent what I actually mean is a home-made job of a couple of filthy pieces of canvas sewn together and held up with a thick stick. And when I say <u>crammed</u> I mean <u>crammed</u> for the tent can't be meant for any more than three and if one of us wants to turn or so much as move an inch then we <u>all</u> have to and even though I've only just begun writing Dylan is already moaning and groaning and harping on about how I'm shining the torch in his face and disturbing everyone. And despite the gap around the edge I am suffocating for the air in here is disgusting and it doesn't help that just after we'd settled down one of the guides came and threw these <u>filthy</u> blankets down on top of us which I'd swear have almost certainly <u>never</u> seen the inside of a washing machine so that when any of us moves even the tiniest bit this cloud of dust rises up.

It's just impossible to sleep and I have to do <u>something</u> to occupy myself as otherwise I'll simply <u>go out of my mind</u>! And anyway what does Dylan expect me to do? Just lie here listening to goodness-only-knows-what prowling about outside?

When we first got into the tent I figured it'd be best not to get stuck in the middle what with my claustrophobia and all but what I hadn't noticed was the gap all around the edge and now I'm shoved right up against it and who knows what could come crawling in on top of me. And there's an unmerciful draught blowing in as well so there's no doubt but that I'm going to wake up with an awful crick in my neck tomorrow. That's if I wake up at all and am not <u>frozen to death</u> during the night. But maybe I should try again to get to sleep for at least morning will come faster that way.

God Almighty! That Dylan is giving out again and demanding that I turn off my bloody torch. For crying out loud! I've only turned it on this second. Would he ever give over! Why doesn't he go out and smoke some of that dope for himself and that'll settle him.

I did turn off the torch only because I couldn't be listening to him moaning on and on but now they're all dead to the world while I'm left <u>wide-awake</u> and Dylan is driving me out of my mind with these funny popping sounds he's making as he breathes in and out and in and out. Pop-pop pop pop pop pop-pop pop pop pop pop-pop.

I can definitely get the smell of horses from the blankets but at least they're on top of our sleeping bags so I can avoid actually touching them though I'm definitely going to have to wash out my sleeping bag at the first opportunity. But what's even more disgusting are our so-called pillows which are in fact just our saddles with some more dirty blankets thrown over them. I've tried to arrange my sleeping bag in such a way that my head is not in direct contact with the "pillow" but the sleeping bag keeps slipping off so my head is beginning to get all itchy. I don't really know though Dad would if he was here but I suppose horses can carry lice and fleas and the like.

God I'm being driven <u>crazy</u> with the itching. I think I used to be asthmatic when I was younger. I hope all the dust won't set it off again.

"Turn off the bloody torch!" God Almighty! There's no need for Dylan to be so rude. I'd only just turned it back on and he was shouting at me and it was him and not me who woke the others up with all the fuss he was making. And it's all right for him, he hasn't been awake half the night. And I don't care what he says but I can't just lie here doing nothing. And he's already sound to the world again – pop-pop pop pop pop pop-pop – but I still <u>cannot</u> get to sleep even though I'm absolutely knackered. It must have been about ten-thirty when we went to bed and it's not even one yet but it feels like I've been lying here for hours and hours. And the feet are practically frozen off of me though I've two pof my thickest socks on.

If I get an asthmatic attack I'll be in <u>serious trouble</u> for we must be hundreds of miles from a hospital. I should just try and keep calm and not think about it as that might bring one on. If I had a brown-paper bag I could use it to breathe in and out which might be of some help.

Some people can be just so cranky! It's not like I woke them on purpose and besides they'll all be asleep again in no time which is more than can be said for me. Anyway it was Debbie's fault for if she'd left my bag where I'd put it instead of shoving it into the corner then I'd have been able to get out another pair of socks and a bag for breathing into without disturbing anyone. She can be such a whinger! Sticking into her indeed! Sure we all have things sticking into us! What does she expect when we're squashed in like this?

I am <u>dying</u> to go to the toilet but I'm just not letting myself think about it.

There was <u>definitely</u> a mouse or something scuttling around in here. It's not as if I'd make something like that up and what with my father being in the business he's in I think I'd know better than most what a mouse sounds like but of course none of them believed me and were all fierce ratty because I woke them again. But what did they expect me to do? Lie there listening to it creeping about the place. I thought they'd be as anxious as me to get rid of it. And it was hardly too much to ask one of them to come outside with me when I went looking for somewhere to do my business. I mean they were already awake. And how can they just drift back to sleep like that knowing that there could be a rotten dirty mouse in here somewhere?

What if an attack did come on? How would they get me to

the hospital? They'd have to sling me on top of that mutt and take me back down the mountain for I can't see any other way.

It'll be bright again in a couple of hours so maybe I can hold off going until then though it won't do my bladder much good. I just remembered a story Debbie was telling us a few days ago about some Dutch girl she was talking to back in Chengdu who told her how she'd used fruit-scented shampoo once when she was camping somewhere and during the night her tent was invaded by mice and being attracted by the fruity smell, they all made a <u>beeline</u> <u>straight</u> <u>for</u> <u>her</u> <u>hair!</u>

I don't really fancy going to hospital. I'd probably end up catching some kind of infection and getting all sorts of complications if I was admitted with my asthma.

There wasn't any water in that hellhole in Songpan so I didn't wash my hair there but the shampoo I used back in Chengdu was definitely kind of fruity. And how would Theo manage to get out to see me if I was admitted? Or my parents? This time of the year is always one of the busiest for my father, and my mother took all her leave when her sister came to stay back in August. But then for all I know they mightn't even let patients have visitors in the hospitals over here.

Pop-pop pop pop pop pop-pop. All night long he's at it.

Imagine having mice crawling all over your head! It just doesn't bear thinking about.

My feet are still like blocks of ice. And I really am going to burst. I'm sure that mouse is in here somewhere. I just have this feeling. It really is just as well Theo has no idea of what I've been going through these past few weeks.

My feet <u>still</u> haven't really warmed up. But at least I haven't heard that mouse for a while. And what if I died in the hospital? Mam and Dad wouldn't know the first thing about arranging to bring a body back.

Maybe the authorities arrange everything.

I wish I could get to sleep. I swear I have never felt so tired in my whole life. Honestly, I don't think I've had a proper night's sleep since we left Andrew's. I really am coming to my wits' end.

Now it's pop-pop pop pop pop pop-pop from Dylan and zzzz zzzz zzzz from Debbie. How on earth can Laura or Maeve sleep through such a racket?

What I wouldn't give to be back in that lovely room in Andrew's apartment.

It's like they're deliberately setting out to drive me bonkers. The <u>second</u> one of them stops, the other one starts up. And I'd swear they're getting louder too.

It'd probably be better not to say a word to the others about my asthma. I wouldn't want to have them worrying about it too.

At last I think I can hear the two guides getting up which is just as well as the batteries in my torch are beginning to run out. What I wouldn't do for a decent cup of strong tea though needless to say there's fat chance of getting that out here.

I hope I haven't done any permanent damage to my bladder what with holding things in for so long.

An Asian Diary

Whenever Deanne says, "Listen girls, I have this great idea," it's sure to mean trouble.

This time her great idea was the worst ever. This time her great idea was to go horse trekking. For three days. In the snow. Or, in the "bloody snow" as Geraldine keeps muttering.

To make matters worse, the trekking company Deanne elected to go with is pretty slipshod. Our horses are so down-and-out they'd be turned away from a knacker's yard. Our guides aren't much better, equally as long in the tooth and as malnourished-looking and, though the weather is hovering around freezing, all they're wearing is plimsolls, light canvas pants and skinny jerseys. As for our accommodation, it's pretty lacking to say the least and the less said about our food the better.

But a right sight we must have made today as we trooped across the mountains on our horses. First, the two guides, cigarettes hanging from the sides of their mouths, puffing away like chimneys, all togged out in their threadbare clothes. Next, Deanne, dressed in so many layers of protective clothing she could hardy move, all the while pestering the guides with questions about their lives and their living conditions. The fact that they do this for a living for the mere pennies we're paying should tell her enough. Then, me, and I think it's fair to say I look pretty good on horseback – straight-backed, my long shiny blonde hair swishing rhythmically back and forth. Then, Mags and Wannabe; Mags going on and on at the top of her voice about just how mad all this is and Wannabe singing awful country and western songs at the top of his. And, lastly, Geraldine holding on for dear life; horse riding does not come naturally to her. I've seen more graceful sacks of potatoes. In fact, I pity her poor horse, she nearly pulled its head off today with all her yanking at the ropes as she kept calling the reins.

And two more days of this!

23rd November

Further into the mountains. Lunchtime.

Debbie

12.30 p.m. We've just stopped for lunch. Cooking isn't our guides' forte but all the fresh air has given me a huge appetite.

I could get used to this. It's like we've been doing it all our lives. Ambling along on our horses by day and sitting around our campfire by night. Hee-har! as Dylan – John Wayne – O' Donnell keeps hollering as we ride along when he isn't crying out in a twangy country and western accent that he was "born under a wandering star," and that we're not to "fence him in".

Genevieve

I think I'm going to get sick. I haven't even the energy to write. And we still have the whole afternoon to get through.

Around the campfire. That evening.

Maeve

Had our share of excitement this afternoon.

When things were starting to get dull, G's horse obliged us by rearing up & galloping off with her.

Don't know which was louder – G *screaming* in fear for her life or her *screaming* at Dylan when he told her she wasn't to go showing off with any more of her daredevil antics.

To which she replied – "Show off! Show off! Couldn't you see I was very nearly KILLED! STONE! DEAD!"

Genevieve

The others are all stuffing their faces but not me for I really have come to the end of my tether. It's true for Laura when she says it was completely irresponsible of Debbie to decide on this trip without looking into it properly for it really is very badly-run. For one thing the food we're being served up is just shocking! It all looks like cabbage to me. Not that I'll be eating any more of it after what I saw this lunchtime.

You see I should have thought to bring my own food along with me of course but I didn't and I really have been doing my best and trying to eat whatever disgusting stuff that was being served up to us though I was finding it almost impossible to stomach any of it. But I won't be even trying from now on that's for sure. I don't think anyone would if they'd seen what I'd seen when I happened to be sitting by the fire trying to warm myself while the two guides were cooking.

And what I saw was this. I saw the skinnier of the two men lean over the pot he'd just thrown the cabbagey-looking stuff into and then with my very own eyes I saw his nose dribble and a string of snot drop into the pot! And if that wasn't bad enough he just wiped his nose with the back of his hand before plunging it into the pot to give the cabbagey stuff a good whirl around.

As well as being plain disgusting, such disregard for basic hygiene has to be downright dangerous.

An Asian Diary

What can I say, dear reader? Only mea culpa. Or rather me and Wannabe. That's right. Me and Him. I've no excuse. It was a moment of weakness. Or boredom. And I can hardly be blamed for wanting a little light relief; having to listen to Geraldine moaning and groaning, especially since we set off on this horse-trek, would send anyone around the twist.

And, besides, Wannabe has been coming on to me ever since he arrived out from Ireland. The reason I hadn't given in thus far is because he's Mags' boyfriend. And of course there's the little matter of having no particular interest in him, good-looking though he may be.

Perhaps I should feel guilty but I don't. I know Mags is pretty serious about him at the moment but she's not a complete idiot and I'm sure she'll eventually realise that Wannabe and a happy picket-fence future are mutually exclusive. Not even Mags could be foolish enough to consider him husband material. And it wasn't like I slept with him. It was just a kiss although, if he'd had his way, it would've been a lot more and I thought I'd choke with laughter when he started singing into my ear, "Let's make love on the white, white snow, so that we can be with nature, be in nature, feel nature all around." Sadly his talent as a songwriter is as lacking as his talent as a singer. He's quite a talented kisser however, but, if being with nature, being in nature, feeling nature all around, meant getting my naughty bits frozen in the wet snow, not going any further with him was an easy choice.

And, besides, there'll be plenty of other opportunities in more conducive surroundings.

24th November

**Assorted bedrooms back at the International Hotel, Songpan.
Evening time.**

Genevieve

It just goes to show what we've had to put up with these last few days to say I'm pleased to be back in this crappy place.

I am aching all over and if I never set foot on a horse again I won't be sorry for Laura and myself were very nearly <u>killed</u> <u>stone</u> <u>dead</u> today no exaggeration. It was just such an awful day I don't even want to write about it.

All I'll say is that this whole trekking business was a ridiculous notion in the first place and a highly dangerous one too and the others especially Debbie have a lot to answer for in making us go on it.

Maeve

More drama today – Serious Drama.

Late this morning when were making our way up this (v.v. steep & icy) path these farmers appeared out of nowhere herding 40+ yaks along in front of them. We'd have passed one another fine too 'cept that L's horse suddenly slipped & she & it went crashing to the ground which spooked the yaks and they all began stampeding like crazy.

Definitely L would have been trampled on 'cept that while

the rest of us sat there gaping – G (her horse's legs going in <u>all</u> directions) somehow managed to get to L & then put herself & her horse between L & the yaks & whenever one of them looked like they were coming their way G kicked out her leg & yelled & yelled like some kinda crazy lady.

She was fantastic!

Funny but I'd forgotten how stubborn G can be sometimes but what she did next brought it back.

When it was obvious L was OK, G got down off her horse & began marching back down the mountain, leading her horse behind her & cos she walked, like, *every* step of the way, it took hrs & hrs & hrs & hrs.

Nothing we could say would make her get back on again.

And L wasn't even hurt.

Not a scratch nor a broken bone.

But boy! Will she be bruised tomorrow!

Hotel rooftop. A little later.

Genevieve

Dylan keeps calling me, "Genevieve, The Mighty!" after that whole thing with Laura and the horses and the yaks today. The eejit! He really is a terrible one for teasing. It's funny but I'm actually sort of beginning to get to like him a bit. I'm not saying I can understand why anyone would fancy him what with him being a druggie and all but I suppose I'm getting used to the way he goes on and how he's forever joking. Before I used to take offence too easily but now I can see he's only having a laugh with me. And the fact he takes drugs doesn't make him a bad person per se just a bit stupid. I've just told him I can't understand what either Maeve or Debbie see in him which I suppose was a bit

256

cheeky and he might have taken offence but he didn't but just said we were quits since he can't understand what Theo sees in me either!

The stars look really bright tonight and really near and it seems like if I just reached out I could touch one of them but then if I stretch too far I might go toppling over the edge and go splat down to the ground below and there'd be an awful mess but it wouldn't matter because everybody would probably think it was from the abattoir next door which is what I just said to Dylan and he's laughing really loudly now even though I keep telling him to shut up as he'll wake up the whole town if he's not careful. He says Laura is bound to be awake anyway as witches don't sleep at night. I must tell her that tomorrow. On second thoughts maybe I won't. She probably wouldn't think it was very funny.

What I wouldn't do to be able to have one of those stars for keeps.

An Asian Diary

Poor Geraldine nearly met her end up there in the mountains which is why we all had to come rushing back to town a day early.

Of course it was all a little scary for her and, genuinely, she could have been killed though I'm not sure she realises just how close she came or realise that the only thing that saved her was my quick intervention.

What happened was this. At one stage this morning, these peasant farmers came against us, herding some yaks along in front of them but, as they started coming down this steep incline the yaks began slipping on the icy ground which frightened them and caused them to start stampeding. No doubt they'd have settled down again and none of us would have been in any real danger except that Geraldine got into a flap and started screaming and shouting which of course upset her horse so it started to bolt which sent Geraldine toppling to the ground. I can see her still, lying prone on the ice in the direct path of the stampeding yaks, her eyes the size of saucers, her bottom lip all a-tremble.

And that's when I came in. Even though the ground was like a skating rink I managed to get my horse between the stampeding yaks and where poor Geraldine lay quivering. In retrospect I can see it could have ended badly and I could have been very seriously hurt or even killed but when you're put in a situation like that you just act on your own instincts no matter how crazy.

But, ever since, Geraldine has been going on about how I'm her hero (sic) and how after what we've been through we're now as close as sisters. She used to fawn all over me before today's events but that was nothing compared to what she's like now. As for Wannabe, he's been hovering around me ever since, asking me if I'm okay and telling me how terrified he'd felt for me – not that that prompted him to come rushing in to help. But then he's not exactly hero material himself.

25th November

Stuffed Dumpling Restaurant, Songpan. Mid-afternoon.

Genevieve

I made up my mind last night that I'm going home as soon as I can organise things though I haven't told the others yet. If I'd <u>any</u> idea what this whole trip was going to be like then wild horses wouldn't have got me going on it but it all sounded so exciting especially as I'd never really travelled much before apart from that time I went to London with Mam at Christmas three years ago. And I'm not saying that I wasn't content with my life in Portrea for I was or am rather and as a matter of fact more than content. Of course I'm not saying it was perfect but then whose life is and it's not nearly as boring as Laura likes to make out and even if it is, well it still suits me fine. And if Laura's life is so perfect then what was she doing coming away with us in the first place? Actually I think it must've been four years since I was in London with my mother for it was the same year Theo traded in his old Volkswagen.

My poor head has been aching since I got up this morning and I just hope there's nothing the matter with me but I really don't feel quite right. There's certainly nothing wrong with my appetite anyway that's for sure and I must have had at least nine dumplings which are absolutely delicious. They don't call this place the Stuffed Dumpling Restaurant for nothing for I really am stuffed!

Now Debbie has come in and has sat down beside me and is yakking on and making it very hard for me to concentrate and though I'm doing my best to ignore her she doesn't seem to even notice. But she definitely is the last person in the world I want to talk to after what Laura told me about her this morning which is what I was just going to write about but I can't now not with her around. But I swear it makes my blood boil to even think about what she did and I can hardly bear to look at her. I'd better leave before I say something I'll regret.

Debbie

4.00 p.m. I don't know what's the matter with Genevieve. She's acting very strangely. I came in to join her when I saw her sitting in this restaurant next door to our hotel but she left almost as soon as I sat down without so much as a goodbye. I think this whole trip is beginning to unhinge her.

Assorted bedrooms, International Hotel.
Several hours later.

Maeve

G's dropped a bombshell and announced she's going home. Course she's been moaning a lot but none of us took her seriously. That's what she does – she moans. Be more worrying if she didn't.

When I told her I'd no idea she was *so* unhappy she demanded to know how could I when the only person I was interested in spending time with was Dylan.

Says I've hardly had a decent conversation with her or with the others since he arrived out.

Which is not *entirely* untrue – I guess.

But he *is* only here for a short time.

At least I think so – doesn't seem to have much of an idea himself what his plans are exactly whenever I try asking.

Will have another go at talking some sense into her tomorrow.

Prob. won't do much good.

When G decides on something, it's, like, impossible to change her mind.

Genevieve

I guess what they actually mean is that the dumplings are stuffed and not the customers but I wish I hadn't eaten so many for now my stomach doesn't feel quite right and I still have that headache and in fact it's getting worse.

Anyway I've told the others about making my mind up to go home and I think they were a bit taken aback especially Laura who's fierce upset and has been trying to persuade me to stay but there's no budging me now that my mind's made up. She says it's a shame seeing as how we've been getting on so well lately and what with me having saved her life there's a special bond between us now and that you could almost call us sisters. I wouldn't go quite <u>that</u> far but it is touching to see how anxious she is for me to stay. I think I might go back to bed soon for I really am dying. At least there isn't much in this town for a tourist to go and see so maybe Debbie will leave us in peace for a change until the bus comes tomorrow. Either way I'm not budging from the bed until that bus is outside the door.

Hopefully I'll feel better in the morning and I'll have the energy to write all about what Debbie got up in the mountains and I'll have the energy to decide that I'm going to do about it for there's no way I can go home without doing or saying something though Laura says leave it to her and she'll take care of it.

An Asian Diary

One other thing did happen up in the mountains which I've neglected to mention. Wannabe and I were almost caught by Geraldine when, on that last night, she went searching for somewhere to do her business as she euphemistically refers to it. We would have been caught too only that, as she came trundling along, I could hear her fretting aloud to herself as she searched for a suitable spot and, not wishing to bear witness to that particular spectacle, I quickly extracted myself from the arms of Wannabe and emerged from where we'd secreted ourselves.

As soon as she saw me, she wanted to know what I was doing and though the obvious thing to tell her was that I was there for the very same reason as herself, I was thrown off-guard by her sudden appearance and, instead, found myself saying I couldn't explain things just then but that I'd tell her everything in the morning and, taking her by the arm, I swiftly guided her back to the tent.

The following day the incident with the herd of yaks pushed the episode to the back of my mind and I'd almost forgotten about it totally but, Geraldine, being Geraldine, hadn't and, this morning, out of the blue, she reminded me of my promise to explain everything and I found myself telling her that the reason I'd hurried her away was because I'd stumbled across Deanne and Wannabe in one another's arms. I know, I know, but it was the first thing to come into my head.

But now in her nosy-parker way she keeps demanding to know when we're going to tell Mags but, in her cowardly way, she wants me to be the one to break the bad news. Needless to say, it's the last thing I've any intention of doing for obvious reasons though I'm not sure exactly how I'll keep stalling her.

But maybe I won't need to for long as she announced today she's going home. All I have to do is to stop her interfering until it's time for her to leave.

26th November

Maeve

Poor G is *just* dying!

This morning when I asked her if she was coming for b'fast she couldn't lift her head off the pillow & only barely managed to whimper how she was feeling a "bit off-form" & how she didn't think she could eat a thing.

So we left.

Can't say any of us took her near-deathlike demeanour seriously.

But – about a $1/2$ an hr later – when we were at our own b'fast, this Norwegian girl burst into the restaurant, looked around, then made a beeline straight for our table.

1st off, she asks us are we friends of Genevieve Price's, & so we say yeah, we are, so she asks us if we, like, know how sick G is & so L tells her that you have to, like, *know* G, that she *exaggerates* & that – the day before – in the one sitting she ate enough dumpling to keep an average family going for a week.

This makes Blondie lose the rag *completely*. She starts telling us how she found G (all sweaty & shivery – hardly able to stand) crawling up the stairs to the toilet on the roof.

So Laura explains that G:

a) is a hypochondriac;

b) has been complaining about not feeling well since we left home; and,

c) is as strong as an ox.

So then Blondie asks L if she's, like, a doctor & L is all like – no, I'm not, are you? – so Blondie tells her she is & tells her that even hypochondriacs can get sick from time to time & that Genevieve is v.v. sick.

So there!

Poor old Genevieve.

Debbie

1.00 p.m. So much for Genevieve's plans to go home. I think she's going to have to defer them for a while. Up to yesterday she could hardly bear to set foot in that horrible toilet on the roof and now she's spending half her time up there.

I don't think she's going to be going anywhere for a while.

That evening in Genevieve's room.

Maeve

I swear I'm beginning to think the patient has it easier than the person who has to look after them.

At least they don't have to watch themselves puke or wipe up afterwards.

Cos I was feeling a tiny-weenie bit guilty 'bout G saying I was neglecting her I *stupidly* sent Dylan off on his own & have spent the rest of the day minding G.

Christ! It's a full-time job.

Between feeding her the horrible mixture of salt & sugar Dr

Blondie recommended, emptying the basin every time she throws up &, helping her up & down, up & down, up & down, up & down the stairs to the toilet on the roof.
I am definitely *not* cut out for the life of a nurse.

An Asian Diary

So delighted was I at first to hear of Geraldine's decision to go home on the grounds that it was going to get me out of a tricky situation, I failed to consider its other implications.

Like what I'm going to write about in my column once she's gone? Without her, things will be far less interesting. Dull-as-ditchwater Deanne never does anything of interest. And Mags and Wannabe don't provide a whole lot of interest either. Mags just spends her time asking him, "Is everything okay, hon?" and, after our love tryst, Wannabe spends his time gazing at me mournfully and furtively asking me to come slip away with him.

And it's not like Geraldine's going to do anything interesting between now and when she leaves for the poor traumatised thing can't go on and has taken to the bed for she's "just dying sick".

It's just as well she's happy for me to be the one to tell Mags about Wannabe and Deanne as Mags has appointed herself Geraldine's nurse so they've been together practically all day. Now guilt is not an emotion Mags is generally well acquainted with but, for some reason, she's been feeling guilty about neglecting Geraldine which is why, to make things up to her, she spent all day keeping an eye on her and ministering to her every need and, Geraldine being Geraldine, there are quite a few.

But if only Mags knew what Wannabe had been up to

she'd realise that she'd be better served keeping an eye on him. Foolishly perhaps, I assumed Wannabe would understand that what happened between him and me was a once-off but we're operating on different wavelengths and, while Mags is busy tending Geraldine, I've been desperately trying to escape his clutches. I'd wager, however, that Mag's enthusiasm for nursing will have dissipated by morning and I'll be able to breathe easily once again.

27th November

Genevieve's room, International Hotel. Early morning.

Maeve

G's still puking her guts up.

Room stinks of sick people.

No catch in the window.

Only air coming in is thro' the hole where I pulled out the old sock plugging it.

G's a funny one really – stuff that goes on in her head would baffle a psychiatrist.

Like, when she's awake she keeps bringing up all these silly worries of hers.

How Dylan thinks she's bonkers

How the only reason we're friends is cos we've known each other for so long.

How I've always been closer to Debs than to her.

How I never invite her up to Dublin for the weekend.

How . . . How . . . How . . .

Doesn't matter how much I try to reassure her.

She doesn't listen to a word &, like, what does it matter how or why we're friends?

The NB thing is we are.

Course I like Debs more but (now that I think about it) G is prob. my 2nd best friend.

271

And of course Dylan thinks she's bonkers – who wouldn't? Not that I said that to her but that doesn't mean he doesn't like her.

And the reason I don't ask her up for weekends is cos cardies, cups of tea, & long cosy chats don't exactly go hand in hand with seedy pubs, ear-splitting music & Sunday morning hangovers.

Boy!

Such Angst!

Not sure how much more of this sick room (& more esp. the sick) I can put up with.

Debbie

11.10 a.m. Maeve has got over her guilt complex and is nowhere to be seen leaving yours truly to look after Genevieve who doesn't seem at all appreciative of my attention. In fact, she's hardly said a word to me all morning but then I guess she is pretty sick.

11.50 a.m. Genevieve's even sicker than I thought. When I asked her would she like something to eat she told me she thought she might be just about able to manage something plain & light, "but nothing with beansprouts for they seem to stick them in everywhere but maybe something like a boiled egg might do but only if it's boiled just the bare three minutes and don't forget the salt. Oh, and a couple of Cokes as well for I'm gasping. And maybe a few slices of toast but only if they're not too well done and they have lashings of butter on them."

But the worrying thing is, she didn't eat a bite of what I brought up.

12.30 p.m. The Norwegian doctor's headed back to Chengdu so we have no one to turn to for advice and Genevieve's still as sick as ever.

2.30 p.m. Genevieve nearly had a relapse when I suggested that we get the local doctor in to see her. She seems to think that leeches are bound to be a part of any cure he's likely to suggest.

5.00 p.m. Hail! Our hero, Mr Clancy! When Maeve eventually turned up again, I managed to persuade her to ring him for some advice regarding Genevieve and whether we should take her to a local hospital but, before Maeve had even finished explaining things to him, he was interrupting her, telling her he was coming down straight away. He says he thinks he'll be able to get here early tomorrow.

I imagine the chance to show Maeve he's there for her is the reason for his mercy mission and that the state of Genevieve's health is secondary.

An Asian Diary

I know I said Geraldine was unlikely to do anything further of interest before going home but I was wrong.

When I popped in to see how she was doing this afternoon, she burst into tears as soon as she saw me and told me she just needed to talk to someone for she was worried out of her mind. It turns out she thinks that what lies at the root of her illness is the fact that she smoked one of Wannabe's joints. I repeat, Geraldine smoked one of Wannabe's joints, up on the rooftop of our crappy hotel the other night. I am not joking. The only reason she told me was because she was so terrified that that was the reason she's been so sick and wanted reassurance from me that she wasn't going to die or become an addict.

I guess I could have reassured her. I guess I could have told her that all she was suffering from was a bit of gastro. and no wonder for she did eat nine dumplings the other day in that crummy restaurant – in the one sitting.

I think what drove Geraldine to do something so out of character as to "take drugs" as she kept referring to her few puffs on a joint, was because, to quote directly from the horse's mouth, she was "just feeling fierce down". Everything had hit rock bottom for her. Everything was just piling up on top of her. Being stuck on a horse for so long. Having to sleep in that makeshift tent. Having nothing to eat for days. Having no opportunity to shower. Coming back to this crappy hotel. Not to mention her near brush with death.

Once she'd made her little confession to me, she started fretting. What if she was already an addict? How would she support a drug habit on her wages? Would it be better to seek counselling sooner than later? Would counselling be expensive? What if her boyfriend turned his back on her? Or if her parents did? Where would she go? Who could she turn to?

Sometimes Geraldine truly is her own worst enemy. Only she could manage to turn a few puffs on a joint into a fully blown addiction. And she didn't even need my help.

28th November

Andrew's rented car, en route back to Chengdu. Morning.

Debbie

9.00 *a.m.* Somehow Mr Clancy managed to get himself on a flight to Chengdu last night where he rented a car and arrived in Songpan at the crack of dawn this morning having driven through the night.

There isn't room for everyone in the car so Mr Clancy, Genevieve and I, in my role as nurse, are now on our way back to Chengdu to try and catch an afternoon flight to Beijing. The others will catch the bus back to Chengdu tomorrow then wait there and see how things pan out before making any plans to meet up again.

10.00 *a.m.* Genevieve's all nestled up in the backseat with her sleeping bag pulled right up to her chin and a cushion tucked behind her head looking the picture of contentment.

11.00 *a.m.* Genevieve is definitely odd with me. At first I thought that maybe the reason she has so little to say to me is because she's so sick but she seems to have plenty to say to Mr Clancy but anytime I try talking to her, she just stares through me like I'm invisible.

11.45 *a.m.* I just asked Genevieve if I'd done anything wrong.

"Well, what do you think, Deborah? If you had then I'm

276

sure you'd know. You'd hardly have to ask."

So clearly I have though I've no idea what. But what I do know is that her calling me Deborah is an awfully bad sign. But I should have known better than to ask her directly what was up for that's the one way of making sure she won't tell. In fact, the only way to find out what terrible deed I'm supposed to have committed is to simply bide my time and wait until she's good and ready to divulge.

Back at the International Hotel in Songpan, Maeve and Dylan's room. That evening.

Maeve

OK, so, Dad isn't *that* bad after all.

Have to admit (here in writing in any case if *not* to his face) that he was quite the hero arriving like that to whisk the ailing G back to Beijing. And there wasn't a mention from him of the difficulties or the money involved in getting plane tickets or of hiring a car at such short notice.

Think both G & Dad expected me to go back with them but I couldn't.

Like, I don't even know how long more Dylan is going to be around – doesn't seem to have much of an idea himself.

First time Dad & Dylan ever met. Sad to see Dad so obviously weighing up Dylan – deciding whether or not he was good enough for his daughter (& making it pretty clear he thought he wasn't).

For some reason G seemed dead set against Debs going with her.

Don't think Debs was exactly enamoured with the idea herself. She's the one most anxious to see everything & going back to Beijing means she'll miss out.

An Asian Diary

Desperate to get on his daughter's good side, Mr C travelled overnight and turned up here first thing this morning to rescue poor, sickly, Geraldine.

I'm not sure who was more put out – Deanne or Geraldine – when Deanne allowed herself to get roped into going back with Geraldine as her nurse. Having weighed up the possibilities of the pleasure to be had with Mr C with the sheer awfulness of having to tend to a puking Geraldine, I certainly wasn't volunteering. And, Mags being Mags, she wasn't going to either.

But what fun it was to watch Wannabe and Mr C together. I think Wannabe actually thought he was making a good impression and Mr C's desperate willingness to be open and to try and accept Mags' choice of partner faltered pretty quickly. Possibly around the time Wannabe asked him if he lived near the *"Going, Going, Gone Bar"* where, he then proceeded to tell Mr C, he'd got, "hammered" on his first night in Beijing and ended up staying there until six in the morning. Or, maybe, it was when Mr C asked him how work was going. Apparently it's going "Shite!" But, as Wannabe explained, though the pay's rubbish Mags makes a fortune on tips and that keeps them going. Exactly the kind of long-term financial planning any father would look for in a prospective son-in-law!

And when Wannabe saw how well Mr C and I were getting along he was positively green. I have to say it was rather odd to have both Mags' father and her boyfriend vying for my attention. It was just as well there was too little time for Mr C to try and resume where we'd left off back in Beijing. Mags' father and her boyfriend in the same week? Even I'd feel a tiny bit guilty. A very, very tiny bit guilty.

Geraldine was of course oblivious to all this. And, cruel though it may be especially when she was so sick, I just couldn't help but point out to her the significance of Mr C travelling all the way here to bring her back to Beijing. Clearly he had feelings for her, I told Geraldine and, the scary thing is, she looked like she might actually believe me.

29th November

Debbie

9.00 a.m. I am so bored.

Genevieve might not be talking to me but she still wants me at her beck and call even though she also has Mei dancing attendance on her.

10.00 a.m. She won't leave me out of her sight. I just mentioned I was thinking of heading out for a couple of hours and you'd swear by her reaction I'd told her I was going to leave her stranded here on her own for evermore, without a bite to eat or a drop to drink.

Maeve

Arrived into Chengdu a couple of hrs ago.

Things seems v. quiet without the other 2.

Kinda miss G rabbiting on all the time.

Dylan seems v. outta sorts.

L isn't much better.

I've started trying to organise a trip for us on the Yangzi River.

Hate having to do the organising.

280

Debs is always way better at this sort of thing than I am.

And back at Andrew's, Genevieve's room.
Debbie

12.55 *p.m.* Mei brings Genevieve her lunch.

12.56 *p.m.* Genevieve stares at it, wonders aloud what on earth it could be, announces that she doesn't think she could eat a thing and pushes the tray away.

12.57 *p.m.* Little Shao reaches out to take some.

12.58 *p.m.* Genevieve grabs the tray back.

1.00 *p.m.* Not a trace of food is left on the plate.

[Save Address(es)][Block]   [Previous][Next][Close]
From: "Tobin, Laura"<lauratobin@hotmail.com>
To: "Wilson, Felix"<felix@fmsounds.com>
Subject: Realising what I have . . .
Date: 29 Nov, 21:23:10
[Reply][Reply All][Forward][Delete]

Felix,
A couple of days ago I had one of the scariest incidents of
my life and I very nearly died whilst saving a friend from a
stampeding herd of yaks.
It made me appreciate my life and what I have. Especially
you. I love you.
Laura.

[Save Address(es)][Block]   [Previous][Next][Close]
From: "Tobin, Laura"<lauratobin@hotmail.com>
To: "Mee, Marsha"<dailyimpact!@compuserve.com>
Subject: Possible series of articles.
Date: 29 Nov, 21:39:12
[Reply][Reply All][Forward][Delete]

Marsha,
Just wondering if you got my e-mail of the 20th regarding a
possible series of articles. I have been having some trouble
with my palmtop which I think is sorted now but if my e-
mail didn't get through you might let me know.
Regards,
Laura

30th November

Terrace, Andrew's apartment. Evening.

Debbie

6.00 p.m. When I came into the kitchen a little while ago, Andrew was sitting at the table and Mei was standing behind him, gently stroking the back of his neck but as soon as they noticed me, she pulled away and he started talking loudly about the weather in this clumsy and woefully obvious attempt to pretend there was nothing happening between them. I don't know why they're being so coy. Maybe he assumes that because I'm friends with Maeve I'll be on her side and I'll disapprove.

7.00 p.m. I still can't figure out what I've done to upset Genevieve so much. She's hardly said a word to me for days now.

Apart from giving me orders, that is.

"Deborah, could you fill up my water jug and pull the blinds before you go.

And pass me over that spare pillow.

And bring this glass back down to the kitchen

Oh, and the towel there, it needs to be taken down for washing."

283

8.00 p.m. "Deborah, can you please pass me my diary if it isn't too much trouble."

I think that must mean she's finally on the mend.

Genevieve's room.

Genevieve

This is the first time I've been able to write for ages for I've been too sick to write not that I've fully recovered yet so I'd better keep this short as I don't want to wear myself out as I really have been in the most dreadful state with a very high fever and the most awful diarrhoea and vomiting and whatnot.

But now that I'm getting better again I just want to write down what happened back in Songpan and what happened was this.

Just when I'd started to like Dylan and think he wasn't too bad after all and that, even though he still has a bit of growing up to do, he and Maeve might actually have a future together, I find out just what a dirty double-dealing crosser he is. You see he and Debbie have been carrying on behind Maeve's back all along. Laura came across them at it on our last night of that dreadful horse trek. She says it wasn't their first time either as far as she knows and that she's had her suspicions about them for quite some time. I know Debbie was very upset when Dylan broke if off with her but to turn around and do that to Maeve is just the <u>pits</u> altogether. I'd never have believed that Debbie would be such a rotten cow.

What with me falling sick and all and Andrew arriving like a knight in shiny armour to take me back to Beijing, I didn't get a chance to do anything about the whole sad sorry mess. But what Laura suggested just before I left Songpan is that she's going to tell Maeve what went on behind her back when the time is right but until she does I'm to hold off letting onto Debbie that I know. But I swear it bloody well kills me not to be able to say anything to her and it's no exaggeration to say that I can hardly bear to look at Debbie for she makes my blood boil. Poor, poor Maeve.

Nightman Bar, Chengdu. Around the same time.

Maeve

Dylan asked me for a loan of $100 a little while ago.

Got into, like, *such* a snot when I said no that I gave in.

Don't know why he's being such a complete pain in the arse.

He's disappeared off now and left me here on my own.

Laura's in foul form too – over Felix I s'pose.

I asked her today how he was & if she'd been in contact with him, just to see if she'd tell me about the big bust-up.

Not a word.

Just said he was fine & thanks very much for asking.

But it's no skin off my nose if she doesn't want to tell me about it.

[Save Address(es)][Block]   [Previous][Next][Close]
From: "Tobin, Laura"<lauratobin@hotmail.com>
To: "Wilson, Felix"<felix@fmsounds.com>
Subject: I AM NOT HARASSING YOU!
Date: 30 Nov, 20:34:55
[Reply][Reply All][Forward][Delete]

Christ Almighty, Felix, I hardly think sending you an e-mail
after I nearly died could be considered harassment.

From the way you're going on, you'd think I was pestering
you non-stop from the moment I left home when, in reality,
it's only been the occasional e-mail and phone call. And it's
not like you're ever even there when I ring. And nobody is
forcing you to open my e-mails.

And yes, I do understand that we're not going out together
any longer but I didn't realise that meant we couldn't still
be friends. You can hardly fault me for thinking we could be
mature enough to at least be that.

[Save Address(es)][Block]   [Previous][Next][Close]
From: "Tobin, Laura"<lauratobin@hotmail.com>
To: "Chunn,Bryan"<bchunn@westernalliancebanks.co.uk
Subject: My Visa limit
Date: 30 Nov, 20:49:37
[Reply][Reply All][Forward][Delete]

Dear Bryan,

As you will see if you check my statements on your
computer, I do still have a regular income from the column
I write for *The Idol* so I don't see why there should be any

problem with increasing the limit on my Visa card. In addition I'm writing features regularly for several other publications but just haven't got around to invoicing them yet.

The only reason I'm looking to increase my limit is for convenience.

I trust this clarifies matters.

Regards,

Laura Tobin

[Save Address(es)][Block]   [Previous][Next][Close]

From: "Tobin, Laura"<lauratobin@hotmail.com>

To: "Colette Turner"<thechronicle@btinternet.com>

Subject: Possible articles

Date: 30 Nov, 21:11:18

[Reply][Reply All][Forward][Delete]

Dear Colette,

Belated congratulations! Look at you now! Features editor no less! Little did I think when we were time-sharing a desk in that grotty back office you'd rise to such dizzy heights within *The Chronicle*! Gone are the days, I guess, when you could sit in the pub after work with the junior staff and get absolutely hammered or make a complete show of yourself at office do's.

But I guess we've all moved on. At the moment I'm in Asia carrying out research for a book I've been commissioned to write. But I'd like to keep my hand in, not in political journalism per se but in something a little different, and I've been giving some thought to writing a series of articles on the history, architecture, culture, that sort of thing, of the various countries I'll be spending time in including China, Vietnam, Thailand and at least three or four other Asian countries, depending on where my research for my book takes me.

Would you be interested in running such a series? I thought I'd approach you first given your paper's extensive travel section. And for old times' sake. Remember the time you broke into Frank Wyse's office during the Christmas party and photocopied his contact book. I don't imagine you'll be bringing that up at an editorial meeting! Let's hope he never finds out . . .

Regards,

Laura Tobin.

1st December

Andrew's apartment, terrace. Evening.

Debbie

7.00 p.m. I am fed up. Maeve rang to tell me that herself, Dylan and Laura are spending the next couple days on a boat trip on the Yangtze. One of the reasons I wanted to come to China in the first place was to do precisely that.

Genevieve's room.

Genevieve

I just had a visit from Andrew's doctor who Andrew seems to think the world of and I'm sure he is very competent medically and no doubt highly intelligent but I definitely did <u>not</u> take to him. His bedside manner left an awful lot to be desired and his hands were like blocks of ice and his attention kept wandering and I don't know how he could have been so quick to diagnose Bacillary Dysentery seeing as how I was only halfway through describing all of my symptoms to him. You'd think he'd at least wait until I was finished. I wonder if Laura has told Maeve about what her rotten friend got up to with her rotten boyfriend.

Debbie

10.00 p.m. I wouldn't mind missing the Yangtze trip so

much if I thought Genevieve wanted me here but she doesn't, except to carry out all the little chores she's forever setting me.

The only person she seems happy to have around is Mr Clancy. She has no time whatsoever for little Shao though he's in and out of her room all day long, trying to cheer her up. For some inexplicable reason he's really fond of her. He's a real sweetheart and, having the skin of a rhinoceros, he takes no notice when Genevieve hunts him out. As for Mei, Genevieve acts as if she barely exists despite all she's been doing for Genevieve.

Genevieve

I know I'd like to be married one day but I'm not so sure about the children part. They seem to be very demanding. I can see why my parents stopped at one. That Shao for example is an awful nuisance and his mother seems to have no control over him whatsoever.

One thing I must say is that I don't know how I'll ever be able to thank Andrew for all he's done for me as he really has been <u>extraordinarily</u> kind. I don't think I've ever met anyone so kind-hearted <u>no</u> <u>exaggeration.</u> The way he flew down to Chengdu at a minute's notice and rescued me from that hellhole and even now though he's up to his eyeballs in work he's forever ringing to check if I'm doing okay and to see if Mei is looking after me all right which I have to say she is but despite that I still can't warm to her, not when I know she's the kind of person who would read another person's diary. Needless to say I'm more careful where I put it this time around.

Maeve just rang. From the way she was going on I

wouldn't say Laura has said a word to her about Dylan and Debbie's antics and I was very tempted to say something to her myself but I didn't for I'd better wait like Laura told me to.

But I really would love to say something to Debbie but I'm not going to until I've got the word from Laura that she's put Maeve in the picture. It's a pity that Laura wasn't around when Maeve rang for I'd have liked to have got a chance to talk to her and to find out when she does intend talking to Maeve especially as they're going off on some boat trip tomorrow and I won't get another chance for a couple of days.

[Save Address(es)][Block]   [Previous][Next][Close]
From: "Tobin, Laura"<lauratobin@hotmail.com>
To: "Colette Turner"<thechronicle@btinternet.com>
Subject: Congratulations Mrs Wyse!
Date: 1 Dec 21:09:32
[Reply][Reply All][Forward][Delete]

Who'd have thought! You and Frank Wyse! Married! And there I was thinking you couldn't stand the sight of him like the rest of us! So it's true, water does always find its own level. Now, not only do you get to spend all day with him at work but every night at home as well. I can't think of anything either of you deserve more. And really, there was no need to tell him how you photocopied his contact book before I got the chance. I can't believe you thought I was threatening to!

And please do pass on my kindest regards to Sally Hill. I should have known you'd still be in touch with one another. It figures. I'm sure she must have made a charming bridesmaid. Almost as charming a bridesmaid as you made a bride. Where on earth did you both find dresses to fit? And how liberal of you not to mind that your darling groom has been sleeping with your bridesmaid for the last couple of years on and off! Word has it that, right now, it's more on than off. But I guess I'm not telling you anything new seeing as how you and Sally Hill are such good friends these days.

2ⁿᵈ December

Boat somewhere on the Yangtze River. Evening time.

Maeve
Advertising this trip as a Super Luxury Cruise was stretching it – just a bit.
More like a trip on a busted-up, clapped-out old ferry.
Cannot *wait* to get off.
It's, like, *totally* doing my head in.
Nothing to do.
Scenery's boring.
Food's horrible.
Dylan & L are no company whatsoever – they're both in *foul* form.
Just as well G isn't here to complain – don't think I could stand listening to that.

Genevieve's room, Andrew's apartment. A little later.

Genevieve
    One thing I am glad about is that I now have a name for my condition. For a while there I was worried out of my head for I thought I might be strung out or whatever the phrase is for you see I smoked some of Dylan's dope the night before I got sick and I was terrified that that might be the cause of me feeling so bad.

I know it was a stupid thing to do and it was something I wouldn't have dreamt of doing in normal circumstances. But that night I was feeling all out of sorts what with having lived through the worst few days of my entire life on that stupid trek and hardly having eaten a bite for goodness knows how long and then there was the fright of Laura nearly getting killed and of course my Bacillary Dysentery was probably in its early stages though I didn't know that then. So between one thing and another, I wasn't feeling myself <u>at</u> <u>all</u>. So when I came out of that cesspit of a toilet and saw Dylan sitting there on the roof strumming away on his guitar and smoking his head off and looking so contented with life, I sat down beside him and then he started kidding me and we were getting along fine and before I knew what I was doing I'd asked him for a drag. I was just curious I suppose.

But needless to say all this was before I found out about him and Debbie. And I blame him as much as her of course for it takes two to tangle. I mean to say what a creep Dylan is pretending to be absolutely crazy about Maeve yet carrying on like that at the same time. Honest to God he's nothing but a wolf in cheap clothing.

But I must admit I liked the dope. It made me feel sort of free and relaxed and I stopped worrying about everything and suddenly it was like I hadn't a care in the world. Nothing seemed scary any more. All I wanted to do was to laugh out loud though God knows there was precious little to laugh about at the time. Of course I know it was a stupid thing to do and as I say I certainly won't be doing it again for the last thing I'd want is start on that particular slippery slope. Of course nobody but Dylan knows about all this.

Except Laura that is. I was so worried that I just had to confide in someone. In a way I wish I hadn't for I know she was only trying to help but she definitely made matters worse. She started going on about how if my condition deteriorated I was to be sure to let her know straightaway as there was no telling what could be mixed in with the stuff I'd smoked and no way of knowing where Dylan had got it from. And then she started on about how if I had to be admitted to hospital I wasn't to worry about my parents or Theo for she'd make sure to contact them and to break things to them as gently as possible. To be honest I don't think she really knew what she was talking about for the last thing she said to me was to keep an eye out in case I started seeing spots before my eyes. Despite all her sophistication, I'd say she's as clueless as myself.

But it's no lie to say I was never so scared in my whole life as I was after listening to her. I hardly slept a wink and my mind was just buzzing and I know it seems stupid now but I couldn't stop myself worrying about dying and I kept on thinking about how Theo would feel if he learned that his girlfriend had died of an overdose in Asia.

And out on the terrace.

Debbie

8.30 p.m. Genevieve is calling out for me again.

She wants me to go and tell Mei to bring her supper in to her a little earlier than usual as she's anxious to turn in.

A "please" wouldn't have gone amiss.

Doesn't she know that us servants are always happier with our lot when we feel appreciated?

I can't believe I'm stuck back here in Andrew's playing nurse when there's just so much I want to see before leaving the country.

I am going insane!

And back on the Yangtze River.

Maeve

Think Dylan's run outta dope – can't imagine that this boat is awash with suppliers exactly.

Wish he wouldn't smoke so much – esp. here in China.

Don't fancy the idea of him being caught and sent off to some gulag.

But at least he realises he's being crabby. When we stopped off at this town earlier this afternoon he bought me a brooch.

Course I know he bought it outta my money – but still – it's the thought that counts.

L's mood has picked up a little – Thank Christ!

Funny thing was she was acting like she & Felix were still together again today & started telling me some story about him & her & was making out as if there were still a couple. Weird!

Which is why I *finally* told her I'd overheard their splitting up conversation back in the train station in Xian.

Think she was a bit taken aback at 1st but (being L) she made a quick recovery & explained to me that I'd clearly misheard & that they'd been fighting about something else entirely & that they were still very much together. End of story.

Très weird!

And complete bullshit.

An Asian Diary

Since Deanne and her patient went back to Beijing, it's just been Me, Mags, and Wannabe – our little love triangle.

Mags asked me today if I thought Wannabe's mood of late had been rather strange and had he said anything to me about what's been bothering him. Needless to say I shook my head and changed the subject as quickly as possible for I don't think she'd have welcomed the truth. I mean who wants to hear that their boyfriend is lusting after their friend?

But it is an odd situation. There she is, catching his hand, trying to whisper sweet nothings in his ear whilst he's looking over at me with this hangdog expression.

What I can't believe is that he thought there could be a future for him and me. But he seems he did, or does rather, and despite the fact that I've taken him aside numerous times and tried to explain that there isn't going to be a him and me he still doesn't get it. He's even thicker than I thought. I can't go as far as the toilet but he's following after me, pleading with me, telling me that what happened between us must mean something.

He even bought me a little antique brooch today though no doubt the money came from Mags, not that that's my concern. It is a nice trinket however even if a little on the cheap side for the tastes of a woman who was once sent 24 dozen red roses just because her amour of the time woke in a good mood one morning. But then I don't think it's fair to expect someone who subsists on the meagre wages of a courier and the few pennies his girlfriend throws him from time to time to be in a position to compete for the affections of a woman who has been wooed by several millionaires.

Of course it probably isn't going to be too long before our little love triangle is blown to smithereens. You see, Geraldine is quite likely to confront Deanne before Deanne leaves to join up with us in Wuhan tomorrow though I have told her to hold off until I've told Maeve first.

But what if she has told Deanne already? And what if Deanne then persuades Wannabe to tell Mags nothing happened between him and her? Will Mags believe him? Why should she? But what reason would Geraldine have to lie? And what would Wannabe have to gain by confessing to what really went on? Questions. Questions. Questions.

3rd December

Andrew's apartment. Evening time.

Genevieve

Well Debbie's gone and good riddance for I can't say I was all that sad to see the back of her. Before she left I'd decided I was going to have it out with her and tell her that I knew all about her and Dylan but I think she was a bit fed up what with me hardly talking to her since we left Songpan so that when she came in to tell me she was leaving and I told her I'd something I wanted to get off my chest, she got all snappy and said I'd left it a bit late and that she'd no interest in listening to anything I had to say and then just stormed out.

But maybe it was just as well in any case for if Laura still hasn't told Maeve yet then I might have ended up doing more harm than good but I just hate it when things are left hanging and I'd much prefer to get everything out in the open.

Mum and Dad rang earlier. Dad thinks I'd be foolish to come home despite my illness but it doesn't matter what he says for I'll be on a plane the minute I'm well enough. He says they're coping fine in the warehouse without me and it seems my cousin Caitríona is getting along grand as my stand-in though I think he'd probably say that even if it wasn't true so as not to worry me. I can just imagine

299

Caitríona showing off and sucking up to everyone especially Dad though it won't do her much good as that position always has been and always will be mine and she'll be getting her walking papers as soon as I come home no matter how much she busts a gut trying to make herself indispensable.

Dad says that Theo's called in to him a few times and that he's in good form. I just hope Caitríona doesn't go getting any ideas about Theo. She's at least five years older than me and she's never really had a proper boyfriend so I'd say she must be getting pretty desperate and I can just see her setting her cap on Theo now that I'm out of the picture but much good it'll do her.

It's a pity I didn't think to ask Debbie to get me some deodorant before she left for I've run out though she probably wouldn't have anyway given the mood she was in.

Oasis Hotel, Wuhan. Evening time.

Maeve

We've come off that goddamn barge – finally.

Debs is finished playing Flo Nightingale & is on her way down to meet up with us – should be here by tomorrow.

Dylan's now started talking about heading off on his own.

Nearly wish he would.

He's in rotten form again today.

What is the matter with him??????

Train, Beijing – Zhengzhou – Wuhan.

Debbie

9.00 p.m. Going back to Beijing with Genevieve was such a waste. And talk about appreciation! When I went in to say goodbye to her, the first thing she came out with was that she had a bone to pick with me so I walked straight back out. There was no way I was taking a lecture from Genevieve, not after the way she's been ignoring me.

I think a little thank-you speech might have been more appropriate. Something along the lines of, "You really are a brick for coming all the way back to Beijing with me, Debbie. Especially as it caused you to miss out on the Yangtze River trip and I know how much you were looking forward to that. And now to meet up with the others you're going to have to travel all the way down by train on your own. I really have put you out a lot. And I've been so demanding as well. But, really, I do appreciate it, I just want you to know that."

Sitting-room, Andrew's apartment.
Around the same time.

Genevieve

Now that I'm on the mend I'm beginning to appreciate being back in Andrew's. This evening I got up after eating the supper Mei brought in to me before she went to pack the young fellow off to bed and Andrew and I got a chance to sit for an hour or so on our own and chat. He agrees with Dad and says I'd be foolish to go home early and suggested I stay here with him until I'm fully recovered and then when the girls reach Vietnam I could fly down and meet them there. I get the impression from the way he was talking that Vietnam is far more civilised than China and that I wouldn't find it such tough going. But even though I appreciate everything Andrew is doing for me and appreciate his advice I'm still going to go home as soon as I'm well enough.

[Save Address(es)][Block]   [Previous][Next][Close]
From: "Tobin, Laura"<lauratobin@hotmail.com>
To: "Adam Nicholson"<adam@weekendmail.co.uk.>
Subject: Possible series of articles
Date: Dec, 19:20:55
[Reply][Reply All][Forward][Delete]

Dear Adam,
Just taking time away to do some research for a book I'm
writing and to see some of the world.
Juggling your own lovely missus and Peter Paterson's missus
must keep you busy but I'd appreciate it if you could spare
some time to consider a proposal I have to make.
Although it's a bit removed from my usual style, I've been
giving some thought to writing a series of articles on the
history, architecture, culture, that sort of thing of the
various countries I'm visiting. I'll be spending some time in
China where I am at the moment as well as Vietnam,
Thailand and at least three or four other Asian countries,
depending on where my research takes me.
Would you be interested in running such a series?
Regards,
Laura Tobin.

4th December

Genevieve

Andrew's forever telling me not to be shy about using the phone so I finally gave Theo a ring even though he hasn't bothered to phone me not even once and I know we agreed we wouldn't ring each other but he could have made an exception seeing as how I've been so sick and all and it's not like he wouldn't have known where to contact me either for Dad would have told him I was staying with Andrew.

But he had the <u>most</u> <u>amazing</u> <u>news</u> for me and that's that he's arranged to come to Vietnam for a week which is the most extraordinary thing I've ever heard for Theo <u>never</u> goes anywhere and he wouldn't be coming to Vietnam now either only that when Trevor was in town last week he spotted some cut-price flights to Hanoi and without even telling Theo he went in and booked seats for them both. I'd say Trevor's main reason for coming out is to see Debbie but I wonder if he'd feel the same way if he knew about the carry-on between herself and Dylan. I tried to tell Theo about it so that he could warn Trevor but he interrupted before I could and told me not to be wasting time talking about Debbie not when every second was costing a fortune

But I did tell him about how I'd been thinking about cutting my trip short but he said he'd probably still go to

Vietnam even if I wasn't there as he's always had an interest in the Vietnam War and was keen to visit some of the places he'd read up on and since the flights were on special offer they'd lose their deposit if they cancelled at this late stage. So much for coming to see me!

Oasis Hotel, Wuhan. A little later.

Maeve

NEWSFLASH NO 1!!

Just been on to G & learned that her Theo is coming to Vietnam!

This is Truly Incredible News.

The last time I met Theo he was going on & on about how he just didn't get the point of travelling, not when you can see it all on the telly.

NEWSFLASH NO 2!!

Theo is bringing his brother Trevor with him.

This has sent Debs into shock.

Since we were in school, Trevor has been *"in lurve"* with Debs. She (on the other hand) is *completely* allergic to him. I can't wait until they get here – it's going to be great fun.

G sounded *soooo* cosy in Dad's – next thing she'll be getting him to adopt her.

Overnight Bus, Wuhan – Yangshuo.

Maeve

This bus is the business.

Très cool indeed!

The driver is dressed like a pilot.

We were welcomed on board by a smart hostess.

There's a toilet (spotless), air con (cold), T.V. (working), & luxurious seats (reclining).

G would be in her element if she was here – it's *heaps* better than anything else we've travelled on.

Dylan's still in funny form. He nearly bit the head off L earlier when she started teasing him about the state of his hair.

At least he's perked up since we met up with Debs.

Debbie

10.00 p.m. I could swing for the others. As soon as I arrived into Wuhan, the first thing Maeve tells me is that she's booked us on this overnight bus to Yangshuo which was just about to leave. That getting onto a bus straight after spending over twenty-four hours on trains would be the last thing in the world I'd feel like doing didn't seem to have occurred to any of them.

I thought I'd at least have a day to look around Wuhan as my guide book mentions lots of sights but when I said as much to Maeve she told me I wasn't missing a thing. Like she'd know!

They're all in foul mood. Maeve and Dylan are nowhere near as lovey-dovey. Maybe Maeve has finally realised that Dylan isn't worth the bother though probably not and no doubt they'll be all over one another again tomorrow.

The second thing Maeve tells me is that Theo and Trevor are flying out to meet up with us in Vietnam which is something I really don't want to dwell on right now.

4.00 a.m. I just woke up in a cold sweat. I was having a nightmare and Theo and Trevor were . . . actually I don't even want to think about it.

I don't think my vocabulary of expletives is anyway near extensive enough to express exactly how I feel about the news that Theo and, more especially, Trevor are coming to Vietnam.

[Save Address(es)][Block]   [Previous][Next][Close]
From: "Tobin, Laura"<lauratobin@hotmail.com>
To: "Adam Nicholson"<adam@weekendmail.co.uk.>
Subject: The Patersons and you
Date: 4 Dec, 21:10:31
[Reply][Reply All][Forward][Delete]

Dear Adam,
I could have approached several other publications first but
I was giving your rag a chance for old times' sake.
If I were you I'd give Peter Paterson a wide berth for the
foreseeable future. China isn't as remote as you might think.
They do have telephones here too. What I wouldn't give to
be a fly on the wall of the Patersons' living-room right now.
Are your ears burning?
Laura.

5th December

Andrew's apartment. Early evening.

Genevieve

Last night Andrew had a dinner party. There were eight people altogether. Andrew and me, this fat middle-aged Chinese couple, an American couple with horsy faces, a young colleague of Andrew's with terrible acne who was from England and Mei.

It's funny but I never noticed before how much more interesting older people can be than people of my own age but all that young English fella for example could talk about were all the different pubs and nightclubs and whatnot he'd been to since moving to Beijing whereas I noticed Andrew covered a huge range of different subjects from cooking to architecture to music to goodness-knows-what and you could see that everyone who was there last night was really interested in what he had to say.

Something has just dawned on me. I must be the world's biggest eejit for not spotting it before. <u>Mei is in love with Andrew</u>. How did I not see it until now? Whenever he comes into the room her whole face lights up and when she's talking to him she's looks lively and almost pretty in her own way and youngish even though she's plain and must be practically in her forties.

I suppose you couldn't blame her for fancying him. I think part of Andrew's appeal lies in the fact that he's a good listener as well as a good talker and is really interested in what people have to say and he's so nice to people as well even Shao who I'd say must really get on his nerves.

Anyway enough about Andrew. If anyone were to read all this they'd think I had an eye on him myself! Well just one other thing. At some point during the dinner party he mentioned he'd decided he was going to fly down to Vietnam to see Maeve. I get the feeling he wasn't very happy with the way things were left standing between them and that he just wants to spend a little more time with her before she goes back home which is understandable. He hasn't said anything to Maeve about his plans as he wants to keep them a surprise.

I have an idea that he might also want to suss out Dylan for I don't think he was very taken with him when they met up in Songpan. And who could blame him? And he'd be even less taken with him if he knew what a drug-taking, two-timing dirty rat Dylan was.

Good Company Inn, Yangshuo.
Around about the same time.

Maeve

Dylan's still being a *complete* pain in the arse. He keeps snapping my head off for, like, *no* reason.

If he's going to keep carrying on like this then he might as well take off on his own like he keeps threatening to.

And he'd the cheek to turn around & ask could he have a loan of money again today & yeah, yeah, I gave it to him. Yeah – I know – I'm a fool.

Debbie

9.00 p.m. Dylan's just asked me if he could come on a cycling trip I've arranged to go on tomorrow with some Germans who're staying on the floor above us. Seeing as how I think one of them who happens to look scarily like Boris Becker has his fair-lashed, baby-blues on me, I told Dylan he's more than welcome as long as he doesn't start hitting on any of them for money.

I know Genevieve is always going on about how fit I am but that's only in comparison to her. These Germans however are serious outdoor types so it could prove very embarrassing. At least now I'll have Dylan to fall behind with for he's even more unfit than I am.

[Save Address(es)][Block]   [Previous][Next][Close]
From: "Tobin, Laura"<lauratobin@hotmail.com>
To: "Sandra Martin"<sandramart@weekendtimes.co.uk>
Subject: Series of articles
Date: 5 Dec, 21:21:43
[Reply][Reply All][Forward][Delete]

Dear Sandra,

I hear congratulations are in order and that you've now been made Travel Editor. Fantastic news indeed!

I doubt your new bosses could ever guess what lies beneath that professional reserve of yours and you've certainly come a long way from the days when you started out as a freelancer and had to supplement your income working in that dreadful lap-dancing club. Let's hope they never find out!

I guess you're probably anxious to put your own stamp on things at *The Weekend Times* and are eager to bring in some fresh voices which is why I thought you might be interested in giving some thought to publishing a series of articles I'm doing whilst over here researching a book. The articles are on Asian history, architecture, culture, that sort of thing. Let me know what you think.

Regards,

Laura Tobin.

6th December

Good Company Inn, Yangshuo. Evening time.

Debbie

7.00 p.m. It's been years since I cycled so much and I ache all over but I really enjoyed the day. Dylan and I had a good laugh like we used to once upon a time. Or at least we were having a good laugh until the journey back.

As to be expected, we'd fallen way behind the Germans and were just cycling along, fooling around, when Dylan suddenly got all serious and said he needed to ask me for some advice as he'd got himself into a tricky situation.

Which is something of an understatement. It seems that himself and Laura got up to no good while we were horse-trekking back in Songpan and now he doesn't know whether or not he should tell Maeve and he wanted to know what I thought he should do.

Him coming to his ex-girlfriend for advice on affairs of the heart is a bit rich, something he didn't seem to understand, not even when I pointed it out to him but just kept on and on at me until I promised him I'd think about it.

Andrew's apartment. A little later.

Genevieve

I've changed my mind and decided I'm going to go to

Vietnam after all. Every time Maeve has rung she's been on at me, begging me not to go home but to meet up with them in Vietnam. And it's not like my Dad needs me urgently or anything seeing as how Caitríona is doing such a fine job as he's gone to such great lengths to point out to me. And besides it wouldn't really be fair to have Theo come so far and not be there for him and I wouldn't even have to go on my own for I could fly down with Andrew. He's going to be flying business class to Hanoi which is really the equivalent of first class but it's just not called that any more and he's offered to pay for my flight and for the hotel in Hanoi which is bound to be fierce classy so in a way I'd be a _fool_ to say no. And if I find I don't like Vietnam then there's nothing stopping me from getting on the plane and going straight home. It's a pity Andrew has made me promise not to say a word to Maeve on the phone about him coming too for I'm just bursting to tell her but I suppose I can understand him wanting it to be a surprise.

Back at the Good Company Inn.

Debbie

8.35 p.m. Dylan came to me just now, wanting to know if I'd thought things over so I told him I had and told him that as far as I could see he'd no choice but to tell Maeve about him and Laura.

So he started going on about how terrified he was of losing Maeve and how he'd never loved anyone even a fraction of how much he loves her which wasn't exactly the most diplomatic thing in the world to say to an ex-girlfriend but then, that's Dylan for you.

And then he started on about how he'd no interest in

Laura and never meant for anything to happen and that it was she who came on to him.

But would he be any less of a rat if he'd cheated with someone he had genuine feelings for? And who's to say he's telling the truth? It's very hard to imagine that Laura is interested in him or that she came onto him.

[Save Address(es)][Block]   **[Previous][Next][Close]**
From: "Tobin, Laura"<lauratobin@hotmail.com>
To: "Wilson, Felix"<felix@fmsounds.com>
Subject: Let's get a couple of things straight . . .
Date: 6 Dec, 18:17:21 ·
[Reply][Reply All][Forward][Delete]

I suppose I should be grateful that for once you took my call. So, finally, we're getting to the root of things. It all goes back to *The Argus*. I can't believe you still think there's going to be a court case and that you're so terrified by the prospect of being associated with me in any ensuing publicity. So much for standing by your woman! But, as I've already told you, they paid Lily Buchan's brother to drop the case which I feel they were wrong to do since I never fabricated anything or made up a single quote.

And while I'm at it, I'd like to clear up some of your other extraordinary misconceptions. Firstly, I left *The Argus* of my own volition. Anything you heard to the contrary are rumours spread by Sally Hill and her like. Ever since her name was omitted from the by-line of a story we worked on together at *The Chronicle* she's had it in for me. Secondly, I don't understand why you keep going on about how my situation reflects badly on you. It has nothing to do with you. Thirdly, I did nothing wrong in writing that story. I simply reported the facts as they were. Ronald Devereux has been found guilty of every accusation I levelled. He's the bad guy here, Felix, not me. He's the one who set up a fictitious company in order to embezzle millions from his own government. What was I meant to do? Not report it? Turn my back on what turned out to be one of the biggest stories of the year? I can't help if Lily Buchan was the emotional fallout. That's just the way it is sometimes.

And to say my career is going nowhere fast is the stupidest thing ever and I have no intention of getting out of journalism despite your advice. Why should I? I've never been busier. I've so many ideas and contacts that when I get home and start seriously arranging work, I won't have time to draw breath. If I wanted another staff job I'd have no problem picking one up but that isn't what I want. I've always wanted the independence of being a freelancer but felt it prudent to wait until I was sufficiently well established as a journalist which I am now.

And there's the book as well. They didn't give me such a substantial advance just to sit twiddling my thumbs.

7th December

Bus to Hanoi. Late afternoon.

Maeve

Feel kinda sad to be leaving China – it's like a connection with Dad will be broken.

Really wish things had gone better between him & me.

Don't even, like, know when I'm going to see him again.

Passing all these houses along the road makes me feel – I don't know – lonesome I guess.

Right now it's dark & you can see into all these brightly-painted homes to where families are gathered around looking so, so cosy.

Wonder how Mum is getting on.

Haven't rung her in ages – will tomorrow.

Dylan is *still* as grumpy as anything.

Debbie

6.00 p.m. Dylan's just come down to inform me he's not going to tell Maeve about him and Laura and that if I tell her he'll claim not to know what I'm talking about. I don't know why he ever bothered coming to me for advice in the first place.

6.35 p.m. And there's no point in me saying anything to

Maeve for she'd just think I was making it up out of jealousy.

7.00 p.m. I really feel like confronting Laura and telling her I know about her and Dylan but no doubt she'd only deny everything. But I hate the fact that she thinks she's got away with it.

8.00 p.m. But I'm still finding it very hard to believe Laura could be interested in Dylan. And what about Felix? He may have broken it off with her but she's obviously still keen on him. Why else would she be letting on they're still together?

Andrew's apartment. Meanwhile.

Genevieve

It'll be funny to see Theo again. I know I haven't been away for all that long but it really does feel like a lifetime. If I'd thought of it I could have sent him a postcard listing out some things he might need but wouldn't think to bring himself for it's only through experience you learn what's useful and what's not. I hope he remembers to bring suntan lotion for it'll be hot in Vietnam and I know I'm pale but nothing near as pale and pasty as Trevor and himself. I wonder if the girls have reached Hanoi yet. It'll be great to meet up with them again. Or at least with Laura and Maeve.

[Save Address(es)][Block]   [Previous][Next][Close]
From: "Tobin, Laura"<lauratobin@hotmail.com>
To: "Sandra Martin"<sandramart@weekendtimes.co.uk>
Subject: Club Coco . . .
Date: 7 Dec, 23:20:57
[Reply][Reply All][Forward][Delete]

Dear Sandra,

I always imagined journalists were good at knowing when someone is bluffing.

For such a seedy dive, Club CoCo has a very sophisticated website. And to think they're still using that photo of you. All of you. In glorious technicolour. Isn't technology a wonderful thing?

And isn't it amazing how it's possible to download an image like that and send it to wherever one wishes? From a tiny little internet café, for instance, in the remotest part of China to a bustling newspaper office in the heart of London.

Look around you. Are your male colleagues looking at you any differently this morning? Or are they too busy staring at their computer screens? What can they be looking at?

8th December

Maeve

So far getting to Hanoi has involved 2 (v dilapidated) buses,
1 (banged up) motor rickshaw, 4 (held together with sticky
tape) motorbikes & 1 (v.v.v. crowded) Hiace van – don't ask
– which we're on right now.

Except that we're making a detour to deliver a consignment of
socks to a shop somewhere in the backside of nowhere.

Again – don't ask – but there has to be easier ways.

Oh yeah, there is & G's taking it tho' that won't stop her
moaning & groaning.

But in an odd sort of way I've missed her & all her
complaining.

Glad she's decided not to go home.

Prob. won't be saying that five minutes after we meet up!

Debbie

6.00 *p.m.* Poor Dylan. It turns out things aren't as clear-
cut and final between himself and Laura as he might
wish. He's told me that she's started coming on to him
again which he says is really freaking him out.

What's she playing at? I can't believe she actually fancies
him.

320

Back in Andrew's apartment. Meanwhile.

Genevieve

I wonder what Andrew will make of Theo. Hopefully they'll get along and I think they will too especially when I tell Theo how good Andrew has been to me. I just hope Andrew's right and that Vietnam will be easier to handle than China and if it isn't then I'm going straight home no two ways about it but hopefully it won't be so foreign and the food will be cheaper and someway edible. At least I've managed to sort out all my stuff in my rucksack and find some replacements for the ziplock bags that have burst.

I'd say Maeve is going to get an absolute heart attack when I come off the plane with her dad in tow.

[Save Address(es)][Block]   [Previous][Next][Close]
From: "Tobin, Laura"<lauratobin@hotmail.com>
To: "Tony Howard"<editor@idolmagazine.co.uk>
Subject: Your e-mail
Date: 8 Dec, 20:33:10
[Reply][Reply All][Forward][Delete]

Dear Tony,
I'm not sure I understand your point. It's a diary column I'm
writing so obviously the three girls I'm spending all my time
with are bound to dominate, as they have from the start.
But since you're the editor I'll broaden the scope of it as you
suggest.
Regards,
Laura.

9th December

Miss Loi's Guesthouse, Hanoi. Morning.

Debbie

7.00 *a.m.* I'm lying here with the sun streaming in through our bedroom window and listening to the sounds of Hanoi's people preparing for the day ahead. I know we arrived late last night but I love this place already. From six this morning the street outside has been all bustle and crammed full of flower-sellers, bread-sellers, rickshaw drivers and teems of others, all in their straw hats and baggy-pyjama outfits just going about their business.

This is the life!

The Lotus Café. Several hours later.

Maeve

Dylan is *such* a Bloody Idiot!

Am fit to kill him!

This morning when I went to get some toothpaste from his washbag I found a little stash of dope. Says he forgot he had it! Like, how bloody stupid is that?

Duh?

That nosy custom official yesterday could *so* easily have

found it & when I (quite reasonably) started giving out to him about it, he just kept humming some stupid song to block me out.

Another thing (amongst many others) that worries me is how he doesn't know the 1st thing about the people he buys the stuff from. I read (can't rem. where) about this scam in some country or other (can't rem. which) where crooked police officers get their buddies to sell drugs to tourists then – later – the same officers carry out a search on the unsuspecting dupe, find the drugs, haul him or her off to the local police station where they then casually mention at some point during their interrogation that (for a certain sum) the whole matter can be forgotten.

Dylan's *exactly* the kind of fool to get caught up in something like that.

Debbie

10.45 a.m. We're now sitting by Hoan Kiem Lake on the terrace of a fancy restaurant enjoying the most delicious coffee. It's been a while since we've had such luxury but I think I am going to miss China.

I may as well savour the moment for we'll have Trevor and Theo on top of us soon enough.

Andrew's apartment. Late that night.

Genevieve

I really am going to miss Beijing and the apartment. Despite being so sick I've enjoyed my time here. As tonight is my last night Mei cooked us this lovely meal and afterwards Andrew and I sat around chatting. We'd still be there except that Andrew said he just couldn't keep his eyes open but that I should write a book as I'd so many interesting stories to tell. He said he'd love to hear more but that we'd better go to bed seeing as how we've such a long day ahead of us tomorrow what with the flight and all. I don't mean he was suggesting that we should go to bed together heaven forbid. He just meant we should go to our <u>separate</u> <u>beds</u> but at the same time.

An Asian Diary

*N*ow that Wannabe's little fantasy has come true and he's had his wicked way with me, the guilt is beginning to set in. The poor fellow's terrified I'm going to say something to Mags and he keeps sidling up to me, whispering at me, pleading with me, telling me how there really isn't any need for Mags to know a thing.

To see him looking so pitiful, wringing his hands together, sweating like crazy, terrified I'm going to confess all makes me wonder how I could possibly have let things go quite so far. I plead temporary insanity. Still I have to confess I'm enjoying his anguish – just a little.

Of course his guilt only manifested itself when he finally got my message that there isn't going to be a happy-ever-after him and me. Only when that message sank into his ever-so-thick skull did he begin to dwell on the implications for himself and Mags for even he has the cop on to realise that she might not be too keen to stick around should she find out about our little dalliance. And now, since he's accepted he can't have what he wants, he's anxious to hold onto what he's got. A bird in the hand and all that . . .

But it's not me he should be worrying about but Geraldine for she's beginning to agitate and when I spoke to her on the phone she even dared suggest that if I hadn't said anything to Mags about Deanne and Wannabe by the time she meets up with us again then she was going to have to take matters into her own hands.

But I doubt she will. Knowing Geraldine she'll do nothing but mutter about what she is going to do though, in a way, I nearly wish she would spill the beans, as she might say herself, for I'd like to see how Deanne would react to her allegations. And since Wannabe's hardly likely to tell Mags the truth I'm safe from her wrath.

10th December

Beijing – Hanoi flight. Afternoon.

Genevieve

I've never flown business class before. It definitely beats economy though I must say it's a bit disappointing given how much it costs and I'd have expected it to feel a bit more roomier but at least I'm not paying for it myself. Of course to Andrew flying is just like taking a bus to the rest of us and he was saying earlier that sometimes he flies a couple of times a week and that often he even does a round trip on the same day.

But one plus about travelling business class is that you're allowed to have as many mini bottles of champagne as you want. I've already drunk two which is as much as I can take before I start making a fool of myself and that's the last thing I'd want to do in front of Andrew. But what I might do is ask the air hostess for a couple more bottles if Andrew goes to the toilet as they'd make a nice present to take back to Dad though of course I'll need to get him something else too. I'm not <u>that</u> mean! And I already have the silk painting Laura gave me in Chengdu which I'm going to give to Mam so that's two of the main presents more or less sorted.

Hanoi Airport. Around the same time.

Maeve

G hasn't come yet but T 'n' T have arrived.

Poor Debs is, like, suicidal.

Mean & all as it may be, I'm enjoying watching the lovelorn Trevor in hot pursuit.

As soon as he came off the plane and saw Debs he made a lunge.

She disappeared soon after that – guess she's hiding out somewhere.

They're already driving Dylan, like, *totally* insane.

They can *never, ever* be quiet, not for a second.

They just talk & talk & talk & talk non-stop tho' what they're actually saying seems to be secondary & their only goal is to be heard.

And in the coffee dock around the corner.

Debbie

4.00 p.m. I'm hiding out in the airport coffee shop while we wait for Genevieve's plane because the truly terrible twins have arrived. Trevor's just lumbered past for the fifth time in search of me.

I hope Genevieve won't start egging him on while they're here since it's been her dream for a long time now to see me settled with someone nice – as in Trevor.

Whenever I've been home in Portrea for the weekend, she does nothing but go on about what a fascinating character Trevor is and because he's so very like her own beloved I have to be extremely diplomatic when trying to explain to her that, well, I'd sooner stick pins in my eyes than have Trevor's fat little hands come anywhere near me.

From time to time, she's even alluded to a life in which she sees all four of us, Mr and Mrs Trevor and Mr and Mrs Theo, living in matching houses on side-by-side plots on the in-laws' farm.

But I have never given her any encouragement in this fantasy, quite the opposite in fact, so she's learned to keep it to herself but I know Genevieve and I've no doubt but that it still lurks somewhere in that head of hers.

Miss Loi's Guesthouse. That evening.

Maeve

G didn't arrive alone.

Dad turned up as well.

Not sure how I feel about that.

Glad – I think.

Tho' I would have liked a warning.

And across town, at the Continental Hotel.

Genevieve

It was just great to see Theo standing there waiting as we came through customs although I must say I have definitely seen him looking better. I thought he looked a bit washed out especially when compared to Andrew who of course has a great colour and don't ask me where Theo and Trevor got their outfits but I'm not going to go into them right now.

From the sounds of it, I don't think Theo enjoyed his flight at all. He said that the food they got on the plane was just dreadful and that his earphones weren't working so he couldn't follow any of the movies and in any case he'd already seen two of them and one of them with my cousin

330

Caitríona of all people! Laura says he probably made a point of telling me that so as to make me jealous but I wouldn't think so for Theo isn't really like that.

The girls are in great form altogether and it was just lovely to catch up with them again. Well at least with Maeve and Laura. I have to say Debbie was <u>all</u> <u>about</u> <u>me</u> but of course she doesn't know that I know about her and Dylan. Maybe I should just leave sheepdogs die and try to forget all about the carry-on between the pair of them but I'm not sure I can. What they did to Maeve was <u>inexcusable.</u> I'm going to have to talk to Laura about the whole situation again as soon as I get an opportunity so that we can decide for once and for all what's the best thing to do. But honestly I just couldn't get over how delighted Laura was to see me. She kept going on about how great it was to have her soul-mate meaning me back again! I'm not sure I'd go quite that far but it was nice to meet up with her again and to realise just how fond she is of me. I mean someone like her must have hundreds of friends.

Needless to say Dylan is <u>still</u> hanging about which isn't exactly a surprise for it's not like he even has a proper job to go home to. And the minute I arrived off the plane he started teasing me and coming up to me and whispering in my ear, asking me if I "wanna buy some dope?". I'm going to have to have a word with him at the first opportunity and beg him not to tell Theo about what I got up to Songpan for I'd just die if Theo ever found out.

I must say the hotel Andrew booked us into is <u>very</u> posh. Apparently loads of famous writers and journalists and what-not used to stay here and it's featured in hundreds of books. He offered to put the others up here as well for there seems to be no end to his money or his generosity but only Laura and the twins took him up on the offer and the others stayed where they were though don't ask me why for it sounds like a complete dump. Maeve especially must be crazy. I mean he's her father for crying out loud!

Back at Miss Loi's Guesthouse. A little later.

Maeve
Yeah – definitely glad.

An Asian Diary

O ur party has suddenly increased dramatically. The delectable Mr C has joined us once again. Geraldine's boyfriend, Thicko, together with his twin brother, Thicker, have arrived out from Ireland. Plus, Geraldine herself is back in our midst. I imagine her decision not to go home has more to do with Andrew's presence than her boyfriend's.

But what a picture Thicko and Thicker made coming through customs in their khaki shorts, their Hawaiian shirts and their enormous bumbags hanging just below their little Buddha bellies. On the one hand, I'm not looking forward to the prospect of spending time in their company as they're the thickest country bumpkins you're ever likely to come across. But, on the other hand, they should be good for a laugh since they're so backward they make Geraldine look like the most consummate of travellers. Heretofore their annual holiday has been a day trip to the beach with a packed lunch.

It's amazing how similar they look to one another as adults though nowhere near as similar as they did as kids. Back in our school days, I happen to believe I was the only person in the world, with the possible exception of their mother, who could tell them apart, and just from a glance at the backs of their heads too. By some bizarre coincidence, I had the dubious pleasure of being seated behind them from the very first day they appeared in our class way back in high infants and every year thereafter until they were kept back again in fifth year. There wasn't a pair of heads in the world I was more familiar with. I knew every cowlick and every pockmark. Thicko, for example, has a very distinctive low crown around which his hair grows in a clockwise swirl whereas his brother, Thicker, has a pretty nasty scar just behind his left ear, a relic of an especially nasty boil circa the spring of third year and his dandruff is far more severe than Thicko's. That much hasn't changed.

But at least we have a more pleasing addition to our party in the form of Mr C.

11th December

The Continental Hotel. Early morning.

Genevieve

It's not even eight o' clock in the morning but we're all sitting here waiting for the others who're on the way over from their hotel. Debbie was on the phone at the crack of dawn this morning telling us to be sure to be ready by the time they got here for we've an awful lot to try and get through today. What is she like? I mean you'd at least think she'd give us a chance to recover from our flights yesterday but oh no not her. No, sir!

But Andrew was right in thinking Vietnam would suit me much better than China. You don't have to do half as much walking for you can get about in these little rickshaws which are fierce cheap although the city did seem a bit crowded when we went out for something to eat last night and there were these little boys hanging about outside some of the restaurants and shops hounding the tourists to buy postcards and lighters when they'd have been better served being at home doing their homework for they can't have been any more than eight or nine years of age.

Laura has started on again about Andrew's <u>supposed feelings</u> for me but I just wish she'd give over for it doesn't seem right especially when Theo has come all the way out to see me. She keeps on about how it's pretty obvious the only reason Andrew came to Vietnam was to spend more time with me. I'm not sure about that though it would be flattering to think it of course.

I don't think Laura knows what to make of Theo or of Trevor and when we were all getting into our taxis at the airport yesterday she started laughing at the suitcase the pair of them had brought out with them and started calling it a right old dinosaur. I can see what she means for it's one of those old-fashioned cardboardy ones with the metal corners. I suppose Theo and Trevor must seem a bit countryish to her and I really don't know what they were thinking when they decided to bring the one suitcase <u>between</u> them like some old married couple. But Theo is definitely not cut out for travelling and even though we're staying in such a fancy hotel I swear he's done nothing but complain non-stop since he got here but as I said to him if he'd to put up with what I had to when we were in China, well, then he'd have reason to complain.

There's a knock on the door which is probably the others and I feel tired already even thinking about what Debbie has in store for us today. I haven't had a chance yet to talk to Laura about Dylan and Debbie's carry-on but I definitely must make sure to before the day is out.

Café des Amis. Early afternoon.

Debbie

1.00 p.m. We, the we being the motley crew of Laura, Maeve, Genevieve, Trevor, Theo, Maeve's Dad and myself, have just been to the *Museum of the Vietnamese Revolution*. Theo and Trevor loved it. It turns out they consider themselves quite the masterminds on the subject of the Vietnam War, or the American War, as it's called here though I'm not sure if dressing in combats was entirely appropriate.

We're off to the war museum next, then to Ho Chi Minh's Mausoleum and, if we've time to fit it in and if we can persuade Genevieve to get on her feet again, to the Ho Chi Minh Museum. We stopped for a quick lunch and now Genevieve's refusing to budge.

She's acting as coolly towards me as she was back in Beijing but life's too short to spend it trying to unravel the mysteries of Genevieve's mind and if she's not going to tell me what's up, I'm not going to let it bother me. I did ask Maeve this morning if Genevieve had said anything to her which might explain why she's being so odd but she hadn't. Maeve says I'm probably imagining it for she hasn't noticed anything. But then I wouldn't expect Maeve would.

The Continental Hotel. That evening.

Genevieve

Ho Chi Minh. Ho Chi Minh. Ho Chi Minh. Ho Chi Minh. Ho Chi Minh. God almighty! I am <u>sick</u> to the teeth of Ho Chi Bloody Minh!

First thing after lunch Debbie dragged us off to this mausoleum to see Ho Chi Minh himself though he's been dead for goodness knows how long. What is it with Debbie? What is this fascination she has with dead leaders? She was the very same in Beijing taking us off to see that other dead fella. At least this time I had the sense to wait outside. I mean you'd think one dead leader would be enough for anyone in one lifetime and anyway who wants to see any in the first place? And if that wasn't enough, she then made us go to see Ho Chi Minh's house though why I can't say for it definitely was nothing to write home about and not at all the kind of house you'd expect for a leader of a country. And then she dragged us all off to the Ho Chi Minh Museum which was about as boring as museums go and that's saying something. And of course nothing would do Debbie but to go poking her beak into every room and examining every single exhibit as if it was <u>the</u> most fascinating stuff <u>ever</u>. I can't believe she's really that interested and I'd say she's just putting it on in order to impress Trevor. Speaking of Trevor. I know I've encouraged him in the past when it came to Debbie but not any more. No, sir! When I get a chance I'm going to take him aside and warn him off.

But both he and Theo just loved that first museum we went to which was all about the Vietnam War. Theo said it was the best one of the lot and I think the pair of them would have spent the entire day there if they'd the chance. Theo nearly used an entire roll of film taking picture after picture of the old plane wrecks out in the front which is saying something for usually he's very careful with his money and that.

We're going out for dinner now but hopefully we won't be out too late for we have to be up at the crack of dawn tomorrow to catch a bus to some place where we're going to be getting the ferry out to some island but at least there won't be any museums and that out there and Debbie will have no choice but to let us relax.

She should relax a bit more herself and she nearly bit the head off me a little while ago because I started on about those little boys again, the ones who should be at school but are on the streets selling postcards instead. She was very rude and started on about how I should get some sense since it's not like they were there by choice. I can see what she's saying but she didn't need to be so cross. Laura started calling her Saint Debbie but not to her face of course.

[Save Address(es)][Block]   [Previous][Next][Close]
From: "Tobin, Laura"<lauratobin@hotmail.com>
To: "Wilson, Felix"<felix@fmsounds.com>
Subject: Losing your marbles . . .
Date: 11 Dec, 23:01:01
[Reply][Reply All][Forward][Delete]

Why on earth did you e-mail me that silly piece of writing?
You can't possibly believe I wrote it.

I am a serious journalist, Felix. I am over here, on my own,
researching a book on Chinese literature and culture, as you
know. How could you think for a moment that I'm the
writer of some silly diary about a bunch of girls backpacking about Asia together? And what on earth makes you
think the girls in the piece are the ones I went to school
with in Portrea? The last time I saw them was on the flight
to Beijing.

I think you're losing it, Felix.

12th December

Maeve

T & T have *got* to be the biggest cheapskates *ever*.

Even G's embarrassed by them!

Earlier – when we were checking into our (dinky little) hotel right by the harbour, the pair of them nearly collapsed in a heap when they learnt the price of the rooms but (since Dad had already used his Visa card to put down a holding deposit) G managed to persuade them that they'd no choice but to stay & that it wasn't really all that expensive – something I *never, ever, ever* thought I'd hear G say.

Then – this evening – when it came to ordering wine at the restaurant, Theo announced he didn't want any but then proceeded to drink twice as much as the rest of us & then refused to contrib. anything towards the cost because he hadn't ordered it.

Like *hello*!!!

Mean isn't the word!

Remarkable really, how well-matched himself & G are.

Genevieve

I'd never have thought it before but Theo can come across as being a little bit mean sometimes. Like when we

341

were checking into our hotel today he kept repeating over and over at the top of his voice about how sixty American dollars was daylight robbery. I was absolutely mortified. And I never thought I'd say this but out of his familiar surroundings he can seem almost stupid. I mean to say it's different at home. Everyone knows him there and respects him and the rest of his family are always running to him for advice but over here he really is a fish out of water.

And I'm not even going to go into what happened on the boat on our way over to the island but to tell the truth I was <u>never</u> so embarrassed in all my born days and I just wish they weren't so loud or so noticeable.

Debbie

10.00 p.m. When we went out to eat this evening I thought I might try and deflect Trevor's amorous attentions away from me and get him interested in Laura instead. Back in our school days she was the one all the boys fancied. All bar Trevor it seems for she holds "no appeal whatsoever" as she was always "a bit too clever and a bit too lah-di-dah" for his liking and, anyway, he likes his women with "a bit more meat on them".

So, if he fancies me, does that mean he considers me fat, stupid and the opposite to lah-di-dah?

An Asian Diary

*E*ver since I can remember it's been my ambition to travel. When I was a child I often pictured myself in exotic, far-flung places such as this. Sometimes I even imagined my travelling companions – sophisticated, knowledgeable types, and of course the occasional handsome male.

But never, ever in my wildest dreams could I have anticipated that I'd have the Bunter brothers along with me. The other day as I stood there, looking up at Thicker's khaki-clad backside as he clambered onto the fighter plane in the courtyard of the Museum so that Thicko could get yet another "action" shot of him, I felt like crying. How had it come about that, when I finally got my chance to travel, I end up with these two bozos in tow?

And today, when we were making our crossing to the island we're now staying on, they were truly at their best. Or worst. Midway across, the crew anchored to allow us passengers to take a quick swim in the sea but, afterwards, as we were all dressing, and the crew were starting up the boat again, one of the other passengers called out that there were two whales in the water which sent everyone rushing to have a look only to be met by the sight of Thicko and Thicker gaily splashing about. Since they didn't appear to have any notion of getting out of the water one of the crew began yelling at them but they just continued frolicking merrily, seemingly oblivious to the fact that they were holding everybody up. But even though we all began shouting they took little notice until, eventually, Mr C got so annoyed he told the skipper to start up the boat again.

It was only then, when they saw us pull away, that they began swimming frantically after us and when they finally managed to clamber aboard, puffing and panting and spluttering like they were fit to die for I'd say they must have swallowed their own body weight in water, Mr C began scolding them for behaving like children which they took fierce umbrage to, especially Thicko. I don't think it helped that Geraldine seemed to be taking Mr C's part.

No, they haven't changed a bit since our school days.

13th December

On the beach, Cat Ba Island. Early afternoon.

Maeve
I just *love* this place.
Done nothing but get up late, eat, swim, laze around, then eat, swim & laze around some more.
Funny to see Dad & Dylan together.
Dylan is doing his utmost to impress Dad.
He's sitting there all polite, asking these earnest, interested qsts about Dad's work & nodding enthusiastically at his answers (tho' I just *know* he's bored senseless).
For his part, Dad is not being at all nice to Dylan – he's treating him like he's some kinda teenage scumbag.

Debbie
1.30 p.m. This is the life. Sun, sea and . . . sex. Or at least there would be if Trevor had his way!
As soon as he noticed I'd changed into my bikini he remarked on how well I filled it and when I pointed out that I could say the same about him and his bathing trunks, for that's the only way to describe what he's wearing, he guffawed, again the only fitting description of the sound he made, and said "Oh you betcha, baby!"

I tried explaining that I meant the girth of his waist but he wasn't listening.

Maeve

But it *is* a pity things are so strained between Dad & myself. The whole business of him having a girlfriend bothers me – far more than it should. It's not like I expect him & Mum to get back together or anything & Dad's always had girlfriends & it's never really troubled me before.

I don't know.

Maybe it's just that the notion of girlfriends *plural* is easier to handle than girlfriend *singular*.

And it's easy to understand what he saw in his previous girlfriends (youth, beauty & the reflected glory of the middle-aged male snaring the young female) & that made it less threatening somehow.

But Mei is this unknown factor & I just *can't* see what the attraction is

Which makes it a little scarier.

If that makes any sense . . .

Debbie

2.15 p.m. I swear I'll go mad listening to the running commentary from the pair of them on the girls passing up and down.

"She's not bad, eh, Theo?"

"Except for her legs, Trev, they're a bit bandy."

"Yeah. I suppose.

"They're too short for the rest of her that's what's wrong and she's got no neck to speak of."

"Hmmm. True enough."

"Ugh! That's disgusting!"

"What Theo? What?"

"That's just gross!"

"What? What's just gross?"

"Look! The stubble on your one's legs! I wouldn't go near her if she was the last woman in the world. "

Like she'd want him to!

Maeve

And Dad & Mei seem to get on so well together. They're kinda like this contented old married couple.

All I rem. about Mum & Dad & when they were with one another was the shouting & the screaming & the doors slamming & the one or other of them forever storming out.

Genevieve

I wish Trevor hadn't come with Theo for he brings out a side of Theo that to be perfectly honest I'm not really all that keen on. When Trevor isn't around Theo is quite gentlemanly but when they're together he becomes what can only be described as boorish and I've never noticed it more so than in the past few days and I think being in the company of someone like Andrew highlights it even more so.

And of course Andrew wouldn't be used to such behaviour and neither would Laura though both of them are far too polite to say much about it although Andrew was driven to saying something on the boat yesterday but I can't say I blame him and sometimes from the look on Laura's face I definitely get the impression that she doesn't really approve of Theo. I just wish they could be a little less loutish.

Debbie

5.00 p.m. When Trevor was changing out of his trunks just now, Laura dared him to drop them which was a big mistake. I don't know what she was thinking of for she should have known he'd be only too happy to oblige.

Theo seems to think it's the funniest thing ever but poor Genevieve looks like she's fit to kill both of them. Dylan of course is delighted with the pair of them and is urging them on all the time.

I'm beginning to think it's time for me to strike out on my own.

Maeve

I guess the problem is that Mei & Shao just seem to be much more Dad's family now than me & Mum.

And if Dad stays with Mei then he'll prob. end up living in China forever.

[Save Address(es)][Block]   [Previous][Next][Close]
From: "Tobin, Laura"<lauratobin@hotmail.com>
To: "Tony Howard"<editor@idolmagazine.co.uk>
Subject: Your e-mail
Date: 13 Dec, 23:01:01
[Reply][Reply All][Forward][Delete]

Dear Tony,
You asked me to broaden the scope of my writing so I did.
That last piece I sent you was almost entirely about two new
people but you're still not satisfied.
I'm not sure you know yourself what you're looking for.
Regards,
Laura.

14th December

Meeting Café, Cat Ba Island. Early morning.

Genevieve

Another thing I've noticed about Theo is how he's not half as confident when he's away as he is at home but tries to hide it with all the blustering he goes on with. And Trevor is as bad. And they can be so rude too. They really took the biscuit last night in the restaurant where we were having dinner. All the other customers were chatting quietly amongst themselves but Theo and Trevor were talking so loudly they were <u>practically</u> <u>yelling</u> and of course everyone was turning around to see what all the commotion was about though neither of the twins seemed to care and went right on commenting on everyone else at the tops of their voices and didn't even notice that some of the other people there could definitely understand English. And then they began taking turns at reading the menus aloud in pretend Vietnamese accents and laughing at one another as if it was the most hilarious thing ever. And then when their meals arrived down they started poking at everything and holding up bits of food and asking each other what they thought this piece was and that piece was. <u>It</u> <u>was</u> <u>mortifying</u>. Heaven only knows what Andrew must have thought of them.

Maeve

Last night Dylan & I had *the* worst fight *ever*.

Over T & T – of all things!

Imagining I'd find it as funny as he did, he started telling me how he'd given both of them a joint before we went out to dinner – he says they'd been pestering him non-stop & (being curious to see how they'd react) he gave in.

Like, how stupid is that?

So then I ask him what if G had noticed.

So then he starts laughing like crazy – so crazy he can hardly talk. There were these, like, tears rolling down his face and I was, like, what? what? until finally he came out with it – he gave G some pot back in Songpan!!

And there I was trying to hide Dylan's bad habits from *her*!

Room 22, Cat Ba Hotel. Evening time.

Genevieve

When we got back to the hotel this evening I tried talking to Theo about how I didn't like the way he and Trevor have been carrying on but he just told me to give over and not to be putting on such airs and graces. But I know they're getting on the girls' nerves for between them Maeve and Debbie must have told them to shut up about a hundred times when we were on the beach today not that they took any notice. At one point I thought Debbie was going to hit Trevor when he announced that the only reason girls wear bikinis is so that men will gawk at them.

And if that wasn't enough to have to deal with, Dylan has gone and told Maeve about me smoking pot that night in Songpan and of course she thinks this is the biggest joke ever and keeps going "hey man!" and making stupid peace signs at me and calling me dude and then falling about all over the place laughing and I'm afraid of my life Theo will hear her and want to know what she's on about. I think I'd <u>die</u> if he ever found out. He'd be so disappointed and of course there'd be no point in trying to explain how bad things were back then and how I just wasn't myself. If I had been things would <u>never</u> have got to that stage. And what if Maeve tells Andrew about the drugs? I'd be <u>mortified.</u>

I keep asking Laura what we should do about the Dylan and Debbie situation but she just says I'm to leave it up to her and that she'll deal with it. When I asked her did she think Debbie and Dylan were still carrying on she said she thought they probably were. I really hate to see poor Maeve being made a complete fool of and if Laura doesn't do something soon then I'm definitely going to have to take matters into my own hands.

[Save Address(es)][Block]   [Previous][Next][Close]
From: "Tobin, Laura"<lauratobin@hotmail.com>
To: "Ivers, Gillian"<gillyivers@indigo.ie>
Subject: What a surprise!
Date: 14 Dec, 19:21:50
[Reply][Reply All][Forward][Delete]

Gilly,
Such a surprise to get an e-mail from you out of the blue! I
didn't even know you had my e-mail address.
If you're so concerned about how myself and Felix are doing,
I suggest you ask him. You are in the same country as him
after all.
Laura.

[Save Address(es)][Block]   [Previous][Next][Close]
From: "Tobin, Laura"<lauratobin@hotmail.com>
To: "Hull, Chloe"<chloehull@hotmail.com>
Subject: [none]
Date: 14 Dec, 19:28:33
[Reply][Reply All][Forward][Delete]

Dear Chloe,
Your sudden and, I have to say, rather unexpected interest
in my welfare is rather surprising but I'm very well, thank
you.
As for how Felix is keeping, all I can suggest is that you, and
Gilly Ivers form a posse and make it your business to go and
ask him. If you don't already know.
Laura.

15th December

Beach, Cat Ba Island. Afternoon.

Genevieve

I've been doing nothing but worry in case Maeve goes and says anything to Theo about me smoking pot in Songpan so on our way down to the beach I decided to ask her not to but she just started laughing and laughing like it was the funniest thing she'd ever heard and started slapping me on the back and going on about how I "like, kill her totally" and no matter how much I asked her she just wouldn't say what was so funny. All she'd say was that Theo and I were well suited and I don't think she meant it in a nice way either.

Debbie

3.00 p.m. I can't figure out what I've done to Genevieve but she's still not talking to me.

Just now I complimented her on how well she's looking in the bikini she borrowed from Laura and she seemed to think I was teasing her and got very huffy. But I wasn't. It does look fantastic on her, far better than the granny bathing suit she usually wears. Theo can hardly keep his eyes off her.

Room 21, Cat Ba Hotel. Evening time.

Maeve

While the others went in swimming this morning, I found myself on my own with Dad so it seemed like the perfect opp. to bring up the subject of Dylan.

Just wanted to know what Dad thought of him (well, not *strictly* true – guess I wanted to hear Dad tell me what a *wonderful* fellow he thought Dylan was).

So when all Dad would say was that he didn't really know Dylan well enough to give an opinion I kept on & on & on at him (fool that I am) until – eventually – he caved in.

In a nutshell he thinks Dylan's a scruffy, stupid, unreliable, feckless, jobless, futureless layabout.

Hearing this, I did the obvious thing & stormed off.

So then – for the rest of the day – I was giving him the cold shoulder or at least I was until he caught a hold of me & started on about how it was a bit rich of me wanting his approval for my boyfriend when I *so* didn't approve of his girlfriend. (I *hate* when he calls her that! She must be, like, in her 50's!)

So then I shrugged & went, yeah, yeah, yeah, whatever & started to walk away again but he yanked me back (like I was a bold child or something) & started going on & on & on.

How by choosing to ignore Mei I was ignoring a really NB part of him.

How as long as I kept doing that I could never fully know or understand him.

How I was missing out by not allowing myself to get to know the really special person Mei was.

Oh yeah, & how I should stop acting like a selfish spoiled baby!

At this point I said something like how at least that was better than acting like a fool & how it was *sooooooo* obvious to anyone with even $^1/_2$ a brain that Mei was using him & how I just couldn't see what he saw in her for she was plain & boring & so quiet that you'd have to wonder if she was quite right in the head.

So he's, like, livid. Like, *seriously* red in the face.

So I say to myself – Maeve, it's time to get outta here.

So I get up.

But he, like, shoves me back down on the seat & starts on this long spiel.

All about the hard life she's had.

And boy! Did he lay it on!

He starts off with her parents "disappearing" for daring to criticise communism when she was a kid.

And he went on from there.

All about her being sent to live with her Gran 100's of miles way up north.

All about her Gran's farm being taken away & being made into part of a collective.

All about the Gran dying, broken-hearted and penniless after the loss of her farm & the loss of Mei's parents.

All about Mei being sent to live back down south with heartless relatives.

And things didn't get much better for her when she grew up.

When she was in her 20's (& preggers. with Shao) her husband was sent away for re-education and when he came back a yr later he was a broken man & died the following year leaving her a widow.

And there was loads more bad stuff too. Something about a

long-lost daughter and a sister who died when Mei was only 8.

It just went on & on.

All that was missing was the sound of violins in the background.

Which is what I said to him

It just sort of, like, slipped out – I *swear* I didn't really mean it.

But his reaction was *frightening*!

He just stood up, give me this awfully, awfully, *awfully* disappointed look, turned & walked away.

Course it's sad that all those things happened to her and I do feel sorry for her but what I was trying to make him understand was that that's not going to make me like her or want her for a stepmother.

Meanwhile in Room 22.

Genevieve

I just don't get Maeve at all! On the way back from the beach I decided to ask her again what was so funny about telling Theo about me smoking drugs and this time she just turned on me completely and told me to f*** off for myself for she'd a lot more important things on her mind and would I ever stop bugging her.

I don't know why she should be so moody. I know I can be annoying sometimes but there really was no need for her to turn on me like that.

And back in Room 21.

Maeve

Really, *really* wish I hadn't said what I did to Dad.

357

Feeling *very* guilty.

Did try talking to Dylan about it but I don't think he was paying too much attention – seemed a bit strung out.

Seems like he's that way a lot lately tho' when I try saying as much to him, he tells me to shut up & stop nagging.

At least I don't think Dad has noticed.

Prob. just thinks Dylan is that way all the time.

An Asian Diary

*H*onestly it was positively embarrassing the way Mags' boyfriend and her father were drooling over me today. From the time I changed into my skimpy white bikini on the beach until I changed back out of it, I don't think their tongues were in their mouths, not for a moment.

But I have to admit I looked pretty good, even if I say so myself. Geraldine too was all admiration for the bikini I was wearing and wondered how she could never find anything to fit her so well. I could have told her there were a few reasons. Amongst them, the fact that manufacturers don't make the same exciting range to fit people like her as they do to fit the perfect size 10; and, also, *S'Wear Boutique* tends to carry a slightly better range of swimsuits than say, Mrs O' Toole's on Main Street P– which is where Geraldine proudly told me she bought her own unfortunate ensemble.

So, jokingly, I asked her did she want to borrow one of the seven I'd brought for though I did pack lightly there are certain things a girl can't do without. Immediately she said yes and, somehow, managed to squeeze herself into one of my bikinis. I won't even go into what she looked like but it was not a pretty picture. That she was lying right beside me made matters even worse and only served to highlight the difference between our respective figures.

And I swear she actually believed me when I told her Mr C could hardly take his eyes off her. Sometimes I almost feel guilty she's so gullible. Sometimes I'm tempted to see just what I could make her believe.

Anything I'd like her to, I imagine. It's all too easy.

16th December

Residents' lounge, Blue Star Hotel, Hanoi. Evening time.

Genevieve

Debbie dragged us all off to some temple this afternoon though to be perfectly honest I was exhausted as we'd only arrived back from Cat Ba at lunchtime. I really must remember to buy some deodorant for I keep forgetting to and the bus we got on the way back from the temple was absolutely sweltering so I was all sticky and it's a wonder I didn't get heat-stroke which would be just my luck on top of the crick I got in my neck from sitting in a draught on the ferry. But the worst thing of all is that Andrew was suddenly called back to Beijing on business and I hardly got a chance to say goodbye as he left for the airport as soon as we arrived into Hanoi.

Laura has started on again and is trying to tell me that these supposed feelings he has for me are probably the reason for his sudden departure as he probably couldn't bear to see me and Theo together but I don't know. I don't think anyone looking at Theo and me at the moment could be jealous for we haven't exactly been getting on all that well. I'm sure something came up at Andrew's work exactly as he said but when I said as much to Laura she started tapping her nose and acting like she knew something I didn't but wouldn't say what. I hate it when she goes on like that.

Debbie

9.15 p.m.   Maeve's Dad has gone back to Beijing. She says he was called back to work unexpectedly but I think they might have got a serious falling-out judging from the mood Maeve's in.

In one way it was probably just as well for I noticed that Laura had begun playing the femme fatale once again and was making advances in Andrew Clancy's direction. What is she playing at?

Maeve

Dad left today.

He barely spoke to me 'cept to say (as he got into the taxi) that the only reason he'd told me all that stuff about Mei was cos he'd hoped it might help me understand her reticence & her vulnerability (his words) & that I might be a little more sympathetic to her.

He wouldn't even let me go to the airport with him.

Actually he did say a couple of other things.

That – on reflection – even a strung-out, no-hoper like Dylan (also his exact words) was prob. too good for the likes of me.

And – that as well as being crap (my words) at picking boyfriends, I was crap at picking friends too for L was the biggest bitch he'd ever met.

The only one he'd a good word to say about was Debs. He said he couldn't understand what she was doing still hanging around with me but guessed it was out of some misplaced loyalty cos we'd been friends since way back.

Genevieve

I've just realised that I might never see Andrew again.

An Asian Diary

Mr C left today. He and Mags had a big falling-out. When I pressed her to tell me what happened, she wouldn't say much but I gather she was being nasty about his dowdy old girlfriend. But what does he expect? If he chooses to take up with someone like her then he's just letting himself wide open for comment. And, given that he's forever ogling at me, it obviously can't be love. And he's certainly not with her for her money either judging by her sad, old sorry appearance.

But I have a confession. I was a tiny bit naughty today. Well very naughty in fact. As soon as Mr C had left, I gave in to temptation and started making out to Geraldine that Mr C had hinted that the reason he was leaving so suddenly was because he couldn't bear seeing her and Thicko together. And did she believe me? Of course she did. This is Geraldine we're talking about. She's so easy to manipulate, it's scary! Despite all evidence to the contrary and the very obvious fact that Mr C has eyes for only me, I think I actually convinced her that he's madly in love with her.

But though she's feeling very down in herself over Mr C's departure that hasn't stopped her turning her attention again to other matters, namely Wannabe and Deanne. She started on at me again today, wanting to know if I'd said anything to Mags about the "situation" so I told her I was waiting for the time to be right but she wasn't satisfied and started mumbling about how it seemed to her that since the time was never going to be right she was just going to have to start taking matters into her own hands. Not that she will of course.

But strangely, an hour later, Deanne, who rarely has much to say to me for we tend to get along best when we avoid one another, asked me if I knew why Geraldine doesn't talk to her any more. I told her I had no idea.

17st December

Residents' lounge, Blue Star Hotel. Early evening.

Debbie

7.00 p.m. Dylan's just told me that Laura is still coming onto him. I know opposites are meant to attract but there are opposites and then there's Laura and Dylan. I can't believe she fancies him.

And what was she doing flirting with Andrew Clancy so much if it's Dylan she's interested in?

Maeve

Dylan can be *so* thick sometimes.

Like, just now he started going on about the good impression he felt he'd made on Dad & how well he thought they'd got along together!

What planet is he on?

And now – as a by-the-way – he's just happened to mention he's heading off on his own for a couple of days.

Tomorrow!!!!

If he'd any cop-on, he'd see I really need him around right now.

Like, how selfish is that???????

Debbie

8.15 p.m. Things aren't going well for Maeve. Dylan's

just told her he's going up north on his own tomorrow for a couple of days.

I'd say one of his reason for leaving is to get away from Laura. It'd be just his style to run away although the north's reputation for opium could well be his reason for choosing to go there in particular.

An hour later.

Genevieve

The others have all gone out for a drink as Dylan's going off on his own tomorrow and good riddance to bad rubbish I say! I only wish he'd take Debbie with him! But at least they won't be able to get up to anything what with him being out of the picture. There was no way I was going out with them even though Theo kept on at me to but I was feeling a bit down and upset in my stomach and tired out and not at all in the mood to talk to either Dylan or Debbie. I really wish Laura would say something to Maeve about them soon or else I'll be forced to take matters into my own hands but she keeps telling me to give her time and that she'll deal with it.

Anyway it's just as well to have an early night tonight seeing as how we're not going to get much chance of sleep tomorrow night as we're getting an overnight bus to some place called Nha Trang which will be a nightmare of a journey no doubt but at least it'll mean we won't have to pay for accommodation which is something as I'm way over budget.

I think Theo is a bit jealous of how friendly Laura and I have become and I don't know how many times he's asked me what I'm doing being so pally with her when she was always so rotten to me in school and he keeps trying to make me remember all these terrible things she's supposed to have done to me back then but he's exaggerating of course and she really wasn't all that bad and anyway people do change and whatever about before we get on really well together now at least most of the time. And anyway what business is it of his? I wish people wouldn't go poking their nose in where it's not wanted.

[Save Address(es)][Block]   [Previous][Next][Close]
From: "Tobin, Laura"<lauratobin@hotmail.com>
To: "Tobin, Gerard"<gerrytobinportreatarmac.ie>
Subject: What a surprise!
Date: 17 Dec, 21:45:23
[Reply][Reply All][Forward][Delete]

Hello Gerry,
Surprise! Surprise! I didn't know the Internet had reached
Portrea!
No, I'm not going to be over from London for Christmas.
I'm on holidays, in Asia. Mum and Dad already know this.
Laura.

18th December

Maeve

Dylan left early this a.m.

Would have been nice if he'd asked me if I wanted to go with him.

Not that I would have – but he could've asked.

We're on an overnight bus now to the coast.

Debbie

11.05 p.m. This overnight bus we're getting to Nha Trang is packed. Genevieve's the only passenger fortunate enough to have a seat to herself although Theo did try sitting in alongside her when we first got on but she was having none of it and managed to shove him back out again so now he's sharing with Trevor and looking very dejected.

Genevieve

God Almighty! After I finally managed to shove Theo out I purposely put a bag up on the seat beside me so as to discourage anyone from sitting there so that I'd at least have a bit of room for when I'll want to get some sleep later on but this awful American woman's just plonked herself down

369

beside me without even asking permission and she has this mangey-looking mongrel with her who she's put sitting on her lap and who's now slobbering and drooling all over the place and staring up at me and the woman is staring at me too now and I think she's waiting for me to pat the dog or something and tell it what a nice doggy it is! She'll be waiting!

Debbie

11.55 p.m. After much coaxing, Maeve's finally told me what happened between her dad and herself and why he left so suddenly. I can't believe she said what she did to him. She can be such a self-centred little bitch.

Genevieve

I've a good mind to complain to the driver about the dog. Not that I think he'd take much notice for he's far too busy gaping in his mirror at these two French ones in the seat behind him who are wearing shorts three sizes too small. <u>At least.</u> I mean to say there's no way they can be comfortable. And really the driver would be better served keeping his eyes on the road and if we crash and there's an enquiry later I'll make no bones about laying the blame fairly and squarely on his doorstep.

And he isn't the only one gaping either. Maeve just told Trevor to pick his tongue up off the floor and put it back in his mouth. No doubt Theo would probably be as bad only he knows I'm watching him.

Debbie

1.00 a.m. I can't believe Maeve. She now says she'd be

willing to talk to her dad if he were to apologise to her first. He apologise to her! She's the one who's way out of order which is what I told her so now she's not talking to me.

Genevieve

Whatever about Theo and Trevor gaping at least they're not the ones driving this bloody bus and given the way that lunatic behind the wheel is carrying on none of us will even get to go to the inquiry since he'll probably have us all killed outright. Does he not understand that the first rule of driving is to keep <u>your</u> <u>eyes</u> <u>on</u> <u>the</u> <u>road</u> <u>and</u> <u>not</u> <u>on</u> <u>young</u> <u>French</u> <u>ones</u> <u>wearing</u> <u>shorts</u> <u>that</u> <u>are</u> <u>barely</u> <u>there?</u>

But the last thing I took my diary out to write about was the stupid driver and what I actually want to write about is Theo and how I feel about him and how I feel about things in general.

You see if I'm to be honest and if I can't be honest when writing in my diary then when can I be, I need to face up to what I've been refusing to admit to all along and that's that I am no longer in love with Theo. <u>If</u> I ever was. God Almighty! This woman beside me is insane! She keeps petting the mongrel and cooing at him and calling him "Baby". I'm beginning to think that if people insist on bringing dogs onto public transport then they should be made to put them in the boot. But looking back on our seven years together it's obvious to me now that our relationship has always been lacking in that something special. I like Theo of course I do, maybe even love him, but that's not the same as being <u>in</u> <u>love</u> with him though I suppose I'd managed to convince myself otherwise all these years. But now that I am actually experiencing true love for the first time I can see how much our relationship was lacking. God Almighty! Can't she see I'm just not interested in her or in her stupid dog or in her long rigmarole of a story about how she rescued him from his destiny as someone's dinner? Like I care! And she's really making it very hard for me to concentrate. Anyway the second thing I need to admit is that I'm in love with Andrew Clancy. There. I've finally said it. And it's the truth though I've been denying it all along even to myself. But I'm in love. I am. I, Genevieve Price, am in love with Andrew Clancy. I love him. I do, I really do. I love him because he's the kindest, gentlest, handsomest, most sophisticated man to ever walk the face of the earth and I think about him all day long. He's the first thing to come into my mind when I wake in the morning and the last thing I think about as I drift off to sleep. For the first time in my life I am truly in love and it feels wonderful.

Of course I know there's no real chance of a future for me and Andrew though Laura keeps telling me that I have to believe in romance and that I have to just go for it. And even if he was interested in me how could we ever work anything out what with us living so far away from one another? And anyway I might never even see him again. It's just silly to be listening to Laura and I should make up my mind for once and for all to forget about him. God Almighty! How am I supposed to write all this down when that stupid dog is tearing up and down the aisle peeing wherever and whenever it wants and yapping like mad while his owner sleeps her stupid head off? She's the only person on the bus he's not annoying and while she's snoring away to beat the band he's keeping everyone else awake. Her head keeps flopping onto my shoulder too which is <u>very</u> annoying and it's making it very hard for me to keep writing. And I have hours of this to put up with yet. Anyway I know it'll be difficult but the only thing for me to do is to put Andrew Clancy right out of my mind and to stop daydreaming about him. I guess I should really try to get some shuteye.

It's impossible to sleep for I keep thinking about Andrew. I haven't said anything to anyone about my feelings for him only to Laura of course since after all she's the one who pointed out to me in the first place that he might have feelings for me though I'm still not convinced he has for he certainly has never said anything but I just can't help imagining how wonderful it would be if he was really interested in me.

But why am I even thinking about all this? What's the use? I should just go to sleep. It's not like there can ever be any kind of a future in it. He's gone back to Beijing and I'll probably never even see him again. In fact I think realising that is what made me see clearly how much I'd fallen for him.

I don't think that woman knows the first thing about dogs. When we stopped for a toilet break and don't even get me started on the state of the toilets Debbie asked the woman if she'd had the dog wormed and so ever since we got back on the bus the woman has been picking and poking at the dog's fur, checking to see if she can find any! I don't know a lot about dogs but even I know Debbie was talking about his insides and not his outsides.

Looking over at Theo I just have to ask myself how I ever

thought he was good-looking. Right now he's sound to the world with his head flung right back and his mouth hanging wide open and he's snoring like I don't know what. Of course I'm going to have to break it off with him as soon as I get a chance which will be a very hard thing to do for I'm still very fond of him and I hate hurting him but I'm sure he'll see that it's for the best. It just wouldn't be fair to keep on stringing him along not now when I'm no longer one hundred per cent in love with him.

The dog lady is awake again and has discovered this teeny-weeny pimple right beside her dog's little you-know-what and she keeps asking me to look at it to see if I think it could be something serious. What does she think I am? A vet? All I want is to sleep but it's impossible. "Baby" is stinking the bus out.

I don't even know when I'll see Andrew again or if I will ever even see him again. It makes me very sad.

An Asian Diary

The mouse roars. Suddenly bumbling, half-witted Thicko has become all-protective of his beloved Geraldine and has told me that I'm to leave her alone. With the sort of logic he shares with Geraldine, he told me today that he doesn't know what my game is but he's on to me. Poor old Geraldine. Even her own boyfriend can't believe that someone like me could want to be friends with someone like her simply because I like her.

But what Thicko doesn't know is that Geraldine is no longer in love with him, as she's confessed to me. It's amazing what a little subtle hinting from her new best friend can do. Like turn what was heretofore a boyfriend she was perfectly happy with into someone she can hardly bear to look at.

I don't imagine she's ever had any problems before with the way he slurps his soup or brings his face to his spoon rather than vice versa. I doubt she ever noticed the way he's forever picking between his teeth. I'd wager that, until recently, she considered socks worn with sandals the height of sartorial elegance. And it's funny, it's not like I even have to say much. In fact I hardly say a word. All it takes is an arched eyebrow and a disdainful curve of the lip.

So she's no longer in love with Thicko. In fact she doubts she ever was. But the irony of it all is that if ever there was a perfectly suited couple then it's Geraldine and Thicko. But though that may be, it's Mr C Geraldine's decided she's in love with though she has confided that there probably isn't much chance of a future for them. Talk about stating the obvious! Not least because of his sudden departure.

Nevertheless I think my next challenge will be to convince Geraldine that a rosy future for her and Mr C is not only a possibility but a probability.

19th December

Debbie

1.30 p.m. Ever since we arrived onto the beach Genevieve's been twisting and turning and sighing and complaining about the heat and the sand but at last Maeve's found a way of keeping her quiet.

Whenever her moaning gets too much, she tells her that one of the masseuses working on the beach is heading our way so immediately Genevieve closes her eyes and starts snoring. She's afraid that if they see her awake they'll be straight over to her and will somehow manage to coerce her into getting a massage and, even worse, into paying for it.

Genevieve

Unlike the others I have *never* understood the attraction of just lying about on the sand. At least on Cat Ba it wasn't so hot but it's just bloody boiling today. We've been lying here now for over two hours and I'm sweating like mad and I really must remember to buy some deodorant for I keep on forgetting and I'm all sticky for I've drenched myself in factor 30 though I just know I'm bound to have missed out some bit and I'll probably end up with blisters the size of golf

377

balls like I did that time when my parents rented the bungalow for a week in Co. Clare years ago. And on top of everything the sand is driving me <u>crazy</u> for it's getting in everywhere and even under my togs where it's making me fierce itchy. And if that wasn't bad enough Theo is doing my head in for he's like an overgrown schoolboy chasing these little kids all over the place and of course they just love it and are squealing like mad which is piercing my eardrums not to mind making it very hard for me to concentrate and to make matters worse they're throwing sand up everywhere.

Trevor started slagging Theo off a while ago about how fond he was of kids and how he'll be wanting to start a family of his own some day soon. You'd think Trevor was a real wild boy himself from the talk of him but I don't think Theo minded and in fact he seemed pleased if anything for he just smiled over at me and said something about how it wouldn't be the worst thing in the world. It's funny but I'd kind of forgotten how fond Theo is of kids. That's another reason why we should split up for I'd as soon have a dog or a cat as a child for they're a lot less work and to be honest I've never really got the whole thing with children. They spend years and years wanting this and wanting that and then they grow up and move on. Now if it was Andrew I was with there wouldn't be any pressure for he already has a grown-up family as in Maeve.

Maeve
Just checked my e-mails.
Nothing from Dylan.
No big surprise there & he has only been gone for, like, a day but it feels like *ages*.

There was one from Mum tho' telling me that she'll be flying into Bangkok on the 3rd Jan.

Am *not* looking forward to that *at all*.

And I'm not looking forward to telling the others – they're going to go ape!

Least it's not for a while yet.

Genevieve

But then again I think after last night's experience on the bus with that dreadful woman and her rotten mongrel you can include me out when it comes to dogs. I guess a cat would be the easiest of the lot to look after but then who's to say I'd have a pet of any kind.

I'd say Theo will take our break-up very badly. After all we have been going out for seven years now which is why I've decided that since Christmas is only days away there's no point in breaking his heart more than I have to so I'm going to wait until after Christmas. It's funny but I'd never have taken Theo for the jealous kind before but he was on at me again this morning about Laura and how I should be careful of her.

I swear himself and Trevor are going to fry and I keep telling them that they should really put on some of my factor 30 but they only laugh at me and keep lashing on the baby-oil. It is hard to imagine it's that time of the year again for it's not a bit Christmassy and while we're lying here in the sun like this it's weird to think that everyone at home is rushing about in the cold and the wet trying to buy last-minute presents and decorations and turkeys and whatnot.

[Save Address(es)][Block]   [Previous][Next][Close]
From: "Tobin, Laura"<lauratobin@hotmail.com>
To   "Lewis, Timothy"<lewissolicitors@lineone.net.ie>
Subject: Your outstanding bill
Date: Dec 19, 19:07:31
[Reply][Reply All][Forward][Delete]

Dear Timothy,

It seems there was some glitch on the part of the bank which is why your account wasn't settled.

Obviously I've very embarrassed by this but my bank manager assures me that the money will be transferred immediately.

Regards,

Laura.

20th December

Debbie

2.20 p.m. I think everyone is losing it. Maybe it's the heat. I'd just begun chatting to these Welsh guys who're sunbathing beside us but Trevor kept butting in and acting as if he and I were a couple and then Genevieve started warning them off, saying that I mightn't look like a man-eater but they'd want to watch out as I was notorious!

What they were telling me about before Genevieve so rudely interrupted them was this column they'd read in some magazine on their flight out the day before yesterday which was about four girls backpacking in Asia. They said it was uncanny how like us the characters were and that Genevieve especially was the double of one of them. When Genevieve butted in at that point and started going on about me being a man-eater they started laughing and kept repeating how Genevieve was this Geraldine character down to a tee.

I hope Laura isn't writing about us!

Genevieve

Maybe Laura's right and maybe the way I feel about Andrew is just too strong to be one-sided. The more I think about him and about him and me the more I'd like to think there might be something in what Laura says as regards his feelings.

As she says, there are just so many things that point to him being interested in me. Like the way he came all the way down to Chengdu to bring me back to Beijing when I was sick. As Laura says, it's not like he'd do that for just anyone. And the way he took such good care of me when I was staying with him. And just the way he spent so much time with me when I was recovering. And I can think of heaps of other little things too. Like the time in his apartment, when we were sitting there chatting and he was telling me how he'd come back to live in Ireland if things were different. By different did he mean if he and I were a couple? Laura definitely thinks so. And then there's the time he told me that he was glad I was a friend of Maeve's as otherwise he'd never have got the chance to get to know someone quite like me. And though I might not be a supermodel I know for a fact that some men find me attractive and maybe it's not unreasonable of me to hope he might be one of them.

Of course I know I have a rival in Mei but as Laura says no man in his right mind is going to pick her over me for she's hardly the catch of the century. And of course since Andrew left Maeve's mum he's developed a reputation for going out with younger women which is something I never knew before and the only one I remember is that young American he was living with over Purcell's Newsagents'.

Debbie is driving me mad. It doesn't seem to bother her one tiny bit that I'm not talking to her and haven't been for ages and most of the time she just carries on like normal although she was a bit mean to me earlier. She was having a great laugh with these two fellas from Wales and from the way they kept looking over at me and sniggering there's no doubt but that it was at my expense though when I asked Debbie she just said it was nothing but I just know she was lying. And I don't know what it is about Trevor but the more I try to warn him off Debbie, the keener he seems to get.

The others keep saying they'll pack up and go any minute now but they've been promising that all morning and to be honest I don't think they've really any intention of budging but are only saying that to keep me quiet. Poor Theo and Trevor are like <u>flaming</u> <u>lobsters.</u>

Maeve

Rang Mum before we came down to the beach.

She kept asking me stupid questions like do I think she should buy some sarong she saw in a pre-Christmas sale in Quinns or would she be better off waiting until she gets to Thailand to buy one.

Don't know *how* I'm going to cope when she comes out.

No e-mail from Dylan again today.

Where is he?

When-oh-when is he coming back?

T 'n' T are, like, totally frying.

Room 19, Mini Hotel Eleven. That evening.

Debbie

8.00 p.m. I just bumped into those Welsh guys again coming up the stairs. It turns out they're staying here too. I asked them if they'd look to see if they can find that magazine they were talking about on the beach today.

[Save Address(es)][Block]   [Previous][Next][Close]
From: "Tobin, Laura"<lauratobin@hotmail.com>
To: "Tobin, Gerard"<gerrytobinportreatarmac.ie>
Subject: [none]
Date: 20 Dec, 23:01:10
[Reply][Reply All][Forward][Delete]

No, I didn't know Mum was in hospital. It didn't exactly make the news headlines over here but if you could get it together to tell me which hospital she's in then I could send her a card.

She's not going to die of a broken hip, Gerry, and it's not like planes leave from here every hour on the hour going direct to Portrea – so no, you can't expect me to change my mind and come home for Christmas. Do you have any idea how much trips like this cost?

Laura.

21st December

Hairdresser's, Nha Trang. Morning.

Maeve

Expected that there'd, like, *definitely*, be an e-mail from Dylan this morning but nothing.

Don't even know where he is.

Don't even know if he's going to get here for Xmas.

Dylan being Dylan just about *anything* could have happened to him.

But the BIG NEWS is that there was an e-mail from Dad telling me he's flying to Nha Trang *tomorrow* to spend Xmas with me!

Says that life's too short, that our relationship's too precious, and that we need to try & patch things before we end up becoming completely estranged.

Maybe he's right. And at least he's trying to make an effort.

Decided I deserved an early Christmas present so I'm getting my hair done in millions of plaits.

It's taking forever – must be here over 2 hrs already but it's beginning to look really cool.

It feels a bit tight but the girl says I'll get used to it.

On the beach. That afternoon.

Debbie

2.00 p.m. Maeve's just told me she's got an e-mail from

her dad telling her he's arranged to fly down to spend Christmas with her. He wants to try and make things right between them while he has the chance and she's still in Asia. She really doesn't deserve a father like him. Genevieve is driving her nuts. She keeps asking her if we should try and arrange something special for him for Christmas Day but Maeve just doesn't want to know. I think the plaits she got put in this morning are giving her a headache and Genevieve isn't helping for she keeps going on about how "red-raw" Maeve's scalp looks She does have a point. It does look a little sore where you can see it through the plaits.

Genevieve

Some big news in that Maeve's dad is flying down to spend Christmas with us! Laura has already started going on about how it's pretty obvious what that means but despite what she says I'm sure his main reason for coming is to see Maeve but I can hardly wait to see him again. I doubt if I'll get so much as a wink of sleep tonight. I mean there I was thinking I might never see him again! I've never felt like this before about anyone. Just imagine if he felt the same way about me! But I have to stop thinking like this for I'll drive myself crazy. I should be happy enough with the fact that I'll be seeing him again.

The other bit of news I heard Maeve telling Debbie is that she hasn't heard a word from Dylan since he left. No wonder she got so annoyed when I asked her when he was going to get here for Christmas. Most likely he's met up with more of his kind and is strung out in some awful dive somewhere with all thoughts of her gone clean out of his head. I've seen the film *Trainspotting* so I know the way these types get.

I swear Theo and Trevor are going to have to be hospitalised if they're not careful and even though they're absolutely roasted from yesterday and the day before they're lashing on the baby oil <u>again</u> today and are lying there sizzling. No less than <u>four</u> complete strangers have come up to them in the time we've been here and advised them that they should move indoors not that they took any notice and I'm already killed from telling them but do you think they'd listen? No, sir!

Debbie

3.30 p.m. Those Welsh guys stopped by to tell me they can't find that magazine anywhere and that they think they must have thrown it out.

Back in the dining-room of the Mini Hotel Eleven. Evening time.

Debbie

8.00 p.m. Genevieve is showing some photos she got developed to the others but not to me of course as she doesn't talk to me these days but, from what I can gather, some of the photos date back as far as Theo and Trevor's birthday of the year before last. Nobody could ever accuse Genevieve of wasting film.

Apart from a single one of the Terracotta Warriors, she doesn't seem to have taken any of the places we've visited and other than those birthday shots there aren't any of Theo. She has however taken quite a few of Andrew Clancy in his apartment in Beijing. I don't know why Maeve doesn't believe me whenever I try telling her that Genevieve has a crush on him.

An Asian Diary

This is the life. Christmas in the sun though I have to say I'm sorry to be missing the seasonal social whirl back home. I never look better than I do in a short black party dress. Except perhaps in a skimpy white bikini.

My millionaire is feeling terribly lonesome. When I phoned him today he told me he's planning to spend Christmas at his parents' country pile and that he'd desperately like me to be there, so much so that he's even offered to fly me back for Christmas. I may be wrong but I think he may have had this idea of proposing to me over the festive season. What would I do if he did? Hard to tell really. I think I'd need to see that country pile first.

But much as I love the buzz of Christmas at home, I think I'm going to enjoy spending it here on the beach without a scrap of tinsel in sight especially as Mr C has arranged to fly down to be with his ungrateful daughter. Isn't parental love an extraordinary thing? Why he can't cut all ties and be done with her, I'll never know.

Geraldine, however, seems to be under the misconception that that Mr C is flying all the way down to see her. Now I wonder where she got that idea? You'd think even she might appreciate that it's his daughter he's coming to see. But not our Geraldine. With a little bit of work I think I could even have her confessing how she feels to him.

22nd December

Room 22, Mini Hotel Eleven. Early morning.

Maeve

Dad's arriving in at 2.

G's insisting on coming to the airport.

Think she'd be better served going with T 'n' T to the hospital to get their sunburn seen to. I get the shivers just looking at them.

Trevor can hardly, like, open his eyes – his face is *that* swollen.

Don't know *what* I'm going to say to Dad when he asks where Dylan is.

And where the hell is he anyway?

Terrace of the Mini Hotel Eleven. That afternoon.

Genevieve

Andrew looked so handsome as he came through customs and the hug he gave me was definitely <u>very</u> <u>friendly</u>. He bought Mei and Shao along with him which is just typical of him being the kind man he is and it's no wonder that Mei is in love with him. I don't think even Maeve knew they were coming with him and she definitely was <u>not</u> pleased.

Theo and Trevor still aren't back from the hospital. Maybe I should have gone with them and there's no question but that I would have too if only they were prepared to wait until I got back from the airport but when I asked Theo to hang on until then he got into a right huff and told me I needn't bother coming. But even if I didn't have any feelings for Andrew I'd still want to go to the airport seeing as how he was just so kind to me.

Maeve
Dad arrived.
Thought he was coming on his own – stupid me!
Brought his housekeeper/lover/whatever (all right, all right – I'll be nice), brought Mei with him.
And her sprog. All right – Shao then.
But does he expect we'll be playing happy families just cos it's Christmas?
Duh?

Room 19, Mini Hotel Eleven. Late that night.

Debbie
10.00 p.m. Poor Theo. He's very upset. He came to me today just after Genevieve left for the airport. He wanted to know if I thought it was odd that she'd chosen to go to the airport over going to the hospital with him. He also wanted to know if I thought she'd gone off him and if she'd said anything to me. I explained how she doesn't talk to me much these days and how he'd be better served asking Laura for if Genevieve's going to confide in anyone, it's most likely to be her.
I can see where he's coming from. Genevieve's forever giving out to him about things that never bothered her before.

[Save Address(es)][Block]   [Previous][Next][Close]
From: "Tobin, Laura"<lauratobin@hotmail.com>
To: "Chunn, Bryan"<bchunn@westernalliancebanks.co.uk>
Subject: My Visa limit
Date: 22 Dec, 23:32:06
[Reply][Reply All][Forward][Delete]

Dear Bryan,
In the absence of a reply to my e-mail of the 30st Nov I'm
assuming my Visa limit has been extended as requested.
I hardly imagine you're going to leave me stranded for
money so far away from home during the festive season!
Regards,
Laura Tobin.

23rd December

Debbie

8.00 p.m. Genevieve's just arrived in with news that she's organised for us all to spend Christmas Day on a boat trip. She found out about it from a flyer she picked up somewhere and it sounds fantastic though $8 doesn't seem an awful lot to pay for a "Super Special Christmas Cruise" as the flyer promises.

Genevieve

If Laura's right and Andrew does really feel the same way about me it's unlikely he's going to do anything about it given our ages and the fact that I'm his daughter's friend which is why it's up to me to take the initiative as Laura keeps saying and I guess she's right. She says if I don't speak up then I'll just spend the rest of my life wondering what might have been. I found out about this Christmas cruise today so I've arranged for us all to go on it. It'll make the day that extra bit special. Christmas Day spent on a cruiser on the clear blue sea would be the perfect setting for me to tell Andrew. If I dare. Of course if he does feel the same way about me I'm not so stupid that I can't see that there'll be an awful lot of obstacles in our way. When I started going out with Theo everyone was dead set against that too including my parents but I didn't let that stop me and it won't stop me now either. It's well known that the path of true love never ran smoothly but it's equally well known that nothing can stand in its way when it really is true love.

I'd better go and check on Theo. I do feel sorry for him but himself and Trevor are just such whingers and they've no one to blame but themselves and if they'd used my factor 30 like I kept telling them to then they wouldn't be in the sorry state they're in. Trevor especially looks a fright. He's like a little pig. His face is still so swollen with sunburn he can hardly open his eyes.

I know I should wait until I've broken it off with Theo before I say anything to Andrew but as Laura pointed out Andrew might have to leave suddenly on business again like he did the last time and I might never get another chance. In fact I might never even see him again. I have to say something to him. Yet I can't break it off with Theo. Christmas time when he is <u>physically</u> <u>sick</u> with sunburn even if it is his own fault is definitely not the time to end our seven-year relationship.

[Save Address(es)][Block]   [Previous][Next][Close]
From: "Tobin, Laura"<lauratobin@hotmail.com>
To: "Tobin, Gerard"<gerrytobinportreatarmac.ie>
Subject: [none]
Date: Dec, 23, 22:10:00
[Reply][Reply All][Forward][Delete]

How do I know where Dad is meant to spend Christmas?
You're a grown man, Gerry. I'm sure you'll work something
out. You could inquire at the hospital. I'm sure they do
Christmas dinners for the close relatives of patients and at
least that way he'd be with Mam. Or why don't you take
him with you to your in-laws? I don't think even they could
object to how much he'd eat. Or can't you and the family
have dinner at his house? So what if it's Brona's turn to go
to her parents? I'm sure they'll survive without you lot.

Christmas Eve

Terrace, Mini Hotel Eleven. Evening time.

Genevieve

I am <u>hopping</u> <u>mad</u> with Theo. He almost deserves to have his heart broken at Christmas for the latest is he claims he saw Laura reading my diary which is a big fat lie of course. I don't know why I bothered even telling Laura what he said for I knew there wasn't a word of truth to it. I mean to say, what interest could Laura have in reading my diary? I tell her everything as it is. Laura says that Theo probably just made it up to cause trouble because he's jealous over how close she and I have become. If he does anything else like that again, then I will break it off with him Christmas or no Christmas. Laura says I'm far too soft.

Dylan arrived back today looking like something even the cat wouldn't drag in. He's in an awful state. Maeve of course is delighted and is all over him though I'd say he hasn't washed for days. I know I haven't said anything to Maeve yet but if I get wind of him and Debbie getting up to their old tricks again I'm definitely taking matters into my own hands no matter what Laura says.

Debbie

10.30 p.m. Dylan's shown up looking very much the

worse for wear. Genevieve keeps muttering about trainspotting.

Maeve

It's funny but even when you're imagining *the* worst-case scenario you don't *really* expect it to happen.

This time it did.

Turns out Dylan was lying in a grotty hotel room, all on his own, strung out &, only for one of the staff arriving in & finding him there & getting him to a hospital who knows what might have been the outcome.

He's recovered fine tho' he still looks very rough as G has pointed out to him about $1/2$ doz. times.

But he might not be so lucky the next time.

Fool!

Fool!

Fool!

Dad wasn't at all impressed with him. He'd be even less impressed if he knew the whole story.

Didn't bother telling the others.

[Save Address(es)][Block]   [Previous][Next][Close]
From: "Tobin, Laura"<lauratobin@hotmail.com>
To: "Wilson, Felix"<felix@fmsounds.com>
Subject: Thank you for the best Christmas present ever!
Date: Dec, 24, 10:45:08
[Reply][Reply All][Forward][Delete]

Dear Felix,
Just writing to wish you a very Happy Christmas and to tell
you that, on reflection, the best Christmas present you
could ever have given me was to break up with me.
For I've moved on to far bigger and far better things.
Now I must go. Andrew is waiting. Yes, that's Andrew who
I first stayed with when I arrived in Beijing. He sailed into
Nha Trang today and we're going to spend Christmas on his
boat. So, when I'm lying out on deck, in my skimpiest
bikini, gazing out over the clear blue sea, basking in the
warm sun, sipping champagne and having my feet massaged
by the love of my life, I'll think of you tucking into your
turkey and brussels sprouts, sweltering in your new
Christmas jumper.
Love and kisses,
Laura.

Christmas Day

On the Super Special Christmas Cruise. Morning.

Debbie

    11.20 a.m. Genevieve is in an awful state. All morning she's been apologising to Andrew and telling him that if she'd any idea of what the "Super Special Christmas Cruise" was going to be like she wouldn't have dreamt of booking us on it.

    Even at $8 it's a rip-off!

Maeve

From the way G's been going on & on & on these last few days I thought we were coming on something along the lines of the QE2

Turns out to be a dodgy wooden boat (most likely retired from fishing for safety reasons) which is crammed with rowdy backpackers the majority of whom are proceeding to get drunk &/or stoned as we go from island to island.

Needless to say Dylan is joining in with tremendous gusto – it's like the last few days never happened.

So much for learning his lesson.

So much for promising to be on his best behaviour in front of Dad.

Debbie

12.45 p.m. What was Genevieve thinking of?

Things are really getting out of hand on the boat. Mei just seems mildly amused by everything and little Shao is absolutely fascinated by the carry-on though on the basis of what he's seeing today he'll probably grow up with a very strange idea of what westerners are like.

And I don't think Dylan is exactly concerned with winning the approval of his prospective father-in-law judging by his carry-on.

That afternoon.

Maeve

This has got to be *the* worst day of my life.

Dad has hardly spoken a word to me – has a face on him like thunder.

I think he's furious at the way Dylan's been carrying on – can't say I blame him.

Can't even *bear* to look at Dylan I'm *soooooo* mad at him.

I did try chit-chatting to Mei cos I thought Dad would like that but it's hard going for we have, like, nothing in common.

As for Shao, what can Dad expect me to have to say to an 8 yr. old who doesn't speak English? Besides (for some v. strange reason) Shao adores T 'n' T & just wants to hang around them all the time.

Don't ask me what he sees in them for T 'n' T have *got* to be 2 of *the* most ignorant yobs to ever walk the face of the earth.

Debs & L are fit to kill them.

I don't even think G is too happy with them – she seems to be casting an awful lot of dirty looks in their direction.

Wedding plans don't seem to figure in her conversation quite so much as they did when Theo was far away in Ireland.

And I can see why.

Like, there they are – lying on deck, two great blobs (their enormous bellies visible for miles around) rating every girl on the boat outta 10, oblivious to the fact that even *the* most indulgent of judges would be hard-pressed to give them so much as a score of one tho' it seems they think they're looking particularly good today & keep referring to their 3rd degree burns as their "tan".

Like, *what* does G see in Theo?

But then, guess there can't be too many men who'd be prepared to put up with all her peculiarities. She is definitely a little bats.

Room 20 at the Mini Hotel Eleven. Evening.

Genevieve

This has been the worst Christmas Day ever. It was so bad that I can hardly bear to think about it let alone write about it. Going on that boat was the worst idea I have ever had in my whole life. Most of the people on it were completely out of control and I know Dylan is hyper at the best of times but today he was absolutely manic. And no prizes for guessing why that was! When we were in swimming he kept diving under the water and pulling at my legs and trying to drag me under and laughing like a loony though it must have been perfectly obvious to him that I wasn't a bit happy with such horseplay. And all Theo and Trevor did all day was eat and eat and go on about how they might as well get value for their money. I can only imagine what Andrew must have thought of them.

And then there was this eejit from Kerry who spent the day absolutely <u>hounding</u> me. He was on a month's holidays which he insisted on telling me all about though why he should think a <u>total</u> <u>stranger</u> would be interested in every little detail I have no idea especially since he was <u>obsessed</u> with his gastric problems and his problems in the other department. Given my own recent experiences I could have told him a story or two if I'd had a mind to. Which I didn't. Laura said that Andrew didn't look one bit happy with me being chatted up! Theo of course didn't even notice being far too busy stuffing his face and staring at all the girls in their skimpy bikinis and racing around like a overgrown kid after little Shao and I don't know why he couldn't have covered himself up with a T-shirt or something like I kept telling him to for he looked a right sight and I know Weight-Watchers is more for women but he really should think about going.

But I must say I felt really lonely what with being so far away from home and all and thinking about Mam and Dad and how they must be missing me terribly. But the worst part of the whole day was that between having that yob in my ear as well as all the other stuff that was going on I didn't even get a chance to talk to Andrew about things so he still doesn't know how I feel.

Theo's just asked me if I'd like to go for a walk with him but I told him I can't as I'm going to have to ring home soon and anyway it's pitch dark outside.

A little later.

Genevieve

If I didn't know any better I'd swear Mam and Dad were already after a couple of drinks when I rang though it's still

401

early in the day back home but they sounded very giddy and kept asking me if I had any news as if they expected that I should and it was very hard to hear them over the shouting and the carrying-on in the background.

I'm trying to avoid being left on my own with Laura for I know she'll start quizzing me straightaway and when she finds out I haven't said anything to Andrew she'll start on at me again and saying things like how I haven't the nerve to make things happen. I suppose she's right but I just wish I was as certain as she is about Andrew's feelings for me. What if we're completely wrong and he doesn't care for me at all?

Room 19.

Debbie

10.00 p.m. When I was ringing home from the payphone downstairs just a short while ago, Theo passed in looking awfully dejected. I can't say I blame him. After coming all the way out here to be with Genevieve for Christmas she practically ignores him for the entire day.

I think she's hanging around with Laura too much. She'd never have acted so horribly before to anyone, let alone Theo.

[Save Address(es)][Block]   [Previous][Next][Close]

From: "Tobin, Laura"<lauratobin@hotmail.com>
To: "Hill, Sally"<shill@democrat.co.uk.>
              "Kane, Christopher"<kaneliteraryagents@aol.com>
              "Chunn, Bryan"<bchunn@westernalliancebanks.co.uk>
              "Lewis, Timothy"<lewissolicitors@lineone.net.ie>
              "Mee, Marsha"<dailyimpact!@compuserve.com>
              "Turner, Colette"<thechronicle@btinternet.com>
              "Jefferies, Jeanie" <jeanieje@bbc.uk>
              "Nicholson, Adam"<adam@weekendmail.co.uk.>
              "Ivers, Gillian"<gillyivers@indigo.ie>
              "Sandra Martin"<sandramart@weekendtimes.co.uk>
              "Crean, Sara-Mari"<sara-mari@magenta.uk>
              "Hull, Chloe"<chloehull@hotmail.com>
Subject: Happy Christmas!
Date: 25 Dec, 21:20:54
[Reply]   [Reply All][Forward][Delete]

Wishing you all a very merry Christmas from a very sunny
Vietnam.
Love,
Laura, XXXX

26th December

Nha Trang Beach. Afternoon.

Debbie

2.00 p.m. Not noticing me lying here, Genevieve's sat down on a deck chair next to Andrew, metres away from where I am and appears to be in the middle of confessing her feelings to him.

2.10 p.m. At least I think she's telling him how she feels about him though she's making very little sense as is often the case with Genevieve when she's overexcited. It's pretty confusing between all her hints and euphemisms and the weird way she keeps referring to herself in the third person.

2.15 p.m. I don't think Andrew has any idea what she's on about or, if he does, he's pretending not to, maybe so as not to embarrass her. In fact I think he's got the impression that Genevieve is talking about his and Maeve's troubled relationship.
Like right now she's going on about how, though there are children involved, she's sure everyone will eventually come to accept the situation. By that I think she means that though Maeve might initially be shocked by the

notion of a new stepmother in the form of Genevieve, she'll probably come to accept it in time. But that's not what Andrew is hearing. It seems to me he thinks Genevieve is talking about the difficulty of getting Maeve to accept Mei as a potential stepmother.

At least I think but hell, who knows! It's all very confusing.

Terrace of the Mini Hotel Eleven. Late afternoon.

Genevieve

I have finally told Andrew how I feel and the brilliant news is that he feels the same way! Honest to God I'm nearly sick with the excitement for it's all just so hard to believe. If only I'd taken Laura's advice earlier I'd have saved myself all that worrying.

Of course I shouldn't get carried away for there are still heaps of obstacles to overcome and it's not like anything definite was said or that we're actually going out together and what we really just talked about was all the obstacles that we'll need to overcome. Like him living in Beijing though he thinks there's a possibility he'll be transferred back to Ireland within the next couple of years. He's obviously been thinking about it a lot for he mentioned how he's already decided he's going to bring Mei back with him. To be honest I'd prefer if he didn't for it's not like I'll need a housekeeper. Still, my mother will be very impressed when she hears that her daughter is going to have a housekeeper no less. And then there's our age, or the generation gap as he called it, but I've always been very mature for my years unlike Maeve as he says. He blames himself and Maeve's mum for spoiling her so much when she was young and feels she might've been better able to deal with their break-up if they hadn't been such indulgent parents. He talked a lot about Maeve. I guess he felt I could understand what with her being my friend and us being the same age.

So, at last we've finally been up front as regards our feelings for one another and though we mightn't have come to any definite arrangement about our future together at least we've starting talking about it.

Room 22.

Maeve

Dad's just come in to tell me he's leaving tomorrow.

Pity nothing's been resolved between us.

Pity Mei & I didn't exactly bond over the festive season – my fault maybe but it was *never* going to happen.

Feel really bad.

Back on the terrace.

Genevieve

Imagine Maeve would have to call me Mum! Ha-ha!

An Asian Diary

Well, Christmas was eventful to say the least. For the day itself Geraldine booked us on what she promised was going to be a *"Super Special Christmas Cruise"* but even at a cost of $8 it proved to be a rip-off! From the way she'd been going on and on I thought we were coming on something along the lines of the QE2 but in fact it turned out to be a dodgy wooden boat (most likely retired from fishing for safety reasons) which was crammed with rowdy backpackers the majority of whom proceeded to get drunk and/or stoned as we went from island to island. Needless to say Wannabe joined in with tremendous gusto.

For yes, he's back in our midst once again looking completely strung out and I'd say he dropped a few tabs too many, or whatever it is these druggies do, during his absence. Guess my rejection hurt him more than I imagined. What can I say? I can hardly be blamed for my feminine charms and it's not like I lead him on or anything. Well, maybe a little. But only because he was just too willing to be led.

Speaking of willing to be led, I thought Geraldine was going to show a modicum of sense for once when she baulked at confessing her feelings to Mr C on Christmas Day despite all my coaxing but she's since summonsed up the courage and has revealed all to him. Heaven knows what he made of it.

Geraldine's boyfriend appears to have a little more sense

than her and he came to me today to tell me that, though he and I have never seen eye to eye, he could see what good friends Geraldine and I had become and he wanted to talk to me about her. And how interesting that proved for it turns out his reason for coming out was to propose to Geraldine but now he has doubts as he thinks she mightn't feel as strongly about him as she used and he even suspects she may have a crush on Mr C. He wanted to know what I thought.

As he said himself, he and I have never seen eye to eye so I didn't see why I should tell him anything except that I thought it'd be interesting to see what he does. So I told him that, yes, he might be right in thinking she didn't feel so strongly about him as she once used to and that she definitely had a crush on Mr C. The poor fellow looked devastated. For a second I thought he was going to burst out crying.

So now all we can do is wait and see if he gives up on her or if fights for her. Should be interesting . . .

27th December

Room 20, Mini Hotel Eleven. Late morning.

Genevieve

<u>Who</u> <u>does</u> <u>Maeve</u> <u>bloody</u> <u>well</u> <u>think</u> <u>she</u> <u>is</u>? How dare
she! Ignorant yobs! For crying out loud! I mean to say just
look at who she's going out with! The biggest God-help-us
to ever walk the planet & who's never even so much as held
down a proper job for any decent length of time and who
spends all his money or all Maeve's money rather on dope
and going out and having a fine old time for himself. And
how dare she call them great blobs! At least they have some
meat on them unlike her weedy little fellow who's so skinny
you'd have to wonder if there's anything the matter with
him medically speaking. Maybe all the drugs have had an
effect on his metabolism. And giving Theo one out of ten.
The cheek of her! Well I wouldn't even give her Dylan a
minus one hundred out of ten. I swear my blood is just
boiling. I'm hopping. I really am.

I'd be the first to admit that Theo and Trevor can be a
bit much sometimes but that certainly doesn't give her the
right to be so rotten about them. I've a good mind to say
something to her I really do. And my peculiarities! <u>What</u> <u>on</u>
<u>earth</u> <u>is</u> <u>that</u> <u>supposed</u> <u>to</u> <u>mean</u>?

Things are going from bad to worse. Now Laura's come

in to tell me that Andrew is about to leave for the airport and is looking for me to say goodbye. How come this is the first I heard about him leaving?

Terrace of the Mini Hotel Eleven. Afternoon.

Maeve

I didn't even get a chance to say a proper goodbye to Dad at the airport since G (who, like, *insisted* on coming with us!) kept getting in the way.

At one point she nearly knocked Mei to the ground as she tried to give Dad (yet) another "one last hug".

I think she's finally lost her marbles but at least she provided some light relief at a pretty tense time.

And I don't think she's talking to me now though I've *no* idea what I've done to upset her.

Right now, she's sitting across from me (supposedly writing in her diary) but every time I happen to glance up, I catch her staring menacingly over at me.

Have tried asking her a couple of times if I've done something wrong but she just shrugs & claims not to have any idea what I'm talking about.

Weird, très weird.

And she's not talking to Debs either.

In fact, Debs says she can't remember the last time G started a conversation with her.

And to make matters worse Mum gave me a right earful when I rang home.

Said that the thought of 2 wks in the sun was the only thing that got her through Xmas Day seeing as how her only child didn't even *think* to ring her.

Which isn't true.

I did think to ring – but – when I went down to the phone there was this humongous queue of tourists all waiting to talk to their nearest & dearest so I didn't see the point of waiting. I *was* going to come back later 'cept I fell asleep.

Genevieve

Just when I finally get to tell Andrew how I feel about him he has to leave so now everything's been left up in the air. I'm feeling <u>very</u> <u>low</u>. And Maeve's doing my head and it makes my blood boil to know that even though she's as nice as pie to my face, she doesn't really think a whole lot of me. Like what does she mean by my peculiarities? I don't think I'm any more peculiar than the next person. But I'm glad Laura told me what Maeve thinks about me for it's as well to know where I stand though Laura wishes she hadn't said a word now as she doesn't like seeing me so upset.

And if things weren't bad enough, we're getting a bloody overnight bus back to Hanoi tonight. Debbie's just come in and both she and Maeve are on at me now and want to know if I'm going to go to some café with them to wait there until our bus arrives. Maeve's nearly as bad as Debbie for not noticing when I'm odd with her but the truth is that I'm afraid to open my mouth for fear of what I'd say. I really am <u>hopping</u> <u>mad.</u>

Hiace van, somewhere between Nha Trang and Hanoi. Coming up to midnight.

Genevieve

This is <u>no</u> bus. I know a Hiace van when I see one and this is a Hiace van. Just because they've installed a few rows of seats in it doesn't change things and the price of the tickets was fierce expensive too considering. I doubt if I'm going to get a wink of sleep. And to make matters worse the man in the seat behind me has his feet up on the back of mine and keeps knocking it forward. He is driving me <u>insane.</u> And I'm sitting over the wheel so I can feel every single pothole and bump on the road. My backside will be <u>ruined</u> tomorrow.

But I suppose I wouldn't be getting too much sleep in any case for my head is just buzzing. I hate the way things have been left between myself and Andrew for nothing has really been decided. I thought he might say something to me at the airport about when he expects to be back in Ireland again but he didn't. I guess Laura's right and though he's admitted he has feelings he's probably still reluctant to take things any further given our circumstances. Laura says that's why I'm going to have to be prepared to take the initiative if I want things to go further. But I don't really know what I can do.

It's funny but after I told him how I felt and I was telling Laura about it afterwards things seemed a lot more definite between us but now when I look back on our conversation I'm just a bit worried that I got the wrong end of the stick.

I mean to say how does he expect to be able to get in contact with me again? He didn't even ask me for my address or for my telephone number.

On the side of the road, somewhere between Nha Trang and Hanoi. Later that night.

Debbie

12.30 a.m. The van we were travelling on broke down so now we're all sitting at the side of the road. The driver says his company have another bus that will be passing here within the next hour so we're going to get on that if there's room.

Luxury replacement bus. An hour later.

Genevieve

The van we were travelling on broke down so we had to wait until this other bus came to collect us which was an awful nuisance but the good news is that it's about hundred times more comfortable than that claptrap van and at least now there's a chance of getting some sleep. We've even got a toilet which is just as well as my bladder feels like it's about to explode and as soon as Trevor comes out, I'll be in there like a shot.

But Laura's right about one thing. While we were waiting to be picked up she pointed out that it's not like there are millions of families with the name Price living in Portrea and Andrew does come from there so he'd know that and then there are such things as telephone directories of course! Stupid me!

[Save Address(es)][Block]   [Previous][Next][Close]
From: "Tobin, Laura"<lauratobin@hotmail.com>
To: "Accounts"<officeoffers.co.uk>
Subject: Get a life!
Date: 27 Dec, 17:34:11
[Reply][Reply All][Forward][Delete]

Dearest Jo,
You're e-mailing to tell me there's €3.48 owing on my
account! Two days after Christmas!
Why don't you sent a debt collector after me!
Regards,
Laura.

28th December

Dormitory No.3, Railway Tourist Hotel, Hanoi. Mid-afternoon.

Genevieve

This place is the pits! I can't believe the only accommodation we could find is this <u>mixed</u> dormitory. The fella in the bunk above me is chewing on a gob of bubble gum which must be the size of a golf ball going by the sounds he's making. I've never heard anything so disgusting! And he keeps humming on and off to the stupid music on his stupid Walkman but he's way off-key and it's impossible to even know what song he's meant to be singing even though every now and then he comes in with a couple of words when he <u>thinks</u> he knows the lyrics and all the while he's chewing and chewing and chewing his fat head off. And anyway what's he doing stuck inside, lying about in bed in the middle of the afternoon especially when it's so fine outside?

At least I have an excuse and if it wasn't for him keeping me awake I'd be sound to the world right now for I didn't get a wink of sleep last night on the bus that picked us up after the Hiace broke down and all because of Theo.

At about two o' clock or thereabouts when everyone had more or less settled down to sleep I decided to pay another trip to the toilet before settling down myself but after I'd done my business I discovered the door of the toilet wouldn't open but I wasn't too worried for I presumed that someone else would be coming to use it soon and they'd find me or that Theo would notice I was missing as I had to wake him up to let me out of the seat. What a joke! As soon as he'd let me out he fell straight back to sleep and because nearly everyone else was asleep at that stage not one single person came to use the toilet until <u>six o' clock in the morning</u> when this old lady came and freed me and when I did get back to my seat <u>eventually</u> Theo half-opened his eyes when I gave him a dig to wake him up and muttered something about how I'd been very quick and got up to let me back in as if I'd only been gone a couple of minutes. The bloody eejit!

And honestly <u>I thought I'd go out of my mind</u> cooped up like that in the toilet for it bloody well stank and I don't even want to get into what it did to my claustrophobia! The only way I managed to stay sane was by daydreaming or night-dreaming I suppose you'd have to call it about Andrew. I was thinking that even if Andrew didn't get home to live in Ireland straight away then going to live in China though it mightn't be my cup of tea mightn't be as bad as I first thought especially if it was only for a short while. I mean to say Andrew's apartment in Beijing is very nice and all and what with having Mei to help me it would be easy enough to run and it wouldn't matter so much that I don't have the language but of course I'd start learning it straight away although it has to be said that languages were never my strong point in school. But there I am jumping way ahead of myself as usual. What am I like? But then I've always been like that.

I think that fella on top of me has fallen asleep. I hope he doesn't choke on his huge wad of chewing gum. The last thing I'd want to get involved in right now is having to give a total stranger mouth-to-mouth resuscitation.

Theo just came in and asked if I'd like to go for a bite to eat with him. Maybe if he'd been a bit more observant last night then I wouldn't be so tired and I might have said yes.

Dormitory No. 3. That evening.

Maeve

Funny I've known Theo for yrs but tonight was the 1st time I've ever had a real conversation with him.

Found him sitting out in the back, all sad & on his lonesome-ownsome so (for something to say) started asking him about his holiday – how he was enjoying it, that sort of thing.

Boy!

It was like a dam suddenly burst.

Everything came *gushing* out.

How G had hardly paid him any attention.

How she'd changed so much.

How she seemed to find fault with everything he did & said.

How she seemed to have time for everyone but him. Esp. my Dad & L.

But then came the BIG! BIG! BIG! NEWS!

His main reason for coming out to Vietnam was (. . . drumroll . . .) to PROPOSE TO GENEVIEVE!!!

He says that within hrs of her leaving Ireland he was missing her *so* much that he went into town where he bought an engagement ring for G & plane tickets for himself & Trevor. Between the (last min.) tickets & (a rock

417

of an) engagement ring he must have, like, spent a fortune, but when I said as much he just shrugged & said it's only money (Like – *Hello!!* – this is Theo who's talking here).

So that G wouldn't suspect anything he pretended coming to Vietnam was all Trevor's idea but the only reason he brought Trevor along in the 1st plc. was cos he's terrified of flying & wanted company.

But he says everything has changed & now he's going home tomorrow with the ring still in his pocket.

I tried & tried to change his mind but no luck.

Genevieve

I'm not sure what I'd do with myself if I moved to China. Maybe I could think about trying to extend Dad's business for there must be absolutely millions of rats and the like given the size of the country.

I really would love to talk to Maeve about her Dad and how I feel about him but of course I'm not talking to her right now not that she seems to even notice and anyway I guess Laura's right and it's best to wait at least until I've sorted things out with Theo for I don't want Maeve blabbing to him before I've had a word with him myself which I really must do soon for I can't keep putting it off but I'm dreading it for I am still very fond of him and I hate the idea of hurting him.

[Save Address(es)][Block]   [Previous][Next][Close]
From: "Tobin, Laura"<lauratobin@hotmail.com>
To: "Wilson, Felix"<felix@fmsounds.com>
Subject: Are you insane?
Date: 28 Dec, 22:15:33
[Reply][Reply All][Forward][Delete]

You're crazy if you think I'm going to send you so much as a penny. Why should I pay half of a Sept/Oct gas bill when I wasn't even in the apartment during October?

29th December

Genevieve

I feel bad that I didn't even realise that this was the last day of Theo's holiday until he and Trevor came downstairs with their suitcase all set for the airport. I wish I'd had a chance to talk to him for I'd have liked to have got things sorted between us before he left but now it's going to have to wait until I'm back in Ireland. But as Laura says nothing's actually happened between myself and Andrew so it's not like I've been two-timing Theo or anything so I shouldn't feel too guilty but I can't help feeling a little bit for even though I might not be in love with Theo any more I did go out with him for seven years and that's not something you can easily forget which Laura doesn't seem to understand. But I'm sure he must feel the same way as I do about things and see that we've outgrown each other. It's funny how our relationship just seems so childish now that I know what true love feels like.

Debbie

10.00 p.m. The twins went home today. Genevieve didn't seem half so upset as she was the day Andrew left. I overheard Dylan asking Trevor for a loan of some money just before they caught the bus to the airport. Dylan is such a bum but I can't believe he could have thought that there might be a chance he'd squeeze something out of Trevor. He must be very desperate.

Maeve

T 'n' T have gone home.

Sad really about Theo & G.

I did try talking to her this morning but she wouldn't listen. Whatever I've done to upset her is obviously still bothering her. She kept going on about how it was *peculiar* that I should want to talk to someone as *peculiar* as her and if she wasn't careful, I'd be marking her outta ten.

Like, what's she on?

She's right about one thing tho'.

She is peculiar – very, very, *very* peculiar.

In fact – completely bats.

But I've enough to worry about right now besides her.

At b'fast, Dylan mentioned how he thought Laos sounded like a really cool place to visit.

At lunchtime, he said he was definitely going to head there sometime.

By teatime, he'd his bags packed & was sitting in the lobby, waiting to be picked up by his "friends" – guys he'd met in the pub the night before.

My coming with him was *not* an issue.

I am *so* fed up with him.

When he *has* been kind enough to grace me with his presence, he's been too stoned $^1/_2$ the time to be much company & whenever I've tried talking to him about how *stupid* he's being, he just covers his ears (& does that annoying humming thing of his).

But I am worried about him.

Like, he used always smoke a bit of pot but now it seems like he's almost constantly stoned.

Course he gave no indication as to when I might expect to see him again.

Just hope he manages to stay outta trouble this time.

He asked me for money just before he left.

And I gave him it to him – yeah, yeah, yeah stupid me.

But he was, like, going to go whether I gave him the money or not so at least by giving it to him there's a chance he'll spend *some* of it on food & proper accommodation.

A slim chance.

Genevieve

I'm really annoyed at myself for forgetting that Theo was leaving today. But why didn't he remind me? I mean to say he'd plenty of opportunity.

Dylan went off again on his own. I think Maeve was really mad at him especially as she was probably feeling down already what with her Dad leaving and all.

[Save Address(es)][Block]   [Previous][Next][Close]
From: "Tobin, Laura"<lauratobin@hotmail.com>
To: "Tony Howard"<editor@idolmagazine.co.uk>
Subject: Your e-mail
Date: 29 Dec, 23:01:01
[Reply][Reply All][Forward][Delete]

Dear Tony,
I can't agree with you that my entries are getting
increasingly vitriolic. Poking fun at Geraldine/Genevieve
and the others is done in a light-hearted way and I'm sure
that's how your readers read it.
I think I've been writing long enough to be able to gauge
the readers' reaction. And I don't know how you can say the
readers aren't taking to me. I just write the diary. I don't
feature in it. You need to stand back a little, Tony, and give
me a free rein and trust my judgement.
Regards,
Laura.

30th December

Rooftop of the Railway Tourist Hotel, Hanoi. Late afternoon.

Maeve

Just checked my emails.

None from Dylan. Big surprise – not!

Why did we waste *so* much of the time when he was here fighting?

It's so hot today that we're all just lazing about writing postcards & reading – that sort of stuff.

Don't know *what's* with G. She's looking v. hot under the collar.

She keeps throwing me these, like, dark, menacing looks.

Debbie

4.15 p.m. All hell has erupted. Ten minutes ago, Genevieve broke the silence of what was up to then a perfectly pleasant afternoon and out of the blue began demanding that Maeve tell her just who the hell she thinks she is giving Theo one out of ten and how dare she call him an ignorant yob and that she wasn't peculiar so she wasn't and that, as a matter of fact, lots of people were interested in her and Maeve would be surprised to learn just who and that she wasn't bats, so she wasn't.

To begin with, Maeve looked completely baffled but

424

realisation gradually began to dawn and she accused Genevieve of reading her diary. And, while Genevieve was stuttering in protest, Maeve went right on, telling Genevieve that everyone knew she was the biggest snoop ever born and that reading someone else's diary was exactly the kind of thing she'd expect from her.

Dumbfounded at first, Genevieve finally managed to get some words out and told Maeve that she would never stoop so low as to read another person's diary and that Maeve should know her better than that. And out she stormed.

4.30 p.m. And now she's come storming back in again and has just come out with the startling news that Dylan has been carrying on behind Maeve's back with . . . me!

Dormitory No. 3. That evening.

Debbie

7.00 p.m. Things have gone crazy. Genevieve is sticking to her story about Dylan's and my "affair". Nothing I say makes any difference. Apparently it's been going on for ages, ever since we were in Songpan.

Unbelievable as it was to hear Genevieve coming out with such rubbish, what's even more unbelievable is that, as soon as Maeve got over the initial shock, she'd the gall to turn around and ask me if it was true. How could she even think such a thing? After all these years I'd have assumed she'd know me a little better than that. Genevieve has been trying to get Laura to back her story up but Laura keeps repeating that she's staying out of it as well she might given that it's her and not me Genevieve should be accusing.

Genevieve

At first I was really annoyed that Laura wouldn't back me up when I finally told Maeve about Debbie and Dylan's carry-on but having talked to her about it and having had time to think, I can see her point of view. She's probably right. I probably shouldn't have interfered like that especially when Dylan isn't here to face the music and of course Debbie is denying everything so Maeve just doesn't know who to believe.

But I was just so angry with Maeve when she accused me of reading her diary out of the blue and for no reason and all that stuff about Debbie and Dylan just came pouring out. But it's not like I'm making it up or anything and it's probably about time she knew anyway so in one way I'm not sorry I said it. I mean to say if I kept leaving things up to Laura then there'd always be some reason not to tell Maeve.

But I still can't get over how Maeve could believe I've been reading her diary. I mean how dare she! I would never ever do a thing like that. Never.

Debbie

10.00 p.m. All night I've been debating as to whether or not I should tell Maeve that it's Laura and not me she should be fighting with but I'm not sure there's any point. It's almost like she wants to believe that nonsense Genevieve came out with about Dylan and myself.

And it's not like Laura's going to suddenly turn around and own up to what she got up to with Dylan

Genevieve

Well maybe if it was lying there wide-open on the table

426

I might have a quick peek. Just maybe. But I don't even think I'd do that though I'd be tempted of course. I mean to say, who wouldn't?

Debbie

11.30 p.m. I think I'm going to wait until Dylan comes back and make him own up to what really went on.

An Asian Diary

oday was just priceless. There we all were, just sitting about quietly on some loungers up on the roof garden of our hotel, soaking up the sun, relaxing.

Or rather, everyone bar Geraldine was relaxing. Like the others, I was trying hard to ignore the loud sighs and constant fidgeting but it was proving difficult for Geraldine was getting more and more bothered by the second.

Finally it all came gushing out and she started accusing Mags of saying some pretty nasty things about her and Thicko, not least that Geraldine was bats and that Thicko was an ignorant yob.

I don't think Mags had any idea what Geraldine was talking about to begin with but realisation gradually began to dawn and now it was her turn to lose the rag and she accused Geraldine of reading her diary and, while Geraldine was stuttering in protest, Mags went right on, telling Geraldine that everyone knew she was the biggest snoop ever born.

Dumbfounded initially, Geraldine finally managed to get some words out and told Mags that she would never stoop so low as to read another person's diary and that Mags should know her better than that. And out she stormed. And then she came storming back in again and, to get back at Maeve I guess, she suddenly came out with the news that Wannabe has been carrying on behind Mags' back with Deanne.

For once Deanne lost her composure. I've never seen her look so shocked especially as I think she knows it's me Mags should be having this fight for I'm pretty sure Wannabe has been confiding details of his and my little tryst to her. At first I thought she might try putting Mags straight but she's smart enough to know that without Wannabe, who headed off on his own a couple of days ago, to back up her story she hadn't a hope of getting Mags to believe it. But I don't think he'll be backing her up when he gets back. Not after I've spoken to him. Not when I tell him that, if he owns up, I won't deny it but I'll make sure to tell Mags he's also been fooling around with Deanne.

So whilst I got to have the fun, it looks like Deanne's ending up getting the blame. It couldn't have worked out better.

31st December

Bus tour of The Mekong Delta. Morning.

Debbie

> 10.30 a.m. We're on this tour we booked before the big
> bust-up yesterday. It's probably just as well we're with all
> these other people seeing as how none of us are talking
> to one other. I can't believe that either Genevieve or
> Maeve could really think I'm carrying on with Dylan.
> What I really hate is that Laura thinks she's getting away
> with it. She looks so smug.

Maeve

G claims that Debs & Dylan have been carrying on behind
my back so I'm not talking to Debs.

Debs denies it – of course.

Dylan is in Laos so I can't ask him.

Who/what am I to believe?

Debbie is my best friend. But she was mad about Dylan &
even if she was the one who actually broke things off
between them she was still heartbroken for ages after.

And I'm not talking to G either for she's been snooping in
my diary & she's not talking to me for she read some pretty
nasty stuff I wrote about her & Theo.

Debbie

1.00 p.m. I could strangle Maeve. I mean we've been best friends for fourteen years and apart from when she started going out with Dylan after I warned her not to for her own sake, we've never had a full-blown falling out before.

Surely she should know me better than to think I'd carry on with Dylan behind her back? I know I'll never be completely over him but I have no interest in getting back with him again. I wouldn't have gone through the whole hardship of breaking up just to get involved again months down the line especially as he's even more messed up than ever.

Maeve

In some ways what G says doesn't come as a huge surprise for I had this feeling that Debs was holding something back from me all along.

And (now that I think about it) Dylan was acting a bit odd too.

I really, really, *really* wish he was here – least then I could get his side of the story.

But what if he denies everything as well?

What do I believe then?

But what reason could G have to lie?

This is going to be a great New Year's Eve – not!

Wonder how Dylan will be spending it?

Course I haven't heard a single word from him since he left.

I didn't even bother e-mailing him to remind him that we're flying out to Bangkok tomorrow evening.

Don't really care if he shows.

Genevieve

I wish Debbie would give over. She's doing my head in. She keeps on and on at me, wanting to know why I made up that stuff about her and Dylan. Why can't she just give me a break? Laura told me to say "no comment" to her like they do on the news the next time she starts on at me. Apart from giving me that advice Laura wants nothing to do with the whole sorry mess and says that since I got myself into it, I'm going to have to get myself out of it again and that I wouldn't be in such a mess in the first place if I'd listened to her and not said anything to anyone until the time was right. But when was the time going to be right, that's what I'd like to know.

But at least the stuff our guide is showing us is interesting and it's taking my mind off things a bit. Honestly it's been all go all day and the guide has us in and out of the bus like yo-yos and on and off boats like nobody's business. And who'd have thought fish farms could be so interesting but then they're not like any fish farms I've ever seen or heard about before. We visited this one family, of people that is not fish, who live on this thing that looked to me like a houseboat but right in what I suppose you'd call their living-room for it was where the telly and the couch and whatnot were, there was a trapdoor in the floor and when the guide opened this trapdoor and threw in some fish food <u>thousands</u> of fish no <u>exaggeration</u> came rushing to the surface in a <u>frenzy</u> all pushing and shoving to get at the food and I swear I thought they'd all come leaping out at us. The guide explained that there was this huge cage underneath the houseboat where the young fish grew up feeding on the fish food the family gave them plus whatever came floating in through the gaps of the cage until they were old enough to be harvested if that's the word and then sold off which is how this family earned their living which seems like a nice way to do so if you ask me. I wonder if you could set up something like that in the sea off Portrea.

Debbie

4.00 p.m. I've tried talking some sense into Genevieve but it's no use. She just keeps insisting she's telling the truth and that I'm to leave her alone and that she doesn't want to talk about it any more. "No Comment!"
What a great end to the year!

[Save Address(es)][Block]   [Previous][Next][Close]
From: "Tobin, Laura"<lauratobin@hotmail.com>
To: "Lewis, Timothy"<lewissolicitors@lineone.net.ie>
Subject: Your fee
Date: 31 Dec, 20:35:59
[Reply][Reply All][Forward][Delete]

I don't know why the bank didn't transfer the money. You know it is very difficult to keep after them from here. It's not like I can nip down to my local branch and sort it out with the manager. I am in Asia you know.

But don't lose any sleep over it. Your account will be settled.

1st January

Debbie

7.00 p.m. We're at the airport waiting to board our flight to Bangkok. For a while there it looked like Dylan wasn't going to show but he turned up twenty minutes ago looking very rough.

Before he'd even a chance to put his bags down, Maeve started giving him the third degree which he didn't look up to at all. He's quite sick, from food poisoning or so he claims though I'm inclined to think it's due to something more illicit. He arrived back minus his guitar which he says he lost though Maeve accused him of selling it and I think she's probably right.

As might be expected, he claims that nothing whatsoever happened between himself and myself back in Songpan or since. Unfortunately he wasn't at all convincing. He looked shifty and as guilty as hell when he was protesting his innocence. I guess that's because he is guilty, just not with me. If I didn't know any better I'd have said he was lying about him and me too.

On the plane to Bangkok. A couple of hours later.

Maeve

Dylan showed up.

435

Quizzed him big time about him & Debs. He swears &
swears nothing happened between them.
I want to believe him.
But just don't know *what* to believe?
Aaaaaarrrrrrrrrggggghhhhhh!!!!!!!!!!!!

Genevieve

I'd hate to be the man Maeve asked to swap seats with
her so that she wouldn't be sitting right next to Dylan for
now Dylan is leaning over him and is trying to catch
Maeve's hand and to stroke her hair and kiss her and he's
pleading and pleading with her and doing his utmost to
convince her that there's nothing going on between him
and Debbie. I don't think he cares who hears him and right
at the top of his voice he's going on now about how she's the
only woman for him and how he'd die for her though I don't
think anyone's asking him to do quite that. You'd swear they
were Romeo and Juliet the way he's going on.

I only hope Debbie can't hear for now he's moved on and
is giving Maeve a list of reasons why he wouldn't dream of
having an affair with Debbie. The expression on Debbie's
face hasn't changed so hopefully she hasn't heard but then
you can never tell with her.

Maeve

I wish Dylan would give me some space.
He is very convincing but I need time to think.

Debbie

Apparently I'm the biggest mistake of Dylan's life.

[Save Address(es)][Block]   [Previous][Next][Close]
From: "Tobin, Laura"<lauratobin@hotmail.com>
To: "Tobin, Gerard"<gerrytobinportreatarmac.ie>
Subject: [none]
Date: 1 Jan, 22:12:33
[Reply][Reply All][Forward][Delete]

Gerry,
I don't know why Mam didn't get the Christmas card from
me. I did send it. And ringing her from here isn't quite as
easy as you seem to think.
Why don't you buy her a get-well card and sign it for me?
And you might as well get some fruit as well or a nice box
of chocolates. I owe you, Gerry. Hope Brona and the kids
are keeping well.
Laura.

2nd January

The Crusty Loaf Bakery, Bangkok. Mid-afternoon.

Maeve

Had to get out on my own for a while

Dylan's done nothing all day but hang about in the lobby of our crap guesthouse watching crap movies.

The only indication that he's alive is the occasional flicker of his eyes when gunfire erupts on the screen or the lethargic movements involved in brushing away an (equally lethargic) fly.

He won't talk to me about Debs – says that I have to decide whether I believe him or not & that he's said all he has to say on the matter.

A change from yesterday or *what*??? Like, he was practically on his knees then.

Rang Mum. She's going to be arriving out tomorrow.

She's all I need right now – between everything that's been going on I'd $1/2$ forgotten she'll be descending upon me so soon.

I should *never* have let her talk me into letting her come – she's going to drive me *insane*!

And she's going to love seeing Dylan & me fighting – never, ever liked him.

I bit the bullet & told the others as soon as I came off the phone about her imminent arrival.

They're not exactly happy about it.

Surprise! Surprise!

Debs started going on about how it was typical of me to spring something like this on them.

This I do *not* need from her of *all* people right now.

Room 20, Clean and Calm Guesthouse.
Later that afternoon.

Debbie

5.00 *p.m.* Dylan spent the entire day right smack bang in the middle of the crowd watching videos downstairs where I can't get at him. I'm sure he knows that as soon as I get him on his own, I'll start giving him grief and start on at him to come clean about himself and Laura.

Maeve's mother is arriving out tomorrow. The first we heard of this was a couple of hours ago which is just so typical of Maeve but I don't want to go into that right now for I'm mad enough about things as it is.

Genevieve

If Debbie asks me once more why I said what I said about her and Dylan I don't know what I'll do. Would she ever just give over!

But my big news is that I rang Andrew today but to be honest he seemed a bit taken aback when he finally realised it was me on the other end and the connection wasn't great so I didn't get to say much to him and of course it didn't help that he was just on his way out when I rang.

I've been thinking that if his company send him back to Ireland then it'll probably be to Dublin so it might be a good idea for me to move up in the meantime. And in any case with Portrea being such a small place I'd be forever bumping into Theo which would be awkward for both of us. Laura says it's a pity she doesn't live in Dublin for then I could move in with her to begin with.

She's on at me now to go have a look around Bangkok with her. Maeve was going to come too until she heard I was coming and then she changed her mind and said she was particular as regards the company she kept. Well so I am and I certainly don't want to have anything to do with someone who thinks so little of me that they'd believe I'd stoop so low as to read their diary.

Back again in Room 20. Late that evening.

Genevieve

Laura and I had a good look around the centre of Bangkok this evening and I must say there was a great buzz to it. Of course she was expecting me to be scandalised by all the go-go bars with their dancers gyrating around poles and whatnot but to be honest most of the dancers just looked a bit sad to me and I've seen happier faces on pensioners in a bus queue.

There's a lot to see in Bangkok such as the floating markets and the wats and whatnot and a lot of the locals have a bit of English and it makes a nice change to be understood and the place caters very well for the tourist which is more than can be said for some of the other places we've been to. When Debbie overheard me saying that to Laura she started going on about how it was far too tame in comparison to China and that China was a far better place to travel in but then that's Debbie for you.

One thing I noticed is that there are an awful lot of stalls selling cheap knick-knacks so it's a good place to buy presents especially since we don't really have all that long left and I'm fast running out of money. I only hope I have enough to last till it's time to go home. I already have the two mini bottles of champagne I got on the flight with Andrew down to Hanoi to give to Dad and the silk painting Laura gave me back in Chengdu will do my mother so that's the two main presents out of the way. I'm in two minds whether or not to buy Theo anything. When I asked Laura what she thought she said there was no need to since I'm going to be breaking it off with him but I don't know. I mean to say I am still fond of him.

On our way back in the tuk-tuk as they call their little three-wheeler taxis we passed by a wedding party and it was funny to see how different everything was although the bride was wearing a long white dress just like you might see in Ireland though it was a bit on the fussy side if you ask me and I thought she was far too slight to carry it off. I'd definitely go for something less elaborate myself. There I am writing about weddings again which I know is just plain stupid but it is a diary after all and it's not like I go around telling other people about the nonsense that goes on in my head apart from Laura that is.

An Asian Diary

Oh! Oh! In old-fashioned parlance, I've been rumbled. Today Wannabe's, who's back amongst us once again, presented me with a bunch of my articles he picked up from some English backpackers he'd met somewhere along the way.

Flinging them down in front of me, he demanded to know if I'd written them. Like what did he think? That there was another party of four Irish girls, made up of a journalist, an insurance saleswoman, a nightclub hostess and a pest-control person, all travelling together who were joined along the way by the hostess's druggie boyfriend, her father, the father's girlfriend, the girlfriend's son, the pest-control person's country buffoon boyfriend along with his twin brother. Sure! Bound to be loads of groups with that exact configuration!

I took one look at him and asked him what did he think. Well, he said, he thought that, yeah, they were us, and that I'd written them. A veritable Sherlock Holmes! So then I asked him what was he going to do about it. Tell the others, he said. Really, I said, and did he think that was wise? So he looked at me, confused. Honestly, it's scary to think how many brain cells he's killed off to-date and I'd be there still waiting for him to get what I meant but I painstakingly pointed out to him that I didn't think Mags would be too happy to read about him and me getting up to no good or to read that he fancied me from our very first meeting. Finally the problem dawned on him.

Caught by the short and curlies!

3rd January

The Crusty Loaf Bakery. Mid-afternoon.

Genevieve

Maeve's mum arrived out today. It's funny to think that she was once married to Andrew. Back home I never really took all that much notice of her though I often saw her in the pub of course. She's not bad-looking considering her age and how much she drinks and smokes and that though I can't say much for her clothes and Laura's right when she says she looks like mutton dressed as a lamb. Laura says I should make use of the opportunity to pump her for information about Andrew but I don't know if I could. She might be good at that sort of thing being a journalist and all but I know I'd be hopeless. And anyway I doubt if it would be much use for I don't think Mrs Clancy likes me. When she came off the plane for example and was hugging and kissing Maeve she spotted me over Maeve's shoulder and straightaway started laughing like mad and wanting to know what was the point in someone like me going abroad when I was as white as I was the day I left Portrea. Then she started asking me was I very lonesome for Portrea and how did I stick all the foreign food and of course she was only mocking me but didn't seem to think I'd realise it though it was hard not to. She must think I'm a complete idiot.

The other news is that Dylan's headed off on his own.

<u>Again.</u> And no harm either. Maeve should have given him his walking papers the minute he came back from Laos even if he did deny that anything happened between himself and Debbie.

Tattoo parlour. About the same time.

Maeve

Mum arrived out today.

Which was the last straw for Dylan.

Said his head was already being done in (with me going on & on – trying to find out what happened between him & Debs) without having to put up with my mother too.

So he's caught a train.

He even gave me an ultimatum before he left – I'm going to have to decide whether or not I believe something happened between him & Debs.

If I do – then I'm *never* to bring it up again.

If I don't – then he just doesn't want to be with me.

How is it he's, like, the one who's giving the ultimatums?

Wouldn't even say where he was going exactly other than it was somewhere up north.

Or how long he'll be away.

Or if he's even coming back.

He could be flying straight home for all I know.

Which is why I'm sitting here, waiting to get a tattoo.

I need *something* to cheer myself up. I'm getting this cute little fish done on my left ankle.

Back at the Crusty Loaf Bakery. A couple of hours later.

Genevieve

Laura's headed off to do some shopping so I'm waiting for her in this restaurant. I'm surprised they haven't asked me to leave for I only bought a single cup of coffee and that was over two hours ago. Before she went Laura was asking me how many bridesmaids would I like if Andrew and I were to get married which is a silly question really for as I say, that's just not on the cards right now. I wish she'd stop asking me those kinds of questions for I don't need any encouragement as I'm bad enough as it is.

We're getting a train to some place down south tomorrow where we're going to catch a ferry over to an island. Because I'm worried about my money running out I've been as careful as I can all along but the price of the train ticket was astronomical so I'm going to have to be even more careful from now on. Of course it didn't help that I bought Theo this hand-painted mask yesterday despite Laura saying I shouldn't. I thought the price was ten euro but when Laura saw the price tag she started going on about how she couldn't believe I was being so extravagant and it was only then I realised that the bloody thing had cost me almost seventy euro which has practically wiped out my budget. I don't know how I'm going to survive until the end. Laura has been gone for ages and I really don't want to splash out on another coffee for why waste money when I don't feel like one just for the sake of it.

But just say we were to get married then three bridesmaids would be the absolute minimum I could have. Even if she did accuse me of reading her diary, Maeve is Andrew's daughter so I suppose she'd have to be one. And of course I'd have to ask Caitríona as she's my first cousin though we've had our differences over the years and I'd really like to ask Laura. Of course marrying an older divorcé wouldn't be what my parents would have in mind for their only daughter but as Laura says it's not like you can pick who you fall in love with and they weren't happy with Theo either so there's just no pleasing them.

But what am I like? I'm going to have to give up thinking about such nonsense.

[Save Address(es)][Block]   [Previous][Next][Close]
From: "Tobin, Laura"<lauratobin@hotmail.com>
To: "Wilson, Felix"<felix@fmsounds.com>
Subject: You have some cheek!
Date: 3 Jan 20:40:29
[Reply][Reply All][Forward][Delete]

How dare you open my mail! I don't care how urgent it was marked. You had no right.

For your information it's just a cock-up by someone in their Accounts Department and I paid the €235 in person the day before I left for Asia.

4th January

Room 20, Clean and Calm Guesthouse. Late morning.

Genevieve

First thing this morning I went back to the shop to try and persuade them to take back Theo's stupid mask but the woman behind the counter acted as if she'd never set eyes on me before and wouldn't hear of giving me a refund and no big surprise there I guess but the thing is I happened to get talking to these English girls in the shop who'd only left home the day before yesterday and they were <u>amazed</u> to hear how long we'd been away. I suppose it is pretty amazing when you think about it and it definitely is a once-in-a-lifetime opportunity as one of them kept saying as if it was news to me or something. And of course when they heard we'd been to China and Vietnam before coming to Thailand they were all agog and started asking me all these questions but after a while they began giving each other these funny looks and giggling and going on about how they just couldn't believe it though just what they couldn't believe exactly they wouldn't say despite the fact that I kept asking them over and over and in the end I just left them there giggling like a pair of fruit loops.

Express train to Ban Phe. Afternoon.

Genevieve

It doesn't bear thinking about how many bahts <u>per</u>

448

<u>minute</u> this train journey is costing. If Maeve's mum wasn't with us we could have taken an overnight bus which would've been way cheaper <u>and</u> we'd have saved on tonight's accommodation as well but we couldn't on account of how we can't expect her to rough it as she's not as young as the rest of us as she keeps reminding us. But all I can say on that score is that it's a pity she doesn't remember that a bit more and not just when it suits her. Honestly the carry-on of her sometimes is something else and she keeps flirting with all the darling Thai boys as she calls them. I know she's Maeve's mum and all but I have to say I'm not really all that gone on her. Like she was just horrible to Maeve yesterday when Maeve showed her the tattoo she got done on her ankle which is supposed to be a fish though it's not much like any fish I've ever seen and it's all a bit blurry really. But all Mrs Clancy kept harping on about was how it was a pity Maeve had her father's ankles and not hers but at least she had nothing much to lose to begin with by getting the tattoo.

Maeve
Mum's doing my head in.
She & L are getting on like a house on fire – birds of a feather & all that.
The little fish I got done is très cool despite what Mum says.

Debbie
6.00 p.m. We're on our way down to an island called Koh Samet. All of us. I thought I was going to get off on my own for once when I signed up for a diving course run on the island but I made the mistake of reading out the

description of it from my guidebook which makes it sound very idyllic so much so that Mrs Clancy has decided she's coming with me, not to dive but to bronze herself as she puts it. So then Laura decides she's coming too. And then Maeve says she'd better as well. And, not wanting to be left on her own, Genevieve jumps on the bandwagon. So now I've the full entourage accompanying me. All bar Dylan that is. All the while he was with us, he managed to avoid being on his own with me so it was impossible to confront him properly and, in typical Dylan fashion, he's run off again, leaving behind a sorry mess.

[Save Address(es)][Block]   [Previous][Next][Close]
From: "Tobin, Laura"<lauratobin@hotmail.com>
To: "Wilson, Felix"<felix@fmsounds.com>
Subject: [none]
Date: 4 Jan 20:41:01
[Reply][Reply All][Forward][Delete]

Dear Felix,
You can send me copies of your bills until you're blue in the
face but I'm not paying any of them. If being short of cash
is your problem, Felix, why don't you get rich Daddy to bail
you out?
Laura.

[Save Address(es)][Block]   [Previous][Next][Close]
From: "Tobin, Laura"<lauratobin@hotmail.com>
To: "Accounts"<officeoffers.co.uk>
Subject: Really, Jo, you need to get out more.
Date: 4 Jan 20:52:11
[Reply][Reply All][Forward][Delete]

Dear Jo,
I've only two words in response to your ongoing requests for
the payment of the €3.48 owing. And the first once rhymes
with duck.
Regards,
Laura Tobin.

[Save Address(es)][Block]   [Previous][Next][Close]
From: "Tobin, Laura"<lauratobin@hotmail.com>
To: "GeoffBarker"<barkingmaddebtcollectors.co.uk
Subject: [none]
Date: 4 Jan 20:59:01
[Reply][Reply All][Forward][Delete]

Get in line, buddy!

5th January

Debbie

5.00 p.m. How does Maeve stick her mother? She's driving me crazy already even though she's only been with us a couple of days. At least I'm doing the diving course so that means I don't have to spend too much time in her company but even after an hour I feel like covering her mouth with sticky tape to shut her up. She is such a bitch, especially to Genevieve and it's not at all surprising to find that her and Laura are getting on so well together.

No wonder Andrew left her. I can understand why someone as sensible and down-to-earth as Mei would appeal to him after her.

Genevieve

I don't know what Mrs Clancy was on about yesterday for she's wearing a pair of shorts today and if you ask me her own legs are nothing to write home about. And there's no doubt about it but she has a fierce set against me. Just a while ago I started asking her about her and Andrew's wedding and how many people were at it and what kind of dress she wore and that sort of thing but honestly after <u>very</u>

453

<u>begrudgingly</u> answering three questions at the very most, she gave this really big sigh then closed her eyes and pretended to be asleep. How could anybody be so rude? I suppose I can be a bit annoying at times but that still doesn't excuse her.

I know I should give myself a good kick in the backside for being so silly and daydreaming about weddings and the like and of course it's plain stupid to be writing about Andrew and about marrying him and all that and carrying on like it's all settled because I know only too well that nothing has been settled but I can't help it. That's just the way I am. I've always been like that. I always get carried away but it's not like it's doing anybody any harm. I was the very same with Theo. On the night of our school debs which was our first proper date I must have spent at least an hour in my white dress standing in front of the mirror before he came to collect me pretending it was my wedding dress and that it was my wedding day. Will I ever learn?

An Asian Diary

M ags' mother has arrived out. Honestly she's nearly as bad as Geraldine for fawning all over me. What with my buzzy life in London, I'd say I live the kind of life she feels she'd have had if only Mr C hadn't got her pregnant; she's still harping on about that though Mags is now 23 years old. Sad really.

But she does seem to have a lot of issues which I imagine are either the cause of or are caused by her drinking, for I'm afraid she's a bit of an old soak. If she were my mother I'd be mortified but Mags doesn't seem to be particularly bothered.

I have to confess to being that tiny bit naughty. Right from the start it was obvious Geraldine was driving Mrs C crazy and she kept muttering about that dreadful pest-control girl as she calls her. So, for sport, I told Geraldine she should pump Mrs C for information vis-à-vis her and Mr C's wedding and, later, when I overheard Geraldine asking Mrs C where they'd held their reception it was all I could do not to burst out laughing.

No doubt Mrs C thinks Geraldine is bordering on the insane.

Not quite perhaps but her mind does work in mysterious ways. Once she gets a notion into her head she mulls and mulls over it until an impossibility becomes a possibility then a probability and finally a certainty.

One minute she's sanely telling me there's no future for

her and Andrew. The next, she loses it and is asking me if I think lilies or roses look better in a bouquet and if I've ever been a bridesmaid before.

She truly is like a pendulum.

6th January

Poolside. Late afternoon.

Debbie

5.15 p.m. I'm glad I'm spending most of my time out diving for Maeve's still odd with me and her mother is insufferable. Both she and Laura are and they seem to regard Genevieve as their own personal servant. I doubt if they've budged from their sun loungers all day and it seems every time they want something from their cabins they tell Genevieve to go fetch and off she toddles. When I pointed out to her how they were using her, she told me to mind my own business. I should have known better than to interfere especially as she's still convinced that something went on between Dylan and me.

If Dylan doesn't tell Maeve what really went on as soon as we meet up again then I'm definitely going to tell everybody everything. I am sick of being cast as the bad guy when it should be Laura.

Genevieve

Laura says that the reason Mrs Clancy hasn't taken to me is because Andrew must have hinted about himself and myself but I doubt it as I'm sure I remember Maeve saying her parents are hardly ever in contact with one another

457

these days. Since I couldn't get a bit of information out of Mrs Clancy about Andrew we've decided that Laura is going to be the one to pump her instead as Laura puts it for Mrs Clancy is just stone mad about her.

I have the most terrible toothache and I swear I was awake half the night with it. I don't think I've ever been in such pain in my whole life no exaggeration. I know I should go to a dentist but I just do not want to for I hate them at the best of times and having to go to one in a foreign country who probably won't have a word of English and won't have a notion of what I'm trying to say and will probably start drilling away on the wrong tooth and not take a blind bit of notice when I try telling him to stop would be the pits altogether. And heaven only knows what he'd end up charging me and I'm broke enough as it is.

At least the pain has calmed down a bit for the moment but I don't know how I'm going to get through another night like last night.

Debbie

5.40 p.m. Laura is now asking Genevieve if she'd get some ice creams for herself and Mrs Clancy.

Maeve

G is driving Mum *nuts*.

Mum says she keeps bringing up the topic of Dad which is just about the last thing in the world she wants to discuss on her hols – esp. with G, of all people.

L & Mum are getting on really well which isn't surprising, I guess.

The 2 of them are happy to spend the whole day just lying out & working on their tans & talking.

Or rather L talking & Mum listening.

Mum loves hearing about the exciting life L. leads in London.

I imagine it's the kinda life she dreamt about living herself before she got stuck in Portrea (as she always puts it).

For her part – I'd say L's delighted to have a fresh audience to impress with all her stories for there was a limit to how many times even G was prepared to listen to them.

Funny thing is she hasn't talked about her book for a while now and when I mentioned it to Mum today L quickly changed the subject. I know she's forever tapping away on that little computer of hers but I haven't seen her do any, like, practical research.

Debbie

4.45 p.m. Genevieve is off again. To the shop again. Laura and Mrs Clancy need some moisturiser.

I think Genevieve is looking off-form but when I asked her if she feeling okay she told me to mind my own business.

Chalet No 3. That night.

Genevieve

My head is fit to burst with the pain. It's throbbing like mad. There's <u>no way</u> I'm going to get any sleep. And I've only got two paracetamol to last me until the morning. Why didn't I think to buy some earlier? It's not like I wasn't in the shop enough times. I think Laura and Mrs Clancy were using me a bit today and I was really getting sick to the teeth of running back and forth fetching things for them. Despite all her talk Laura didn't manage to find out a thing from Mrs Clancy today and to be honest I don't know what exactly she thinks she is going to find out.

I swear my head will explode. I am just <u>dying</u> and I'm now down to my last paracetamol.

Great! That's all I need right now. A party has started up in No. 2.

Which seems to have woken up every single gecko on the island. They're going flaming mental! No wonder they're called geckos for that's exactly the sound they make and one of them sounds <u>very</u> near indeed. Too near. I hope it doesn't get into our cabin and despite all Debbie's talk earlier this evening to her friends from the diving course about how cute geckos are and all her oohing and aahing over them they're nothing but dirty little lizards if you ask me. I think it's time I took my last paracetamol though it'll never last till morning.

[Save Address(es)][Block]   [Previous][Next][Close]
From: "Tobin, Laura"<lauratobin@hotmail.com>
To: "Wilson, Felix"<felix@fmsounds.com>
Subject: [none]
Date: 6 Jan 23:14:51
[Reply][Reply All][Forward][Delete]

How dare you put my things in storage! Where do you expect me to live when I return? You haven't heard the last of this, Felix. I've already been in consultation with my solicitor over the matter.

[Save Address(es)][Block]   [Previous][Next][Close]
From: "Tobin, Laura"<lauratobin@hotmail.com>
To: "Chunn, Bryan"<bchunn@westernalliancebanks.co.uk
Subject: [none]
Date: 6 Jan 23:32:06
[Reply][Reply All][Forward][Delete]

Dear Bryan,
I feel your e-mail was rather severe in the circumstances, particularly in light of my track record with your bank.
As you know, I have been banking with Western Alliance since I first moved to London just over seven years ago without, I'm sure you'll agree, a single problem until this current one. The last thing I'd want is to take my business elsewhere and I'm sure my fiancé, Felix Wilson, and his parents, Conrad Wilson and Jocelyn White-Wilson, would feel the same way but, in light of the rather shabby way you're treating me, I can't guarantee they won't. I doubt

you'll be named "Employee Of The Month" if you're the cause of the bank losing such highly-valued customers.
Regards,
Laura.

7th January

Chalet no. 4. Early morning.

Debbie

7.00 a.m. I might as well get up for I'm wide awake ever since Genevieve woke me at the crack of dawn on her way out to the pool to lay out some towels on a couple of sun loungers for Mrs Clancy and Laura. I hate seeing her being taken advantage of like this but when I said as much to her she just told me to mind my own business. And she looked wrecked. I don't think she slept a wink last night but totally ignored me when I asked if she was okay. I don't know why I bothered. She's still mad at me because of what she thinks I got up to with Dylan.

Poolside. A couple of hours later.

Genevieve

A load of Scandinavians have arrived onto the island. God they are just so loud. They're taking the whole place over completely and I'm going to have to put the towels out even earlier tomorrow morning to be sure of getting a spot. There's no point in even trying to swim in the pool when they're in there playing volleyball and splashing about like overgrown children and yelling their heads off. Not that I'd even want to go in for a swim in any case as I am still in agony with my tooth. Now two of those Scandinavians have taken the top half of their bikinis off and are swimming around like nobody's business with not a care in the world as to who's looking at them. Just as long as they keep their bottom halves on.

It's no exaggeration to say I was awake the entire night with the pain and it didn't help having those geckos parked right outside my window geckoing away all night or having those drunken louts in the cabin next door partying to beat the band like there was no tomorrow and I'm sure I heard Maeve in the middle of it all singing <u>"I don't like Mondays"</u> of all things.

The first thing I did this morning as soon as I'd put the towels out was to go and buy myself another box of paracetamol but now I think I've already taken as much as you're allowed to in the one day and it's not even lunchtime yet and though they haven't made the pain go away I'm beginning to feel a bit woozy so I'd better not take any more for the last thing I'd want on top of a toothache is an overdose for I most certainly do <u>not</u> want to have to go getting my stomach pumped. I've always thought that that must be a terrible thing to have to go through. And of course if I say anything to the others even Laura they'll just think I'm making a mountain out of a moleskin. But I really don't know how I'm going to carry on.

Now Maeve's mother of all people has whipped off the top half of her bikini which I suppose is no great surprise really and the wonder is she didn't do it before now. God I am <u>dying</u> with the pain.

Train en route to Bangkok. Evening.

Debbie

10.00 p.m. We had to cut short our stay on the island.

This afternoon when I came back from the diving course I found Genevieve in the changing rooms crying her eyes out. She's had a really bad toothache these last few days but didn't say a word to any of us about it. I've never seen anyone in so much pain.

Since there's no dentist on the island, we're heading back to Bangkok.

Maeve

Poor G.

She's been suffering with this toothache for days now but was afraid to say anything to any of us in case we hauled her off to some backstreet dentist-cum-butcher who'd charge her the earth.

1st thing tomorrow we're going to take her to this ex-pat healthcare centre in Bangkok recommended by our insurance people.

Mum didn't come with us.

Didn't see the point in wasting her holiday going back to the city when she could be enjoying herself by the sea.

Or rather with this German guy who I'd have considered even too young for me.

What is it with my parents?

What can't they behave like everyone else's?

Not sure why I bothered but I e-mailed Dylan before we left to tell him I was heading back to Bangkok.

[Save Address(es)][Block]   **[Previous][Next][Close]**
From: "Tobin, Laura"<lauratobin@hotmail.com>
To: "Tony Howard"<editor@idolmagazine.co.uk>
Subject: I hope you don't regret your decision
Date: 7 Jan 21:24:11
[Reply][Reply All][Forward][Delete]

Dear Tony,
I'm well aware that we don't have a contract per se. I guess
I was foolishly relying on old-fashioned trust and courtesy.
My decision to come to Asia was largely based on the fact
that you'd agreed to take my diary/column. Flying here was
quite an expense. Plus there's the loss of income as a result of
turning down work back home in order to be here.
However the monetary implications of your decision aren't
my main concern. What is, is the way you're undermining
my professional integrity.
Laura Tobin.

[Save Address(es)][Block]   **[Previous][Next][Close]**
From: "Tobin, Laura"<lauratobin@hotmail.com>
To: "Tony Howard"<editor@idolmagazine.co.uk>
Subject: And another thing . . .
Date: 7 Jan 21:40:21
[Reply][Reply All][Forward][Delete]

And what are you going to tell your readers? That I
suddenly disappeared without trace?

[Save Address(es)][Block]   [Previous][Next][Close]
From: "Tobin, Laura"<lauratobin@hotmail.com>
To: "Howard, Tony" <editor@idolmagazine.co.uk>
Subject: And another . . .
Date: 7 Jan 21:51:19
[Reply][Reply All][Forward][Delete]

But get one thing straight. By writing for your little heap of
crap, it was I, and not you, who was doing the favour.

8th January

Genevieve

This morning at the dentist's, Maeve showed us an article she found in this magazine she came across in the waiting-room. It was written by this girl who was keeping a diary whilst travelling around Asia with her friends one of whom was this real dozy eejit who was fierce mean and who Maeve had the <u>cheek</u> to say was my double! I have <u>never</u> been so insulted in all my born days. I mean this girl was <u>the pits</u> and I don't know how her friends put up with her for she seemed to do <u>nothing</u> but moan the whole time.

Honestly it's been a really rotten day all around what with Maeve upsetting me like that and going on about that horrible woman in the magazine being my double and then having to get my tooth fixed and of course having to pay the dentist <u>through the nose</u> for the privilege though he kept telling me to stop fretting and that I'd get my money back from the insurance company but I'll believe him when I see it. I don't think he really cared either way. He just wanted me out of there as quickly as possible so that he could bring in the next poor sucker and fleece them too. It's not through kindness those dentists get to own such big fancy cars and whatnot.

And what's more this place we're staying is the <u>pits</u> but it's dead cheap which is saying something. It was the only place we could find at such short notice. I swear our room's like a prison cell for there isn't so much as an outside window and all we're missing is the toilet in the corner though the one down the corridor smells so bad it's easy to imagine that it's right here in the room with us.

Maeve

While we were waiting for G at the dentist's this a.m. I started thumbing through some magazines & came across an article in this British one written in diary form.

And it was *just* that little bit spooky – could have been about us there were so many similarities.

It was written by this girl – an absolute witch – who was travelling through Asia with these 3 friends & one of them was *scarily* like G. We're, like, talking twins here.

I showed it to the others but only Debs saw what I meant.

L just got all sarcastic & started going – Yeah, like, right! 4 girls travelling in Asia. What an amazing coincidence!

G couldn't see the similarities either – she just got all hurt & said I mustn't think v. much of her.

Guess I can see her point – wouldn't have been exactly flattered myself.

Got an e-mail from Dylan telling me he's coming back today & that I'm to meet him in Bar Zero's at 9 this evening.

Genevieve

I'm not mean. I'm just careful with my money and I really only whine when there's reason to. That girl Maeve said I was like was really horrible and if that's what she thinks of me then I don't know what's she doing being friends with me. But then it seems she's never thought all that much of me only that I'm peculiar.

Debbie

8.00 p.m. Maeve came across this article today in a magazine about four girls travelling through Asia who are almost certainly us. There are just too many similarities for it to be coincidental. And, curiously, we do happen to have an out-of-work journalist travelling with us. I think I know now what those Welsh guys were going to show me back in Nha Trang.

Of course Laura denies she's written it and it is hard to imagine how anyone could be such a bitch. Even Laura.

Bar Zero's. Coming up to midnight.

Maeve

I've been waiting for Dylan for hours now.

Hasn't shown up yet.

Surprise! Surprise!

Course if that article *was* about us then obviously Laura is the author – a fact she's not going to want to broadcast exactly.

Debs kept going on about it for ages after we left the dentist.

But would L stoop *so* low?

[Save Address(es)][Block]   [Previous][Next][Close]
From: "Tobin, Laura"<lauratobin@hotmail.com>
To: "Tobin, Gerard"<gerrytobinportreatarmac.ie>
Subject: [none]
Date: 8 Jan, 21:45:23
[Reply][Reply All][Forward][Delete]

I've no idea why my mail is being redirected from my London address to Mam and Dad's. No doubt it's some kind of glitch but not something I can sort out from here. Just tell Dad to hold on to it until I get home and am in a better position to sort it out.

[Save Address(es)][Block]   [Previous][Next][Close]
From: "Tobin, Laura"<lauratobin@hotmail.com>
To: "Wilson, Felix"<felix@fmsounds.com>
Subject: [none]
Date: 8 Jan, 21:51:13
[Reply][Reply All][Forward][Delete]

How dare you take it upon yourself to start redirecting my mail to Portrea! Don't think for one moment I'm finished with London just because you're finished with me.
Believe me, I'll be back with a bang. Aside from everything else, I'm now working on a story which, when it breaks, will have you along with every other radio personality just begging me to come on their show.
And it's the kind of meaty story that just cries out to be followed up with a book. In fact I'm already in negotiations with my agent.

471

9th January

Maeve

Dylan turned up here this a.m.

1st thing he asked me was if I thought there was something going on between him & Debs – told him I didn't.

And I don't.

I think.

In that case, said he'd stick around.

So we're happy together again – sort of.

Pat Thai restaurant. Lunchtime.

Debbie

1.00 p.m. Dylan's turned up and has been avoiding me since he got here. Maeve's keeping a very close eye on him. In case I try to have my wicked way with him again I guess. I did manage to get him on his own for all of about two seconds and before I could say a word, he started pleading with me to give him a bit of time and that he'd tell Maeve everything. Fool that I am, I agreed. What it is about him?

Ages ago, I booked us all on a two-day walking trek through some of the hill-tribe villages north of Chiang Mai. We're meant to be catching a bus tonight to

Chiang Mai but now Genevieve says she isn't going because it sounds like her idea of hell and Dylan and Maeve have pulled out too so it seems it's going to be just me and Laura. With any luck she'll change her mind as well. I can't imagine she'd want to be stuck on her own with me.

Overnight bus to Chiang Mai.

Debbie

8.00 p.m. It turns out the whole circus is coming trekking with me after all.

Why Dylan and Maeve changed their minds they didn't care to divulge but I think it might have had something to do with the shady character I saw Dylan arguing with outside the guesthouse a couple of hours before we left. The reason Genevieve decided to come was because she realised it'd be far more expensive to stay in Bangkok.

Maeve

This samlor driver whose buddy Dylan bought grass from this afternoon came around to the guesthouse demanding 1000 baht from Dylan & threatened to call the police if he didn't get it.

What a stitch-up!

How could Dylan be *sooooo* stupid?

Dylan told the guy he'd get the money for him tomorrow when the banks open.

Which is why we had to high-tail it out of town.

Genevieve

I think I must have been totting up one of the columns

in my notebook wrongly for I've even less money than I thought which is the only reason I'm on this bus to Chiang Mai to go on this stupid trek for it's an all-in price and very reasonable considering food and that is included. With what little I've left I don't think I could afford to eat in Bangkok for the next few days let alone pay for somewhere to stay.

But maybe this trek won't be too bad for so far I've quite liked Thailand and at least there won't be horses involved. And the people who live in the area we're going to are called hill tribes which means it's <u>hills</u> we're talking about and not mountains like in Songpan.

But I am getting <u>so</u> sick of these overnight journeys. There's a gap where the window wouldn't close so no doubt I'm going to have a fierce crick in my neck tomorrow and I wish someone would go and pick up the empty Coke can rolling up and down and up and down the bus for it's driving me bananas. I really cannot wait until we're back home again and I even rang the airline this afternoon to see if they could get me an earlier flight home but no luck.

Maeve
Dylan's sound to the world.
He looks *so* beautiful when he's sleeping like that.
If something did go on between them it seems stupid to be talking to Dylan and not Debs.
Like, they're both equally to blame so it's nonsense to be talking to him & not her.
And – in the end of the day – *I'm* the one he wants to be with – not Debs.

Debbie

10.45 p.m. Genevieve might not be talking to me on account of what she thinks Dylan and I got up to but Maeve seems to have got over things a little quicker and has just made her way up the bus to tell me she forgives me. For what? To me that implies she still believes there really was something going on between myself and Dylan.

If she does and she's still willing to forgive him then she really is stupid.

11.00 p.m. Maeve might have forgiven and forgotten but I haven't and the first chance I get, I'm going to make sure Dylan knows that. He can't avoid being on his own with me forever.

10th January

Genevieve

All day long I was stuck behind the others, just walking and walking and walking and walking and bloody walking. And even trying to stop to have a drink of water out of my bottle every now and then was pointless for every time I'd managed to take a couple of slugs, the others had marched on ahead of me which meant that I had to run to catch up with them so of course I was gasping all over again and fit to collapse.

And what with all the other heads bobbing up and down in front of me I couldn't see a thing especially as one of the Norwegian girls must be at least seven foot no exaggeration. And I thought I was tall! Not that there was anything to see apart from trees and trees and more bloody trees. And if all that wasn't bad enough, when we stopped in this little village where we're going to be spending the night, the first thing I did was ask could I use the bathroom and so I was shown into this tiny little horrible outdoor shack for want of a better description and as soon as I'd set about my business I thought I heard laughing coming from somewhere close by outside and then I realised that there were holes all over the flimsy wooden walls and that all the kids in the village were peering in at me and having a right old laugh

476

<u>for</u> <u>themselves</u> <u>at</u> <u>my</u> <u>expense</u>. I have never been so embarrassed. And when I came out and tried to shoo them all away they only laughed all the more.

The only others on the trek besides ourselves and our two Thai guides are these six Norwegian girls and as soon as we arrived into the village they just ate their dinner, took out their diaries and started writing though what they could find to write about I just can't imagine for they're still at it. Honestly they haven't a word to say to anyone.

Needless to say our accommodation isn't exactly five star and is in fact more like a shed but I'm not going to get into that right now. All I will say is that I hope the pigs in the pen across the way don't wander in on top of us during the night for they've no proper fence and we've no proper door. And I hope the walls don't fall in for they're made of reeds or some such stuff and there are gaps everywhere and anyone could be gawking in at us when we're changing and we wouldn't even know and after the toilet incident I wouldn't be one bit surprised.

And anyway I don't know why these people are called hill tribes in the first place when what they should be called is great-big-mountains-almost-the-size-of-Everest tribes.

Debbie

8.00 p.m. I don't know when I'm going to get a chance to talk to Dylan as Maeve's sticking to him like glue.
I'm sure Dylan's quite pleased for the longer he can avoid another confrontation with me, the better.

Genevieve

It's funny but I always thought Norwegians would be

quite nice people but these ones are about <u>the</u> most boring people I have <u>ever</u> met in my life. Those endless summer nights back in Norway must really seem endless for they haven't a word to say to any of us and how can they possibly find so much to write about in their diaries?

As well as walking for miles I thought the other reason for this trek was to get an opportunity to meet the local people but aside from a few women who came here a little while ago trying to sell us silver knick-knacks nobody else has come near us. I was saying as much to Laura a little while ago but I didn't know Debbie was eavesdropping until she butted in and started demanding to know what I'd expected and began rabbiting on about how they were real people too with real lives and not just here for our pleasure. Laura said that Debbie's never happier than when she has the moral high ground.

One of the women we did meet hounded me for ages and ages trying to get me to buy some of the little trinkets she had with her so in the end I told her I didn't know where my wallet was but if she was around tomorrow morning before we set off then I'd definitely buy a bracelet from her but hopefully she'll have forgotten by then.

I'd say it must be very hard for that tall Norwegian girl to find clothes to fit her. I don't think I've ever seen a taller woman.

Maeve

This is gone way, way, *way* beyond a fucking joke.
Hash I could deal with but now Dylan is smoking opium.
And not for the first time either.
It's just dawned on me why he was so anxious to travel up

north on his own last week – why buy from a series of middlemen when you can go straight to the source?

And I heard him asking our guide about some leaf I've never heard of before. He was trying to find out if he could get his hands on that too.

What a fool!

Has Dylan *ever* heard of a little discretion?

Genevieve

I suppose she could shop in men's stores though they wouldn't have a great selection.

11th January

Same hamlet. Breakfast time.

Genevieve

Of course I'd say with the good healthcare and the clean fresh air and all those trees and fjords and clear streams and whatnot Norwegians are probably taller than average so there's bound to be a better selection in the shops for tall people in Norway than there would be in Ireland.

The backs of my legs are killing me from yesterday and I'm feeling tired already so what am I going to feel like by the end of the day? I swear I must have been awake since four this morning and I don't know how anyone gets any sleep in this village. I thought the countryside was meant to be quiet and peaceful but the bloody cocks started cock-cocking their heads off at the crack of dawn this morning and didn't let up for hours.

But it seems like people are early-risers around here. At about half past five when I went to use that see-through shack of a toilet as I figured that at that hour there wouldn't be any kids around to spy on me, I noticed three figures miles away in the distance making their way down the mountain path towards the village. I forgot about them again until about an hour ago when they turned up here just as we were finishing up our breakfast and who was it but the woman I'd promised to buy a bracelet from last night and her two children who could only have been about three or four years old tops. I think she must have walked all that way just because I'd promised to buy a bracelet from her last night which was worth less than ten euro.

Debbie

7.50 a.m. I managed to get Dylan on his own for all of five minutes and straight away he started making excuses and explaining how he was going to tell Maeve about him and Laura but that he was waiting for the right time. Needless to say, there never will be a right time which is what I was saying to him when Maeve came along and interrupted things. She's like his bodyguard.

Genevieve

I'd say the reason she came so early was because she knew we'd be leaving soon. To think that those poor children had to walk miles and miles so that their mother could sell me a bracelet. In the end I bought two as I felt bad about making her come back like that. I guess I can give one of them to my mother as well as the silk paintings and I can keep the other one for myself. To think that selling a couple of bracelets could mean so much to that poor woman. To think that people could be so poor.

It looks like we're about to head off and the guides are on at us to start making a move. If only I fell desperately ill right at this minute with something serious which was fixable but only if I was airlifted to a hospital immediately At least then I wouldn't have to go through another awful day of trekking. The thought of it just makes me sick.

**Veranda of the tourist accommodation house in another
hamlet, 12km further on. Evening time. After dinner.**

Genevieve

I remember Debbie going on about those two guides we
had when we were horse-trekking back in China and how
they looked so skinny and how all they were wearing on
their feet were these little flimsy plimsolls. I can see now
why she wanted us all to chip in and give them a tip for I
guess she was right and they probably weren't getting paid a
whole lot and I kind of wish now I hadn't listened to Laura.
I still can't get over the fact that that poor woman had to
walk all that way just to sell a lousy bracelet.

I wonder what Andrew is doing right this minute. It's
funny but the more time passes the harder it is to picture
him exactly. Laura was going on at me today about how I
should ring him when we get back to Chiang Mai for as she
says it's not like he can ring me but sometimes I wish she'd
just lay off a bit on the whole Andrew thing.

I don't believe it! It just gets worse and worse. The guides
now want us all to perform a song or a dance to get into the
holiday spirit like it's bloody Butlins or Club Med or
something but they've got another thing coming if they
think I'm getting up and making a complete fool of myself
though it's no surprise that Dylan's the first to volunteer.
He's in great form lately though he and Maeve are fighting
<u>again</u>. It seems to me they're forever falling out and making
up again and that as a matter of fact they kind of seem to
enjoy it. They weren't arguing about Debbie for they seem
to have put the whole business with her behind them
though if he were my boyfriend I wouldn't be so quick to

forgive him. I think they were fighting about something to do with drugs though what exactly I didn't quite catch.

Maeve

Dylan's making a fool of himself.

He's, like, *completely* wired.

Right now he's doing a 3 hand reel with this tall Norwegian girl.

At least he's stopped trying to make everyone play party games – G went off to bed in a huff after he started trying to get her to clench a coin in her bum and walk over to a cup on the ground and drop it in.

She was having none of it.

In the tourist hut. Meanwhile.

Genevieve

I wish the others would all just go to bed. I'm fed up of lying here listening to them all acting the eejit. How come it took the Norwegians until now when it's middle of the bloody night to prove that they're not in fact quiet after all? They're all roaring out <u>Patricia</u> <u>the</u> <u>Stripper</u> and no prizes for guessing who Patricia is. He really is <u>out</u> <u>of</u> <u>control.</u>

And how am I <u>ever</u> going to face another day trekking tomorrow if the fat one of the guides starts hassling me again like he was today. And Dylan asked me earlier this evening if I was making sure to keep a careful eye on where we were walking especially where the grass is tall or wet as he says the place is just full of leeches. Why did he have to go and tell me that? I'd have been better off not knowing. Leeches are about the last thing I need right now.

Thank goodness there's only one more day left on the trek and then only two before we go home.

And back out on the veranda.

Debbie

11.00 p.m. Poor Genevieve. I think she's beginning to crack up and I don't blame her. All day the guide was at her to keep up with the rest of us and shouting at her to, "Come on, big lady. Move it, move it." At least from the sounds of all the snorting and snoring coming from our bungalow, she was asleep almost as soon as she went to bed.

When the snoring first started, Hannah, one of the Norwegians on the trip, began giving out, saying it was just too much that we'd been put sleeping next to a pig pen for the second night running until the guide pointed out that it was, "not pigs but the big lady with the orange hair". I think Genevieve will be very glad to get home.

12th January

Same veranda. Morning.

Genevieve

God almighty! Dylan is going to get us <u>all</u> into the <u>height of</u> <u>trouble.</u> Not only is he smoking his own head off but he's now quite openly selling stuff to others and I overheard two of the Norwegians say they bought some from him this morning.

Never in all my born days did I think I'd be on holiday with someone who is in fact a drug dealer, no two ways about it. When I confronted him, he just laughed and told me to, "Chill, just chill!" And then he told me he could give me a special price if I was interested for he knew I was partial to that sort of thing. The cheek of him! I know I don't see eye-to-eye with Dylan but I really don't like seeing him abuse himself like that or even more so being the cause of other people abusing themselves. And I really can't bear to think what would happen to him if he were caught by the authorities. Or what would happen to us. I tried to talk to Laura about it but she just told me not to worry and that it was his own look-out.

And why does he keep going oink-oink at me? I really wish he'd stop for it's not funny although for some reason all the Norwegians seem to think it's flaming hilarious and I asked Laura if she knew why but she doesn't. Oh God! It looks like we're about to leave now. I just hope the bloody guide will leave me alone today and I think he really should just let everyone go at their own pace for it's not fair the way he picks on the same people all the time.

By a waterfall in the forest. Lunchtime.

Debbie

12.45 p.m. Things are getting complicated. Maybe one of the reasons I've been stalling and not telling Maeve about Dylan and Laura is because I really believed Dylan when he told me he never intended anything to happen with Laura and that it was she who came onto him. I still believe that. I also believed him when he told me Maeve was the only one for him. That I don't believe any more. This morning, when Maeve inadvertently left us out of her sight for a moment, I started at him again, telling he had to tell Maeve what really happened back in Songpan, but he didn't seem to be taking much notice. And then, out of the blue, he announced that one of the worst things to ever happen to him was us splitting up. His reasons, or so he says, for going out with Maeve in the first place was partly because he fancied her but mainly because he wanted to get back at me for dumping him.

I told him I'd no interest in hearing any of this particularly in light of the way he's been carrying on lately but he says he's only been like that because he feels so wretched over us splitting up.

So then he asked me did I still have feelings for him so I told him I hadn't and walked away.

Genevieve

I hope I don't get an ulcer from worrying about Dylan and the drugs and that. And the leeches of course are another worry which I do <u>not</u> need right now. I know I've thick boots on but how can I be sure they're thick enough to stop the leeches getting at my feet? They're the one insect if you can call them that which I know nothing about and in all the years I've worked with Dad I've never come across them. I'm afraid even to take off my boots to have a look in case any of them have already wormed their way in.

I wonder if smoking some opium would make this hell any better. Not that I'm going to even try of course. I know the doctor said it was Bacillary Dysentery I got back in Songpan but I can't help thinking it was a bit too much of a coincidence that I got sick the day after smoking Dylan's dope. I heard one of the Norwegian girls and Debbie talking about how an awful lot of people in these parts grow opium for a living and that loads of them become addicted to it and that the drug problem is <u>just</u> <u>huge</u> around here. It's hard to imagine really for it's so peaceful and countryish.

<u>What</u> <u>is</u> <u>Dylan</u> <u>like?</u> What can't he just sit there quietly and eat his sandwiches like the rest of us. But oh no! Not him! Instead he's gone and taken off all his clothes and is now standing <u>naked</u> under the waterfall and crying out about how he's feeling nature at its rawest. Somehow I don't think having to watch a naked man cavorting under a waterfall while I'm trying to have my lunch was what Dad meant when he said he hoped travelling would broaden my mind. The guide should really put a stop to him or next thing the Norwegians will be joining in for I'd say it'd be right up their street.

487

Debbie

1.30 *p.m.* Even when I was telling Dylan earlier that I didn't care about him any more, I wasn't one hundred per cent certain I was telling the truth. But now, as I look at him splashing about around under a waterfall with no clothes on, I can honestly say I don't.

Jeep back to Chiang Mai. Several hours later.

Maeve

Dylan is losing it.

He's decided he's going to make a heap of money importing heroin back to Ireland.

He's it all worked out – so he told me.

He says this contact he's made in Bangkok is going to supply him with the stuff and then he's going to seal it in plastic and hide it inside a radio at the bottom of his backpack – claims that way it's undetectable.

And the funding for the operation?

Me – of course.

What is he like?

I told him where to go

At least without money he can't get very far with his plans.

Which is just as well since all the customs guys would have to do is take one look at his face to know he's hiding something – which I pointed out to him. There's no way he could carry it off.

But I don't think he's given up on his plan entirely. He's being especially nice to me ever since but if he thinks I'm going to change my mind about giving him the money he's another think coming.

Room No 13, Imperial Guesthouse, Chiang Mai.
Early evening.

Genevieve

I think Norway was where nudist colonies started to begin with though I'm not sure how I know that.

I swear I have blisters the size of marbles on my feet from all the walking, and welts on my bum from the drive back in that jeep this afternoon. Never, <u>ever</u> again. The others are all gone out somewhere which is just crazy if you ask me for we have to catch a bus to Bangkok at the godforsaken hour of <u>four</u> in the morning which is why I'm now taking myself off to bed.

Thanks God we've only two more days to go.

Room No. 12. A couple of hours later.

Debbie

11.30 p.m. Dylan is such a fool. Even though he doesn't love Maeve, it's obvious from his carry-on this evening that he's happy just to string her along.

How can he act like that? One minute he's telling me I'm the love of his life and, the next, he's all over Maeve. But Maeve should watch out for I saw Dylan and Laura out in the corridor just now as I was coming back from the bathroom. I wonder if he was coming on to her now that I've given him the brush off. It wouldn't surprise me. They stopped talking when they saw me but it definitely looked like he was trying to convince her of something but she looked like she was having none of it.

13th January

Common room of the Foremost Guest House, Bangkok.
Early afternoon.

Genevieve

The first thing I did when the bus from Chiang Mai
dropped us off here at the guesthouse at lunchtime was ring
Andrew for I just wanted to say goodbye to him and let him
know that I'm leaving his part of the world tomorrow. But
to be honest he sounded kind of odd like he was taken
aback to hear from me but Laura says that I shouldn't read
anything into that for men are generally far more awkward
than women when it comes to showing their feelings and
that the deeper those feelings are in a man, the more
awkward he's likely to be.

I swear I'm beginning to think that the drugs must have
Dylan's brain completely addled. After I'd rung Andrew I
decided to make a start on sorting out my rucksack for the
journey home but as soon as I'd begun Dylan was in on top of
me and the first thing that struck me was the strange mood he
was in. He was real fidgety and it's no lie to say he must've
asked me at least a dozen times where the others where and
when they'd be back and though I kept telling him over and
over that I didn't know, he didn't seem to hear me for as I say
he was acting very weird and all distracted. But then as I was

490

in the middle of telling him <u>yet again</u> that I didn't know anything about the others' whereabouts he just walked out of the room which is the kind of thing you'd expect from Dylan so I didn't take too much notice and went back to my packing.

But almost straightaway he was back in again and telling me that it was actually me he wanted to talk to and that's when he came out with <u>the most ludicrous thing I have ever heard in the whole of my life.</u> He asked me would I take some drugs home to Ireland for him in my luggage. I am not joking. He said that no one would ever suspect anyone as dowdy and as sensible-looking as me of drug-smuggling which wasn't exactly a nice thing to say and he certainly wasn't out to curry flavour. So I pointed out to him that sniffer dogs aren't going to know how dowdy or otherwise I look but he said they don't use sniffer dogs in Bangkok Airport and that even if they did the dogs wouldn't be able to smell anything for his plan was to seal the drugs in plastic and stash them inside this radio which I would then carry in my luggage so they'd be completely undetectable.

Needless to say, I told him I'd no interest whatsoever in his crackpot scheme and to leave me out of it and that if he wanted to stay out of trouble he'd forget all about it.

Mrs Clancy has just arrived off the train from Koh Samet with this boy who looks about half her age. Maeve is going mental. She's absolutely killing her mother no exaggeration. Now she's stormed off to her room. Now Mrs Clancy's stormed off to hers. And now Frank as he's called has stormed off too though I don't know where he's going for he didn't say. I'm glad they've all cleared out for they were making an unmerciful racket or at least Maeve and Mrs Clancy were. They have the exact same awful high-pitched screech when they're angry.

Room 13.

Maeve

Mum's arrived in from Koh Samet.

Didn't come on her own either but with her new boyfriend Frank.

Frank?

Like what kinda name is that for someone from Thailand?

And what happened to the German I left her with?

Doubt if Frank's even outta his teens though Mum insists he's a youthful-looking 25.

Sure he is!

He's as much 25 as she is herself.

And back in the common room.

Genevieve

But I'm not finished with the Dylan saga yet. The next thing was he started on about how he'd make it worth my while to take the drugs through for him so I asked him where on earth was he going to get the money in any case and that's when he said he was glad I'd brought it up and that if I was prepared to put up the money he'd double it for me. He must be <u>stark</u> <u>raving</u> <u>mad!</u> Does he really think I'd risk my own money not to mind risk getting caught? And anyway all I've left is the equivalent of forty euro and out of that has to come the price of a taxi to the airport and tonight's accommodation.

He must think there's one born every minute and anyway if he'd any sense he'd have just tried to borrow the money without saying what it was for, bought the drugs and then slipped them into my luggage without me knowing a thing about it. That way I'd have sailed through customs without a care in the world and not in the least bit nervous which is how, as I was telling Laura afterwards all about what he had said to me, I'd say most drug-smugglers give themselves away.

Anyway I got rid of him eventually and I went back to sorting my stuff out but I still hadn't finished when in came Maeve who was in a foul mood because of her mother I suppose and I guess she felt like taking it out on someone, so in her nosy-parker way she started asking me what I was doing so I told her and so she started laughing and started going on about how it hardly mattered what way my things were at this stage and how doing something so pointless was just so typical of me. What I should have pointed out to her and I don't know why I didn't but I guess I was afraid of upsetting her any further was that one of the reasons I needed to sort through everything was to see exactly what I'm missing for I think quite a few of my things have found their way into her rucksack. I'm not saying she stole them of course but she's just careless and doesn't have much regard for other people's property.

Room 12. That evening.

Debbie

8.00 p.m. Dylan is something else. The other day when I told him I'd no interest in him, he seemed to take it so badly that I was worried about him but he certainly did get over it very quickly.

I just bumped into him out in the corridor and what he said was this:

"Course I was disappointed at you knocking me back like that, Debs, but it's your loss in the end. By the way, I couldn't borrow some money from you? I'd have it back to you, say, within a week of getting home. With interest. Think of it for old time's sake."

Needless to say, I passed.

Genevieve

And I don't think it's fair of Dylan to call me dowdy. Doesn't he realise that I have feelings too? One of the mini bottles of champagne I was going to give my dad has broken and spilt all over the place and now I'm going to have to get him another present though I've <u>no</u> idea what and of course it'll eat into what little money I've left.

[Save Address(es)][Block]   Previous][Next][Close]
From: "Tobin, Laura"<lauratobin@hotmail.com>
To: "Tobin, Gerard"<gerrytobinportreatarmac.ie>
Subject: You were right as usual!
Date: 13 Jan, 11:54:31
[Reply][Reply All][Forward][Delete]

Hi Gerry,

I've been thinking. It must have been a really hard time for Mam, especially with Dad being the way he is, and it's occurred to me that some help when she comes out of hospital wouldn't go astray which is why I've decided to come home like you suggested right from the start. I guess I should listen to you more often for you really have a knack for talking sense. Sometimes it just takes me a little time to see how right you are.

I do have one problem. This trip has cost me an absolute fortune for I've never been one to stint on luxuries as you know. More is the pity your financial wizardry isn't shared by your spendthrift sister! So, unfortunately I'm stony broke, but just temporarily, for I do have a considerable sum of money owing to me – just nothing I can get my hands on from over here. Which is why I'm now coming to you, big brother, to ask could you loan me the fare home. At such short notice, it'll cost me a fortune, €4999 to be exact for they have only one seat left and that's in first class. I'd really appreciate it if you could help me out.

Transferring money overseas is a lot easier than you'd imagine, Gerry, as the bank will do everything and don't worry about any costs incurred for I'll cover them. And I promise I'll have the entire sum back to you within the week. One other thing, it'd probably be easier for you to withdraw the money from your business account though that's up to you of course. My own account number is 1243 3434 3774 34019.

The available seat is on a flight going out early on the morning of the 15th so you'd really need to go into the bank at the very first chance you get. I'd like to surprise Mam, so don't tell her a thing.

No doubt Brona will be pleased not to be stuck with doing everything for Mam when she comes out of hospital. Between work, the four girls, the baby, she has enough to cope with right now.

Laura.

14th January

Debbie

1.45 p.m. Dylan came barging in here just now, wanting to know if I'd thought any more about lending him money so I told him I hadn't and began pushing him back out again but he managed to shove past me and came right into the room, closing the door behind him And then he began threatening me! If it wasn't so ridiculous it'd be almost funny. Dylan of all people acting the heavy! He told me that if I didn't give it to him, he'd go straight to Maeve and tell her that I've been coming on to him ever since he and Maeve got together. I told him he could tell Maeve whatever he liked which floored him a little but then he started on about how Maeve and I were meant to be friends so why was I suddenly acting like I didn't care about her any more.

The truth is I don't. I'd hoped that when we started out on this trip it would help Maeve and me get over the problems we were having and back to the way we used to be but now her friendship doesn't seem quite so precious to me any more.

Room 11.

Maeve

Started off the last day of our trip with a fight with Mum when I stumbled upon her & her *boyfriend* having a lovey-dovey b'fast in the restaurant next door.

Told her that seeing a mother & son on hols together looking *so* happy would warm the heart of any onlooker.

Don't know where Dylan is.

He'd better not think I'm doing his packing for him.

At least he's forgotten about his stupid plan – I hope.

Room 12.

Debbie

2.00 *p.m.* I think it's about time Maeve found out just what a rat her boyfriend is.

Genevieve

The room is like a bomb hit it. Debbie's things are all over the place and I still haven't finished my packing yet but at least we've plenty of time for our flight isn't until one this morning which is a ridiculous time if you ask me. I think I'll wear my baby blue tracksuit on the plane for I know it's not exactly stylish but it is comfortable which is the most important thing seeing as how long we're going to be stuck on the plane.

From the sounds coming from the room next door, I'd say Debbie is in danger of being strangled by Maeve. Debbie went barging out of here just now and must have gone straight into Maeve's room for now there's a huge fight going on between the pair of them but I can't hear what they're saying exactly for Mrs Clancy and her boyfriend are in the room on the other side and he's pleading and pleading with her to marry him even though she keeps shouting at him that all she was looking for was a holiday romance.

Room 11. An hour later.

Maeve.

Debs told me what happened 'tween L & Dylan.

Didn't believe her at first & went looking for him to see what he had to say.

Found Laura instead & when I accused her of going off with Dylan, she just gave me this, like, blank stare & went, "Yeah! And *this* comes as a surprise to you? Wake up, Maeve!"

And then she just walked away – she didn't, like, care one bit.

And now Mum's just come in to tell me she's staying on in Thailand for a while.

Of course the 1st thing I told her was that lover-boy was sure to dump her as soon as someone better came along.

But it turns out he's got *nothing* to do with her decision to stay.

She's doing a Shirley Valentine & is heading back to Koh Samet on her own to work in some restaurant for a couple of mths!

Downstairs in the foyer. Late that night.

Genevieve

Andrew might find it hard to communicate his feelings for me verbally as Laura put it but about twenty minutes ago a present of this gorgeous big teddy arrived here for me with a note saying, "Can't wait to see you when I'm back in Ireland in early March – Andrew XXX". Just when I'd resigned myself to thinking I'd got the wrong end of the stick and now this! What does it mean? I don't know <u>what</u> to think any more.

The taxi should be arriving any minute now though there's one problem which is that Dylan has disappeared and nobody has any idea where he's got to. In the middle of her own packing this evening Maeve went out to buy some cigarettes though why she couldn't wait until we got to the airport I don't know but I suppose she's right and only a smoker could understand but by the time she got back up to her room Dylan's stuff had been cleared out completely.

Maeve is now saying she's not going to budge until she finds out what's happened to Dylan and is ranting on about how someone else could be involved in his disappearance. Now Debbie has started shouting at her, telling her not to be so stupid and that obviously Dylan's just fecked off on his own. She could be right for it's not like he has an awful lot to come home to. I'd say the courier company he worked for have long since taken him off the roster and he doesn't even have his guitar any more so it's not like he can make money playing gigs.

And he isn't the only one who won't be on the plane for when I asked Maeve where her mother was she told me where to go in no uncertain terms but Debbie told her not to be taking her temper out on me and explained that Mrs Clancy had decided to stay on for a while and that she's got a job in a restaurant in Koh Samet. I can't say I blame her for she's another one who doesn't seem to have a whole lot to go back to.

I think Dylan must have taken my woolly hat and one of my jumpers with him or else Maeve still has them but when

I tried asking her just now she nearly bit my head off and said for once couldn't I focus on the bigger picture and that her boyfriend had disappeared. I know things aren't going well for her but that doesn't make it right for her to take her bad mood out on me. The taxi is due to arrive in ten minutes' time so I've time to pay a visit to the bathroom before it comes for goodness knows when I'll get the chance again.

15th January

Debbie

1.00 a.m. Poor Genevieve has been hauled away by the airport police. Nobody will tell us a thing.

Maeve

Everything is just falling to bits.

First I learn 'bout Dylan & L having it off together b'hind my back.

Then I learn what a Total Bitch my *friend* L is.

Then my mother announces she's not coming home with us.

Then Dylan disappears without trace.

And then G goes & gets taken away by the airport police!

I'm *not* joking.

When we were going thro' customs, these 2 guys came up alongside of her & escorted her away – have, like, *no* idea what's going on or where they've taken her.

She looked so, so *sooo* frightened.

She wasn't crying but her bottom lip was all a-tremble & her eyes were the size of saucers.

And now they won't let us see her.

None of us were allowed on the plane either but were

502

brought into this little room to wait & we've these 2 guards sitting across from us watching us like hawks.

I hope Dylan hasn't had anything to do with the mess G's in – wouldn't put it past him.

Debbie

2.15 a.m. We still don't know what's happening to Genevieve. No one will tell us anything.

Maeve and Laura are like cat and dog but at least Laura's trying to be of some practical use and has got one of the guards to take her out to a phone so that she can get onto her journalism buddies to see if any of them have contacts here who might be able to help.

Maeve

Debs is making a huge fuss & demanding that they let us see G or at least tell us why she's been arrested.

Don't think they're taking too much notice.

Debbie

3.00 a.m. They've just informed us that Genevieve was caught with drugs on her and that they're about to charge her. I can't believe this is happening.

Maeve

G's been arrested for (*really* can't believe I'm writing this) attempted drug-smuggling!

Nobody has come near us for hrs – we've, like, *no* idea what's happening to her or even where she is.

I can't help thinking Dylan's behind it.

But where could he have got the money?

And it doesn't really explain why he's suddenly disappeared either.

Debbie

4.30 a.m. An official has just come to tell us they're putting us on the ten o' clock flight to London. He's kidding himself if he thinks we're going to leave without Genevieve.

6.00 a.m. They're still not letting us see Genevieve. We don't even know if she's still in the airport.

7.30 a.m. Still no news of Genevieve. Laura's contacts haven't been of much help.

Maeve

Debs just rang Theo & told him – he's going to break the news to G's parents.

Debbie

8.00 a.m. There's no way any of us are getting on that plane, despite what they might think. They can't force us.

Flight to London.

Debbie

11.45 a.m. Famous last words! Here we are on the flight home. But without Genevieve. At least Laura managed to persuade them to allow her take a few things to Genevieve before we were put on the plane.

Maeve

I can't believe they frog-marched us onto the plane like that – *everyone's* eyes were like Out-On-Sticks.

Have *never* been *soooooo* mortified.

Some of the passengers are *still* staring at us.

These 2 (frightened-looking) old dears in the seat opp. haven't taken their eyes off of us since we sat down.

Do they, like, suddenly expect us to pull a gun on them?

At least L got to visit G before we left & was able to bring her a few bits and pieces.

And we had to leave without Dylan too. I still have no idea where he is. Or if he was involved.

16th January

ALTHOUGH LESS THAN twenty-four hours since her arrest at Bangkok Airport on suspicion of drug-smuggling, Genevieve Price, the twenty-four year old woman from Portrea, Co Cork, is already showing the ill-effects of her detention. When I visited her in prison this morning, her baby-blue tracksuit was filthy, her carrot-red hair greasy and her plain, broad, freckled face was streaked with grimy tears.

Prison cell 13. Evening time.

Genevieve

Before the girls were put on the plane they let Laura come to see me though I have to say she was the last person in the world I needed arriving in on top of me like that. I mean I know I can be a bit stupid at times but I'm still kicking myself over how long it took me to see her for what she really is and though she was all questions I just said as little as possible. I can only count my lucky stars that I got talking to those English girls in the bathroom at the guesthouse just before we got the taxi to the airport for I just can't imagine the <u>awful boat</u> I'd be in right now if I hadn't. Meeting them let me see Laura for what she is and really saved my bacon and only just by the skin of my teeth too.

But at least Laura brought a change of clothes for me which was something as my tracksuit was absolutely <u>mangy</u>. Of all the luck to be wearing baby-blue on the day I get sent to prison for you just couldn't get a worse colour. She brought my diary and a toothbrush too though why she didn't think to bring toothpaste as well I have no idea for one's not much good to me without the other and it's not like this place is some holiday camp or the like where everyone gets along cosily and we're all borrowing each other's clothes and toiletries and whatnot. To be honest there are few enough people in here that I'd even <u>dare to look in the eye</u> never mind ask for a loan of toothpaste and the sooner I'm out of here the better.

If only people knew what this <u>hellhole</u> was actually like they just wouldn't believe it for it is the <u>pits</u>. I thought the floors in some of the places we stayed in over the last couple of months were <u>filthy</u> but they're nothing like the floors in this <u>dive</u> and there isn't so much as a piece of lino covering the concrete in our cell. And all I'll say about the toilet is that at least you don't have to go far to get to it. In fact just to the other side of the room! It is just <u>humiliating</u> and the smell would <u>knock a horse out</u>. And don't even get me started on the mattress for it is <u>crawling</u>. And I've never seen <u>anything so disgusting</u> as the food they're serving up and I'd swear the stuff we got this morning at breakfast had <u>maggots</u> in it for I definitely saw something moving but when I tried telling one of the guards she suddenly couldn't understand a word of English yet I notice she's well able to say <u>shut up</u> and <u>hurry up</u> and <u>lock up</u> and <u>belt up</u>. I don't know what's eating her but she has a real set against me and she spent the whole of today pushing me about and <u>yelling</u> and <u>screaming</u> at me and I swear my head was just done in from her.

The minute I get out of here the first thing I'm going to do is make an <u>official</u> <u>complaint</u> against her.

I'm glad Laura gave me my diary though for at least it gives me something to do as otherwise I think I'd go out of my <u>tiny</u> <u>little</u> <u>mind</u>. Of course I'd say she read as much as she could before she handed it over but then again she probably hadn't any need to for no doubt she's seen it all already.

For crying out loud! The lights have all gone out without any warning whatsoever apart from the ones out in the corridor which are throwing a tiny bit of light through the gaps in the hatch but even still I can't see what the blazes I'm writing and I'm probably making a complete mess on the page so I'd better call it a day but it's bloody <u>ludicrous</u> to expect grown-up women to go to sleep at this hour.

17th January

Yet underneath the tears and the grime there lay a frightened, innocent-looking face, a face hard to conceive as belonging to a criminal. But then there are, it seems, many faces, many sides to Genevieve Price. That of lover:

"I'm in love with Andrew Clancy. There. I've finally said it. And it's the truth though I've been denying it all along even to myself. But I'm in love. I am. I, Genevieve Price, am in love with Andrew Clancy. I love him. I do, I really do.

Prison cell 13. Early morning.

Genevieve

I don't know why they're so anxious to have us up at the crack of dawn for it's not like there's exactly a lot to do in this place and even though we were all sent to bed when it was practically daylight outside I still didn't get much sleep for Khun who's the woman in the bunk opposite must have used that tin toilet at least five times per hour <u>all</u> <u>night</u> <u>long</u> no exaggeration and you'd be surprised how loud the sound of someone peeing into tin is. I'd swear she has a problem with her kidneys and she should really get the prison doctor to have a look at them.

Khun's quite nice really once you get over her appearance which is a bit off-putting to begin with for she hasn't a tooth in her head and she's got fierce acne scars and I'd say she's at least triple my weight no exaggeration which is unusual for a Thai woman as most of them are skinny out and I'm glad I'm not the one sleeping in the bunk under her for I wouldn't feel very safe. She can speak some English though how much I don't really know but when I asked her what she was in here for she said it was for killing her father but then she laughed so I don't know if she was just pulling my leg or what.

One of the guards who speaks English was telling me that there's another westerner in here who's Finnish. I don't think I've ever met anyone from Finland before though you'd get the impression that they're very clean living-people and the last place you'd expect one to show up is somewhere like this!

Some hours later.

Debbie rang and the first thing she had to say was that she was certain Dylan put the heroin in my bag which is exactly what I thought herself and Maeve would think but which of course isn't the case at all and I'd say he just decided to stay on in Bangkok for that would suit him far better than going home and having to find a proper job for himself. What he'll do for money I don't know but I certainly won't be losing any sleep worrying for he's the kind who'll always make out. The authorities are keeping an eye out for him in case he goes back to Ireland for the last thing they want is him messing everything up. The second thing was that though Debbie didn't want to go upsetting me she felt I should know that Laura had a full-length article about me in the *Daily Democrat* today. When I agreed to stay here until everything was cleared up I never considered something like that happening though I don't know why for how else has Laura been making her living these past few months but by writing about me so why should she stop now when she actually has something real to write about.

At first Debbie didn't want to read it out to me and I had to make her but honestly it was so awful I can hardly <u>bear</u> to write about it for she just <u>couldn't</u> have painted me in a worse light. Like going on about how I had a broad freckled face for instance! I mean she might as well have just called me ugly and be done with it. And nobody has ever called my hair carrot-red before and why would they when it's strawberry blonde? And going on about how I had a dull façade and that I was remarkable for being especially unremarkable. Like what's that supposed to mean? And I don't see what need there was to mention I was wearing a tracksuit. When I put it on thinking it'd be comfortable to wear on the plane home the last thing I could <u>ever</u> have imagined was that the whole world would be reading about how dirty it was over their cornflakes. Of course it was dirty. How could it have been any other way what with me being stuck in prison?

That I was wearing a tracksuit was probably the only true fact in the whole bloody thing and other than that it was packed full of lies. I swear she made it sound like I was a drug-addict and she called me a criminal and a deceiver. How can she get away with writing that stuff? Doesn't anyone check these things to see if they're true or not?

At least when she was making a fool of me these past few

months in that magazine she wasn't using my real name and I'd say the *Idol* hasn't anywhere near as many readers as the *Daily Democrat*. I know it's a <u>rag</u> and all but everyone buys the *Democrat*. All of Portrea does for sure including my parents and all my aunts and uncles. It's probably the most popular paper around. And she was horrible about everyone else as well. Calling Theo my jilted boyfriend and Mei an ageing oriental mistress

Before she hung up she told me that Maeve wanted me to know that her Dad has been ringing all his contacts to see if any of them might be able to help which is the sort of thing you'd expect from a gentleman like him though it's not really necessary of course but I couldn't tell her that.

I must say I feel a right eejit when I think of Andrew. How could I ever have thought he was interested in me? I guess if Laura hadn't been encouraging me all along then I wouldn't have imagined such a thing for a second. I'd say the reason Laura wanted me to believe he was interested was just for a laugh and it had nothing whatsoever to do with anything else like the events leading up to why I'm in here for example. Seeing me pestering him like I was and making a fool of myself and hearing me go on and on about him was probably a big joke to her and an even bigger one when she could write about it in that stupid diary of hers for all the world to see.

It's funny but when those two girls back in the bathroom in the guesthouse started calling me Geraldine I just assumed that they'd misheard me when I'd introduced myself for Geraldine is sort of like Genevieve I suppose. But then they started squealing laughing and saying, it has to be, it just has to be, so of course I kept asking them what on earth just had to be until one of them finally calmed down enough to go and fetch a copy of the *Idol* from her room and that's when she showed me the page with Laura's diary.

At first I couldn't understand why they wanted me to see it and it wasn't until I came to the bit about a temple being a temple being a temple and a statue being a statue being a statue that bells began to ring and when I checked my diary I saw that they were <u>my</u> <u>very</u> <u>own</u> <u>words!</u> My very own words that I had privately written in my own diary but which were now here before me as plain as day in black and white for all the world to see in a magazine. I just can't describe the feeling I felt but it felt awful. And there were other bits in there as well that I hadn't written personally but which were based on <u>confidential</u> conversations between Laura and myself, things I would never have said to anyone but Laura and only to her because I thought we were practically best friends. But I swear everything she'd written from start to finish just made a complete <u>mockery</u> of me and made me out to be a right <u>loop-de-loop</u> and it's no lie to say I was <u>gutted.</u>

They're making us all go and do some exercises now though it's the last thing in the world I feel like doing.

18th January

That of deceiver:

"Genevieve changed once she started travelling and met up with Andrew Clancy. Before that she wanted the same things as I did – a big wedding, a nice little bungalow, children. But once Andrew Clancy came on the scene it was like her head was completely turned"

– Theo Whitlam, Price's jilted boyfriend, in conversation with this reporter.

Prison cell 13. Morning.

Genevieve

I don't know who's worse, the prisoners or the guards. When the prisoner sitting beside me at breakfast this morning saw that I wasn't eating my bowl of mush, she'd it whipped off me without so much as a please or a thank you which I was about to point out to her but then I saw that the poor thing had this scar all the way down the other side of her face so I felt a bit sorry for her and let her off and anyway it's not like I was going to eat it or anything.

I was allowed another phone call today from Debbie. She told me that Theo is very upset over what's happened to me and wanted me to know that he's been trying and trying to ring the prison but for some reason he hasn't been able to get through. Knowing him he's probably doing something stupid like using the wrong code or something like that. He told Debbie to tell me that he's there for me which is touching really considering what Laura wrote about him and me and after everything else that's happened. He's on standby now to fly out but I told Debbie to tell him that he's not to come for to be honest I don't think I could listen to him moaning and groaning about how bad the flight was and whatever else he'd find to complain about which would be plenty no doubt. Anyway there's no point in him flying all the way over here only to find that I'm on my way home which could easily happen since I'm only going to be in here for another day or two.

Even though nothing's ever happened or will happen between Andrew and myself, I've decided I'm still going to split up with Theo that's if he doesn't decide to split up with me first and I could understand if he did. I hope we can stay friends however for he really is a good person and we've an awful lot in common and at a time like this it's touching to see how much faith he has in me. It's that sort of thing that's important and not the small things like the way he slurps his soup or the way he's a bit loud despite what the likes of Laura might think. Of course it would be nice if I could get back to feeling the way I used to feel about him before I went away but that's not going to happen for I just think I've changed too much.

After Laura I've had just about as much as I can take of journalists and magazines and whatnot but shortly after Debbie hung up another call came through for me and this time it was from a journalist called Sally Hill who works for some English newspaper but who's just been posted out here and who right now is working on this piece all about what it's like for westerners in Thai prisons. She said she did an interview with Rakel, the Finnish girl, yesterday and that Rakel happened to mention I was in here too so now she wants to interview me for her piece. Needless to say I told her I'd no interest whatsoever for once bitten, twice as shy and if Laura's anything to go by, journalists are a very cunning crowd and the last thing I need right now is to go getting ensnared by another one.

I don't know how I didn't cop on to Laura earlier. It was only when those two English girls had gone and I was left standing there in the bathroom <u>completely</u> gob-smacked that I started remembering things. Things like Theo telling me how he'd caught Laura reading my diary but how I hadn't believed him. But I guess I should have had more sense than to think that someone like Laura could be really interested in being friends with someone like me. When I think of all the times I confided in her when no doubt she was laughing on the other side of her face and drawing me out and making me tell her all the silly stuff that was going on my head though I'm sure I really didn't say half those things I said and even if I did say them then I was definitely misquoted.

Several hours later.

Well they arranged for me to ring Laura which wasn't something I enjoyed doing <u>at all.</u> I kept things short but though I know it wasn't what I was meant to be talking about I did tell her I was very upset at how she'd exploited me all along and especially in the article she'd written for the *Daily Democrat*. Once I'd got that out of the way I went on to tell her that I was sure I'd be found innocent as soon as the authorities tracked down Dylan and made him confess to planting the radio with the drugs in my bag. That certainly shook her. I'd say she couldn't believe what she was hearing for she was silent for a few moments and then when she recovered she began asking me all these questions but I interrupted her and continued on with the rest of what I had to say. I told her that I wouldn't be asking for help from her of all people but that I'd no choice given my circumstances and then went on to explain that I'd given Debbie Andrew's teddy before we checked through our luggage as I didn't really have room for it in mine but that now I wanted her to ring Debbie and ask her to post it over to me. I said I was sure that she of all people would understand how much it meant to me and understand how it would give me some comfort to have it here with me in prison and that it was the least she could do for me considering everything.

Now all I can do is wait and see what happens.

19th January

That of the other woman:

"It was obvious right from the start that Genevieve was interested in Andrew but I didn't take it seriously. I mean Andrew and I have been together for such a long time and I never imagined he would be interested in Genevieve as she's an awfully silly girl."

– Mei Fan, Andrew Clancy's ageing oriental mistress.

Prison cell 13. Early afternoon.

Genevieve

I'm just wrecked. They're far too fond of making us do exercises in this place and for what I don't know for it's all a bit pointless and I have to say that walking around and around and around with a bunch of other women in a tiny little yard is not exactly my idea of a nice way to pass the time. I thought that at least with Debbie out of the picture I wouldn't be subjected to any more of that sort of thing. It reminded me of the time we were trekking in those hills up by Chiang Mai and all I could see were the backs of the heads of all those tall Norwegian girls stretching out in a line in front of me. And if they're going to make us exercise like that then the least they could do is let us have a shower afterwards for believe me sharing such a small cell with Khun especially on a sweltering day after all that exercising and without the benefit of showers is not pleasant to say the least.

One thing that's been bothering me is how I acted with Mei and I really wish I'd been nicer to her. That first time when we were staying with Andrew I knew someone had been at my diary when I found it in the wrong pocket in my bag and I have to confess that I was one hundred per cent certain it was Mei especially when Laura was so quick to agree with me which is why I never gave Mei a proper chance. Of course now I know why Laura was so happy to point the finger at Mei seeing as how it took the suspicion away from her.

It's funny but now that I know Mei is Andrew's girlfriend nothing seems clearer to me but of course that's with the benefit of twenty-twenty hindsight and it wasn't like the thought hadn't ever struck me before for I remember near the start of our trip asking Laura if she thought Andrew and Mei could be together but she just started laughing like it was the most ridiculous thing ever so I didn't think much more about it until that second time I stayed with Andrew and then I just thought it was all one-sided on Mei's part.

This morning when I was talking to Rakel the Finnish girl who I've become quite pally with I happened to mention about that journalist Sally Hill wanting to interview me and how I'd turned her down but much to my surprise Rakel got very cross and said I was being selfish and that I owed it to all western prisoners to let the world know what conditions are like in here. I suppose she's right. It's okay for me for I'm not going to be here for long but it could make the difference to others who find themselves in my position but on a more permanent footing. So bearing in mind what she said I asked one of the guards to contact this Sally Hill and to let her know I was prepared to talk to her. One thing I am going to tell her about is that rotten guard with the set against me for people like her deserve to be exposed for what they are. I really don't know what I ever did to her for she's been mean out to me again today and she was in here just now and was on at me to straighten out my bedclothes. Like what's the point when I'm lying on top of them for there's nowhere else for me to go and I didn't hear her saying anything to Khun or the others.

20th January

And that of drug user:

"I like it. It makes me feel sort of free and relaxed and I stop worrying about everything and suddenly it's like I haven't a care in the world. Nothing seems scary any more. All I want to do is to laugh out loud though there's precious little to laugh about."

Prison cell 13. Early afternoon.

Genevieve

If they don't let me out of here soon then the whole deal is off. I tried saying as much to one of the guards but I don't think she knew who I was and started <u>laughing</u> at me and when I tried explaining to her that I was innocent she just sniggered and said that that's what they all say.

Rakel was telling me that the woman with the scar all down one side of her face who stole my breakfast from me the other morning got the scar from her husband. Apparently she was in the middle of killing him with a knife and after she'd stuck the knife right into his heart he mustered all his energy together and somehow managed to pull it back out again and gave her one swipe across the face with it before he finally kicked the bucket. And apparently he wasn't the first husband she'd killed either but in fact the third though they never found the bodies of the first two but the men just disappeared one day and were never seen again! Needless to say if she wants my bowl of mush at breakfast tomorrow I'll happily hand it over to her. Let her have the maggots.

One of guards told some of the other prisoners that I was caught with a load of heroin on me and the worrying thing is that now some of the harder nuts in here are fierce impressed and are telling Khun to just let them know if I need anything and by that I think they mean drugs for I'd say the place is just <u>walking</u> with them. I can tell you that the last thing I need right now is attention from their sort and I'd be happy just to get through these few days without drawing too much attention on myself. When Rakel heard the rumours going around about me she came rushing in and started saying to me, you poor thing, you poor thing, and started hugging me and holding my hand. She says that being caught with that amount of gear as she put it carries a life sentence at the very least and maybe even execution and she should know for that's the sad sorry future her boyfriend is facing which is why she tried to bust him out of prison which is why she's now in here for she wasn't very successful.

Her brother came in to see her today. I only caught a glimpse of him but he looked nice and sort of wholesome and healthy in a Scandinavian way. Rakel says he's furious with her for letting herself get caught up in such a mess but he's still doing all he can to get her out of it. Apparently the only person who can pardon her boyfriend now is the King of Thailand so now the brother who's called Rieti or something like that is on to everyone he can think of to start lobbing the King and I'm going to do the same when I get out of here for I really like Rakel though I've only known her for a few days.

Somehow I don't think Khun was joking when she said she was in here for killing her dad. Just a few minutes ago this mouse ran across the floor of our cell and she was out of her bunk like a shot and had crushed its little body to a pulp with her <u>bare</u> <u>heel</u> before I even knew what was happening.

One of the guards has just come to tell me that the journalist Sally Hill got back onto them and is going to come in to interview me tomorrow. I wonder if she ever came across Laura for the world of journalism can't be that big.

21st January

So many sides to Genevieve Price, sides which this reporter finds almost impossible to reconcile with the Genevieve Price she's known since childhood.

For I grew up with Genevieve But that Genevieve was just your average, small-town girl and if she was remarkable for anything it was perhaps for being especially unremarkable. But maybe that was just one more face she wore, one more mask, and who knows what was really going on behind that dull façade she portrayed.

But, in light of recent events, it seems likely to have been a lot more than any of her old classmates, myself included, could ever have imagined.

Prison cell 13. Morning.

Genevieve

I wonder where that woman with the scar who killed all those husbands put the two that were never found. I mean to say a body wouldn't exactly be the easiest thing in the world to hide. Apart from the whole business of her husbands I must admit I find her a bit weird. She seems to be always sidling up alongside me without me even noticing and whenever I turn around she's standing there behind me, just staring. It's hard to imagine that there could be so many oddballs under one roof and the sooner I'm out of here the better. I don't think I can stand much more of this place. I thought I'd be long gone by now and don't ask me what the hold-up is for nobody's bothering to tell me a thing despite all their promises back in the airport.

Rakel says her brother Rieti was telling her it's unlikely her boyfriend will get a full pardon so what they're hoping for now is that he gets a life sentence which would be better than execution for the obvious reason but as well the life sentence would probably be reduced to a couple of years so why it's called a life sentence is beyond me. Rakel says that her brother thinks that this boyfriend of hers might even be allowed to serve the reduced sentence back in Finland where the prisons are top-class.

In a way Rieti sort of reminds me of Andrew especially the way he's stepped in and is doing all he can to help. And he even looks a little bit like him too in a way though Andrew is a good few inches taller than him and a bit heavier but there definitely is something similar in the set of their jaws and maybe about the eyes as well.

Late that afternoon.

That journalist Sally Hill turned up here a couple of hours ago and the first thing I told her was that I wasn't prepared to talk about the events leading up to my arrest. I also told her that I wanted to remain anonymous for there's been enough about me in the papers and as it is people in Portrea are probably already going around saying there's no smoke without fire. She said she had no problem with either for she was just interested in what I had to say about the prison conditions.

So after she turned on her little tape recorder I started talking and I'd say I didn't stop again for at least an hour and I told her everything. All about the tin toilets and the maggots and how it seemed to me that the place was awash with drugs and of course all about the guard with the set against me and all sorts of other stuff. When I finally stopped I told her I wanted to see exactly what she'd written before it goes into the paper for one thing I've learned is to be wary of journalists after the way Laura twisted my words and the facts to suit herself. Somewhere along the line I must have mentioned my own diary and how it has kept me sane in here for just before she left she asked me would I consider letting her look at what I'd written about my time in prison and at first I said no way but she kept on badgering me until finally I agreed but only if I was with her and I could pick out the pieces for I don't want her reading stuff she's not meant to see especially all that stupid stuff about Andrew.

Our time was up by then so she's going to come back in tomorrow for me to go through the diary though of course I might be gone by then though I didn't say that to her for I didn't want to have to get into explaining things to her.

22nd January

How could we have foreseen that one day Genevieve Mary Price would be languishing in a Thai prison, her fate resting in the hands of the Bangkok courts? How could anyone ever have imagined such a future was in store for her when she set off just three months ago to Asia on what was to be a trip of a lifetime? A trip she's now looking unlikely to ever return from, for, if the Thai authorities decide against her, as seems likely, then Genevieve will face a charge of execution though as a foreigner it's possible that her sentence will be commuted to life imprisonment.

Execution or life imprisonment, such is Price's bleak future now.

Plane home to Ireland. Late afternoon.

Genevieve

I think I'm going out of my mind! By rights I should be sitting in the window seat for it says so on my ticket but the rotten man who was already in it when I arrived down refused to budge and being foreign he just pretended he didn't know what I was on about. And to make things worse his wife or his girlfriend or whatever is sitting on the other side of me in the aisle seat so I'm trapped in the middle and they keep reaching across me to kiss and whisper things which I can't understand but no doubt it's just stupid lovey-dovey in Russian for I'd say it's Russia or whatever it's called these days they're from judging by their overall appearance.

For the life of me I don't understand why they won't swap seats for at least then they'd be together and I tried saying as much but they just don't understand. And why they won't take off their fur coats is beyond me for they're fierce bulky and I'm beginning to feel very claustrophobic what with being swamped on either side by bloody fur. And it's not like it's cold in the plane either and in fact it's sweltering. I wonder what business they had in Thailand and why they aren't flying back to Russia now. Maybe they're on an extended honeymoon though how they can afford it I just don't know for as far as I know the Russian economy is very weak which is why they're always having to queue up in little corner shops to buy tights and toilet paper and whatnot from abroad. Of course if they were in the Mafia or whatever then that would account for their money. I'd better stop staring at them or they might put a hit out on me when we land. After what I've been through this past week <u>nothing</u> would surprise me! But really what am I like writing about the <u>Russian</u> <u>Mafia</u> of all things when I have so much more important stuff to write about.

Well first of all I'm on the flight home. Obviously! And what a day I've had! It's been non-stop since Sally Hill came in to me in the prison just after breakfast to go over my diary with her. Making sure to leave out all the silly bits about Andrew and all the stuff about Laura and the events leading up to my arrest I started going through it and reading out pieces I thought might be of use for her article but pretty soon she seemed to lose interest for she said something like how I really was <u>obsessed</u> with the mundane and that she probably had enough details from our talk the day before to go on and that she didn't need to bother me anymore. But as she was gathering her things together who should walk in but the Prison Governor and a bunch of other top-notch types to tell me I was free to leave and that Laura Tobin had been arrested for the possession of heroin. Well Sally Hill's eyes nearly <u>popped</u> <u>out</u> <u>of</u> <u>her</u> <u>head</u> when she heard this for it turns out she and Laura know each other very well from the world of journalism where they've had quite a few run-ins over the years and to say Sally Hill <u>hates</u> Laura would be <u>no</u> <u>exaggeration</u> though I'd say Laura probably hates her a lot more for it seems Sally Hill was responsible for Laura having to leave *The Argus* and apparently it's all got to do with the famous Devereux Affair which I'd heard of before of course though I never really got what it was all about but Sally Hill explained it all to me.

She told me that though everyone in the world of journalism suspected that Ronald Devereux a one-time British Minister was a bit dodgy it was Laura who uncovered the whole story behind him and how she did it was as follows as Sally Hill explained to me. Somehow Laura found out that this Ronald Devereux was having an affair with his secretary and so pretending to be a politics student doing a project she contacted the secretary for help. Now the secretary who was called Lily Buchan was a very obliging sort of person and gave Laura all the help she needed and pretty soon they struck up a friendship. I think this Lily Buchan must have been a lonely sort and very gullible for within no time at all Laura was calling around to her apartment and next thing you know they were going to the cinema together and to plays and dinner and whatnot. So of course poor lonely Lily Buchan started confiding in Laura. First about her and Ronald Devereux's affair and as time went on about all sorts of other things as well. Such as how Ronald Devereux set up a made-up building company and then paid out thousands maybe millions of pounds from the government coppers for work this pretend company had supposedly carried out for the government but of course the money was going straight into Ronald Devereux's own pockets. So Laura had her scoop as they say and she wrote a huge piece all about it and quoted poor Lily Buchan all over the place for sometimes when they'd met up she'd secretly brought along her little tape-recorder so she'd all Lily Buchan's words down on tape. Oh for crying out loud! The Russian is now videotaping his girlfriend or his wife or whatever and it's not like she's doing anything interesting for she's just sitting there and smiling and waving at the camera. If he thinks I'm going to bend down to keep out of the picture he's got another think coming. It's hard enough to write as it is and between one thing and another I've got a lot to get through. Needless to say poor Lily Buchan was distraught for as well as having her affair with her beloved Ronald Devereux exposed she was also the cause of his downfall and what did she do next only commit suicide. Poor, poor Lily Buchan. I feel so sad when I think of her and so mad when I think of the part Laura played in her death

Anyway the reason Laura now hates this Sally Hill is because a couple of weeks later Sally Hill did this feature on what she called morals in the media and as an example discussed the rights and wrongs of what Laura had done and how it had led to poor Lily Buchan's suicide and, as Sally

Hill explained, her piece caught the public's imagination and what followed next was a whole load of discussion in the media and there was an absolute avalanche of letters to the editor and that sort of thing and all the papers were just chock-a-block with it for days.

So then who pops up only Lily Buchan's brother who never had much time for her when she was alive but now that she was dead he started seeing dollar signs and started threatening to sue *The Argus* for causing her to take her own life though whether or not he'd have been successful who knows for *The Argus* settled before it got anywhere near court and apparently he got a fortune which was the cause of Laura falling out with *The Argus*. And that's about the sum of it. Needless to say I was gobsmacked.

The Russian is now videotaping out the window of the plane though of course there's nothing to see only clouds and clouds and more clouds and I'd hate to be one of the poor souls he brings around to look at his holiday video when he finally gets home.

But getting back to Laura being arrested with all that heroin in her possession. According to the Governor what happened was this. Laura turned up at Debbie's yesterday and after giving some excuse as to why she was over in Dublin she went on to explain to Debbie that I'd asked her to collect the teddy and to post it over to me. Of course Debbie handed it over without question for I'm sure she was only too glad to be able to do something to help me though I'd say she must have been surprised that I'd asked Laura of all people given her recent article about me. But what Laura didn't know was that she was being tailed from the moment she left Debbie's by the detectives who'd been watching the house waiting for Laura to show and I'd say Laura must have got <u>the</u> <u>shock</u> <u>of</u> <u>her</u> <u>life</u> when the carload of detectives pulled up alongside her after she'd stopped into a laneway and was in the middle of ripping the teddy open to get at the drugs.

Needless to say Sally Hill's ears were <u>out</u> <u>on</u> <u>sticks</u> when she heard all this and nothing would do her but that I'd tell her the whole story from start to finish and so as soon as I'd collected my few bits and pieces and said goodbye to Rakel and Khun and everyone she insisted on taking me to this most beautiful hotel where we stayed until it was time to go to the airport and while I ate my fill of cakes and drank my fill of tea I told her everything.

God I must have talked for hours. I told her all about how the morning before we left for the airport I received that present of the pink teddy with the love heart from Andrew Clancy and how I thought it a queer sort of present from a man as classy as him. I told her how after we'd got to the airport I noticed that sign asking if you'd packed your own bags and how, because of a recent approach from a <u>certain</u> <u>party</u> as I called Dylan for I didn't want to reveal his identity to a journalist of all people, to smuggle drugs through for him I was probably more tuned in to this kind of thing than I might otherwise have been. And I told her how I'd started thinking about the teddy and how when we were passing by a toilet on our way to the check-in I told the others I'd catch up with them and then slipped into a cubicle and very carefully plucked open the teddy until all these bags of powder came tumbling out which I just knew had to be drugs of some sort. And how I just <u>nearly</u> <u>died</u>!

And I told her how my first reaction was to flush them all down the toilet and be done with them but how I'd then started thinking about who could have put them there unbeknownst to me, about who could think so little of me that they would risk me getting caught like that? And the person who came to mind was the very person who thought so little of me as to spend months encouraging me to feel we were friends so that I would confide in her and give her lots of entertaining material to write about in her stupid column. But if I hadn't bumped into those girls in the toilets in the backpackers I would never have known about the column and probably would never have seen Laura for the low-down toad-faced frog she is. And so I told Sally Hill how I'd got madder and madder and madder at the thought of all that Laura had done to me until I finally decided it was time to get even. Nobody was going to treat me like that. It was time to put my thinking cap on.

Of course the more I talked the more interested Sally Hill became. So I went right on talking. I told her that I'd stuffed the drugs back into the teddy and the teddy back into my rucksack and had then come out of the toilet and put the rucksack in a locker and then went straight up to a couple of the airport police and demanded to speak to their boss. I told her how at first they tried to fob me off but I kept on and on insisting but I could see I was getting nowhere so I just sat down on the ground and refused to budge until they either brought me to see him or him to see me.

And so that's how I got to see him and to tell him everything ending it with the part about the drugs being in the locker but needless to say he thought I was a complete nutter so I told him that if he'd just come with me to the locker he'd see I was telling the truth. At first I thought he wasn't going to budge but then he told me to lead the way. And so I did. With him and five others in tow. And then when we got to the locker I showed them the teddy with the bags of powder stuffed inside it. It must have been about then one of his goons started getting worked up and kept going on about how they'd all these bags of heroin right in front of their noses and the obvious person to arrest for them was me! At least I think that's the gist of what he was saying for he was switching back and forth between English and Thai.

And so I told him not to be such an eejit and that I'd hardly be trooping around the airport leading a bunch of gorillas to my stash of drugs if I was really a drug-smuggler and that it would be worth their while to listen to my plan to catch the real smuggler for I was one hundred per cent certain I knew who it was. And my plan was as follows. First, they should let me go back to the girls and give me time to give the teddy now empty of all the drugs to Debbie when Laura wasn't looking and get her to mind it in her bag for me. Second, when we were going through customs, they should arrest me for drug-smuggling but not give the others any more details than that. I knew Maeve and Debbie would immediately assume Dylan was responsible for the drugs on me and that Laura would think they were hers.

After an awful lot of humming and hawing and nit-picking over the finer details they agreed to my plan on two conditions. One, that they got the agreement of the Irish customs to keep Debbie's house under surveillance from the minute she got off the plane. Two, that I'd stay in Bangkok for if the true smuggler didn't turn up at Debbie's to claim the drugs, they needed someone they could pin it all on. So I agreed. Which is how I ended up spending almost a week in a Bangkok prison which I must say came as something as a surprise as I thought they were going to let me stay at a hotel or something but they wanted the smuggler, meaning

Laura, to feel confident that I was locked away and that her path to the drugs was clear.

So as I say I talked for ages and ages and Sally Hill was just <u>agog</u> and I must have eaten at least half a dozen cakes and had as many cups of tea and I'd say that if I'd wanted she'd definitely have stood me a full meal even though it was a real posh place but then she was probably on expenses. I wish I'd asked her now for I feel a bit queer after eating so much rubbish and the stuff we're being served up on the plane isn't doing me much good either and I'd say I'll be lucky if I manage to last the rest of the flight without throwing up.

But I must say Sally Hill was fierce impressed with what I'd done and I think she was a bit surprised that someone like me could have thought up such a plan but with my back up against the wall like that I don't see that I had any choice. There was <u>no way</u> I was letting Laura get away with screwing me again.

I think what I'm going to do now is spend a week or two in Portrea making things right with Theo for I wouldn't want to lose him as a friend and I'm also going to have to sort out the office. Of course I'm sure Caitríona did her best but there's bound to be heaps of things that need looking after for I can't expect her to be able to run the office as efficiently after three months as I can myself when I've been at it for seven years. After that I'm not sure what I'll do. It's not that I don't enjoy living in Portrea or working in the world of pest control but in a way I've learned all there is to learn about the business and maybe it's time to move on. Rakel did say to me that while she's in prison her brother Rieti is short of a pair of hands on the family fish farm and that if I liked I could go and stay with her family for a while and help out and who knows but I just might.

Journalist Arrested For Drug Smuggling

By Sally Hill, Bangkok   **23rd January, 2002**

Dismissed from The Argus following her part in the so-called Devereux Affair and the tragic suicide of Lily Buchan. Dumped by long-term boyfriend, hot young radio star and supermarket heir, Felix Wilson. Snubbed by her influential friends in the media and politics. Reduced to writing for the failing Idol.

Laura Tobin had lost everything. And she was desperate to get back. Desperate enough to plant a whopping 150 grams of heroin on unsuspecting old school friend, Genevieve Price.

The cunning part of Tobin's plan was that she stood to gain whether the heroin got through or not and at no risk to herself.

If Price was caught then Tobin was well placed to report on her "scoop" – a story that could turn around her ailing career in journalism.

If Price got through then all Tobin had to do was coolly reclaim the heroin, offload it and, once again she could afford the parties, the designer clothes, the expensive restaurants that were once part of her extravagant lifestyle. Only unsuspecting Genevieve Price stood to lose .

But what Tobin didn't count on was Price's cunning and earlier today a spokesman commended Price's bravery and acknowledged that their daring operation was made possible only by her co-operation.

Tobin's arrest came as the result of a unique international operation carried out by top officials from the Thai and Irish police and customs.

Price was released earlier today without charge.

FULL COVERAGE INSIDE!

A PROFILE of Genevieve Price, the girl Irish gardai describe as a heroine; and, life in a Bangkok Prison – excerpts from Price's diary. Pages 2 & 3

A CAUTIONARY TALE of betrayal and of ambition gone mad – events leading up to Tobin's arrest; and, how Laura used her mother's ill-health to con brother Gerry into funding her heroin purchase – exclusive interview with Gerry Tobin. Page 4

A LOOK at the extravagant lifestyle Felix Wilson and Tobin once shared and a recap of Tobin's part in the so-called Devereux Affair. Pages 7 & 8

"*LAURA* stole my idea," claims Dylan O'Donnell. Full interview with O'Donnell. Page 31.

THE END

536